JULIET'S
NURSE

ALSO BY LOIS LEVEEN

The Secrets of Mary Bowser

JULIET'S NURSE

LOIS LEVEEN

VINTAGE CANADA

VINTAGE CANADA EDITION, 2015

Published in Canada by Vintage Canada, a division of Penguin Random House Canada Limited, Toronto, in 2015. Originally published in hardcover in Canada by Random House Canada, a division of Penguin Random House Canada Limited, in 2014. Distributed in Canada by Penguin Random House Canada Limited.

Vintage Canada with colophon is a registered trademark.

www.penguinrandomhouse.ca

Library and Archives Canada Cataloguing in Publication

Leveen, Lois, 1968–, author
    Juliet's nurse / Lois Leveen.

ISBN 978-0-345-81400-5

    1. Angelica (Fictitious character) —Fiction. 2. Shakespeare, William, 1564–1616.

Romeo and Juliet—Adaptations. I. Title.

PS3612.E824J84 2016   813'.6   C2014-902436-3

Interior design by Jill Putorti
Cover design by Terri Nimmo
Image credit: © Chiara Fersini / Trevillion Images

Printed and bound in the United States of America

2 4 6 8 9 7 5 3 1

 Penguin
Random
House

For Fred Barnes and Betty Acreman Barnes,
for welcoming the American who fell in love with their son
without putting up the kind of fuss the Capulets made
over a certain Montague

PART ONE

1360–1363

ONE

Two nights before Lammas Eve, I go to bed believing myself fat and happy. You will think me a fool for being so deceived, at my age. But in our hearts, we all wish to be fooled. And so we make fools of ourselves.

For months, Pietro and I have finished dinner with a sampling of his latest confections: candied cherries, quince marmalade, muscatel-stewed figs. Though he still cannot afford sugar, Pietro's begun gathering honey from hives in the groves and fields beyond Verona's walls. This frightens me, for I was badly stung as a child. My face swelled so large, villagers crossed themselves when they passed me, as though I was a changeling. But whenever Pietro returns from his hives he hums like he's a bee himself, insisting this will be his good fortune at last. With the honey, he can make, if not the bright,

3

hard confetti candy the apothecaries offer, at least such treats as we might sell ourselves.

Though I warn he'll put us in the alms-house by squandering any of the precious spices for our own pleasure, each night I let him pull me to my feet and feed me an unnamed delight. Standing close behind me, he covers my eyes with one broad hand, and with the other slips some new delicacy upon my tongue like a priest placing a communion wafer. "Why do you look for a sting," he asks, his words soft in my ear, "where there is only a sweet?" So I swell not from the sharp sting of a bee but with the many dainties he's made from their honey. Or so I believe, my body spreading and slowing while the spring's warmth deepens into the summer's heat.

The delicate flavorings my husband brings to my mouth seem to sharpen my sense of smell, so that I cannot abide any off odor. I scrub and air everything in our meager rented rooms. And the week before Lammastide, I launder our linens. Every coverlet and pillow-casing, all the sheets stored within our musty marriage-chest—they get such a laundering as I've not found time to do in many a year, killing every louse, flea, and bedbug upon them. It's three days' work, and I struggle with each basketful of bedding as I walk to the public fountain, and even more when I carry the linens wet and heavy back to the Via Zancani, and haul them up the ladder to our roof. Once they're hung along the wooden window-rod under the bright July sun, the sheet-corners catch on the wind like the black-tipped wings of the gulls chasing each other over the Adige River.

My Pietro has never been one to waste a clean bedsheet—nor even a new-swept table-carpet or a leaf-strewn patch of ground within a sycamore grove—without taking me upon it. And so every night of the week, he climbs on me with the same merry lover's zest with which he connived me of my maiden-head thirty years before. About this, too, I fool myself: that we could laugh and lust as though we are still such youths as when we first lay together. As though we'd never left the countryside to enter city gates, and the plague had never come.

For seven nights, we sleep snug and satisfied on those sheets. Until the earliest hours of the day before Lammas Eve, when I awaken to find the bedding soaked.

Pietro is a man who rouses neither quickly nor easily, so I give him a knee to where I know he'll most remember it. "You pissed the sheets."

He wakes, and swears, and says, "It's not me who wet it." Pushing off the coverlet, he traces the damp spot with the cinnamon-smudged nail of his stout finger. The stain forms a little sea around the buxom island of me, yet reaches not halfway under him.

Fat and happy. Could I believe myself those things, and nothing more? Could I think myself only old and corpulent, glad just to rut with the same hoary goat I long called beloved husband? In the months of shortened breath within my tight-pulled dress, had I not felt the truth of what was happening?

I had not. I could not. Until Pietro traces it on the sheet, and him still not understanding what it is.

Now it's my turn to swear. "By my holidame, go get a midwife."

He's more stunned by this second, spoken blow than the first, physical one.

"Husband, will you not see? It's not age that's stopped up my bleedings these seasons past." I pull his hand onto me. "It was a quickening, so long done that here's my water, broke. Blessed Maria and Sainted Anna, I am about to birth a child."

This brings him full awake. He kisses the last of the words from my mouth, and kisses my full belly, and kisses each of my broad haunches. The glad fool even kisses our puddled sheets, he's so pleased at the news.

"A midwife," I remind him, as the church bells ring for lauds-hour.

He dances his way dressed with even greater glee than that which with he usually undresses me. The way he sways and hoots, it seems as if he's still drunk on last night's wine, until he stops before the picture of the Holy Virgin suckling her babe. He crosses himself three times and mutters a prayer to her to keep me well while he is gone. Then my great bear of a husband, forgetting to duck his head, smacks his broad brow hard upon the beam above the doorway. He reels like a buffoon before galloping down the stairs and out into Verona's still-dark streets.

Alone, I look to the Virgin, not sorry it is too dim to make out her familiar features. Whatever apprentice painted her had no great gift, for she is a cockly-eyed thing, the black pupil within one pale blue orb gazing down upon her infant, and the other looking straight out at whoever passes before her. Pietro gave her to me when we married. At twenty he knew no better than to pick her, and at twelve I knew no better than to find her lovely. In the decades since, I've fancied myself worldlier, snickering at her ill form. But there's no snicker in me now, as I ask the most unlikely of mothers how this could be, and will she bless me, and why do my pains not come, since my waters are already loosed. It's a one-sided conversation, like all I ever have with her. Lonely and terrified, I lie flat on my back, kneading the thick flesh of my sides but afraid to touch my belly. Waiting for Pietro, and the midwife, and my own last and least expected infant to arrive.

"No birthing chair?"

By the time Pietro returns, the day's light is already stealing into the room, and there's no hiding that the midwife he's brought is gnarled like a walnut, with a palsy shaking her hands and head. I cannot imagine where my husband unearthed such a decrepit creature, though I suppose we are lucky that at such an hour he found anyone at all. She sends him away as soon as he shows her in, leaving only me and her assistants, twin girls so half-witted the pair of them do not seem the equivalent of a singleton, to listen to her complaints—the first of which is the absence of a birthing chair. Her only solace in hearing I have none is to say it is just as well, as I am too fat for a baby to escape me seated upright.

Next, she demands to know when my last bowel movement was. Too many days past for me to remember, is the best I can answer. I've not marked each bodily passing like it's some holy feast. Not with such wind, such colic, and such loosing and then stopping-up of bowels as I've had these years past. Why keep careful count of all the troubles that time, that thief of youth and health, works upon my body? We are not wealthy. Though Pietro would insist on seeking out physick and apothecary if ever I spoke of these ailments, I know such things are beyond our means. So I've taken what comfort I could in having Pietro's honeyed sweets in my mouth, and tried to find in my husband's doting some relief, if not remedy, for everything I suffer.

The midwife seizes on my constipation as though it's the only care either of us has in all the world. Displaying a gleaming desire to purge my bowels, she sends one twin off for common mallow, borax, and dog's mercury to be boiled into a soup, while she sets the other to rubbing chamomile and linseed crushed in olive oil into some hidden nether place where front and back join between my legs. It's not hard to tell which of those girls she favors.

Only when at last I shit to her satisfaction does she turn her attention to delivering my child. She produces a small dowel for the kitchen-twin to coat in chicken fat, then has the other twin open me with it so the midwife might survey my insides. She tells me to scream, loud as I can. I do not find this hard to do, with a fat-coated dowel shoved in me. I shout till I am hoarse, which finally brings on the first birthing pains. A fine trick that, no voice left for howling just when you want to howl most.

From time to time, my banished Pietro calls up from the street, saying he has a gift for me. One twin or the other runs down, returning first with a tiny woven pouch containing a Santa Margherita charm, then with a marten's tooth, then with a wooden parto tray rubbed so smooth with use, I cannot make out which sainted mother is bearing which holy babe in the scene painted upon it. Though I curse the money-lenders and the marketwomen so eager to prey upon my worried husband, I wrap my hand around charm and tooth, and tell the twins to set the tray where I can easily see it. Fourteen years it's been, since he last had cause to lavish me with parto gifts. A dozen years since, in my maddened grief, I burned up all the ones he'd ever given me upon a plaguey pyre. I can feel the heat of that fire now, am bathed in the sweat of it, as I beg Santa Margherita and the figure on the parto tray and our cockly-eyed Holy Virgin to make this baby come.

The day is already past its hottest when Pietro sends up three eggs. One tawny, one spring-sky blue, and the last a purest white. The midwife spins the eggs one by one atop my belly, snorting with approval when each comes to rest pointing to my woman-parts. Pricking a hole on the top and bottom of each egg, she bids me blow out the yolks. The twins fill the first shell with amaranth, the second with fennel seed, and the third with sow thistle, each of which the midwife says I am to rub upon my breasts every night to keep my milk thick and plentiful. Setting the shells in a varie-gated row beneath the Virgin's picture, she beats the eggs till the golden yolks stain all through the glossy whites. In the next pause between my pains, one twin feeds me raw egg swirled in red wine. As I struggle to keep the loose, thick mixture down, the other twin greases my nether end with the rest of the eggs combined with oil of dill, while the midwife lights a votive and mutters an abraca-dabra of prayer.

After the candle burns low, she orders me to kneel wide-kneed on the floor. The twins heap pillows behind me, and the midwife instructs me to arch back over the pile until my head touches the worn wooden floorboards. I tell her I saw an acrobat once that might have contorted backward like that, but he was a strapping young lad, which I most certainly am not. The twins each grab one of my shoulders, stretching and pushing according to the midwife's commands, until I'm as close to that improbable position as a woman my size and age can get.

Once I'm stretched neck to knees like racked linen, the tight globe of my belly pointing up, the midwife lays one icy hand atop the great mound of me, and works the other inside. Palsy shakes her so furiously, I feel the tremors deep within me. I lie folded back like that until my shins are numb, my back cricked, and the upside-down world no longer unfamiliar, before her bony hands jiggle the baby loose. I swear it stands straight up within me, my belly-button a brimless cap upon its hidden head. It balances like that a short minute, then pitches down again facing the opposite direction. But still, it will not push its way out of me.

All my other babies, conceived as they were from Pietro's randy youth and my ready young womb, were eager to press their way into the world. Nunzio came just two months after quickening, and Nesto only three. Donato barely brought me any birthing pains, and Enzo kicked and pushed himself out while Donato was still at my breast. I'd not begun to bleed again before I was carrying Berto, so I cannot say how many months he grew inside me, though it seemed a scanty few. And Angelo, my littlest angel, began to drop from me as I bent to blow out a candle, and was halfway into the world before we had the wick relit. But this baby feels the slowness of our ages. Though I try to fill the time with hopeful prayers,

I cannot help but think of certain horrors. The widow in the village where I grew up, who swelled four years before she was delivered. A young bride startled by a fox on the way to her wedding bed, who bore a pointy-faced child whose body was thick with reddish fur. The cousin of Pietro's who birthed twins, one as perfect as an orchid bloom, the other a ghastly bluish-purple beast.

The midwife quizzes her assistants on what they think she ought to try, to pry the baby from me. "Girdle the laboring mother with vervain leaves gathered before dawn on the feast day of San Giovanni," recites one. She sounds quite convincing until, picking with a grimy fingernail at a freckle on her chin, she adds, "Or is it plantain leaves, gathered at evening on the feast day of San Giorgio?"

The second twin shakes her head. "Have her wear her husband's shoes upon her hands and his pants upon her head," she insists. "Perch his hat upon her abdomen, while she recites the name of his mother, and his mother's mother, and her mother before her, backward, and begs forgiveness from all their saints."

They go back and forth like that, until at last the midwife claps them each on the ear with a satisfying smack. She informs them that it is time to fumigate my womb, as the smoke from a fire of salt-fish and horse hooves should surely get the child moving. This, I think, is clever true. What being would not vacate where it lay, once the stench of herring and hoof reaches it?

We have some small bit of salt-fish in our store, but as I've never found much call in my kitchen for horse hoof, one twin is sent off for that, while the other scrounges up the last of our apples. This is a disappointment for the midwife, who would prefer an artichoke.

I'm not sure it matters much, as she shoves it inside my behind, saying it will tip the womb to help slide the baby free.

But it does not, and neither does the fumigation. The day turns to slant-light, then twilight, then dark, and still the baby is not born. The midwife mutters incantations over me while the twins doze in a heap in the corner and Pietro, having snuck back inside, snores from the kitchen floor. In these small hours, I sink into a wet chasm of pain. Muddy, bloody walls undulate high on either side of me, threatening to cave in if I struggle too hard to claw my way out. From this place I pray, not to the Sacred Madonna or any of the blessed saints or even to the Most Holy Trinity, but to my own child. *Come out to me, dearest lamb. If the world is so cruel you are frightened of it, I will hold you, and protect you, and teach it to love you as I already love you.* Words I dare not say aloud but form in my mind, so that my little one alone can hear.

By the next ringing of matins bells, I fear there is no baby in me. Had I not bled four days in a row, some time this past spring? But as the sun slowly rises I feel that my belly is indeed full, though what is waiting to be birthed is not a new babe. It must be one of my well-grown boys, come back to claim the mother-love that floods through me once again, a love I thought I'd buried in the single grave that swallowed all of them. In such delirium, I do not mark the new ways in which my body is stretched and twisted by the midwife's apprentices, what is rubbed or dripped or shoved onto or into the varying parts of me. I come to my senses as the sext bells ring at midday, to find myself standing with an arm over each twin's shoulders, the three of us walking a circle like blinded mules turning a mill-wheel. We grind on and on for hours. When, bathed in sweat and mad with thirst, I beg for water, the midwife gives me only wine. But when I plead to be numbed by wine, all I get is tepid water. You can pray to God and holy saints for compassion, but do not bother to ask it of this midwife.

It is the afternoon of Lammas Eve when the baby finally arrives. A daughter, the first I ever bore. I am so grateful when she passes from me, I croak out an exhausted, "Hosanna." But "Susanna" is what the ancient midwife hears. She bathes, swaddles, and bundles my babe. Worn as I am, I can barely raise my head to steal a glimpse of my precious girl before the midwife calls out the window for Pietro, who she chased back out of the house at daybreak, to take Susanna to be baptized. Then she orders one twin to shove hellebore petals up my nose until I sneeze the afterbirth into the other twin's waiting hands.

Delivered of my daughter, I sleep. When I wake the night is late, the fire out, the room empty. I might believe the laboring and birth all a dream, but for the soreness between my legs, the animal stench of blood and sweat and secundine that hangs in the dark. And the terrific ache that swells my breasts, my hardened nipples ready for Susanna's mouth. Swollen and tender, I hear Pietro's sobs filling the dark house.

A man will cry for joy when his wife has born his son. A soft-hearted man will even weep astonished tears over the delicate beauty of a new daughter. But this animal sound Pietro makes is different. I know it, and the knowing stings spear-sharp through my waiting breasts.

This is why the midwife sent her off so quick, that my child's tiny soul might fare better than her tiny body would. What ill-formed thing did the midwife sense in my newborn that, with a mother's heart, I missed? I cannot know. And I'll not forgive myself for not knowing.

In my sleep, I'd clutched the Santa Margherita charm in one hand and the marten's tooth in the other. Cupping my belly against the crude stigmata they've pressed into my palms, I wonder how, in all the months my daughter lived in me, babe and mother a single breathing being, I'd not let myself know her. Such a fool I was, not to even admit that she was there. And now, when I most crave her, crave the hungry suck with which she would crave me, she is gone.

What's tomb is womb. That is what the holy friars preached when Death with his plaguey army robbed us of so much, more than a decade past. Worms will turn dead leaves, dead trees, dead men into new soil. But what can worms do for a living, grieving woman?

Let the brown-frocked friars tremble with awe over how the tomb of earth sprouts seedlings. Such wonders are no comfort when you birth a babe who dies.

When next I wake, the room is filled with golden light, and all Verona smells of yeasty bread. It is Lammas Day, a harvest feast. Sown seeds reaped as grain, then ground and baked to rounded loaves. Pietro, red-eyed and bewildered, kneels beside our bed, tearing small pieces of the blessed bread. Dipping some in honey, some in wine. Feeding each to me. Could anything be so sweet against the metallic taste of grief?

A Lammas Day procession winds past, its drums and shouts

and trumpets echoing against the tight-packed buildings, resonating across our floor and up our walls. After the noise passes away, Pietro slips his hands beneath me, his palms warm against the ache across my back. "Susanna is—"

I shake my head, cutting him off. I will not let him say the word. Will not make myself listen to it.

Why could we two not just be alone, like we'd been the seasons past, and happy? But there they are, the portrait of the Holy Madonna suckling sacred babe upon our wall, and some saint or other being newly born upon the parto tray that holds the honey, bread, and wine. Icons of what we cannot have, blessed mothers such as I'm reminded I'll never again be. The plague that stole our other children laid half the city dead. But this fresh loss comes to us alone. This is grief's great trick: you think you have faced the worst of it, not dreaming of all that is yet to come.

Somewhere outside a lonely kitten mewls, and my milk begins to run. Pietro catches the first weak drops on his pinky finger, a too-delicate gesture for a lustful husband. He wets a cloth and washes me, dresses me, rebraids the great length of my hair, and covers it. Then he guides me to my feet, and leads me down the stairs and through Verona's crooked streets. Sore and stiff, I move slowly. But what aches most drives me on, as I hold Pietro's arm, repeating to myself the promise he whispered as he lifted me from our bed. There is a baby waiting. Needing me as much as I need her.

We leave our familiar parish, Pietro guiding me past the towers and guild-halls and churches that mark the way to the Piazza delle Erbe. Even with the merchant stalls closed up for Lammas Day, the air hangs fragrant with basil, rosemary, and fennel, the last reminding me that I left my herb-filled eggshells behind. But I'll not turn back. I need no remedies, no potions. I need only a child to draw out what is already thick in me.

We cross below the Lamberti tower, to where the piazza narrows into the Via Cappello. This parish is not a place I ever come, for what have I to do with the Scaligeri princes and the wealthy families who guarantee their power? Nothing. Until today. This holy-day when, stopping midway along the Via Cappello, my husband raises a grand carved knocker and swings it hard against the wooden door. The door opens, and beneath an archway tall enough to admit a man on horseback, I enter Ca' Cappelletti.

The Cappelletti house does not smell of yeasty Lammas Day offerings, nor of the goods sold in the herb-market. There is no hint of the fetid waste that fills Verona's streets or the hogs roaming loose to feed upon it. Those odors cannot breach these walls, thick as a cathedral's. I breathe in the miracle of it, as a house-page no older than an altar boy nods a curt dismissal to Pietro, then leads me alone through the cool air of the ground floor, perfumed by the household's stores of wine and grains, cured meats, hard cheeses, and infused oils. I follow him up stone stairs to a storey so full of wool carpets, fur robes, and lit perfumers, their rich smells settle as tastes on my tongue. The walls and even the wooden ceiling beams are painted with holy images here, and exotic beasts there, and everywhere repeating shapes and dancing patterns that dizzy me.

We wind past the great sala and through the family's private apartments to an intimate corner of the house. The page stops before a heavy pair of curtains, scraping agitated lines along his neck and stammering out that he's not bidden to go any farther. I part the curtains and, passing between their woven scenes of hinds and hares frolicking in some imagined forest, I enter the confinement room.

A maid-servant weaves through the room with trays of roasted capon and sweetmeats, serving a dozen gossiping women who circle around the new mother's bed. Most of the guests wear jeweled overdresses heavily embroidered with the crests of the city's finest families. The others have the full-skirted habits of Verona's wealthiest convents. No one notices me enter, except a sharp-eyed midwife's assistant, who slips a swaddled bundle into my arms, whispering, "Juliet."

Juliet—a little jewel. No ruby, no sapphire, no diamond could dazzle more. My little jewel and I are as eager for each other as young lovers. Settling upon an enormous pillow on the floor, I cradle her in one arm, loose my milk-soaked blouse, and offer up a breast. She takes it with such lively greed as makes me smile. When she's sucked that, and then the other, to her satisfaction, I lay her down before me on the silken cushion. I snug her head between my calves, her swaddled feet tucking into my plump thighs, my thumbs tracing the soft smooth of her tiny cheeks. Sainted Maria, the very sight of her bursts my mother-heart.

Juliet is my earth, and I am her moon, so caught in our celestial sphere we exist entirely apart from the rest of the bustling confinement room. Invisible even to the new mother lying in the parto bed, who lifts her slender arm, coral bracelets jangling down her wrists. With no more signal than that, silver goblets and flasks of trebbiano are brought out for the guests. Bright maiolica bowls appear, their lids hiding spiced stews. Trays come piled with sponge cakes and marzipans and fine salts. All eaten with a set of delicately worked silver forks brought by Prince Cansignorio's aunt, who repeats to each woman who arrives how they were chosen from the Scaligeri inventories by the prince himself.

I care nothing for the lavish confinement gifts, nor for any of the room's fine furnishings, except the heavy silver tub in which I wash Juliet, and the iron brazier over which I warm the swaddling bands to wrap her. To tend, to touch so little a living delight. I lean close to smell the delicate baby scent of her, and know it is my milk on her breath, my kiss on her downy hair. *Dearest lamb,* I whisper with those kisses, *do not worry or wonder what all those other noises are, who makes them and why. They do not matter, now that I am here. Here for you.*

Juliet has a ferocious hunger, rousing herself six or seven times during our first night to nurse. I do not bother to lace my blouse, keeping a breast ready so that she'll not cry and wake the house. But to feed her, I must be fed. In some quiet hour, hungry from her hunger, I steal up to the table beside the parto bed, where remnants of Lady Cappelletta's supper remain. A taper flickers beneath a portrait of Santa Margherita. Is it any wonder the saints favor the rich for offering up such extravagant devotions even while they sleep, when the rest of us can barely afford to keep a candle lit upon a worktable when we are full awake?

In the dancing light, I pick the darkest of the meat. Even cold, it is the finest I've ever eaten. I close my eyes, sucking poultry-flesh from bone, savoring the flavors until I feel another set of eyes upon me. Lady Cappelletta's.

I slip the purloined bone inside my sleeve, so I'll not be called a thief. But well-fed as Lady Cappelletta is, she does not seem to mark what I've taken.

She stares at my untrussed breasts. "Is that what they do to them? Suckle like piglets till they fall flab?"

Standing so close beside her parto bed, I see she is hardly more than a child herself, consumed by girlish fear at what her body is, what it will become. "Time will do what time will do," I say. "No one stays"—I peer at her and make a careful guess—"fourteen forever."

She looks down at the bumps that even after pregnancy barely bring a curve to her nightshirt. "I'm already turned fifteen."

"An age when bud turns into bloom." An age that is but a third of my own. Her face, her neck, are smooth as a statue, her bead- and braid-strung hair shining. Lady Cappelletta is that beauty the poets call a just-plucked rose, and gossiping old dowagers call a coin that's not yet spent. Wondering that this is not enough to please her, I add, "And blessed that your child is healthy." She cannot know what those words cost me.

"So what if it is?"

"Not it," I say. "She. A beautiful daughter of a beautiful mother."

Some hard emotion pulls at the edges of her pretty mouth. "Who should have borne a son."

"You are young. There will be sons yet."

"I am young, but my lord husband is not." She shudders when she speaks of him. "Neither is he patient."

Surely tonight all her husband's thinking of is how much it costs to dower the daughter of so fine a house—that will shrivel more than a man's impatience. But who am I to tell her so?

"He'll climb right back upon me," she says, "to make a son."

Fear tinges her words. Perchance it's more than age that makes them ill-matched. He must run hot, as men do, and she cold, as I for one do not. Although never having seen her husband, I cannot say whether there is anything in him that might please any woman. Especially one barely out of girlhood.

"The midwife will tell him he must wait, as all men do," I say, thinking of how Pietro brought me here out of our marriage bed.

Her fingers, heavy with pearl rings, tug at the gold-and-garnet cross that hangs around her neck, then turn the coral bracelets upon either wrist. Extravagant talismans, doubtless from her husband's family, which no one thought to unclasp at night so she might sleep in comfort.

She's sorely in need of mothering herself, new mother though she is. I could sit upon this grand bed, stroking her hair and whispering soothing words until her hands lie calm. I might tell her that many a wife whose husband gives her no pleasure in the getting of babies still finds great joy in the children she's borne. But Juliet begins to stir, and I turn my back to the parto bed to take up the child who is my charge.

TWO

For the first five weeks, I see nothing of the Cappelletti compound except the confinement room. But Lady Cappelletta is not wrong about Lord Cappelletto's eagerness to make a son. The day after I arrive, her breasts are bound in squash leaves to dry their milk and keep her fertile. And at five weeks to the hour of when her labor ended, her husband—who's not bothered to make a single visit to the confinement room—orders her brought back to their marriage bed. The fire in the confinement room is put out, the parto linens and sumptuous wall-hangings folded away for when she'll bear again. The handsome walnut-and-ivory cradle, with its fine white Levantine silk and gold-fringed coverlet, is moved through the family apartments to what will ever after be Juliet's room.

Her own room. Bigger than the one in which my whole family

slept, and hung with fabrics I cannot even name, fabrics so mysterious and beautiful I know they're not from Verona or Mantua or any land where anyone I know has ever been. It has art like a grand parish church, paintings of the Blessed Maria and the Sainted Anna, and a niche as big as a man filled with a statue of San Zeno. All smile their holy approval onto a bed that's wide enough for a bride, a groom, and half their wedding party. The headboard and footboard rise so high, it's like a little fortress when the bed curtain closes around them. Outside the footboard sits a cassone-chest longer than I am tall, its sides and cover carved with chubby angels. When I open it, the woody scent of rosemary seeps from the dresses stored inside. Garments sized for a child of two, of four, of six, each more elegant than the next—a bishop's ransom worth of clothing, waiting for my tiny Juliet to grow big enough to wear. And beside the massive bed, a narrow, low-slung truckle-bed for me.

Juliet's chamber glows with light, a perfect setting for my little jewel. There is a window that stretches from below my knees to high above my head, broad as my open arms. My fingers are greedy to touch its thick, warbled panes. Real Venetian glass, nothing like the waxed-cloth windows on the Via Zancani. These panes are set within a heavy frame hinged to swing wide, to let in air from the Cappelletti's private arbor. In all the years I've lived among the city's crooked, crowded streets, I've never known that such trees grow within Verona's walls, their ripe fruit so fragrant. This is what the rich have: the prettiest smells in all the world, and the means to close out even those whenever they want.

It is a bright September day, so I keep the window open while I sit in a high-backed chair and sing to Juliet. I sing, she sleeps. Surely no harm if I sleep too, dreaming the golden sun is Pietro come to warm me, inside and out. It's a dream so real, I wake certain I feel the very weight of him, and find a poperin pear lying in my lap.

I might believe Pietro is here withal, when I see that. *Pop-her-in*, he calls the bulging fruit, wagging a pear from his breech-lace whenever I bring some home from the market. But shut within the Cappelletti compound, it cannot be Pietro who pranks me.

A boy of nine or ten perches on the bottom of the window frame, watching me. His light brown hair falls in loose, soft curls to his chin. His face stretches long for a child's, as if the man in him is already struggling to make his way out. His arms and legs are thin and strong, although not pinched by work like my sons' were. He pulls his head high and announces, "I am the king of cats."

I've not forgotten how to manage a playful boy. Picking up the pear by its round bottom, I wave the peaked tip at him. "A cat who hunts fruit instead of mice?"

"Cats climb," he says with feline pride. "I heard whistling outside our wall. When I climbed over to see what it was, a man asked if I would bring that to you."

I ask who the man was, as if I do not already know.

The boy describes my strong bull of a husband to the very mole above his left eyebrow, while I bite deep into the pear. "He said to tell you that if you like that, he has something even juicier for you to eat."

Though I blush, the child seems ignorant of what charming filth Pietro bade him speak. "How did you know to bring this here, to me?"

He laughs, raising both knees and rolling back. Backward out the window. My heart goes cold, the pear-flesh stuck in my throat.

But in an instant two small hands appear on the bottom of the window-case. The child vaults himself into the chamber, turns a somersault, and leaps up. "I am Tybalt, king of cats. I climb, and I jump, and I know all that happens in Ca' Cappelletti." He struts back and forth like the Pope's official messenger proclaiming the latest Bull. "That is my cousin, and you are her nurse, and tomorrow is the Nativity of the Blessed Virgin, and before you go to be shriven the man will meet you, and he will give you three almond sweets to give to me, as long as you give your sweets to him."

"Tybalt my king of cats," I say, careful to hide my surprise that Pietro has trusted this strange boy to bear me these naughty tidings, "how clever you must be, to keep such delicious secrets."

The mention of secrets sets off another round of acrobatics. "I know every hidden passageway in Ca' Cappelletti, and which alcoves to stand in to overhear what somebody is saying." He gives his narrow chest a proud thump. "I've climbed all the way to the top of our tower, as high as the campanile of Sant'Anastasia. The perch is filled with rocks I carried up myself, some as big as a man's head, to throw on any enemies who pass below."

"Any enemies?" I raise the pear to my mouth, to hide my smile.

"The Cappelletti have many enemies," he says. "Because we are so brave and pious."

A man makes more enemies being cruel and quick-tempered than brave or pious. But there's time enough for this Tybalt to learn such things, so I only nod and tell him I can see how gallant he is, and bid him finish off the pear as his reward.

He takes the knife from his belt, assaulting the pear as though it has offended his honor. He carves the pale fruit-flesh with the same coat-of-arms that is painted along the corbels and patterned in golden thread into the Cappelletti linens. Neither Pietro nor I were born to families who had so much as a surname, let alone a scroll-worked crest to herald that name to all the world. But the Cappelletti coat-of-arms is a bewildering thing. Unlike most shields one sees around Verona, which feature eagles or dragons or other formidable beasts, this one boasts only a peaked mitre-hat.

"Does your family make hats?" I ask, though I doubt that even the most gifted milliners could ever amass such a fortune as built Ca' Cappelletti.

Tybalt scores the air with his dagger to correct me. "Not hats, chapels. Our family endowed so many of them with all we earn from our lands, Pope Innocent III himself decreed we should be named for them."

"I see the joke," I say, the word for the Pope's mitre-hat sounding in our Veronese dialect almost the same as the word for chapel.

"It's not a joke," Tybalt insists. "It is a shibboleth."

I do not know what a shibboleth is, cannot guess why Tybalt's so proud that some long-dead Pope gifted his Cappelletti ancestors with one. But from the way he swaggers out the word, I know how best to answer. "A shibboleth. How clever."

This brings another smile to the boy's face, and he lists the names of a half dozen bygone emperors, telling me how they hated the Popes and the Popes hated them. How this emperor warred against that Pope, and the next Pope plotted against the subsequent emperor. On and on for a hundred and fifty years, the Cappelletti always siding with the Pope, supplying knights and horses to capture whole towns from rival families named Uberti and Infangati and Montecchi. A catalogue of bloody conflicts this Tybalt's been taught to recite like a poet singing a love-ballad.

How much easier it is to be poor than rich. We are too busy scrambling to find enough to eat each day to worry ourselves over the centuries' worth of slaughtering that consumes a boy like Tybalt, who chews thick slices from the pear as he schools me about his esteemed relations. His father is Giaccomo, and Juliet's is Leonardo, and they are brothers. Very cunning, very courageous, and very rich, ever plotting against anyone who dishonors their noble family. Just like all the Cappelletti who came before them. When I ask which man is the elder, Tybalt laughs and tells me they are too old for anyone to remember. From this I figure that his father must be the younger, for an older brother never fails to impress his son about his rightful place in the family line.

"And your mother?" I make my words sound light, so they'll not betray my worry. Tybalt's mother cannot be near so young as Juliet's, to have a son of his age. If she is cruel or jealous, she will make life hard for her sister-in-law. And for Juliet, and me.

"My mother is with the angels." Tybalt turns to throw the pear core out the window. He keeps his back to me, his voice unsteady as he tells how his mother passed just before Michaelmas, birthing his sister Rosaline.

Not yet a year gone. The air of death still lingering in the confinement room when young Lady Cappelletta was brought in for her own recent childbearing.

"You must love your sister very much," I say, to ease any resentment Tybalt might have for the baby whose birth brought the death of their mother.

"I've never seen her. My father sent her away to be nursed, so that he'd not be reminded."

Only a man could have such sentiment: to love a departed wife so much, he banishes the child she bore.

Juliet stirs in her cradle, giving a little cry as if to confirm the folly of men. Every wisp of her first golden hair has fallen out. But even bald as an ancient abbot, Juliet is still my beauty. I take her into my arms, telling myself I only want to check her swaddling, to be sure each limb is wrapped tight.

Tybalt sees how needy I am just for the feel of her. "My uncle thinks my father is a fool. He says not even a daughter should be sent off as a newborn."

Much as I agree, I know better than to confirm aloud that his father is a fool. Instead, I motion the boy close and place his tiny cousin into his arms, hoping she'll make up for the sister he does not know. He wiggles one of his small fingers before her face, and she smiles up at him. "You must protect your cousin Juliet, and your sister Rosaline."

He nods, touching that same eager finger to where his knife hangs at his waist, as if he might need at any moment to ward off some grave threat. My Pietro was a motherless boy, and it was the love of his doting older sisters that taught him to love me. Why should I not give this serious, tumbling Tybalt more to care about than almond candies and ancient feuds?

Juliet sleeps heavily our first night in her bedchamber, but I am wakeful, worrying over how I will contrive a way out of this room and away from Ca' Cappelletti, to meet Pietro. How I miss my husband's snores, the way even in sleep his great bear-paw of a hand cups my rump or hip or the soft curve of my belly. We've never been so long apart, even after my other lying-ins, for we have but one bed. When each of our sons was born, Pietro placed the newborn boy on the bolster above our heads, and entertained me by translating their gurglings into wild tales of where they'd been and what they'd seen before coming into this world, as one by one our older boys dropped off to sleep. He spun weeks and weeks of such stories, filling the nights until I was well again.

All that fills the night in this great chamber is the sound of Juliet's small breath, and the church bells counting off the three hours between compline and matins, then the three between matins and lauds. And in between the tolling, the songs of the nightingales in the arbor. Their trillings have barely given way to the first morning lark's insistent chirps when, without so much as a knock, a man strides into the chamber, the dangling ends of his broad silver belt clanging with each heavy footfall. He's of great girth if no great height, and as anyone but a blind man can tell from every gilded stitch upon him, rich. With a rich man's surety of all that is his due, he demands, "Where is my Juliet?"

My Juliet. Hearing him say those words makes me despise him, detesting how his silvery hair grows thick from his ears and nose yet thin upon his head. Holding my milk-sodden nightdress closed, I fold back the coverlet and reveal my darling lamb, perfect in her sleep.

He lifts her up, away from me. I feel the warmth go out of the truckle-bed, the slight hollow where she lay chilling into an abyss as Lord Cappelletto cradles her in his arms. His liver-colored lips kiss her creamy cheek, those bristly nostrils widening to take in the precious scent of her.

His thick fingers draw a tiny cap from his doublet pocket. It is a deep indigo, worked with gold. A perfect miniature of the elegant headpiece Lady Cappelletta wears, though with fewer rows of pearls. Too delicate in its silk and jewels for an infant. But when he puts it on Juliet's new-bald head, she strains against her swaddling as though she means to raise her own tiny hand to settle the cap in place.

"Juliet Cappelletta di Cappelletto," he says to her. Not in some foolish cooing singsong, like my doting Pietro would. But Lord Cappelletto's deep voice betrays an adoration that does not seem to fit a man who'd not bothered to make a single visit to his wife's confinement room.

"Your milk is fresh?" He asks me this the way a man fingering his coin purse might inquire about the strength of a plough-ox.

"It came the same day she was born." I turn my back to him as I lace my nightdress, to keep him from surveying me in the way I've surveyed him. Though in truth he's not raised his gaze from Juliet.

"You sent your own child off?"

This is what he thinks of me. That I would pay some peasant in the hills to take my just-born child, so I could earn a few soldi more by nursing his. I turn to him with a stare that could vinegar whole casks of wine. "Susanna was not sent, she was taken." I cross myself. "God rest all Christian souls."

He crosses himself, repeating my prayer before adding, "I christened Juliet for my most cherished, departed mother, God keep her in His rest." This surprises me. I'd not known she'd already been baptized, being but a day old when I came to her. He presses a thumb gently to her forehead, just as the priest must have done. "The prince himself stood for her, and so did Il Benedicto."

Two godfathers, and well chosen. Prince Cansignorio Scaligero is the most powerful man in the city, having killed his own brother this winter past to seize the rule of Verona. And Il Benedicto is the most pious, as resolved to be poor as the prince is to be rich. Il Benedicto owns nothing but a haircloth shirt, sleeps in the doorway of whichever church he finds himself nearest to when the curfew bells are rung, and eats only if some stranger, moved by some mixt of guilt and charity, presses food on him. No one knows his true name or his family or where he came from, nor why he chose, longer ago than anyone can remember, to evangelize in our streets. Some say Il Benedicto is too devout to abide the petty corruptions of a monastery. Others whisper he's too unschooled to be allowed to join a religious order. But not one of the tens of thousands of souls in all Verona doubts that this pauper is the nearest of us to God. No man could do better than this calculating Lord Cappelletto has, guaranteeing his family the protection of both God and government by binding his daughter to such godfathers.

His daughter, their goddaughter—but my darling lamb. And easier for me to scheme a way out of Ca' Cappelletti with her, now that I know how much Lord Cappelletto wants the world to think him pious. "Bless the saints," I say, and I do bless them, for giving me my chance to see Pietro, "if she is already baptized, she can join the children's procession for the Nativity of the Blessed Virgin." Making myself as big-eyed as a cow, I offer to carry her, if his lordship wishes it.

He purses those liver lips, unsure. So I add, "Il Benedicto leads the procession, kneeling." It is only a guess, but surely a good one, as Il Benedicto never misses a chance to inspire Verona with his bloody-kneed piety.

"Make sure Il Benedicto blesses her on the steps of the Duomo, once everyone is assembled just before the procession starts," he tells me. "And carry her toward the front of the cortege, near Prince Cansignorio's favored nephews."

I nod my feigned obedience. What trouble is it to me to keep her close to the swaggering little counts, at least until I can slip away to see Pietro?

But Lord Cappelletto will not leave me and Juliet be. He points to the empty cradle, with its sumptuous layette. "My daughter is not to be taken into a servant's truckle-bed."

"She naps in the cradle. But nights are long for a child to be alone." As they are for a full-grown woman. "If I keep her close, she'll not cry."

Juliet gurgles a smile at him. Already she knows how to rule a man. Nestling against Lord Cappelletto, she softens him from an imperious father into something closer to a doting grandpapa. "I suppose if Juliet prefers it, you may put her down for the night in her bed, and lie there yourself," he says. "Only until she is old enough to mind you sleeping beside her, but that will be some time yet."

Some time. I hold his words tight in my chest, guarantee of all the hours they promise I'll have with Juliet.

My breasts are hard and full again, and I reach for my nursling, needing her to suck the ache away. But before Lord Cappelletto will let me have her, he says, "Make sure Juliet wears the Cappelletto headpiece, always. Not only when you take her out, but whenever she is awake."

He means for me to know she is above me. But surely it is only him who is above, too certain of his superiority to see that silk and pearls and all King Midas' piss-streams of gold could not equal the worth of what flows between my milk-babe and me.

Juliet begins to work her mouth into the demanding circle I know so well. As her lips curl in and out, I wait, knowing that when the first cry comes Lord Cappelletto will have to give her back to me. Only I can give her what she most wants. What she truly needs.

When you make the circuit of a city's churches following a kneeling supplicant, you move with God's glory, but not with God-speed. The Nativity Day procession forms a snake of many parts, slithering slowly away from the Duomo, a thousand Ave Marias swallowing the rhythmic slapping of the Adige against the city's edge. Juliet begins to fuss as soon as the cortege turns south. By the time we reach the Chapel of the Sainted Apostles, her tiny lungs hit full howl.

You might think the celebrants of the birth of the Holy Mother would greet an infant's cry with *alleleuia* and *amen*. But we're surrounded by a rivalry of mamas, each trying to push their little ones closer to the head of the procession in the hope of winning the Blessed Virgin's favor. Or at least of having something to brag over, when they gather tomorrow at one or another of the city fountains to haul water home for their daily round of chores.

Marking what tart looks and bitter murmurs we get for disturbing the solemn rite, I pinch Juliet's swaddled bottom to be sure she'll keep up her wailing, which I take as my excuse to steer us out of the piazza. Once we're free of the crowd, I slip the jeweled cap from her head, hiding it in my sleeve so no one will know her for a Cappelletta as I carry her toward the Via Zancani. Toward home.

Pietro meets us in the doorway, gathering me and Juliet together in his big arms, his thick chest absorbing the last of her howls. "How I've missed you, Angelica," he says, guiding us inside. "These have been the loneliest weeks of all my life."

He's kept house as best he can in my absence, which even in what little light steals through the waxed cloth that covers our window-holes, I see is terribly. This should please me, for what woman is not glad to know how helpless her husband is without her? But here in our dim little room, the loss of Susanna cuts even more sharply than it has during all the weeks I've been gone.

In the familiar nest of our marriage bed, I bury myself against

Pietro, and he buries himself inside me. As though we could lose our freshest grief in pleasure taking. This is the crudest comfort we can offer each other, and like beasts driven by their heat, we take it.

After we are spent, I lie in Pietro's arms with Juliet at my breast, breathing in the warm scent of the straw mattress. For a few precious moments, it is as if Susanna lived, and we are a family. Until the noise creeps into the room. A steady, droning buzz, coming from the opening to the roof, a sound I know in my bones.

"You brought a hive here?"

"It's too quiet, all alone." His voice tremolos against the hum of the bees. "Not in all the years of my army did I ever think this house could be so quiet."

Pietro's army. That's what he called our boys. Half a dozen sons, each a head taller than the next, from Angelo, not yet two years and squirming in one of his older brother's arms, to Nunzio, at fifteen already of a height to look Pietro directly in the eye. These little rooms could hardly contain them all, and whichever way I turned I'd find one of the older boys tickling a younger one until both shrieked with joy, or one of the littler ones stomping and strutting in proud imitation of his bigger brothers. If Enzo began to sing, soon enough you'd hear a chorus, and if Berto let slip some wind, the others would join in to make a stinking cacophony. Once when I sent Donato to bring my loaves to the public oven, he passed a preacher who drew a crowd by imitating a tree-frog's call, and for months afterward our home sounded with a pond's worth of rib-biting. This little house was never still, never silent, with Pietro's army. Until, within a single ugly week, every one of them was dead.

I tell Pietro that all day the Cappelletti compound is noisy as a little village. "But at night, if I wake, I hear only Juliet. Her breath." I shift her from my breast and lay her down between us, show him how I turn my head over hers, holding a cheek above her dainty nose and milk-wet mouth to feel that breath on me. Then slowly, slowly, I lower my head onto her chest, laying my ear over her heart. Careful, always, not to burden her tiny body with the weight of me. How many hours I've held myself like this, just to be certain of her during the darkest of night.

When I lift my head, Pietro props himself on his elbow and rests his own cheek onto Juliet's small body. He closes those beautiful eyes of his and listens, squeezing my hand with gentle pulses that echo the beating of her heart.

Lying entwined with them beneath the portrait of the Holy Madonna, all I want is to feel her cockly-eyed blessing on us. But I cannot ignore the bizz-buzzings shimmering up my spine. "You know it frightens me to have bees so near."

Pietro drops my hand and rolls away from me and Juliet. "They may be near, but you're not." Lying on his back, he stares up at the ladder-hole to the roof, watching the bees crossing above.

I wish now that Lord Cappelletto shared his sorrowful brother's sentiment. But with all his prideful love for Juliet, he'd never allow her to live in the cramped quarters of a wet-nurse. Not when he could summon any of a hundred peasant women to Ca' Cappelletti, to nurse her there.

All around the city, churchbells begin to ring. Knowing the Virgin's procession must be nearing its end, I rise from our bed. I pull my veil and my gown and Juliet's pearl-beaded headdress from where they're heaped with Pietro's clothes, and begin to dress. I count out three almond comfits to bring Tybalt, leaving all the rest behind as I bid my husband good-bye.

Before returning to the Via Cappello, I carry Juliet to the Franciscan friary, ready to cover her innocent ears while I confess the bittersweet pleasures I've just taken with Pietro. Though the Pope may go to Babylon and back proclaiming that it's a sin to revel in any pleasures of the body, the Franciscans are forgiving sorts, if you make sure to sprinkle *blessed husband, conjugal duties,* and *matrimonial bed* throughout your shrift. Even so, I'm careful in my choice of confessors.

Friar Lorenzo fancies himself a man of never-ceasing learning. He is writing a treatise on marital relations. Or so the rumor goes, the whispered explanation for why he leans so eager an ear to any penitent who divulges what Friar Lorenzo in his chaste state cannot know directly. Lovesick boys, naughty girls, and many a full-grown man or woman wearing well-rumpled shift or smock—they all warm the cool air of Friar Lorenzo's stone cell with details of their hot lusts. Although the friar is a thin man, practically swimming within the folds of his cassock, he has rather large ears even for a cleric. Between those ears brims the greatest gift for a penitent, a natural history of healing herbs and cordials. When a lady finds herself more harmed than charmed after a visit from the raunchy Mab, in the space of the same shrift with Friar Lorenzo she can confess her sins, be forgiven, and be dispensed some flowery decoction to rid her lips of what blisters she earned playing her lover's trumpet. No wonder Friar Lorenzo is regarded as a treasure without equal in all Verona.

"God give you peace, Angelica," he greets me. "It's been so long since you've come to be shriven, I'd not known which to fear for more, your mortal body or your immortal soul." He lays a hand of blessing on Juliet. "But I see what has kept you away. Lord Cappelletto has already made several generous altar-gifts to celebrate this new member of the Church, and he honored me by choosing my hand to sprinkle her holy baptism." He smiles encouragement at me. "A pleasure, always, to absolve a sin."

I take the holy hint, telling him I hope I'll not disappoint him, having only an hour's worth of lovemaking with my husband to confess. He nods gravely, urging me to unburden myself of every copulatory detail. When I finish, he raises a single eyebrow and asks if that is all.

I bow my head like a dog caught helping himself to a cutlet while the cook's back is turned. "I deceived Lord Cappelletto. I let him believe I only intended to take Juliet to join the procession for the Blessed Virgin. Which I have done. Before I did Pietro."

"And what else?"

"Only Pietro."

"No other bedmate, of course not. But what other sin, my child?" Friar Lorenzo would call even Methuselah himself *my child*, if they ever happened to meet. "Not only in deed, but in thought, we sin."

He means my darling lamb. He can mean only her, for what

other secret do I carry? "Sometimes when we are closed up alone together, I imagine she is my own. My Susanna."

Though he hunted for a sin, I mark from the way he pinches at his ear that he does not care to catch me at this one. It was Friar Lorenzo who baptized Susanna, and blessed her shroud. He's the one who told my grief-struck Pietro of the Cappelletti being in need of a wet-nurse, then arranged the terms of my service with them. "Never question the wisdom of God, or of Church," he tells me. "Do not deceive yourself or the child, about what she is and to which family she belongs."

Wise though Friar Lorenzo is, at this moment I realize all he'll never know. Whatever lusty pleasures I take with my husband, he finds forgivable. But my wishing my dead daughter alive, a mother's most urgent desire—that the celibate cleric cannot possibly understand.

After I bow my head, bend my knee, and say my penance, I step from the friary into an afternoon grown gray. When the first fat drops of rain begin to fall, I stop beneath a narrow archway, steadying my back against the rough stones while I slip Juliet inside my dress to keep her dry. As we make our way through the crooking streets to Ca' Cappelletti, she nestles into the warmth of my body. Nothing comes between us. Nothing.

THREE

Every house has its rhythms, and the first I learn of Ca' Cappelletti's is this: Lord Cappelletto rises before the morning bells. He dresses and washes in the dawn's first streaks of light, then breaks his night-fast in the sala beside Juliet's chamber. By the time the prime-hour bells toll, he's guttled himself full. He comes in and takes Juliet from me, holding her so long that when he hands her back she stinks of Lodi cheese and liver pie. Then he rushes downstairs to hear the first of the day's news cried through the streets, before he disappears into some corner room on the ground floor.

"We're free of him," I tell Juliet, though by my mickled saints, I'm as bound as she is, as I wrap her in fresh swaddling. Shut up in this chamber hour upon hour, as two days, three days, four days have passed, all the same.

But as I rock Juliet in her cradle late in the morning on the fifth day, I see Tybalt crawling out the window opposite, on the far side of Ca' Cappelletti. He slithers on his belly across the kitchen roof, then inches atop the arched entry to the arbor. Passing hand-over-hand along the ledge beneath Juliet's chamber, he pulls himself in through her window.

He carries a toy bird in his mouth, which he drops at my feet. "The king of cats has brought a present for his cousin."

"Even a cat can use a door," I tell him.

"My tutor pushed a cassone against the door, to keep me at my lessons while he goes drinking at the tavern."

Tybalt can escape a room. His tutor can escape the Cappelletti compound. All I can do is stare out the window at what grows within the walled-in arbor. "When your father learns you've disobeyed your tutor—"

"My father is in Mantua, serving at the court of the Gonzaghe. And my uncle is in his study buried in accounting books, except when he's called away to some meeting of the prince's council. And my aunt is in her bedchamber, always in her bedchamber." He pounces on the bird-toy, tossing it into the air and catching it in his mouth. "But now you're here to play with me."

Though the bird's feathers are real, its eyes are dull beads. Flightless, lifeless—like I feel, cabined here.

But I see what the bird-toy cannot: how to play Tybalt by letting him play with me.

"We could have a hide-and-go-a-seeking," I say, "if we could find a place far from your uncle and your aunt."

Tybalt puffs his chest like a blackcock grouse before a hen. "I know the best hidey-hole in Ca' Cappelletti. No one will look for us there."

He pulls back the wall-hanging beside the statue of San Zeno, straining under the weight of the thick weave. Underneath, where I expect bare wall, there's a door with a bolted lock.

A whole world opens off this chamber, and I'd not known it. A world that surely must be full of wonder, if the door is hidden, and barred to me.

Tybalt bids me hold the wall-hanging while he draws his dagger. He works the pointed tip into the lock, twisting it this way and that until the metal working clicks into place.

The door swings open, revealing not gold or marble or any sumptuous thing, but only the interior of the Cappelletti tower. Dank and bare, and of no interest to me. But Tybalt snatches Juliet from her cradle, whisking her through the heavy-beamed doorway. Bounding up the stairs, he calls down to me to hurry.

Inside the tower it's dark, the air a damp chill. The walls are thicker than my Pietro is tall, narrow lines of sunlight barely stealing through the sparse bow-slits. The winding steps are worn shallow in the middle, and the wooden landings groan beneath my weight. I keep my shoulder pressed against the rough stone wall to steady myself. But the stairs stretch on and on like nothing I've climbed. Not since I was Tybalt's age, herding my family's flock up and down mountainsides.

As I rise, my calves burn. And then my thighs. Hot pain twinges across my hips and up my back. I'm not caught halfway up to Tybalt, and already there's no breath left in me.

"I cannot," I call to him. Or try to, gasping out the words.

Not that it matters, as Tybalt pays me no mind. "I'm old enough to climb to the top," he says, "and so are you." As though age is only what makes us able to do, and not what steals the doing from us.

His footsteps grow fainter the farther I am left behind. I'll not be stranded here, partway between unseen ground below and whatever lies above. Not stop to imagine what might happen to Juliet in this dark place, without me to protect her. And so I cross myself and snail up the steps after Tybalt.

My head is light by the time I reach the final landing. But the landing is light too, bathed by the sun pouring through the arched openings that crown the tower. I'm like a blind man startled to regain his sight, blinking at all the bright as I pick my way across the wooden platform. I gather Juliet from Tybalt's thin arms, the tiny warmth of her spreading against my chest.

"Let me show you," Tybalt says. He pulls me to the tower's edge, where I see the city as I've never before seen it, stretching below as though Tybalt, Juliet, and I are angels looking down from heaven.

I know Verona as I do my own body. Every labyrinthed passage and each loose paving stone along my parish streets. The smell of tanneries, of public ovens, and of offal-piles. The snorting hogs upon the piazze, and the rush of the Adige beneath the bridges. But I've never imagined this: that I could stand as tall as the church campaniles, watching the city's roof tiles glint in the sun, the people and animals moving between them as small as crawling insects. The world spreading beneath me glows with the sublime beauty you see in paintings of the Annunciation. And that same holy terror that widens the Blessed Virgin's eyes and flushes her cheeks beats sharp within my own awed breast.

A golden-bellied thrush soars by, so close I lose my footing. I grab at Tybalt to catch my balance, ripping his silken doublet. As he reaches out to steady me, sunlight catches the flesh beneath the tear. It's raised in angry welts, his torso purpled with bruises.

"Who did this to you?"

"Did what?" He asks as though the beatings come so regularly, there is nothing astonishing about them.

My finger circles his discolored skin. Still child-soft, despite the ugly mark. "Who hits you, Tybalt?"

"My tutor, of course. He says that I am slow with Latin, and with the abacus. But he's the one who's slow, and dull. Why should I be bothered with book-lessons, when I can teach myself to jump and joust and parry like brave knights do?"

Pietro's army was true enough to its name, our boys staging epic battles or wrestling like the gladiators of Ancient Rome. But not one of my unschooled sons ever earned a bruise in the way Tybalt has.

No matter how hungry we were, Pietro never put any of our boys to work for masters who beat them. "You cannot treat a boy like he's a beast," he'd say, "and expect he'll grow up to be a man." Having spent his childhood coddled by his sisters, Pietro saw no need to allow anyone to cuff and thrash his children. Having spent my childhood terrified by my father's beatings, I agreed. But despite all of our indulgence, not one of our boys ever grew to be a man. Who knows what Tybalt, born to wealth and power yet marked with what my sons never had to bear, might come to be?

I tell Tybalt I must sit and nurse Juliet. I let him lead us back down the tower stairs and into our chamber, as I carry her wrapped within my careful arms. I'll mend his doublet while she sleeps.

Lord Cappelletto dines in the sala just before sunset, offering barely a word to his wife, who sits on one side of him, and endlessly haranguing his nephew, who's seated on the other. He speaks of ventures and profits, which bore the boy, and sieges and skirmishes, which thrill him. Lord Cappelletto tells Tybalt that he must learn to move the silver king upon the chessboard in the corner of the sala with cunning care, if he's ever to understand how his uncle moves the young prince who sits upon Verona's throne. Through all Lord Cappelletto's endless lecturing, I'm made to stand beside the table holding Juliet, so that if he happens to look up from his meal, he may gaze upon her.

Though the aromas of the rich foods growl my stomach, I get not one bite of what the Cappelletti eat. When Lord Cappelletto lets out a belch to show he's had his fill, the preening serving-man rushes forward to clear the trencher, and without a word I am dismissed. As soon as we're outside the sala, the serving-man sneers at me, scooping through their leavings with his bare hand to gull whatever he can for himself. I carry Juliet back to our chamber, where I find my own meal: overly boiled farina that's grown cold long before I dip my spoon to it, which I'm to wash down with a jug of wine that's so diluted it tastes more of well-water than of grapes.

It's no mystery what makes a rich man rich. They have what

we poor do not: money. This money of theirs is not like what we earn with honest sweat. It has its own magic, by which it is forever making them more of what they've already got. When Pietro and I first came to Verona and were in want of a place to sleep, we pawned everything we'd brought except a single cooking pot, yet had barely enough to rent a narrow little house from a man who was so wealthy he owned more buildings than all his relatives could ever inhabit. Every year since, the rent on our house has come so dear that the landlord grows richer and richer while we stay always poor.

Living within Ca' Cappelletti, I realize a rich man's food is not unlike his money, for I'd swear I can see Lord Cappelletto growing fatter while I am always famished.

So in the middle of a morning hour when he is gone from the compound, and Lady Cappelletta is yet in her bed, and poor Tybalt is at what no right-minded person would call the mercy of his tutor, I gather Juliet in my arms and steal down from our chamber. The autumn day is dry, and the air in the courtyard smells of the acrid odor of olives being pressed to fresh oil, mixed with the heavy must of strong wines aging in barrels in a nearby storeroom, and the fragrance of loaves baking in the Cappelletti oven. The bready scent draws me to such a kitchen as I've never imagined any house could have. Set in its own stone building, it has two open fires along with the oven, and pots of every size hanging from the ceiling and stacked along the walls. A table as big as an ox-cart sits in the center of the room ringed with mysterious jars and jugs, its top covered with sprigs of fresh-pulled herbs.

The man standing at the table does not glance up when I enter.

He's got the drawn face of a hare, the skin beneath his eyes shaded from want of sleep. His quick-bladed mincing of parsley does not slow, even while I complain my food's too bland.

"That's no fault of mine," he says, snorting in all the sharp, sweet, thick flavors of the meal he's making. "Lord Cappelletto told me you're not to have any sauce or spice, no hint of flavor that might taint your milk."

This is how I'm spoken of, like I'm some cow being pastured. "I nursed six sons while eating savory dishes, and none of them—"

"None of them is Lord Cappelletto, who is the man who pays my wages." He reaches for a head of garlic, and, sliding his thumb up the dull side of the blade, begins to peel it. "Meager wages they are, for everything I'm got to do to get his meals cooked, the arbor fruit and all the vegetables that are brought in from his country estates preserved, and a winter's worth of meats cured. They do not keep a man-servant in this house I can trust to send to the market to buy a decent round of cheese, or a pantry-maid with sense enough to keep the mold from growing on it once it's brought back here."

Cribbed as I've been within Juliet's chamber, still I know the truth of what he says. Tybalt's tutor is not the only hireling seeking his own pleasures. The serving-man'd slurp the dregs out of a dead man's cup, or so I suppose from how often his face is flushed with drink. The maid-servant is such a doltish thing she truckles more grime into a room than she ever manages to clean out of it. Tybalt tells me there's no need to grumble over her, for she'll doubtless be gone in a month or two, like all the other maids before her. And whenever I catch sight of the house-page, he's scratching so furiously at himself that I'd not let him within twenty paces of Juliet, to keep whatever infests him away from her, and me. For all the poor are in want of good masters, it's the wonder of Ca' Cappelletti that the rich can be so in want of good servants. A fine riddle that proves for me to puzzle over whenever Juliet's soiled swaddling needs washing, and I must haul up the water bucket from the courtyard well myself, balance the tub above the brazier fire in our chamber to heat it, scrub the strips of fabric clean, and lay them in the sun to dry, all before my babe cries once more to be fed.

"Lazy and insolent," I say, to show him I agree. "It must be trying for so skilled a cook to have to rely on them."

He pitches the peelings into the fire with a flourish, as if to confirm how worthy he is of my compliment.

"So skillful a cook," I continue, "could easily prepare a bowl of hearty broth, and send it up to me with fresh bread and oil. And a bit of cheese, which after all is made from milk. Surely that would do no harm."

For the first time, he raises his eyes to take me in. "Lazy and insolent," he repeats. "And witless as well, if you think I take orders from a common servant."

My quick tongue is ready to tell the cook I'm not some common servant. But Juliet wriggles in my arms, and in the moment I take to soothe her, the cook turns his back to me to toss the garlic into a sizzling pot upon the fire. Then he bends to stir the parsley into a bubbling sauce, and a hole gapes in his breeches, revealing a hairy part of him that I'd just as soon not see.

What use is it to argue with such as him?

I carry Juliet out of the kitchen. Before I make my way back upstairs, I slip into the arbor. Though the trees are nearly bare, I hunt out the last three apples that've fallen from the branches. Closed up again in our chamber, I gobble the fruit so fast, my stomach twists in pain. But I'm not sorry to have eaten my fill, defying Lord Cappelletto despite the cook.

From the time I could first grasp my mother's skirts, I've always done my part of a household's work. I began as any girl does: mashing herbs, shelling beans, and kneading dough, though soon enough I was stirring ashes back to fire, drawing water by the bucketful, and tossing scraps to hens and hogs. By the time I was eight, I could lay a trap to kill the mouse that'd gotten into our grain, or tell with a single whiff when the cooking oil was near to turning rancid. I stank of manure when the fields were tilled, of lye when we did our laundering, and each night of whatever simmered in the pots I stirred. There was not a chair in my father's house for anyone but him, so I stood even through the long hours when I spun and sewed.

Once Pietro and I were married, I'd barely finish one chore before I had to set my roughened hands to the next. To keep my husband and our growing army of ever-hungry sons fed took such hours of buying and storing and preparing food, there hardly seemed enough light left in the day for all the scrubbing and salting, sieving and weaving, sorting and mending a household requires.

I'd not imagined during any of those work-worn years that one day I would sit for hours in a high-backed chair within an ill-run house with nothing to do but watch a single infant sleep. Would I have believed then that I could feel as dulled by it as I do now? But we are what our life makes us. Hard as I've always had to work, I've never been any good at being idle.

Besides, in the hole exposing the cook's hind-part I glimpsed a portent of something I'll not let come to pass. And so I plot my way into Lady Cappelletta's chamber. Young as she is, younger than five of my six boys would be if they lived, still she is the lady of Ca' Cappelletti. Whatever else the gulling, gadding, tippling, scratching servants do, or do not, to look after the larder and the cleaning and the grounds, the household linens are her responsibility. If she'll not tend to them, by spring not a one of us will have a proper cloth to wipe withal when we relieve ourselves, nor hose or breeches to lace back up once we are done.

This does not occur to Lady Cappelletta until I come into her chamber carrying the spindle, needles, and hoops that Tybalt hunted up among his mother's things. "We should begin while the light is still strong," I say. She's a-bed, eyes red above her lovely cheeks. She nods, barely, and I busy myself with lifting the lid of the nearest linen-chest and surveying its contents, while Tybalt carries his cousin's cradle into the chamber.

Lady Cappelletta grows so distressed at Juliet's presence, I mean to distract her with some comment about how much needs mending. But before I can, Tybalt plucks up her cap and puts it on his head. Letting it fall in front of one eye, he lifts Juliet from the cradle and dances her in her matching cap along the edge of the broad bed, warbling nothing-such words as Lady Cappelletta laughs. This is Tybalt's gift, to himself and to us. Hungry for a mother's love, he mines affection from this aunt who shows none for her own child, just as easily as he does from me, bereft of every child of my own. By the time his tutor calls him to his lessons, Lady Cappelletta is, if not delighted to be left with Juliet and me, at least willing to abide us along with her household duties.

At first she and I speak only about the inventory of linens, what tasks we need to do. I've always liked to work the spindle, the certainty of the spinning, dropping, and catching as wool or flax turns to yarn. The weight and rhythm anchor me. She is more suited to the needle, her young eyes and slim hands working such delicate stitches as I'd never manage. We are ill-matched in many ways, Lady Cappelletta and I, but that is what makes us well-matched for our tasks.

As the weeks of autumn pass, the wool oil seeps into my hands, its sheepy smell staying with me even when I sleep. I begin to spin stories while I spin thread, stories of tending my family's flock when I was a girl. I tell them as cradle-tales for Juliet. Lady Cappelletta shows no sign that she listens, until I soothe Juliet through one colicky suckling by recounting an early blizzard that caught me and my sheep the year I turned twelve. The storm was fierce as well as sudden, purpling the sky and turning the world so dizzying white I'd not believed we'd ever find our way back to my village. I was shivering as much with fear as cold, when a rowdy band of hunters happened across the hill where we'd been stranded. Three of them eyed my plumpest sheep, debating which one to kill off for supper. But the fourth smiled kindly as he eyed me instead, and he convinced the others he'd lead the flock back to my family, for what he was sure would be ample reward.

"Reward it was, and he took it long before we reached my father's house," I say, shifting Juliet from my left breast to my right. Is it any wonder the scent of wool moves me to tell such tales, given how at Pietro's gentle urging I bade my virtue fond farewell before an audience of baaing sheep? "We were married before the spring snowmelt, and soon enough I was at my own lambing."

Lady Cappelletta looks up from her sewing as though she's noticing me for the first time. "You've borne children?"

"Barren women cannot suckle." Does she really need me to tell her such things? "And neither can virgins. Except for the Sainted Maria."

She listens only for what she wants to hear. "Sons? You've been delivered of healthy sons?"

I tell her my children were all boys, and all born healthy. "Except the last, which was neither. God rest them, every one." I mark the sign of the cross against my face and chest, before pretending to busy myself with unraveling Juliet's soiled swaddling.

Hard as it is to speak of all my lost little ones, what pricks most is how Lady Cappelletta disregards their deaths. "How? How did you make sons? If I can bear just one . . ."

I made sons easily, without thinking of it. Made them with Pietro, in all the warmth and strength of his youth. Not a bit like Lady Cappelletta, with her repulsion over the getting and having of babies, nor like Lord Cappelletto, bulbous and spotty with age.

"I did not lie too long in bed," is what I say, "either before my husband came to me, or after." True enough, for each boy I bore only increased the load of my household work.

She nods at my words, though giving up the hours she spends under her bed's rich, heavy covers'll not come easily to her, even if all she does instead is sit robed in furs sewing before the fire. Still, she might as well stop wallowing about like a sow in the mud. So long as a wife loves her bed only when her husband is far from it, she'll not help herself in the getting of a son.

"And I ate sparingly." Again, the truth. We were often hungry, more with each mouth we had to feed. But that's not why I say it.

Lord Cappelletto is a man whose opinions grow as his hair does, only where you'd least want to find them. Though I'd not dare raise a plaint with him about what the cook told me, I take some small pleasure in forbidding Lady Cappelletta from having her fill of all the foods that are forbidden me.

She gives another nod, though this one is slower, worry widening her amber-flecked eyes. "The apothecary sent balsam and peony seeds. Not to take by mouth, but to put inside me, there." She gestures toward her lap. "Lord Cappelletto read a treatise by a very learned physick, which says that this will help."

Apothecaries. Treatises. Reading. If people put their faith into these things, is it any wonder they never get around to the making of children? The only remedy I've ever known, ever needed, was simply doing what we without money always do, to take a little pleasure in our lives. We romp, and we rut, and we leave it to the saints to decide when the babies come.

"Plant salves? Flower seeds?" I snort at the idea that those are what she needs inside her. And then I tell her things she'd never imagine, about how to draw a husband's salve and seed into her. I let my eye catch bolster, carpet, pomander—whatever lies around the chamber. Imagining some copulatory use for every object, I describe these acrobatic feats as though they're common practice to all but her. I do not know if any of the acts I describe make a womb more likely to form a boy. But seeing how she looks at me, like a veal-calf watching its fellow herd-mates being slaughtered and then eyeing the butcher as he turns, knife in hand, its way—that's grand amusement to me.

"And if your husband, once he is in that position, can balance with his left leg up," I say, "then you might reach across and slip your mouth about his—"

A small, horrid gurgle cuts me off.

Juliet, my dear babe, shudders in my lap.

She's open-mouthed, her breathing stopped. Her face a ghastly blue.

Blue against the indigo of the cap that, unswaddled, she's pulled from her head. The silk border of the cap is wet. The last two pearls that rowed its edge are missing.

I crook my littlest finger into her tiny mouth and pry out a pearl. Tossing the precious bead to the floor, I fish my finger in again. But in the small, wet cave of her mouth, I cannot feel the second pearl.

I lift her and turn her upside down, smacking the heel of my hand hard against her back. Nothing. Not a whimper, not a gasp. Not any sign of the deadly jewel.

Lady Cappelletta shrieks. But I'm too terrified to utter a sound.

I turn Juliet face up again and bend closer over her, opening my mouth to cover hers, and her nose as well. I suck in, as deep as I can. Deeper than I thought I could. My great, fat body fills with what I suck from her. A grim reversal of how her small, delicate body has grown these past months with all she's sucked from me.

Suddenly something thumps against my gullet. The pearl, freed from her throat, hits so hard within my own I nearly gag into her mouth. Juliet begins to struggle, kicking and swatting, straining in her desperate will to breathe. But the air's sucked so tight between us, I cannot lift my mouth from hers.

I work my tongue within my mouth, rolling the pearl forward as I pull fresh air in through my nose. Pinning the pearl between my tongue and teeth, I push this breath deep into her. Push myself in that one great breath away from her.

Juliet howls as I spit the pearl into my palm. She's red-faced and wailing, inconsolable. I'm glad for it. I do not know how many nights the sight of her, blue and still, will haunt me. But for now, I relish this lively, angry red of her, proof that she's not gone to join my other little ones.

"What have you done to Juliet?" Lord Cappelletto rushes in, shouting as though Ca' Cappelletti is under sling-and-arrow siege.

"Saved her," Tybalt says, vaulting into the chamber after Lord Cappelletto. "It was amazing, Uncle. My cousin could not breathe, so the nurse did it for her."

Lord Cappelletto's roiling anger boils off in a vapor of worry. "Could not breathe? Is she ill?"

"She choked on a jewel that came loose from her cap," I answer, letting my gaze drop to the once elegant headpiece, crumpled and saliva-soaked at my feet. I want to make him feel that it's his fault, for ordering that an infant wear such a thing.

"I was in the antecamera, practicing my lute, and I saw it all," Tybalt says. "The nurse was giving lessons to my noble aunt, just as the tutor does to me. My cousin turned blue as a spring sky, and the nurse turned her back to the carmine of the prince's pageant-robes."

His half-lie hits me like a shaming slap. I'd not heard a single pluck of a lute string, and if he'd been practicing in the antecamera, how could he see Juliet turn veiny blue? Tybalt must have snuck close to listen to all the filthy things I told Lady Cappelletta. Filthy things I was so consumed with telling, I'd not noticed him—just as I'd not kept careful enough watch over Juliet.

The boy slips something from his sleeve, holds it above Juliet, and slowly lowers the end into her mouth. Her face puckers around it, and she gives suck with that same determined mouth-tugging that makes my nipples ache. She's so pleased with what she tastes, she forgets her sobs. Her angry fists relax, and the red seeps from her face.

Tybalt shines with boyish pride. "I knew a candied orange peel would make my cousin happy. Candies always cheer me. That's why the honey-man gave these to me."

I understand who Tybalt means, but Lord Cappelletto does not. He asks if a honey-man is something like a straw-man.

Tybalt laughs and does a little straw-man dance, as though he has muscleless limbs propped up by poles. "The honey-man's not made of honey," he explains. "He's a maker of it. Or he is a keeper of the bees that make it, and then he makes it into this." He shakes a rainbow of candied fruit pieces from his sleeve. He smiles at his own treasure-stock, but then his face wiggles into a frown. "The honey-man asked if he might keep a hive inside our arbor. May he, Uncle? He says our trees will bear better fruit, which he can candy for us."

Lady Cappelletta's tongue pinks out between her lips, as though she's tasting first one and then another of the candied strips of fig and pear and lemon that sit in Tybalt's hand. Knowing my husband offers more tempting treats than hers ever will, I say, "I heard once of a treatise that said children fed on honey grow both sweet and rich." I keep my eyes on Tybalt and Juliet as I speak, though I mean the words for Lord Cappelletto.

They hit perfectly upon the mark. He waves a hand, the way a wealthy man does to show he spends money with no great conse-quence, and informs us he is having a dovecote built in the arbor, so Lady Cappelletta can be kept on a breeding diet of dove, and capon and gosling, and eggs and hens of every sort. "This honey-man shall come and place his hive beside the dovecote, in exchange for what-ever delicacies please Juliet and Tybalt." He wraps one wrinkled hand around Juliet's tiny fist and with the other tousles his nephew's long curls. Then he plucks up a ruby strip from the boy's store of candied fruit, tossing it between those liver lips as he leaves the chamber.

The moment he's gone, Lady Cappelletta gestures Tybalt to her, taking careful stock of the sweets that are left. She chooses one to eat right off, and three more to hoard beside her sewing things. Ty-balt turns to offer me a share, but I busy myself with getting Juliet reswaddled. I bend my head low as I unravel the fresh winding strips, to hide my worry about bees being kept so close, and my flush of anticipation for the visits of the man who'll come to tend them.

But then I notice the army of tiny purple specks beginning to appear on the bottom half of Juliet's face. They form a wine-colored version of the beard and mustache Prince Cansignorio wears. They say the Pope himself ordered the prince to grow the hair on his face, to make public penance for killing his hated older brother to become Verona's ruler.

I do not need the Pope in far-off Avignon to tell me that what stains Juliet is not her guilt. It's mine. I barely emptied my mouth of smutted words before I laid it onto her. Though Tybalt convinced Lord Cappelletto that I saved her, these marks across her face will ruin her, if they remain. What man would marry a beard-besmirched girl, no matter how large her dowry?

But I see still worse in those purple prickles. They are ghostly reminders of God's tokens, the plaguey black specks that spread their way across the lean thighs and muscly arms of my boys, and of countless others like them that the pestilence stole away.

Not Juliet. Not so long as I breathe will I watch the breath seep from her. Tucking a blanket to cover her discolored cheeks, I place my gentlest kiss between Juliet's puzzled eyes and ask Lady Cappelletta's leave to take the infant to the Franciscans, to offer a prayer of thanks that she is saved.

I'm barely through the door of Friar Lorenzo's cell before I am begging absolution for my soul, and some herbal remedy for Juliet's body. "I cannot absolve you," he says, pressing the tips of his long fingers together, "until I know your sin." Man of God and science that he is, he bids me repeat every filthy thing I said to Lady Cappelletta, making me admit which are things I've done myself with Pietro, and which were only my depraved imaginings.

When at last I finish, he asks, "And the bead, did you say it was, on which the child choked?"

Surely he knows what I said. Friar Lorenzo never forgets a detail that's confessed to him. "Pearls, two of them."

"Where are they now, these pearls?"

I picture where the crumpled cap dropped during my frantic effort to save Juliet. But I do not know what's become of the jewels she sucked from it. "They must've fallen somewhere in Lord and Lady Cappelletti's bedchamber."

His nose twitches like he's a hound scenting rabbit. "Can you find them?"

I cup a hand around the cradle blanket covering Juliet's bare head. She feels so small. Even more fragile than she was on the day when I first met her. The day I lost Susanna. "Can you not offer her some cure without them?"

"A cure? Of course, of course." He does not even bother to examine her before going to his cache of petals, leaves, and seeds. He grinds up some sickly-sweet smelling remedy, which he spoons into a pouch, securing the drawstring with a tiny cross. He tells me to mix two pinches of the herbal with a thimble-full of still-warm goat's milk and rub the paste onto Juliet's chin and cheeks, first thing in the morning, again when the sun is at its highest, and finally after it sinks entirely from the sky. Three times each day I am to pinch and mix and rub, until the guilt-rash goes away.

"Come back then, with the pearls. As a token of thanksgiving to the Holy Church that she is spared."

This many pinches, that many times a day for who knows how many days, and all the while needing to hide Juliet's besmirched face from even Tybalt's curious eyes. My muddled brain is so occupied with trying to remember all of that, it's only after I leave the friary that I stop to wonder where I can get warm goat's milk. Though hogs and chickens, donkeys and wild dogs fill Verona's streets, there's not a goatherd within the city gates. And if Friar Lorenzo knows of some miracle that turns solid cheese back to flowing milk, he's not shared it with me.

But I'll not let Juliet bear that mark. Back in Ca' Cappelletti, I lay her on her big bed. I loose the string that holds the tiny cross and drop two quick pinches of Friar Lorenzo's powdery herbal into a thimble. Pushing off my dress, I squeeze myself like I'm a goat, catching my own warm stream of milk to mix the paste. I coat Juliet's face with it, praying to Sant'Agata to leach the stain from her. I do the same come evening, working with an apothecary's care.

The measuring and mixing vex me even in my sleep, and I wake early, urging Juliet through her suckling so I can begin to work my flow into the thimble.

A cart wheel thumps across the courtyard stones, and Tybalt calls from the far side of Ca' Cappelletti, "The honey-man is here."

I drop the thimble and hurry my lacings closed. Hugging Juliet against me to smother her startled cry, I hie through the sala and down the stairs into the courtyard. But I stop short when Pietro, who's pulling a handcart, turns to me.

I cannot kiss him, cannot even let on that I know him. Not here, where the pompous cook or the prickling page or any other member of the household might peer out and see us. Lord Cappelletto forbids the wet-nurse even a sprig of parsley. He would never tolerate any of her husband's humors tainting her milk.

I nod toward Tybalt, who's dancing with excitement atop the curved ledge of the courtyard well, and say, "You might have sense enough not to wake the whole house, banging about at this hour."

Pietro answers my scolding by shaking a handful of honeyed walnuts out of his pocket and offering them to Tybalt. "Do you know what a swarm is?"

Swarm. Such a soft-sounding word, to carry such threat of stinging.

Tybalt leaps to the ground, stretching himself before Pietro, eager to show off. And even more eager to earn the candy. "That's when bees attack," he says.

Pietro draws back the sweets, shaking his head. "There's no danger in a swarm. They are how new hives are made, like the building of a new church when a parish gets too crowded. When a hive becomes too full, the queen leads some of the bees out to look for a new place to live. That's when the honey-man husbands them. He must make sure they survive in their new home." He pulls the canvas covering off the cart, revealing a log as long as his outstretched arms, capped on each end. "There was a queen whose hive was at my house. But now, she's here."

His words sting in a different way than any bee could. The sting's made all the worse because I do not dare reply, not here.

"Show him where to set the hive in the arbor," I tell Tybalt, "so you and Juliet can watch the bees from her window." And I can see the beekeeper when he comes to tend them, without the rest of Ca' Cappelletti knowing.

I lead the way, settling Juliet onto the bench beside the new-built dovecote while Tybalt and Pietro maneuver the cart through the narrow archway into the arbor. A person could stand within the Cappelletti courtyard all day and not suspect what lies on this side of the passage, hidden behind the kitchen and the chapel. Pietro surveys the copse of fruit trees, amazed, before lifting the hive-log from the cart. Broad-shouldered though he is, still he staggers under the weight of it, his face reddening as he sets it on the ground.

"The honey-man needs a cup of something," I say to Tybalt. "Fetch him some trebbiano."

Tybalt pouts. "I want to see the bees."

"I'll keep the bees sealed in the hive until you're back," Pietro promises.

Tybalt smiles and tumbles off. He's barely out of the arbor before I'm in Pietro's arms. I close my eyes, savoring the feel of his big hands on me, the taste of my mouth on his.

"Angelica, where can we—"

"The boy will be back in only a minute."

Pietro pulls me tighter, as though he means to take me right here, in that single minute. By my troth, were I a younger woman, I might let him.

But age has made me one who savors more slowly. And now that I have Juliet—secluded though the arbor is, I'll not risk having one of the feckless servants bumble in and discover us.

Juliet's chamber is just above us, over the chapel. And beside it is the tower, its dark stair hidden to even the most curious eyes—but opening right into her chamber. "Come to me through there," I say, pointing to the low arch at the bottom of the tower.

I press myself against him for one more kiss, then hurry to the bench and take up Juliet. Crossing back through the courtyard, I climb the stairs to the sala and spirit one of the dinner knives from the credenza. Back in our chamber, I set Juliet in her cradle, making a quick bow to San Zeno before I pull back the wall-hanging. I kneel before the tower door like a penitent before his priest, my lips moving not in prayer but in impatient oaths while I tilt the knife into the lock.

Once the metal working turns and the door heaves on its hinge, I turn back to the window. Pietro is crouching before the hive, Tybalt beside him. My husband points, explaining as he used to do with our boys. Tybalt nods, hungry with questions. But I'm hungry, too. I swing the window wide and wave at Pietro.

He twists a fat cork from a hole in the log. The first bees fly out, turning one loop in the air and then another. As Tybalt spins beneath them, following their paths, Pietro crosses to the tower, his feet quick on the worn stone steps. He is barely in the room before he's inside me.

"Tybalt?" I ask, worried the boy might burst in on us.

"I told him he must count the bees." Pietro runs kisses from beneath my ear all down my neck. "That will occupy him, while I occupy something else." He pulls himself nearly out of me, then plunges slowly in again. Over and over, working up his whetted rhythm, setting off the first tremors deep within me. But as I thrum with pleasure, the prime-hour bells ring.

"Lord Cappelletto." I gasp out the name.

Pietro goes limp inside me. "Angelica, you've let Lord Cappelletto—"

"No. Never." I cannot find words fast enough. "He's a shriveled old thing. But he'll be coming here now, to see Juliet."

I push my husband off me so fast, he rolls to the edge of the broad bed. I give him one more shove, sending poor Pietro tumbling to the floor, and whisper for him to stay there. Working my way back to the other side of the bed, I pull Juliet from her cradle just as the door from the sala opens and Lord Cappelletto stalks in for his morning visit.

I tip my head, making doe-eyes at Juliet in a grand show of my innocence. Only then am I reminded: the prickle marks still taint her.

"She's just started to give suck." I pull Juliet to me, rubbing my breast against the corner of her mouth. She burrows into me as though she is a rooting pig, and I work the folds of my nightdress to hide her face from Lord Cappelletto.

But he jabs a hairy-knuckled finger at something behind me. "What's that?"

My throat tightens as I turn. Pietro is pressed against the bottom of the bed, hidden from view. The tower door is pulled shut, covered by the wall-hanging. But there, at the feet of the statue of San Zeno, is the dinner knife.

"Tybalt brings things in to play," I say. "He'd invent a broadsword out of anything, to pretend that he's a knight at jousting."

"The Cappelletti have foes enough for him to raise a blade to when he comes of age. But our family silver is not for a child's play. Have Tybalt—"

"Is that the crier, already coming up the Via Cappello?"

Lord Cappelletto, ever impatient to calculate how to turn the day's first news to his family's advantage, forgets whatever was about to trip from his wagging tongue. He makes his daily retreat through the sala, his footsteps echoing down the stairs and into the entryway to Ca' Cappelletti.

Pietro pulls himself back onto the bed. "This is no way for a husband to be with his wife."

"This is the only way for a wet-nurse to be with her husband." I wrap my hand around him, careful not to disturb Juliet. It has never taken much to firm Pietro, and our months apart serve in my favor. As soon as Juliet's had her fill of me, he lays her on the bolster above our heads, as though this was our bed and she our babe.

But once he and I are done and laced back up again, Pietro kneels beside the bed, taking my hand to his lips. "Now that I've a hive here, and the other at our house, I'll harvest more honey and more beeswax. When I sell the wax and what I make with the honey, it will bring enough to pay our rent and keep the two of us, all year."

I am not a stupid woman. I know that when a man contracts to hire a wet-nurse, and another to let his wife serve as one, there is hard bargaining over how much money passes from one to the other, though no one bothers the milk-mother with such details. Whatever Friar Lorenzo said and did when Susanna died to bring me and my nursling together, it was set down as so many soldi to be paid each month by Lord Cappelletto. A sum that is delivered to Pietro by Friar Lorenzo, who keeps some tidy portion as his broker-ing fee. But what ties me to Juliet is worth far more than money.

"It will be summer before there's honey and beeswax to be har-vested," I say. And although I'm not the kind of woman who holds her tongue before her husband, for once I do. I'll not remind him now that it's far longer than that before an infant is weaned. Two years, two and a half—does he not remember how it was with our boys? Would I want any less than that for my last darling?

Before he can answer, the door from the tower creaks open. Tybalt pushes aside the wall-hanging, bounding his way into the chamber as he recites all the many things he's noticed about the hive. How some bees fly, and others crawl along the ground. And some stay within the hive, pushing out the dead. He grabs my husband by the hand, pulling him back into the tower, down the stone steps, and outside.

I leave the window open, listening to their voices in the arbor as I fish the thimble from the bedclothes and prepare Friar Lorenzo's remedy for Juliet.

I've not forgot what else Friar Lorenzo told me I must do. I must bring him those pearls, to give grateful thanks to the Holy Church that Juliet is saved.

I remind myself of this as I sit with Lady Cappelletta in her chamber. While my thick fingers spin a steady rhythm and her thin ones sew, my eyes rove like unleashed beasts, searching the stone floor.

But I cannot find those wayward pearls. Not that first day. Nor the second. As the nones bells ring on the afternoon of the third day, something finally catches my ever-roving gaze. Some lustrous thing wedged within the pebbly crack between two of the large floorstones. Juliet stirs in the cradle, and I reach my foot out to rock her. But I'll not let my eyes leave that spot, certain it's a pearl.

"It must tire you, working such a fine stitch," I say to Lady Cappelletta.

She nods, letting her needle dangle as she rubs her eyes. I sing a slow lullaby about a fast-growing swan, pretending it is meant for Juliet, watching as Lady Cappelletta becomes the bird I sing about, her long, slender neck too delicate to bear the strain of holding up her pretty head.

Once her chin dips down, I say three silent Pater Nosters. When I'm sure she's deep in her sleep, I slip from my chair and lower myself to where the pearl lays. My breath stills as I work a thick forefinger and my fatter thumb into the crevice. The pearl is curved and smooth, and the rough floorstones scrape my knuckles raw as I pry it loose.

Tucking the gem inside my dress, I survey every inch of all the rest of the floor. But search as I might, I cannot find the second pearl. Just yesterday, Marietta took her leave of Ca' Cappelletti. Or Maddalena, maybe she was called. The latest of the serving-maids, she'd not stayed long enough for anyone to be certain of her name, and was gone so quick there'd not have been time to shout it after her even if we'd known it. Perhaps it was the weight of a pilfered pearl in her pocket that carried her away so fast, well beyond anywhere Lord Cappelletto, let alone the wet-nurse, might find her.

When Juliet and I lie at night in her great bed, I roll my own purloined pearl in my palm, imagining how much it might bring at one of the money-lender's stalls. Who knows how far Pietro and I might travel on that sum, what of the wide world we could discover together. But precious as the pearl is, it is nothing compared to Juliet. No more than a small, hard sphere beside my warm, soft girl.

I go early the next morning to make my shrift. Friar Lorenzo greets me with his familiar "God give you peace" as I pull the blanket from Juliet's head to show him how the purply prickle has faded.

"So dark." His words confound me, until I realize that he does not mean her face. He means her new-sprouted hair.

In place of the blonde down she was born with, this hair is as coarse and dark as mine. And her eyes—they've darkened too, so slowly I've not noticed, from their first pale gray, past Lady Cappelletta's amber, to a deep brown that matches my own. "It must be your milk," he says.

I'm not a woman who blushes easily, not even in a friar's cell. What use is such coyness before your holy confessor? Still, my cheeks redden as I wonder how he knows that I used my own milk to concoct his remedy for Juliet. "The hair came in before that," I say.

"Before? You've nursed her since she was born."

I realize too late that he'd not known. Not until I half-told what now he makes me tell in full. I silently beg forgiveness, not from my saints but from Juliet, as my guilty tongue betrays how I milked myself to heal her, a secret only she and I should share.

Friar Lorenzo frowns and mutters something about seething the flesh of a kid in the milk of its mother. As if goat stew has anything to do with my darling girl. "Remember your place, Angelica. You are only her wet-nurse."

How could I forget my place when it's with Juliet, always with Juliet? I'm the one, the only one, who wakes with her and sleeps holding her, the one who's given up Pietro and my little house and my whole life for her. The one who suckles her, and saved her. "Only her wet-nurse," I repeat, nodding. There's much of Juliet's heart that only her wet-nurse can know.

I draw the pearl from my belt-purse and pass it to Friar Lorenzo.

"Only one?" he asks. That same *only*. Always it is that same *only*, when he speaks of what I am, and what I do, and what I bring.

With a quick tug of his purse string, Lord Cappelletto gives the Church far greater offerings than this lone pearl. Altar-gifts to celebrate Juliet's birth. The cost of a month's fresco painting to commemorate a saint's day. A handsome sum of silver coins, that God might favor the commencement or completion of some business dealing in which Lord Cappelletto has an interest. He'd drop a diadem's worth of pearls into Friar Lorenzo's waiting palm, for he gladly tithes from his vast riches. And, eager to best every other noble family in Verona, even more gladly brags of it.

But this thanksgiving gift for saving Juliet comes from me, alone.

I searched and searched, and found the pearl. And if it was any sin to take it, surely it is absolution to give it over to the Church.

"I prayed to the Holy Mother to help me find the pearl Juliet choked on, and she did," I say. "Only one, so that must be what the Blessed Maria knows the Church should have."

Friar Lorenzo looks at me. Looks, I swear, into my very soul. Then he pockets his precious gem and sends us back to Ca' Cappelletti.

FOUR

During all the years I ran my own house, I never relished how I had to hurry my dough to the city ovens for baking, or bargain for every bent coin's worth of household necessities I bought in the market. How I hefted dirty pots to the fountain, scrubbing them while I sweated under the sun's heat or shivered with the winter's cold or soaked to sodden in the rain that might come any time of year, then hauled them home filled with whatever water we'd need until I returned to the public fountain the next day with another load to clean. With so many tasks pulling me through Verona's teeming streets, I never saw the joy in any of them, until passing the winter within Ca' Cappelletti.

There are braziers to heat every room in this house, and at least the itchy little house-page never lets the woodpile dwindle. But the smoke-thick air that hangs inside is rough in my throat. So rough my eyes tear, and I long to walk in the bone-chill of the fresh winds blowing off the Adige. Instead, I'm shut away like some lord's jealously guarded wife, going out only when I can give excuse to see Friar Lorenzo. And how often can a wet-nurse tell her employer she has sins she must confess?

Juliet is as restless as I am, angry that I can do nothing about the teeth tearing their way out of her gums. Why a babe of six months needs teeth at all, I cannot say, when surely I'm enough to feed her. Or would be enough, if not for the pain those teeth bring her. Sore and sullen, my beloved nursling shoves my breast away like I am no comfort to her.

Only Lord Cappelletto savors these dark days. Some of his seed seems to have settled in his wife, and he's as pleased as she is sick with it. He thunders in as we sit with our sewing, carrying a gilt chest nearly as large as Juliet's cradle. The sight, or perchance the smell, of him makes Lady Cappelletta heave into the bucket that now is always beside her. While he waits for her to finish, he beams just like Tybalt does whenever he has some new trick he wants to show us.

"I've brought your dowry jewels."

"They are not mine," Lady Cappelletta says. "They are yours." Her voice is uncertain. As though she fears that for all her retching, she and the jewels are about to be packed up and sent back to whatever family cared so little for her happiness, they married her off to this old mule.

"They are mine so long as you are mine, and I shall choose which ones you'll wear, and with which gown, on the palio-day."

"The foot race?" Lady Cappelletta eyes go so wide, perhaps she worries that he means for her to run the course herself. A fine show it would be, her huffing along among the teams of well-oiled men nominated each year from the city's assorted parishes to compete in the race, named for the green palio-cloth that's awarded to the winner.

But that's not the spectacle Lord Cappelletto means to make of his pretty young bride. "Prince Cansignorio is hosting a palio-day banquet for Verona's hundred richest men, and their wives. There'll be more than one family there to whom we owe a century-old grudge, and I'll not be outshone by any of them."

He unlocks the little chest, selecting a pile of gold buttons and silver-set gems for us to sew onto her gown and sleeves, and an even larger pile we're to attach to his robe and doublet. It will be no easy thing to work so many fancy stitches, with the palio-day only a week away. But when Lord Cappelletto snaps the chest shut and departs, I'm glad to take up a needle, and to have Lady Cappelletta do the same.

Verona's palio-race has been run along the campo outside the city walls for a hundred years at least. Longer than the Scaligeri have ruled Verona. But Lord Cappelletto's boasted to Tybalt about how he advised Prince Cansignorio, who is ever eager to surpass the brother who ruled before him, to extend the length of this year's race all the way to the Piazza dei Signori. And to richen the prize. The new prince will gift the winner not only with the traditional palio-cloth but with three whole bolts of pale blue samite, thumb-wide bands of gold and silver woven through the thick fabric. Also a riding horse bred from his royal stable, and a brace of fatted geese. Before the race begins, there will be endless delights for the gawking eyes of any who line the course. Musicians. Jugglers. The prince's whole menagerie paraded by. Perhaps an exorcism, if Providence will send some bedeviled soul for the saving. Prince Cansignorio promises Verona a celebration to make even the bishop forget it is a Lenten Sunday.

I, of course, am no bishop. So while Lord and Lady Cappelletti vie with rival nobles for the favor of the prince's table, I'll steal away to watch the race with Pietro, cheering as we always do for our parish-runner. I deserve an excursion outside Ca' Cappelletti, beyond the city gates. And tetchy as Juliet's grown from teething, perchance a few hours of fresh air, and fresh sights, will distract her.

Verona's narrow streets ring thick with different languages on the palio-day. Not just the dialects of Venetians and Tuscans, or Sards and Calabrians. The air is heavy with the guttural languages spoken by those who come from across the Alps and far to the North, as well as the rapid, jagged rasps of Arabian traders. There are those who say the world is broad and wide, and those who say there is no world without Verona's walls. Today it seems that both are right: the broad, wide world throngs within the city walls, separating me from Pietro. As the inns empty of foreigners, I push through the crowded streets, Juliet tight in my arms, and Tybalt close by my side.

He appeared in Juliet's chamber this morning, just after his aunt and uncle left for the prince's castle. Chittering away while he watched me braid my hair, ready my overgown, and slip on my veil, never considering that I might not intend to bring him with me. This is my own doing. From the first day nimble Tybalt came into Juliet's chamber, I've taught him to funnel his love for his dead mother and his sent-away sister onto her. He entertains her for hours on end, delighting in filling her with delight. It is always the bitterest of sweetness to see them together, for he is of an age somewhere between Nesto and Donato, and offers Juliet the same tender affection my sons showered on their littlest brother, Angelo.

How could I leave Tybalt behind? He is so lonely. So sensitive. And he is the closest companion I have within Ca' Cappelletti, as I whisper when I remind him that our outing is to be an especial secret, just between him and me, and Juliet.

Tybalt marvels at the throngs who are turning out for the race, bowing his head in reverence to the clusters of dark-robed priests and priors, then gawking at the eager hands of pickpockets and prostitutes. But even such wondrous distractions do not keep him from asking, "Will my father be here?" as we cross beneath the massive portraits of San Zeno and San Cristoforo that decorate the city gate.

Tybalt's widowed father has been in Mantua longer than I've been at Ca' Cappelletti. Tybalt asked for him on All Saint's Day, on Christmas Day, on the Feast of the Epiphany. Even, out of habit, on a few lesser saints' days. Always there is a letter, with his father's seal. Letters so full of sentiment, Lord Cappelletto refuses to read them aloud, leaving little Tybalt to struggle to decipher his father's

ornate script. Though I cannot read a word, I learn from those letters what Tybalt is too young to understand: why his father left
him. Too attached to the dead wife whose features show in her living son. Too afraid to cherish the boy, lest he be lost as well.

"Do you see Pietro?" Better, I reason, to distract Tybalt with a
question that will delight him, than to give his own question the
same-again answer that shadows even his happiest days.

Pietro comes to check the hive in the Cappelletti arbor as often
as he can, though still not as often as I want him. Whenever he appears, Tybalt follows him like a waggly-tailed pup, reporting all he's
observed of the bees since Pietro's last visit. Young though he is, Tybalt's no fool, and when he asked me how I knew the honey-man,
I made him cross his heart and swear upon his much-cherished
honor to keep the answer to himself. But when I then confided that
Pietro is to me what Lord Cappelletto is to Lady Cappelletta, Tybalt laughed and said this could not be true, for his uncle and aunt
never smile at each other as Pietro and I do. What else we do we
are careful to keep from him, and with each visit, Pietro crafts ever-
more elaborate challenges to distract the boy long enough for us to
sneak our time together in Juliet's broad bed. Or upon the stone
floor of her chamber. Or against its carved-wood door. By my troth,
there's not an inch of that room that Pietro and I've not explored as
we explore each other, hurrying ourselves to be done before Tybalt
bursts in to show off the latest kingfisher feather, or goat horn, or
bear claw that Pietro bade him find.

At my mention of Pietro, Tybalt scrambles ahead, searching out
the spot along the edge of the race-course where my husband has

stretched a bedsheet for us to sit upon as we watch the day's entertainments. It is one of my better sheets, just the thing a man would choose to throw onto the ground, never mind how people to either side will grind their filthy soles into it. A year ago, I would have carped at Pietro for ruining a sheet this way. But now I sleep on far finer linens, stitched with the Cappelletti seal by Lady Cappelletta's own hand. My worn bedding, my musty marriage-chest, the few tiny rooms of our rented house—they've become part of another life, the life I had before I had Juliet.

Tybalt runs to Pietro, who catches him up, swinging the boy in his two strong arms so that Tybalt somersaults high in the air before tumbling onto the sheet with a laughing shriek. Pietro, already red-cheeked and purple-tongued, offers me a swig from a three-quarters-plump wineskin As he lays his stubbly cheek against Juliet's smooth one, he slips a hand inside my dress, rubbing with his thumb in a way that sends shivers all through me.

I give his hand a playful slap. "Best not set a pot to boil, if you've no way to let off its steam."

We settle on the sheet sitting one inside the other like a set of stacking bowls, my back warming against Pietro's broad chest and his big legs curving snug around my hips, passing the wineskin between us to ward off the February chill. Though the ruby barbera's not of so fine a quality as what fills the casks at Ca' Cappelletti, at least it's not watered down like the pale trebbiano Lord Cappelletto allows me to be served.

I pour some of the barbera onto my pinky and rub it along Juliet's aching gums. The wine, and being out in the brisk air, soothe her. She coos at the bright scarf I bob before her, while Tybalt runs along the edge of the raceway, doubling back every few minutes to report on what spectacle of minstrels or stilt-walkers will soon parade before us.

I wait until the boy is out of earshot to tell Pietro about Lady Cappelletta. "It's a mystery how a woman can eat so little yet vomit so much. At least, it is a mystery to her." I lift the wineskin in toast to her ignorance. "I told her it's a sure sign she is carrying a son, a strong boy who wants her belly all to himself. I can be kind to her, when I have a mind to."

Pietro leans back, letting cool air fill the space between us. "What kindness is there in lying to her?"

"You do not know that it's a lie. It might be a son. Or a daughter. Or a hairy mole. Or an overly bilious humor. Or a clever ruse to keep her husband from her bed, though I doubt she is capable of that." How can Pietro chide me? "Why not let her believe she carries his heir, if that makes it easier for her to suffer these months of constant retching?"

He reminds me the rich are spiteful. "If she does not bear the son you've promised, she may take her disappointment out on you."

"Until she bears a son, her husband has her in such a qualmish state, she's not able to do much hurt to me, or to anyone else." I hope this will prove true, that there will be a healthy boy to please the father and relieve the mother, before Juliet is old enough to notice how Lady Cappelletta looks at her.

"I'll make some ginger comfits, taffied with honey and almond milk, for you to give her when her stomach needs steadying."

I do not care to have my husband thinking up treats for Lady Cappelletta. "The Apothecary Guild will come after you, if you start making medicines."

Mischief plays along his face. "Perhaps you can demonstrate what punishment you think the guild master should demand?" He pulls me close, his breath warm. "I miss you, Angelica. The smell of you, the taste of you. That perfumed bed in another man's house—that's no way for us to be together." He draws Juliet away from me. "Let Tybalt watch her for a little while."

It's more than wine that's stoking my husband. Stoking me, too. And it's true, Tybalt is devoted to Juliet. If I tell him to count out the number of monkeys and baboons to her as the prince's gilt-caged menagerie parades by, and to make up a fabulous story to tell her about each of the prince's lions, he'll do it, whether I am watching over his shoulder or not. Perhaps when he reappears, Pietro and I might—

A curse and a splintering crack split the air. Four of the young men who've been calling out bets for the palio-race swear and jump on a fifth, who's broken a cudgel over one of their heads. The foursome topples the culprit, and all five tumble in a mass of angry arms and legs onto our sheet. The broken cudgel swings wildly, smashing the side of my face.

Something jagged catches inside my cheek, and salty blood thicks into my mouth. I spit one molar and then another onto the bedsheet, as a crowd of gangly, coltish youth, some barely past their boyhood, swarm at us.

Pietro pushes Juliet into my arms, wrapping himself around us as he tries to pull me to my feet. But it's impossible to stay standing amidst the angry surge.

Hundreds of them, there suddenly seem to be. Some coming from the campo and others pouring out from the city gates. All of them swinging fists, clubs, whatever they can grab, while decent people struggle to shove their way clear.

I bend over Juliet, my body the only protection I can give her. Pushing my tongue against the bloodied gap on the side of my mouth, I hold to her like a half-drowned person clings to a floating log, as everything we have with us—our bedsheet, the scarf, and my lost teeth—are swallowed up in the press of bodies.

It's impossible to see more than a few arms-lengths in the direction we last saw Tybalt run, away from the city toward where the race was meant to start. I realize there's no way Pietro and I can keep Juliet safe if we try to go after him. And I'm too afraid, for her and for myself, to send Pietro off alone.

A mother of sons knows which boys have to be watched every waking moment—and some sleeping ones as well—to be kept from trouble, and which might wander off but will always return, none the worse for their adventures. Though cat-like Tybalt loves to leap, he always lands on his paws. Or so I've believed. But who knows what might become of such a trusting boy in the midst of a fist-ready mob.

Terrified families pour into the race course. The frenzied mob, hungry for more space in which to fight, follows. Pietro half-pulls, half-carries me in the other direction, into the sycamores edging the campo. The grove seethes with shrieking children, frightened mothers, and uncertain fathers. Near us, a trembling girl of twelve or fourteen sobs. Her mother kneels before her, trying to work some tuck in the girl's torn gown to cover her tiny breasts and belly, which have been badly pummeled in the fray. I turn away and seek the only comfort I can think of, leaning against a thick-branched sycamore to nurse Juliet.

My poor lamb must be half-starved, for she drinks me in as she's not done in the weeks since her teething started, those new-sharp teeth shooting a delicious pain through my too-full breast.

Pietro watches her suck with eyes full of wonder, the way he did when I suckled our sons. When I curse the brawlers, he says, "They are just boys. Their blood is still so hot from the pleasure-filled nights of Carnival, they seek mischief even now that it is Lent."

"Not all boys are so hot-blooded." Our boys, I mean. They might have tussled with each other, but Nunzio and Nesto both had Pietro's tender heart. They kept their younger brothers from any real harm. Except once, that once. It was Berto who led them to it. Or maybe Enzo. I was never sure, for none of them would tell me how it happened. And before I could wheedle or harangue it out of them, death stilled all their tongues. For months afterwards, I pleaded with the saints, cataloguing all I'd do if they would give me back my sons. Even just one or two, if I could not have them all. Who cares which was the first to lead the others into danger?

"It must have been a group of Florentines who started it." I cannot understand what Pietro means, until I realize he's talking not about our boys, but about the brawlers. He repeats what everyone around us is saying, about a bridge in Florence where the young men gather by torchlight to fight. Not ten or twenty of them, as might come to blows in any God-fearing city, but eight or nine hundred at a time, some barely old enough to grow hair on their chins, or anywhere below. All punching and stabbing at once, until they cannot tell friend from enemy in the maddened fray.

"This is not Florence," I say. Verona's not suffered such fighting in years. Not since Prince Cangrande II put down a rebellion early in his reign, ordering every soul in the city into the Arena to watch as he hacked off the heads of a half dozen conspirators. I'd buried my face against Pietro as each condemned man was blindfolded. Like the kneeling, bare-necked culprits, I'd not known when the first axe blow would fall. Though my stomach leapt at each thwacking execution, what haunted me more were the scores of others Cangrande II tortured and left dangling from the old Roman bridge over the Adige. Their cries echoed through the city for three days and three nights as they begged Death to take them, while ravens plucked at their bloodied bodies.

But in the sound and sight and smell of their agony, the rest of Verona knew ourselves safe. After that, the only blood shed in our streets was what Cangrande II ordered to amuse himself. Ambushes followed by savage beatings, mostly. Or a quick-plunged blade of assassination. Such attacks were plentiful, to be sure, for he was a brutal man, but they were aimed only at whatever noblemen the prince deemed too powerful. A prudent mother could easily keep her children locked at home until each spurt of violence was over.

But Cangrande II is dead. And though no one mourned him, not even his widow nor either of his mistresses, as I shiver in the sycamore grove I realize no one knows if Prince Cansignorio is man enough to keep the city's peace. Cansignorio, after all, has never killed anyone aside from his own brother. And after that, he fled to Padova until he was certain he'd be welcomed back as Verona's new rightful ruler. What good is a prince who cannot keep a youthful mob—or the warring Milanese or wily Mantuans—at bay?

Bells ring from inside the city walls, one angry peal answering another. Word spreads through the sycamores that the Franciscans are making their way out to the campo. Walking bare-footed in brown-robed pairs and chanting in Latin, as though godly incantations can stop a fist or club midswing.

All at once, the earth itself begins to rumble. Worry rounds Juliet's eyes as hundreds of horse-hooves thunder against the ground. The angry rhythm sets off a wave of anticipation throughout the grove. Prince Cansignorio must have sent his knights at last. Whether he rides at their head, as the older generations of Scaligeri did, or sits drinking from golden goblets with his wealthy guests, none of us in the grove can guess. But we listen with care to the crashing lances of a hundred mounted knights, and the tormented shrieks of whoever is in their path.

At last the sounds of fighting die away, and the brigade clatters off. Families all around us gather themselves, convincing one another they feel safe enough to leave the sycamores and make their way home. But I cannot take Juliet back to Ca' Cappelletti. Not without Tybalt.

The barbera burns in my belly, my head aching from its vapors. Why did I bring him withal? Why, having brought him, did I not keep him near? Tybalt is neither my child nor my charge. But he's a tender boy. And he is Juliet's cousin, the only nephew of her powerful father. How could I risk not only his little neck but also every tie I have to her?

Juliet, squirming in my arms, begins to cry for Tybalt. By my heart, I know the half dozen ways she shares any unhappiness with me. She cries when she is hungry for my breast, and she cries when her swaddling becomes too full of piss and shit. Cries from colic, though not often, given what Lord Cappelletto lets me be fed. Cries from the cold or the heat or the aching in her gums. Cries when she is too long in her mother's presence. And cries when she is too long from her cousin's.

I somehow believe Juliet's sobs will draw Tybalt to us. When they do not, my wine-soaked worry deepens. "What if—"

Before I can give voice to all I fear, Pietro cuts me off. "He strayed away before the fighting started. We'll find him, and you'll see he's fine."

Pietro is a hopeful man. But that can sometimes wear upon a wife. He knows I have no patience for being told everything is fine, when in truth neither of us can tell how well, or how awfully, something might turn out.

Walking out from among the trees, we pass brawlers and innocents alike, dragging their mauled selves from the campo. Those too hurt to walk howl for friend or stranger to take mercy on them. The gilded cages of the menagerie lie toppled on their sides, the whimpers of the frightened animals inside swelling into the cacophony of human shouts and cries. But we see no sign of Tybalt and no trace of where we sat when he last left us.

"There's no place for him to find his way back to." I raise my voice to make myself heard above Juliet, whose wailing grows louder the longer she longs for her cousin, who could be halfway to Villafranca by now. Or drowned in the Adige. Or carried off by ransom-seekers. "And no way for us to know where to look for him."

"So we will look in all directions," Pietro says. He starts to walk in a circle. Not a perfect round, but an ever-widening curve that slowly grows to take in a greater and greater area.

I taught him this trick years ago. Whenever a sheep strayed off, I'd spiral farther and farther around my flock until I found it. But sometimes what was left to be found was only the mauled remains that a bloody-fanged wolf had left behind.

Pietro keeps walking, the distance between us growing as he circles away. I'm not the sort of wife who follows anywhere her husband leads. But then he begins to whistle. He knows I cannot stand him whistling when I'm worried. I cut in a sharp line across his curving path, scolding him to pray instead, or just to shut up entirely. Anything but that cheerful whistling, which does not seem right until we find Tybalt.

"Until," he repeats, meaning to assure me the boy will be found. Pietro slips an arm around me, and we walk side by side. Curling our way beyond what was crushed in the brawl, we cross winter-bare fields, Juliet inconsolable in my arms. We've walked for who knows how long, my throat aching from calling for the lost boy, when Pietro stops. He hears first what I, soaked in Juliet's crying, miss: the matched cries of Tybalt, pitched as high as those of his baby cousin.

Tybalt is tucked in the crook of an olive tree. Pietro reaches up, murmuring gentle words until the boy crawls into his arms. His big hands run over the teary child, and he shrugs to let me know neither flesh nor bones seem broken.

"The brawl is over." Pietro cradles Tybalt to his chest as I cradle Juliet to mine. "The mob is gone, it's safe to come back with us now."

Tybalt tips his head up. "What brawl? What mob?"

"Never mind about that," I say. I pass a hand through the boy's pretty curls, as much to reassure myself as to comfort him. "Why were you hiding?"

"The other boys said I could not win."

My relief at finding Tybalt ebbs back into worry. "What other boys?"

"There were five of them. We had a contest to see who could piss the highest. I made an arc just like a fountain, I should've beat them all. But one of them, who was smaller than me but wore a fur-trimmed carmine cloak just like the prince's, said I'd not win unless I could make myself into a statue the way he can."

I work the edge of my tongue in and out of my fresh-cracked toothhole, trying to dull the throbbing edge of pain as I puzzle through what Tybalt means. The boy he met must be Cansignorio's nephew, Count Mercutio, who's been sent by the prince's conniving sister and her calculating husband to Verona to serve in the court of his ruling uncle. Everyone knows why, though no one dares say it out loud: if Cansignorio cannot make a legitimate heir, this Mercutio might one day rule our city. Unless he somehow provokes his living uncle, and thus meets the same fate as his murdered one. Such are the prospects of a royal boy.

"Even counts and princes cannot turn themselves into statues," I say, thinking Tybalt is confused by the tombs of the Scaligeri, which rise high above the churchyard of Santa Maria Antica, each with a sculpted likeness of the man whose remains it covers. The sarcophagus of Cangrande I is topped with a statue of the prince astride his horse, his sword sticking up from his lap in such a way that Pietro snickers whenever he passes it, saying all of Verona can see in that extended member why Cangrande I was called the big dog.

"This one can," Tybalt insists. "After he shook his last piss drops off, he turned like marble down there. I shook myself and tried to turn to stone, too. But I could not."

I cannot help but smile at the idea of Mercutio swinging his little manhood at Tybalt like a miniature version of the rock-hard sword sported by the death-statue of Cangrande I. It's welcome relief after all the terror of the brawl to laugh at the way small boys tease each other.

As we walk back to the city gates, Pietro provides the talk that Tybalt's father is too far off to give. If only we could pass a ram tipping its ewe, or a mastiff mounting a bitch in heat. But you never happen upon those things when they are most convenient, and so Pietro gestures wildly to illustrate his explanations. Though I walk a little ways off in the hope Tybalt might forget that Juliet and I are here at all, I mark the way he tilts his ear, struggling to understand what turns a man hard as stone, and softens him back up again.

To me, those things are far easier to grasp than what would bring youth not half a dozen years older than Tybalt and Mercutio to such bloody conflict, leaving the campo trampled, the palio-race unrun, and who knows how many innocents hurt or killed.

FIVE

Shad, eel, perch, carp, pike, trout. Pickled, salted, smoked, breaded and fried. In the forty meatless, milkless days of Lent, the cook dishes up so much fish for the Cappelletti, I swim the Adige in my dreams. I visit whole underwater kingdoms as I sleep, a twitch of what are no longer my human hips sending me gliding headlong through mysterious dark channels. My scales shimmer in the cool rush of river-water, and I want to stay weightless and submerged forever. Until the night between Maundy Thursday and Good Friday, when a whole herd of gaping-eyed sea monsters chase me in my sleep, sinking fangs into my guts as I struggle to swim free. I wake gasping for air, beached on Juliet's big bed.

I need to relieve myself. There is a filth bucket beside the bed, where I'm meant to empty my bladder and bowels. But I just dumped and scrubbed the bucket after supper. Rather than soil it again so soon, I make my way through the dark sala to the privy closet in the antecamera outside Lord and Lady Cappelletti's bedchamber. It's the first private necessary I've ever seen, and I sneak into it whenever I can. Shutting myself inside I always feel, if not like a queen upon a throne, at least like a fat hen on her roost. It holds the cleanest waste pot in the house, the maid hauling off the contents three times a day. Which you'd think is often enough.

Yet as I approach the door, the stink wrenches my stomach halfway to my mouth. Lord Cappelletto must have filled the privy with who knows what ill-humorous excretions. Surely I'd do better to go back to my own bucket.

But then I hear the whimpers. Small, wounded sounds, more of fear than physical hurt. A noise I first heard from a neighbor's puppy, not at the moment my father smacked it hard between the eyes for digging in our field but when, seeing the stick swung high once more, the animal sensed it was about to be struck again.

Pushing open the door, I realize the stench is not of piss or shit. It's rot. The fetid rot of human flesh, which hung so heavy during the great pestilence that no one who lived then can ever forget it. It's coming not from the high-sided privy pot, but from Lady Cappelletta, who lies curled into a sweat-soaked ball on the cold floor.

This is my luck, to escape sea monsters in my sleep only to wake to this.

I kneel in the doorway, one hand covering my nose and mouth, the other gently pulling free the thick locks of Lady Cappelletta's hair, on which she's sucking.

"I reek," she says.

It is so true, I do not bother to disagree. "Where is the pain?"

"Gone. Since last week."

"A week past, and you've not yet sent for the midwife?"

"Lord Cappelletto calls for the midwife, when it is my time." Her eyes swim up, then down, uncertain. "Is it my time?"

Fifteen and lady of a grand house, yet she's still more of a child than I ever had the chance to be. Already delivered of a daughter, she knows less of bodily things than I did even before my first babe quickened in me. I'd tended a herd. Watching my flocklings tup then lamb, I formed some vague understanding of the relationship between the two. Learned, from watching, all the troubles there were to worry over. I saw lambs come out feet first. Or two-headed. Or, twisted up within a bleating, terrified mother, not at all.

"If you're in pain, the midwife should come."

"But I'm not in pain, not since last week."

"That is when she should have come. Now it may be too—" I catch myself. What use is there in lecturing? I lay a careful hand across the rise of her belly. "Has it moved since then?"

She shakes her head, keeping her eyes from mine.

It's not that she does not know. It's that she'll not admit to herself what she knows.

"And the smell, when did that start?"

"Just the last day."

"Have you bled?" I ask, and she nods. "But nothing else has come out?"

She cocks her head at me, like a slow-witted horse.

I try to make my words gentle, but what is the use? "It needs to come out of you."

"They die if they come out too early, that is what my sister told me when she gave me my bridal-chamber instruction. I must keep it in me. Lord Cappelletto needs his heir."

A privy closet is no place for prolonged debate, especially when its inhabitant is putrid. And too terrified to understand what's happening to her. I brush Lady Cappelletta's feverish cheek, wondering how long she's hidden here trying to deny the death inside her. This is the difference between us. I lost an infant I'd not even known I carried. She carries an infant she'll not admit is lost. The two of us, huddling with our separate griefs in this tight space.

"Lord Cappelletto waited this late to marry," I say. "He can wait a little longer to make a son."

"He did not wait. He had sons." Her voice drops. "It is not his fault if I cannot make a healthy boy. His first wife gave him three sons, before she ever had a daughter, as he likes to remind me. He still calls for her in his sleep, thirteen years after the plague took them all."

I slump onto my heels, feeling the weight of what Lord Cappelletto survived. To lose all one's children, this most terrible grief I know too well. But to endure it alone—that I cannot imagine. I would have thrown myself into the same shallow grave that swallowed my sons if Pietro had not held so tight to me, his grief as great as mine. I can only pity Lord Cappelletto for whatever twisted curse of luck kept him alone alive. And Lady Cappelletta—though she'd hardly been out of infant swaddling when the plague ravaged Verona, the ghost of it yet hovers over her marriage bed, festering its way inside her.

"The midwife must come, and maybe a surgeon, too." What more can I say to make her understand? "It's already dead, and must come out of you. To be buried, like his others." I add the last part in the hope of convincing her that Lord Cappelletto will be moved to sympathy by this new loss. But we both know her dead issue cannot be buried in his family tomb, or any consecrated ground, its unbaptized soul condemned to who knows what eternal fate.

She grabs my hand, crushing my fingers with a surprising fury. "She took it. I know she did." She speaks with a lunatic's urgency. "I hate her."

"Who?"

"Juliet."

What is she saying in her madness? "She's just an infant."

"Not the brat, the other one. The one he named her for. His dead wife. I hear it every night: Juliet, most cherished, departed mother. Even in his sleep he taunts me with it, to remind me of what I'm not."

So this is why she loathes my Juliet. A treasured jewel named for a wife Lord Cappelletto may have truly loved, the mother of all he'd lost. All the things he's given my dearest lamb—ivory-inlaid cradle, pearl-trimmed cap, grandly godfathered christening-day—such weak talismans against what he and I and everyone who lived through that awful time knows can so quickly snatch breath and life and joy away.

When death decides to come, neither wealth nor piety can stop it. We know this, and yet we bargain with our saints and ourselves, every moment of every day trying to deny the one great truth of life: loss. It is a fool's bargain, but still we make it.

"You are his living wife," I remind her, "and you've given him his only living child." Given me my only living child as well. A child I need to protect. Protect even—especially—from Lady Cappelletta. "Let them take what stinks of him from you. As long as you survive, that is all that matters."

She gives the slightest nod and eases her grip on me. I fold her fingers around the garnet-studded cross that hangs on a thick chain around her thin neck, to give her something to hold to once I leave her.

She slips the bejeweled cross-piece into her mouth, sucking like a child and rocking herself back and forth. Unsound body, unsound mind. You need not be a midwife or a physick to know which is the harder to salve. I unbend myself, my legs tingling and unsteady as I go to wake Lord Cappelletto.

When I part the curtain around their marriage bed, I see in his sleep-softened face some tender thing I've never before noticed in him. Not so gentle-hearted a man as my Pietro, but one more touched by sentiment than I'd thought Lord Cappelletto to be. A frescoed Virgin covers the wall beside the bed, watching over him like a doting mother over her own slumbering son.

But where care lodges, sleep cannot long lie. I shake him awake. As he makes out my face, he grunts with alarm. "Juliet?"

"Juliet is fine. But Lady Cappelletta—"

"Is it the child she is carrying?"

It's true, this wife means no more to him than the pried-open oyster means to the man that seizes a pearl. Or the man who, seeking a pearl, finds none. "The child is already gone."

The softness sags out of his face, and I recognize the same old man who was too superstitious to visit the confinement room.

Before I can say more, he slips from the bed and kneels beneath the painting of the Holy Madonna, grabbing my arm and pulling me down beside him. His insistence startles me, until I think of how many nights, and days, he must have knelt alone after losing his first Juliet and all their little ones. Word for word I match his prayers, taking comfort in our nearness as we implore the Blessed Maria to keep safe the soul of his never-to-be born babe, along with the many souls of those others taken from us. All our plague-dead children. His first, beloved wife. And Susanna, my terrible fresh loss. Almost too much to bear, such doubled and trebled grief, until I utter that one comfort, the name of our living love. The two of us entreat the Sainted Virgin to keep little Juliet with us and well. "And Lady Cappelletta, too," I say, crossing myself and waiting for Lord Cappelletto to do the same.

He does, calling her Emiliana. It's the first time I hear her Christian name. Those pretty syllables seem to shimmer from his stale-breathed mouth. He calls on Santa Margherita, and the Virgin Mother, on his own patron saint and on Lady Cappelletta's too, praying she will prove fecund. I know that whether we fare well or ill, it's only by the saints' intervening grace, and even the apothecaries will tell you the Pater Noster and Ave Maria are the surest cure. But how long ought a man keep beseeching the heavens to let his wife birth new life, while she lies alone and terrified within a privy closet? I give off a little cough, interrupting Lord Cappelletto long enough to squeeze in a quick *amen* and hoist myself to my feet.

"Amen," he repeats, rising and calling for the page to fetch Verona's most respected midwife, to rid Lady Cappelletta of what she's lost.

Prince Cansignorio and his household ride on horseback at the head of the Easter procession, while all the rest of Verona walks. Or nearly all. Lord Cappelletto strides. Having maneuvered his way to a position right behind the prince's family, Lord Cappelletto wears an expression I first caught sight of while peering out from behind my mother's skirts when Luca Covoni, who owned our village, came to collect my father's rent. A tightness around the jaw to convey impatience at being bothered with such petty matters, a tightness that barely masks what shows in the darting, bulging eyes: a deep sense of pleased possession, as though Covoni owned not just the land, but all of us who lived and labored on it. Striding in the wake of the Scaligeri horses, his vair-lined velvet robe secured by a broad silver belt that wraps twice around his great girth before dangling nearly to the street-stones, Lord Cappelletto exudes the same entitled air, but with an assurance that a man like Luca Covoni, whose hems remained caked with manure from the fields and dirt from our peasant floors, never had.

Tybalt and I follow like a pair of pack-donkeys, me bearing Juliet and Tybalt carrying the silver chalice that will be the Cappelletti's paschal offering. Both held so high that every noble family who walks behind us, and all the less-than-nobles who line Verona's streets to watch the grand procession, see them.

Lord Cappelletto's tasseled hat has slid to one side, revealing his balding pate. Tybalt giggles at the way the glinting sun dances on the sweat that slicks that feeble, hairless spot. But no one else is close enough to notice. And if anyone wonders at the absence of Lady Cappelletta, surely they cannot imagine the state she's in. From the time the midwife arrived with her hooks and pliers, not all the aqua vitae in the city could quiet Lady Cappelletta's screams. I glugged back a good quantity myself in the hopes it might at least dull my hearing, but it's been no help. I've kept Juliet and Tybalt as far from her as I can, though in truth there's no place in all Ca' Cappelletti where her maddened howls do not reach.

But passing outside the compound's walls brings me no solace. A dozen brutal fights have bloodied Verona's stone-paved streets since the palio-day riot. I've not left Ca' Cappelletti during these deadly weeks, and now the slightest jostling from those behind us in the cortege, or the press of the crowd watching us pass, shimmers fear across my back. As the trumpets heralding the prince sound against the buildings that line our route, I'd swear I hear in their reverberations some echo of cursing and crossed swords. The silver chalice flashes like an upraised dagger, and with every turn we make, I wrap myself tighter around Juliet, certain the day's uneasy peace is about to burst.

Following so close to Prince Cansignorio offers faint comfort. Several years shy of thirty, he's barely older than the palio-day brawlers and, it seems, no wiser. Lacking his brother's lust for control, he's not bothered to quell the violence. Mayhap he believes that as long as Verona's bloodthirsty youth are killing one another, they'll be too busy to raise a blade against him. Though the city is in want of peace, he offers only a grand show of his own supposed piety, pledging a thousand candles to each church and chapel in the city. He leads the Easter procession on a three-hour circuit for all Verona to witness his enormous waxy offering, as though we are too stupid to realize that princes pay their tithes out of poor men's taxes.

At last, we reach the Duomo. As we face the rippled marble columns framing the cathedral's entry, the crowd sways before its arches and peaks, its windows carved with more beasts than Noah could've fit within a fleet of arks. I wish I could set my rump upon one of the stone griffins flanking the door and settle Juliet onto my lap, for at eight months she's grown heavy as a good-sized sack of grain. But what do Cansignorio or Il Benedicto care for a woman's suffering? Neither of them offer any balm for my throbbing feet and aching shoulders, as they stand in the shade of the cathedral, taking long turns addressing the crowd. Blessed, the poor are told they are, though not a one of them—with their dirt-streaked nails, callused hands, and bodies still bent from whatever toil swallows the other six days of their week—will gain entrance to the Duomo. Not today, a day so sanctified that prince, counts, lords, and all the new-moneyed merchants turn out in their finest silks and furs, velvets and jewels, to command places in the cathedral. It is Easter. Christ is risen, and so are the profits of every fabric dealer and goldsmith in the city.

I wonder where Pietro might be among the gathering. This was the one hope I carried when I left Ca' Cappelletti: that he and I would find some way to find each other. Foolish wish. For how can I tell if my husband is one of the tens of thousands of people crowding the streets that fan out from the Duomo, when I face only the back of Lord Cappelletto's balding head and the Scaligeri horses' behinds?

The prince's nephews ride two astride the same horse, a broad black beast that, as if to add an *amen* to Il Benedicto's final blessing of the crowd, lifts its tail and looses a mound of slick, brown dumplings onto the cathedral steps. The younger of the boys, the one called Mercutio, digs a quick heel into the horse's flank. The beast turns sideways just as the liveryman steps forward to lift the child from the horse. Swinging his far leg across the animal's hindquarter, Count Mercutio thrusts himself into the liveryman's arms with such force the servant stumbles back into the steaming turds. Sliding across the mound, he loses his grip on the boy, who manages to crash, hands outstretched, into the ample bosom of the bishop's niece.

Surely the liveryman will be put out from service, and probably from the city walls, for such clumsiness, though I see it's all the boy's doing, a prank to amuse himself during the solemn monotony of Easter morning. Tybalt stares at Count Mercutio, worry edging his face. Count Paris, the prince's other nephew, still atop the horse and clutching its mane to keep from tumbling off, mirrors Tybalt's expression. As though each of them knows that while this bit of Mercutio's fun is at the liveryman's expense, next time it might be at theirs.

Lord Cappelletto gives a quick nod to Tybalt to make haste as he follows the prince's family through the massive cathedral doors. Tybalt looks longingly at me, but I give his shoulder a loving push. Shifting Juliet from one hip to the other, I make my way to the smaller northern door with the other women.

In all my decades in Verona, I've never been inside the Duomo. I always offer my confession in Friar Lorenzo's cell, Pietro and I going to full Mass no more than once or twice a year. And that we did at San Fermo Maggiore. Nesto insisted the communion wafers there tasted better than any others he ever had. We laughed when he said that, thinking it a sinless sacrilege for a child to believe such a thing. After he died, I took what small comfort I could in feeling the same circle on my tongue he'd been so adamant about having on his.

If I were at San Fermo now, I would make my familiar way along the nave, slip through the side door in the upper church and down the stairs, passing the corridor that leads to Friar Lorenzo's cell to head instead into the lower church. There, in the cool dark air, I could nestle Juliet to my breast and nurse her as I used to nurse my boys, under the watchful eyes of my most beloved saints. But the Duomo is as strange to me as a Mohammedan's temple. Spread broader and rising taller than San Fermo, the grand cathedral does not make me feel like an angel ascending to heaven—more like a tiny churchmouse dizzily scurrying across its vast, patterned floor. Scores of candles burn upon the altar. Watching them glow, I try to feel Pietro near, to believe it is his bees who birthed the wax that drips, liquid hot, before the image of Our Lord and Savior.

Though I know by rote my Ave Maria, Pater Noster, and Pax Domini, the rest of Mass remains a mystery to me. Not so Lord Cappelletto. Even from across the nave, I mark the proud way he intones in Latin along with the cathedral priests. He pulls sanctimoniously on Tybalt's ear whenever the boy's eyes start to wander to the sculpted swords that frame the rood screen, or the painted scenes along the side-walls of bloodied martyrs glorying in their righteous torments.

Once the last prayer sounds against the cathedral walls and the congregation rises from our knees, the priest signals for the acting out of the Passion, which features a live lamb and three donkeys—a spectacle beyond anything the Franciscans over at San Fermo ever offered. The woman beside me strains to get a better view of every hollow between the would-be Christ's ribs and the shimmering oil on his anointed feet. The Crucifixion is so realistic, I wonder if instead of pardoning a criminal in honor of the holy-day, Cansignorio means to start a new tradition by having this one sacrificed.

But no, the pretend Savior survives long enough to be entombed and then rise up. For what inspiration would there be in death, common as that is? The miracle is in the Resurrection. Or ought to be, though in truth I notice Mercutio snickering and Tybalt slumping with disappointment when they see how the priests playing the Roman guard conspire to block the congregation's view while the pretend-Christ clumsily replaces his brittle band of thorns with a golden crown. Holy chicanery it is, yet it impresses the thousands of Veronese pressing in behind us, whose rippling murmurs of awe fill the cathedral.

After the congregation has gasped and oohed to the bishop's satisfaction, he gives a final benediction and disappears into the sacristy. Cansignorio and the counts follow, Lord Cappelletto close on their heels. He hurries Tybalt along with him, the boy struggling to keep the chalice raised high as a score of men who are the most trusted of the prince's allies swarm forward with the various treasures they are gifting to the church.

The last of them is barely through the rood screen before the congregation begins to press its way from the cathedral, eager to trade piety for pleasure. But I must wait for Lord Cappelletto. Slipping a finger into Juliet's needy mouth, I murmur, "Yes, dearest lamb," matching my words to the familiar, urgent rhythm with which she sucks: three insistent squeezes, then a pause, and then three more. Kissing her dark hair, I smell not the delicate baby scent I crave, but the dank, spicy incense that fills the Duomo. At last the cathedral bell begins to ring, and the bells of all the churches across Verona answer, their high- and low-pitched peals dancing across the city's tiled rooftops. Lord Cappelletto reappears, barely flicking his eyes to me to signal that I am to follow after Tybalt, who's scurrying at his heel.

As soon as we return to Ca' Cappelletti, Lord Cappelletto orders every trencher in the house set out in the sala. There is cabbage loafed with eggs and garlic, savoried with marjoram, mint, and walnuts, baked heavy with Piacentine cheese. Mutton is served stuffed with pork bellies, parsley leaves laced through the meats. Next come liver pies and veal tortes, and platters of aspic shimmering with whole peppercorns and slivered cardamom seeds. Lord Cappelletto possesses the same gusto for breaking the Lenten fast that he'll soon have for breaking wind.

Although Lady Cappelletta still lies raving in the parto bed, he does not seem to mark her absence as he holds Juliet upon his lap and catechizes Tybalt about which men who knelt and worshipped nearest them in the cathedral are allies to the Cappelletti, and which are enemies. He talks full-mouthed of a seducer kidnapping a dowried girl away from her lawfully bound fiancé, or of a drunken insult shouted at a gambling table, quizzing Tybalt about what revenge should be exacted for each wrong, never mind that they were committed three generations past.

The more Lord Cappelletto talks, the more he drinks, until he's had wine enough to drown the Venetian fleet. He pushes first a goblet and then a trencher toward me, and orders me to drink and eat my fill.

But for once, I've no appetite. I'm thinking of the lamb stew I always made for Easter, which my Berto especially loved. Donato teased him as we walked home from church one year, saying there'd not be enough for Berto, which made the younger boy cry. Nothing we said or did could calm him, until Nunzio hoisted him onto his shoulders and ran the whole way home, letting Berto dip a spoon into the cookpot before the rest of us had even turned into the Via Zancani. I'd not believed I could bear to taste that stew again after the pestilence stole our sons, but still I made it that first Easter and ladled out a bowl for Pietro. Pulling me onto his lap, my husband tore off a piece of bread, dipped it into the soup, and begged me to have it for Berto's sake. Every Easter since, we've eaten it like that, with each mouthful recalling another memory of our lost boys. But this year Pietro must be having who knows what for his holy-day meal, alone in our house or out among strangers at some public tavern, his pocket full of honeyed sweets I cannot taste.

Sometime during the week past, a splintered fish bone slipped beneath the tooth that sits beside the gaping hole left by those I lost in the brawl. I push my tongue at the stuck bone, letting the pain throb into my gum and flash along my jaw as I watch Lord Cappelletto giving Juliet tastes of this or that from his finger. When a pinkieful of lemon pottage makes her throw up—not the soft milkish spit she trails every day on me but thick gobs of undigested food—I reach fast for her, glad for the excuse to carry her back to our bedchamber.

Tybalt follows after us. I wish he'd chirrup out some joke or song to cheer me despite myself. But he sinks onto a high-backed stool set against the far wall, plugging his nose with his fingers while I wash Juliet and replace her puke-covered swaddling with fresh bands. He watches like a cat outside a mouse hole until I nurse her to sleep.

"What's the Order of Santa Caterina?" A funny question, even for a boy as odd as Tybalt.

"A convent." The truth. But from the confusion that pulls at his curious eyes, I can see that like so many of life's truths, it's of no particular help. Not until I explain, "A place where nuns live."

This Tybalt understands. He clasps his hands against his chest, fluttering his eyelids and pulling his cheeks taut in mimicry of the dourest abbess, and parades around the room. Then he asks, "What does *weaned* mean?"

I crook an elbow around Juliet's head, to protect her from hearing such a word. "Weaned is when a child grows too big for nursing."

He nods like some great sage. "When they're weaned, they go to the convent."

His words catch me cold. "When who's weaned? Who's going to a convent?"

"It's what the bishop said, when Uncle bade me give him the silver chalice." He screws his voice into a perfect imitation of the bishop's haughty tone: "We shall keep a place at the Cloister of Santa Caterina. Send her as soon as she is weaned."

Something sharp jags inside me. "You're sure that's what you heard?"

Tybalt puts a hand to his heart, swearing on his most prized possessions: three marzipan wise men he's been hoarding since Christmas.

"Was he looking at your uncle, or at another man?"

"He looked at the chalice. It was heavy, and I had to carry it for hours, until he took it from me."

I curse that chalice, which I mistook for a mere paschal offering, never guessing it was the first piece of a convent-dowry. Now I see that the silver goblet is like Juliet herself—a sacrifice Lord Cappelletto will gladly make, bargaining with God to give him a son.

Tybalt's words still turn in my head hours later, as I fall into a tormented sleep in which I dream I search all through Ca' Cappelletti only to discover my girl gone, and Lord Cappelletto laughing over some swollen-headed boy who fills her cradle. This boy is so hideously deformed, his face cannot be called human. He has a spiderish number of arms and legs, which spill out of the cradle onto the floor. Even as I dream, I can hear Lady Cappelletta howling as she lies wakeful with wild-eyed fear that she'll never deliver a living son. Or maybe she howls from the grim realization of all that it will take for her to bear one.

During the next months, I lose more teeth. One into a thick cube of veal fat, another to such rotting that Lord Cappelletto pays his barber to pull it from me. I lose teeth, and Juliet gains them, two tight little rows rising from her gums. Tybalt and even Lord Cappelletto marvel when Juliet opens her mouth and the light flashes on those perfect teeth. Such marvels only taunt me, consumed as I am with what Tybalt never should have told.

Friar Lorenzo, sensing I'm keeping some secret, presses me each time I return to be shriven. I make careful catalogue of every hour I snatch with Pietro, when I stop at the Via Zancani on my way to the friary and whenever he comes to tend the bees at Ca' Cappelletti. I accumulate randy acts to repent, knowing that I'll not confess to the friar what really burdens me. Not tell him how I hate the thought of Juliet being taken from me and sent to a convent, consigned to the same celibate life he lives. What use would it be to confide what is not my sin, when I know already how he will answer? I am only a wet-nurse. A woman who is not to question God or Church or Lord Cappelletto.

So I'll not question, not aloud. Only when I'm alone, with Juliet burrowing asleep against me, do I silently wonder how long we will be able to keep our precious milk bond—and what I will do to protect it.

SIX

Although Lord Cappelletto waited five weeks from when his wife was delivered of her first child before taking her again, she was brought back to their bed only five days after the midwife removed her second, dead one. I thought Lady Cappelletta would cower from him like a caged animal. But instead she shrilled out demands that he mount her once, twice, three times each night, which he was glad to oblige. In the days afterward, she'd remain in bed and rave for Tybalt, of all the household, to come and place a hand upon her stomach and say whether he felt anything stirring there.

What could Tybalt feel at such moments but frightened? The boy who loves to stage bloody battles with toy soldiers, and who eagerly recites every gory detail of a dozen assassinations undertaken by long-dead Cappelletti to avenge their honor, yet who delights in making up songs and tumbling-shows to entertain me and Juliet—this same boy has learned to hide whenever he hears his aunt call. So, for his sake, I go to her instead.

She's not pleased when I come into her bedchamber carrying Juliet with me, as if it is the child's fault, or mine, that she was born a girl. "Where is Tybalt? He is the only one in this whole household who cares for me."

I open my mouth to assure her that's not so. But what good would such lying do her? She's barely older than Tybalt. They might have whiled these last years of childhood as contented playmates if she were not married to his uncle, her lonely fate already settled.

I balance Juliet on my hip while I open the window covering to let the newly warming spring into the room. "Lord Cappelletto chose you for his wife."

"He chose me in payment for a debt."

This seems to me more of Lady Cappelletta's madness, for what man marries a debt-slave, instead of working her for what is owed? But when I turn back toward the bed to tell her so, she cuts me off.

"Lord Cappelletto was visiting one of the Scaligeri castles on Lake Garda. He rode out upon a hunt, and one of the hounds got loose and killed a hind on my family's lands. My sister loved that hind and wept to find it slaughtered, so when our cousin discovered the bloody-mouthed dog, he slit its throat, to please her. Not long afterward, a serving-man from the hunting party came near, calling to the dog. My cousin laughed and told him it was dead. But Lord Cappelletto, as a guest of the Scaligeri, demanded the life of whoever killed the hound. Our family priest advised my grandfather to send away my cousin, and offer Lord Cappelletto a wife instead."

She fingers the edge of the coverlet, as if she's trying to pull loose the thread that binds her to her husband. "I thought he ought to have my sister, for if she'd not wept over the dead hind, the hound would never have been killed. But my father said she was promised to one of the lords in Padova, and he did not care to jeopard what he'd already given for her dowry. So I was delivered to Lord Cappelletto."

A deer, a dog, a daughter: are the rich so muddle-headed from all they possess that they think such things are equal, and ought to be traded one for another? Yet this must be what Lord Cappelletto believes, pledging Juliet like a sack of tithed coins to the Church to please the saints into giving him a son.

When Pietro first made of me a wife, I'd stir myself awake in the smallest hours of the night, watch his sleeping face by whatever moonish sliver rose, and whisper out all the grateful love I felt. Whatever we might declare by day, only in the night, when slumber dulled his ears to me, did I dare show how desperate I'd been for anyone to care for me as he did. Not until Nunzio was delivered of me and exhaustion stole my strength and made me cling to any sleep I got, did I stop rousing myself like that. By then it mattered not. Cradling our first son, Pietro knew the full measure of the ferocious love I felt for him, and I knew he felt the same for me. Lady Cappelletta's wakeful nights and red-eyed days offer no hint of such joy for her.

I nestle my sleeping Juliet into a chair and bring the work basket to Lady Cappelletta's bedside. "Your father must have thought it well to marry you to an ally of the Scaligeri," I say, though such alliances are made only to serve men. If Lady Cappelletta's gained anything by the match, it could only be in measure against how awfully her own family may have treated her.

I search through the basket for a hoop from which emerald-green and ruby-red silk threads dangle. It's the budding floral hedge she was embroidering before the child died in her. But when I hold it out to her, I see her hands are still too twitchy to work a needle.

I sit beside the bed and begin to fasion the slow stitches myself. This is how we'll pass the days. I can care for Juliet, and do the household's sewing. The hare-faced cook will prepare the meals. The cleaning and tending will fall to whatever worthless servants wander in and out of employ within Ca' Cappelletti. But there is one wifely duty that Lady Cappelletta alone must perform.

Through the nights that follow, whenever I hear her desperate pleading for her husband to make his heir upon her, I wonder whether that hind was better off. At least its end came quick, and someone wept for it.

It's the height of summer, but Tybalt does not seem to notice the day's thick heat as he chases a capon around the dovecote, trying to slip one of his out-grown stockings over its squawking head. His father's most recent letter made mention of the expert falconry practiced by the Gonzaghe courtiers. Tybalt read the letter to Juliet and me over and over so many times I can recite it back like a traveling peddler calling out his wares. Tybalt's convinced himself that if he can train a bird—any bird—to sit upon his arm, cast off, and return with some wormish kill, surely his father will come back to see such a feat, or send for Tybalt to go to Mantua to show off his prowess, such as the boy imagines it to be.

I should rescue the stocking, and the dishcloth he cut up for jesses, and the ribbon he's fashioned for a leash. Should consign them all to my work basket, which grows fuller every week. But how can I deny the self-sworn protector of Ca' Cappelletti a chance to play at manhood?

"Look at the castrated little cock," I laugh to Pietro.

"Tybalt may not have a falcon, but the bird runs, and flies, yet it will return." Pietro pinches one of the scarlet-orange blooms on the pomegranate tree, pulling it free without losing a single delicate petal. He dangles the flower in front of Juliet, who opens her pretty pink lips and squeals "usss, usss." It's her first word, or will be once she learns to say it right. I let Tybalt believe it's *cousin*, though I'm sure she's really saying *Nurse*.

Pietro lets the flower drop. "You hold too tight to her, Angelica. At that age, our boys—"

"She is not like our boys." Why must I even say it? Our boys never looked upon trees like these. Never knew their father to tend bees. Never saw him cut honeycomb from a hive, as he's just done. As he did with not a single of his own half dozen sons to help, but only little Tybalt.

I'd watched the two of them from inside Juliet's bedchamber. Even with the window pulled tight to keep the bees out, I could not help but imagine the dizzying smell of ripe fruit going soft in the midday sun. And intermingled with the smell of fruit, a smudgy waggle of smoke, which tapered into the sky from the torch Pietro'd lit to keep the bees at bay. Through the wavering air, I saw how he unsealed the lid from the cut-log hive, deftly slicing and lifting out the combs. How he broke those combs into the deep-sided pot that Tybalt held for him, to begin the slow process in which the wax, which Pietro will trade to a chandler, rises, while the thick honey sinks.

Even with a cloth covering his face, Pietro sang while he worked, to show me he has no fear of bees. He is a barrel-chested basso, and his timbrous notes wavered against the panes as if they meant to steal their way into the room, as Pietro has stolen his way inside the half dozen times he's come to Ca' Cappelletti to check his bees.

After Pietro culled what he wanted from the hive, he replaced the cover on the hewn log. And then my husband dipped his broad thumb into the honeypot and pulled it back out glistening, closing his eyes as he sucked off the golden liquid. At last, he opened those beautiful eyes and dipped his thumb again. This time, he held it up, slowly waving it at me.

My mouth watered for that sun-colored honey, and so I disappeared from the window, carrying Juliet through the tower passageway and down into the arbor.

Pietro pulled me around the side of the dovecote, holding me close as he slipped that thumb into my mouth. But Juliet wriggled in my arms like a kitten wrapped in a drowning-sack, separating Pietro's chest from mine.

I'd taken a half-step back from Pietro, tasting apple and pear and pomegranate, my tongue coated with all the fruits of the arbor condensed into the warm honey, as I commented on Tybalt and his capon.

But Tybalt's not what my husband's thinking of. "It's been a year, Angelica. Time to loose the child's swaddling."

A year. A birth, a saint's day, Christmas, Lent, Easter. Each was Juliet's first. Each, aside from birth, is what Susanna never had. Every holy-day, every season, I feel it.

The first year is the hardest. That is what the black-veiled crones say, the ones who gather like sharp-beaked crows at a stranger's graveside, cawing unasked-for advice at the mourners. The brown-frocked friars, if they bother to murmur any sort of comfort, will say as much as well. But no one says aloud what my mother-heart cannot unlearn: hard as the first year is, harder still is what happens in all the years that follow, when part of you forgets for a moment here or there what you've lost, even as the rest knows that in your deepest bones you can never for a day, an hour, an instant, forget.

I still catch sight of Donato or Enzo or any of my boys, out of the corner of my eye. Sometimes I see them at the age they were when death snatched them, and sometimes as the age they'd be now, every one of them grown tall. Sometimes they're some age in between, so I'm not certain from the fleeting features which son I saw, those beautiful lost faces blending one into another.

But not Susanna. She stays ever a newborn babe, still covered in our shared blood, as she was in that too brief moment when first and last I glimpsed her. If Juliet's grown and gained this year past, it's only in measure against Susanna. How can I be glad for that? Why wish this last child grown enough to be taken from me and sent off to live among cold-humored nuns? Swaddled, she is safe. Suckling, she is satisfied. And so am I.

"It is for Lord and Lady Cappelletti to decide when she is ready to be unswaddled." Even as I say it, I know how Pietro might argue back. Lady Cappelletta has no notion what a child needs. And when have I been eager to obey Lord Cappelletto? Pietro might point out these things, or things much like them, and I ready myself to answer as soon as he does. But instead he says what I never expected to hear.

"We could have another."

My tongue swells in my throat, too full for me to speak. All I can manage is to shake my head. Shake it as though to keep what he says from landing in my ears.

We've never spoken this way, uttering out-loud plans for making babies. There'd been no need for such talk during those first laughing days of lusty love when we made Nunzio. Nor in the fifteen years that followed, when our little house filled with growing boys. And after we lost our sons, I never dared say to Pietro, nor did he dare say to me, that we should make another. This was what the pestilence taught, a lesson too terrible to ever forget: it was not for us to decide what child we got, when they came, and when they were taken.

Month after month, I'd watched the moon grow full, wishing, hoping, my belly would grow with it, but all that swelled me was time, and wine, and sweets. And then, long after I'd given up waiting: Susanna.

Did Pietro say anything to me, or I to him, to make her come? Could we have said anything to make her stay?

This past year, the year since she was lost, is the only time I ever let the getting or not getting of children govern how Pietro and I indulge ourselves. There are countless ways for a wife to please a husband, and a clever husband can match them one for one in the pleasing of his wife. Pietro's not ever remarked on how careful I've become since entering Ca' Cappelletti to keep his seed from landing where it might quicken in me. Not because I do not want his child, but because I cannot bear to lose the child I already have.

For this is what wealthy men dread most in a wet-nurse. I've seen women with smaller waists and faces far gaunter than mine standing in church doorways, milk soaking through their gowns while some sneering notary takes their testimony. But each woman and every notary and anyone who happens by—all know such a woman's sworn-to-God statement will do no good when the court hears the suit her employer has brought against her. The merest suspicion of pregnancy is grounds enough to break a contract with a wet-nurse, no matter if it proves false or true. I'll not take such a risk with Juliet.

I love Pietro. But with what foolishly deluded heart can my husband believe that he and I might yet see even one child raised and wed, when we have buried seven children dead?

"It was you who brought me here," I remind him. "You set your mark on the nursing contract, hiring me away."

"It was Friar Lorenzo's idea, not mine," he says. "He told me there was one other baby born that day in all Verona, and by God's grace the family was in want of a wet-nurse." My strong Pietro quivers like a too-shorn sheep. "I waved his words away, thinking I could not bear to let you go. But when I saw how your body ached, like my own heart, for our dead daughter, it seemed the only way to stop your weeping. The only comfort I could give to you."

I pull Juliet close against my heart, feeling the weight of how much my husband loves me. "You were right, Pietro. She's my comfort for all we've lost. Just as you wanted her to be."

"As I wanted, and you needed, a year ago." He dips his little pinky into the depths of the honeypot, then traces my lips with the golden liquid. Dots it on my sweat-damp brow, his finger lingering between my eyes like Friar Lorenzo offering Ash Wednesday absolution. "But now I need you home with me again."

Instead of answering with words, I lead him into the tower and up to Juliet's room. Laying her in the cradle, I bid him gather back the sun-warmed honey with tongue instead of finger. He savors that and more from me. For the first time in a twelve-month, I let him spend himself deep inside me, and I shiver with the pleasure of it.

Afterward, I steal to the privy pot, as though his seed means no more to me than what else is squatted out here. I mouth a silent plea to the Virgin Mother. *Sacred Maria, you who did not bear your own husband's child so that you could raise the one God gave to you*—a shrewd opening, to remind her of our likened states—*I beg of you, take pity on me. On me, and on Juliet. Most Holy Madonna, keep us together, always.* Then I rouse Pietro, telling him it's time for him to take what he's harvested back to the Via Zancani.

But the pleasures I steal with my husband are not the only delights I must keep secret. Come nightfall, while Tybalt and the other Cappelletti sleep with bellies full of the evening's meal of roasted capon, I do what I've never so much as hinted to anyone, even Pietro or Friar Lorenzo, I've long been doing. I unwrap the swaddling bands, letting Juliet's arms and legs spring free.

She gurgles with pleasure at the rush of air. I match her throaty purrs, nuzzling the delicious plump of her legs and arms, cupping my belly against the soft bottoms of her feet.

This is my secret joy, and hers. It started one half-mooned night before the Pentecost, when I awoke to her crying over having soiled herself. I unswaddled her and wiped her clean, but in my exhaustion I fell back to sleep before binding her arms and legs again. I dozed and dreamt and woke to Juliet grabbing at my hair and ears. She even wiggled her curious hand into my gaping mouth to touch my broken teeth and full, wet tongue. When I laughed, she folded herself and stuck her own toes into her mouth. I gobbled up her other foot, humming as she squealed. In that delicious moment, I knew the same pleasure she'd known months before, my mouth as full of her as hers has been of me.

We slept again, entwined like vines heavy with ripe grapes. When sun and lark roused the house the next morning, I reswaddled her, pressing a finger first to my lips, then to hers. She nodded, sure and solemn, as though she knew we needed to keep anyone from suspecting how free she'd been.

When the next night came and I took her into bed with me, she looked up with such expectation in her dark eyes, I could not leave her bound. I woke terrified through those first weeks, fearing her limbs would go crooked because they were not kept wrapped tight. For that is all we ever hear: the tighter the swaddling, the straighter the arms and legs. But the fear that comes with morning's light is nothing compared to what I feel in the dark, once her arms are free and she reaches for me, or when she tests her uncertain legs by stepping against my thighs. We are lovers of the purest kind, for what greater love is there than the one between a mother and a milk-babe? Happy nights, when we take such simple, secret pleasures.

Swaddled, she is safe. Suckling, she is satisfied. That is all Ca' Cappelletti, or Friar Lorenzo, or even my own dear Pietro need know.

SEVEN

When Juliet is nearly a year and a half old, Prince Cansignorio comes to dine. Lord Cappelletto, eager to please his powerful guest, lets Carmignano flow by the cask, and I do not miss the chance to drink my fill as I hold Juliet for her royal godfather and the other guests to admire. The prince has brought a half dozen musicians with him, and they play different styles of song, some brightly plucked upon the lute and some heavy with the viol's melancholy, to match each course as it's served. While I soothe Juliet by swaying to the melodies, Cansignorio sits at the table-head drinking down one round of the Cappelletti's wine after another. Lord Cappelletto twines compliments over his regal guest until the prince interrupts and, with a tongue heavy as wet wool, announces that he's sent counselors to every ruling-house within a month's travel by horse or sail. They're seeking a woman not too old, not too ugly, with not too many brothers in her powerful family, to become Cansignorio's holy wedded wife.

Lord Cappelletto raises his goblet before anyone else can. "To a goodly, Godly match."

The prince nods and drains his cup once more, as Lord Cappelletto leans forward to suggest that Cansignorio's good fortune would be best served if, before any dowry is negotiated, he dismissed a certain maladminstering Uberti, appointing Lord Cappelletto to oversee his treasury instead.

Though the prince waves in wine-flushed agreement, all Europe knows it's not only by the size of the dowry-portion that a ruler values his wife. I see it in how Cansignorio looks at Juliet, eyes full of pity for Lord Cappelletto, and something else for Lady Cappelletta, who still cannot produce a son. Eggs are eaten, herbs are applied, prayers are said. But nothing quickens. Her blood has stopped and started three times in twelve months, what is purged from her each time not even formed enough to bury beside her other lost one. The fault cannot be in the stars, or something gone off in the year's grain, for bellies spread all over Verona. The prince's mistress is thin and carrying high, so that not even the bishop can pretend not to notice that Cansignorio will have another bastard long before he ever takes a bride. Lord Cappelletto takes careful note, commissioning a finely worked silver dog with sapphires for its eyes as a gift of congratulations to the prince, and an even more ornate silver-and-sapphire cross for the altar of one of the chapels in the Duomo as penance for his envy.

While the thickest of winter's fog twists through Verona's streets, Lord Cappelletto sends the nittish house-page searching through the family's storerooms. It takes a half-day's hunt before he barges into our chamber bearing such a contraption as I've never seen, a thick wooden ring etched with the Cappelletti crest, held up by four carved legs set on a larger ring balanced on wooden wheels. "Girello," Lord Cappelletto calls it. He orders me to unswaddle Juliet and set her inside the frame, as though she's a cork being fitted with feathers for a game of shuttlecock, and he means for me to bandy her back and forth.

Juliet has no need for this strange machine of which Lord Cappelletto is so fond. She is ample-limbed and dimple-fleshed like me, not wan and sullen like Lady Cappelletta. I know how ready her chubby legs are, a sturdy match to her plump, impatient arms. I'd bid Tybalt to teach Juliet to walk as my boys taught their younger brothers, for a ready babe will give toddling chase to an apple rolled along the floor. Pietro's army roly-polied an entire orchard's worth of apples between the six of them. I baked each bruised fruit with parsnip, fig, and turnip, seasoning the mixture with anise, fennel, and a touch of mustard. Then I chewed with my own mouth the portion to feed whichever boy was just out of swaddling. The whole neighborhood could smell the scent, imagine the taste of one of our sons learning to walk.

But Ca' Cappelletti fills only with the dull, grating sound of wood wheels along the stone floors. Juliet careens in the girello, dark eyes flashing wonder at how she can make herself go. But then comes the pause as she turns, looking back to make sure I'm following. I am all she seeks, and she ventures in her walker only so far that she can please herself at being able to waddle her way back to me again.

As Juliet masters the girello, Lord Cappelletto tells me the page is to take the cradle from her chamber. He says it is to make more space for Juliet to practice walking, but from the way his scheming tongue darts at the spittle that gathers in the corner of his mouth, I can tell this is a lie—or at least not all I'd have of the truth.

I piece the fuller truth together hours later when I stand in the sala window, straining in the last of the day's light to sew a border of Damascus cloth onto one of Tybalt's doublets. It is a lurid violet, as costly for the vivid color as for the exotic fabric. Tybalt begged for it in imitation of the new fashion the prince's nephews wear. Lord Cappelletto, ever wanting to outdo his noble rivals, happily indulges anything that ties his household to Cansignorio's. Never mind how my eyes strain to work such careful stitches, attaching the border to a garment that Tybalt, already long in the leg, will soon outgrow.

As I pierce the needle into the precious Damascus cloth, I catch sight out the window of the house-page. He's bearing the cradle along the Via Cappello as though Lord Cappelletto has ordered him to float an infant Moses down the Adige to some unknown pharaoh. But no, just before the page reaches the Porta dei Leoni, he turns into a humble doorway.

It's the house of a pursemaker. He is a man with maybe six, maybe seven daughters. I can never keep track as they pass back and forth on their household errands. However many they total, you do not need an abacus to tally that there are too many of them for a pursemaker to dowry.

Wide-hipped and young, those daughters are. It flashes on me like a lightning bolt: Lord Cappelletto means to have his pick, trying one and then another to fill that cradle with a son.

I store away the discovery like Tybalt stores candies in his sleeve, though it gives me something more sour than sweet to chew. I draw Juliet out of the girello, saying I must go to San Fermo to be shriven, though we head first to the Via Zancani.

"You cannot warm two houses with only one woodpile," I say, after I've shared the gossip with Pietro. Lord Cappelletto will never have heat enough to make a son in his marriage bed, if he spends himself among the pursemaker's daughters.

Pietro, who has heat enough for an ironmaker's furnace, swings himself before me. "But if your fire's big enough, who knows how many pots you can bring to a boil."

My husband is a merry man. It's a truth I treasured when he and I had every night together, for we always made good use of them. But the stolen hour here or there we've had these seasons past to take our quickest pleasures—they are like crumbs of stale bread to a starving man. And worse, to a starving woman.

There are undowried daughters up and down the Via Zancani, the same as on the Via Cappello. And Pietro can easily find time as he travels from hive to hive to stop among the prostitutes who ply their trade in the sun-bleached stands and shadowed corridors of the Arena.

"Have you been bringing many pots to boil?" I ask.

He pulls me to him. "One pot is all a good cook needs to make the most savory of stews." Burying his face in my bare belly, he runs those big hands above and below, touching and then tasting all the places he knows well. What we make is more savory than stew, fills me more than whole loaves of bread. We lie so long together, I have to skip my shrift, carrying my sins along with the precious taste of Pietro on my tongue. The smell of him lingers on me as I bear Juliet through the wintry streets, clinging to Pietro's promise that he passes solitary days and nights while I am gone.

Back in Ca' Cappelletti, Lady Cappelletta is wearing a new gilt-and-emerald brooch and a puzzled look, not sure what to make of her husband's sudden generosity. I remind her it is a rich man's duty to purchase such sumptuous things, for how else are the silver-smiths, gem traders, and silk merchants to keep their families fed?

It's true Lord Cappelletto wants all Verona to know he is a rich man. But there are other things he'd not have his wife know, and that is why he buys what he believes will distract her. During the next months, the Cappelletti wardrobes swell. But Lady Cappelletta's womb does not. Whether the same can be said of the purse-maker's daughters, I cannot tell, their bodies hidden beneath new cloaks as they scurry along the Via Cappello.

The year's first snow does not come until the middle of February, falling just past dawn in great fat flakes that make Juliet press her nose against the cold glass of the window. Tybalt would carry her out into the courtyard still in her nightclothes if I did not stop them long enough to bundle her, and him, and myself as well. Outside, the chill air tingles against our skin, as Tybalt insists we turn our faces up to the sky, open-mouthed like three baby birds waiting for worms to drop from their mama's beak. Juliet giggles at the silver taste of falling snow, but whimpers with disappointment when she watches the flakes melt into moist nothing in her cupped hand. Tybalt lifts her up, spinning with her in his arms until she laughs once more.

A man's boots crunch along the entryway. It is Pietro, come to check how the hive is faring in the blustery cold. Juliet wriggles free of Tybalt and totters toward my husband, half-singing and half-panting, "Po, Po, Po," in perfect imitation of the tone with which I call Pietro's name when he and I lay together. Why does this surprise me? She's heard it enough times, when I've given her a top or doll or just a pot-spoon to bang against the floor, anything to distract her while my husband and I take our tumble. "Po," she says again, insistent, reaching up her arms.

Pietro scoops her up, planting a warming kiss on her reddened ear. But as she shrieks another joyful "Po," Lord Cappelletto appears behind my husband.

"What's this?" he asks.

I'm not sure which distresses him more, to find Juliet outside at this hour and in such weather, or to see her beaming at the bee-keeper with a grander version of the same adoring look Lord Cappelletto believes she saves only for him.

"Where have you been so early, Uncle?" Tybalt asks, juggling snowballs. The four perfect rounds arc up, only to smash apart when he tries to catch them.

Lord Cappelletto blinks once, twice, as though he is trying to conjure the right answer, then says, "A business matter. For the prince."

But his clothes are dry, his cheeks pale, not the wet and pink they'd be if he'd come all the way from the prince's castle, or even one of the lordly palaces that line the Piazza dei Signori. He must have passed the smallest hours of the night at the pursemaker's house, hoping to slip back here before anyone noticed he was gone.

My teeth ache in the wintry air as I reach for Juliet. I mean to hurry her inside, but when I take her from Pietro, she shrieks, "Po, Po, Po," so fiercely that Lady Cappelletta rushes down into the courtyard, asking whether the house is under attack.

"Such a bright child." I speak as though Juliet's recognizing Pietro should please the Cappelletti. "She knows it is the beekeeper, and she asks for a little honey."

I pray the mention of sweets will distract Lady Cappelletta as well as Tybalt, just as surely as needing to deceive Lady Cappelletta will distract Lord Cappelletto.

Pietro, who never comes to Ca' Cappelletti with an empty pocket, pulls out a bundle of candies and passes them to Lord Cappelletto, who doles them to his wife and nephew, and to Juliet, like a guilt-faced priest giving out the sacrament. Lady Cappelletta shivers, blue-lipped in the cold, and lets her husband drape an arm around her, guiding her inside. I follow, carrying Juliet back to our room without any farewell to my husband, who is already answering a new round of Tybalt's never-ending questions.

A child will parrot whatever it might hear, and who knows what the consequences will be, for the child or for the one whose words she innocently repeats. When I was a girl—older surely than Juliet though I could not say how much older—I repeated what I'd heard my father say a hundred times: *pox-faced son of the Devil*. His hateful name for our hated landlord. Yes, a child too easily recites what it does not understand, and that is how I spoke those words when Luca Covoni appeared one summer day to take his share of my father's harvest.

He repeated them, looking not at me but at my father. And before my father could respond, Covoni said the rent on the land we worked would be doubled the next year, and every year thereafter.

Covoni had barely left before my father grabbed a metal cooking spoon and began to beat my face with it. When I asked what I'd done wrong, he bared my buttocks and swung the spoon against that tender flesh, whacking out each syllable of *pox-faced son of the Devil*, demanding I never mock him again.

Though I'd always been quick with words, I'd not known what it meant to mock. And this I must have protested to him. For next he screamed he'd take a knife to my very tongue and cut it loose for all the trouble it caused. My mother went out, leaving me to his rage—or so I thought. She reappeared clutching a clay jug she'd hidden in the root cellar. Even I could smell the heavily fermented contents as she uncorked it. Wine made my father cruel enough. Surely with such evil spirits in him, he'd kill me.

But once he started to drink, he could not stop. By the fifth swig, or the sixth, he'd lost interest in me. My mother just had time to whisper a single command to me before he shoved her down onto the bed. She smiled at him, but she kept one eye on me to make sure I did as she bade, running to my aunt's house on the far side of the village. It was three days before she let me back. My father's rage had faded, though the angriest of the red welts he'd laid on me were still raw. That was my first lesson in the value of keeping things unspoken, or carefully half-told.

I'd not lay a hand on Juliet, would not even threaten it. But by the look upon Lord Cappelletto's face when she called for Pietro, I know I must quell what's dangerous in her mouth, just as surely as my father did what was in mine.

The day is bright from sun and snow, too bright for spinning schemes. I wait until night settles like a great shadow over Ca' Cappelletti. Then I teach Juliet to do what I hope will keep us in Lord Cappelletto's highest graces.

I let her grow hungry and hungrier, before I untruss my left breast. I dance it above her, watching her watch the nipple slick with milk. As her mouth opens, I take her chin in my other hand, gently working her jaw up and down as I say, "Papà."

"Po," she says. "Po," reaching for me with greedy hands.

I pull away. "Papà."

"Pa-po." Closer, but still not close enough.

"Papà, Papà, Papà, Papà, Papà, Papà, Papà." I repeat it so many times it begins to sound like none-such speech to me, until at last she says, "pa pa."

"Yes, my darling girl, yes." I let her take me in her mouth, indulging her only long enough to dull the ache I feel from being too full of milk. Then I pry her from my breast and make her say "pa pa" again, before I let her drink her fill.

I go to sleep thinking myself quite clever. But when I wake, Juliet is kicking at my ribs, calling "pa pa, pa pa," as she pounds her hands against my breast. That is what she thinks "pa pa" means.

This will please neither Lord Cappelletto nor Lady Cappelletta.

Lord Cappelletto's grown so full in the gut, there's a pouch within the household sewing basket filled with buttons he's burst loose. I slip one of the silver buttons stamped with the Cappelletti crest into my blouse, and, sure the saints will smile at such ingenuity, let it settle into place between my breasts. When I gather Juliet to me to nurse, she discovers the button, clutching it with one hand while the other cups the great globe of me that fills her mouth. I kiss her hair, then kiss the hand that holds the button, whispering, "Papà." Every time she nurses, she finds the button, wrapping greedy fingers around its shiny surface and singing out, "pa pa," before she latches onto me.

I bide our time until the prince next comes to dine. While he brags of the fine bride he's at last contracted for—who will come from Naples with a good dowry, a grand title, and best of all, a dead father, no surviving uncles, and a sister who rules the city of Durazzo childless—I let Juliet crawl into Lord Cappelletto's lap. She reaches for the topmost of his buttons, calling, "pa pa, pa pa."

"Papà," Lord Cappelletto repeats, laughing and grabbing her insistent hands before they tear the button loose.

Juliet smiles up at him and says, "Nusskiz," which is how she demands a kiss from me. Lord Cappelletto, who always thinks he understands what he does not, bows his head and pushes his big nose toward her delicate lips, waiting for her to kiss it. I notice what no one else does: how she hesitates. But my good girl does what is asked of her. I nod, letting her know that later, once we are alone, I'll give her what she seeks.

It's harder to herd a well-pastured lamb than one that's never left its pen. Freed first of swaddling and then of the girello, Juliet tumbles and stumbles and grabs at anything she can. We go to confession just before Pentecost, and when Friar Lorenzo bends to bless her, she pulls so hard at his Pater Noster cross that the cord snaps. Beads fly loose, bouncing across the hard floor of his cell. I kneel and crawl, searching out the myrtle-scented beads. He keeps careful count until I find them all.

But Friar Lorenzo'll not scold Juliet. He lays a loving hand on her bejeweled cap and says, "Juliet Cappelletta di Cappelletto, truly you are Heaven's child."

She rewards him by snugging herself into the thick folds of his cassock and trilling out, "Fri-lore-so, Fri-lore-so." The holy celibate, beaming like a proud grandsire at how she forms his name, offers a Latin benediction to show all is forgiven.

When we leave his cell, I take her into the lower church, where she toddles up and down the aisles to touch the brightly colored saints painted upon the square pillars while I say my Ave Marias.

Her delighted squeals echo against the ceiling arches, until I'd swear the icons themselves smile back at her. She insists she can make it up all the steps by herself, and though she uses hands as well as feet in her crawling climb, when she reaches the top, I stand on the landing below and clap to show her she's done well. This sets her squealing again, and she bolts into the upper church—and comes to a smacking stop against a kneeling, sobbing woman.

I hie to them, murmuring an apology to the mourner. As I scoop up Juliet, she grabs at the woman's veil, expecting a game of peekie-boo as she pulls the dark fabric up. But my sweet girl's grin cracks into a gasp when she sees the woman's face, leaden with grief.

The woman reaches to tug the veil free. But no, her fierce hands seize Juliet, snatching the child to her.

Juliet screams. A sound of pure fear, entirely unlike her familiar squeals of joy, or impatient wailing, or frustrated sobs, or any other noise she's ever made.

"So alive," the woman says, clinging tighter as Juliet shrieks louder.

I reach for Juliet. "Let me take her, while you make a prayer for the departing soul of the one the you've lost."

"I've not lost one," the woman says. "I've lost them all."

Her grip is as tight as mine, and we stand together like a single, strange beast wrapped around my screaming Juliet, until one of the Franciscans hurries out from the sacristy as if he's expecting to combat Satan himself. Seeing him, the woman looses her hold. I cradle Juliet to me, bearing her away, out of San Fermo and into the bright sun.

Shushing her terrified cries, I carry her toward the Adige, hoping the swooping gulls will distract her. But even when her screams subside, she'll not forget the woman.

"Who-da?" she asks, "Why-do?"—her worried way of wondering who the woman is, and what made her act so strangely.

How am I to answer? Although I'd never before seen her, I know everything about the woman's agony as surely as, in that horrible year when plague crept across this very bridge into Verona, I knew my own miserable self.

For weeks, for months, as the mysterious pestilence ravaged the city, I woke fearing I felt the gentle swell in the pit beneath my arm or between my legs. I was sure I would be the one taken, and then Pietro after me, our children left orphans. When each dawn found us well, I prayed my thanks, then prayed my beseechment that I might live to pray such thanks the next day, too.

Pietro and I lumbered like blinded mules through the deathly miasma that lay upon the city, struggling to keep ourselves and our boys clear of it. I rose at odd hours so that I could draw water from the public fountain when no one else was there. And I wrapped myself like the wife of a Mohammedan whenever I went to the market, although in truth we stayed half-starved because I feared what sickly airs might coat any eggs or grain or meat I bought.

That spring, Pietro was hired by a confectioner whose apprentices had fled the city. It was against the guild rules for a grown man to be taken into the trade, but in those dismal seasons no one bothered to enforce such statutes, for what man wants to waste what might be his last healthy day just to swear out a complaint against a rival artisan? If you've never lived through plague, you'd not believe how popular clove-soaked candied walnuts or cinnamon-sugared bozolati can be. When disease ravages innocent and guilty alike, there are those who don hairshirts and shout for repentance, and those who drop breeches and call for delights. Appetites for confections swelled along with appetites for every other bodily indulgence, and Pietro was gone long hours from us. When my chores gave me need to go out as well, I bade Nunzio lead his brothers to the roof, to play whatever games they could invent. I never would have believed this safe and right before the plague, but now I thought only of the one great harm that I believed could not find them there.

Any mother of sons knows how boys will entertain themselves watching ants carry off the carcass of a wasp. From our roof, my sons saw Verona's bier-bearers crawling ant-like through the streets, first to the cemeteries and then, once there was not a single square of consecrated ground left unfilled, to any field beyond the city gates where a mass grave-pit could be dug. It was not right for children to gape at those bespotted, boil-ridden corpses being carried off. But what else could I do with them, six sons I dared not let into the street? I always barred the door from the outside, so they could not let themselves out. Returning an hour later, I'd hear their shouts and taunts, the thrumming of a ball against the wall, all the boisterous cacophony of boys kept locked inside echoing along the street. In happier times, a mother might scold her sons for such disturbance to the neighbors. But during those months when pestilence silenced so many, whenever I came back to my boys' noisy mischief, I kissed and hugged them hard, until even little Angelo squirmed away from me.

Half a year we lived like that. Till the autumn day I went to buy the last of the season's onions, hoping they would somehow be enough to get us through the winter. When I haggled over the brown-skinned bulbs, did I forget to beg the saints' forgiveness for my great presumption that there would be eight of us to feed all the way to spring?

As I neared our house, I heard Angelo crying as though his older brothers were tormenting him. No mother is surprised by such things, but Angelo's wail was unusually frightened, and frightening. The door was still shut fast, just as I'd left it. But what tingled in the pit of my arms and between my legs swelled to a throb as I unbarred the door and hurried up the stairs. There was Angelo, redfaced and bawling, bound to the bed with a dishcloth. I stopped only long enough to see he was unharmed, before I searched out his brothers. They were not inside, and when I called them name by name to come back from the roof, there was no answer.

I hauled myself up the ladder, but none of my boys stood upon the roof's sloping tiles. My yells sounded back unanswered from the walls of the neighboring buildings, which rose above our little house.

Somewhere Berto let out a giggle. One of his brothers smacked him back to silence before I could be sure where the sound was coming from. Curving foot to tile, foot to tile, I crept to the edge of the roof. Bracing myself against the corner of our neighbor Luigi's house, I peered out. Though the day was cold, Luigi's shutter was flung back, a patch of faded bigello caught on its hinge. I knew the fabric well. Nunzio, Nesto, and Donato each had worn and outgrown the tunic it was torn from, which now was Enzo's.

Angelo, still bound to the bed, let out a doleful cry. My foot slipped, sending a tile sliding off the roof. It smashed into the street, and Enzo poked his curious head out from Luigi's window like a ground-mole popping up from his hole. Before I could grab for him, his brothers pulled him back inside.

I could not creep hand-over-hand along the awning pole that hung across the windows, as my sons must have. Instead I crawled back up the roof and down the ladder, hurrying down our stairs into the street. Banging on Luigi's door, I called his name, and then the name of each of my naughty sons. None answered. I grabbed the latch, which lifted too easily in my hand.

Luigi was a tanner, and at first I thought the stink inside must have come from a remnant of curing hide. But climbing his stair, I knew the stench was too terrible for that.

I found him lying on the floor. His half-rotten corpse gaped with holes where rats had fed off him for who could say how long. But those devil-toothed rodents would never be so cruel again thanks to my sons, who'd taken Luigi's kitchen pestle and smashed the rats to death. Five in all, one for each boy.

How could they be so impious? As if dying unshriven and unblessed, then being chewed through like some Alpine cheese, was not enough for Luigi to suffer. Though the sight and stench of him turned my stomach, I kept my sons in that room yet longer, ordering them all to kneel and pray for the poor man's wandering soul.

But I could tell already it was too late. I did not yell, or strike, or chasten them. Neither did Pietro, when I told him that night what they'd done. We both knew that what punishment they'd suffer for their savage sport was one we could neither give nor relieve.

Two days passed before Berto began to swell. Within hours, four of his brothers did as well. We tried to keep Angelo apart from them, but where in our little rented rooms could he be hid? The pestilence took but another day to find him.

By the end of the week, every one of our dear boys was dead. Pietro bore them off on a single bier, while I cursed the saints that saw fit to let me outlive my sons.

So alive, the grieving woman in San Fermo said. So alive—the worst thing to be, when you've lost all. But the best, now, as I hold Juliet and coo her calm again.

EIGHT

The dovecote stands one year, then two. Tybalt grows bored with chasing game hens, and Juliet, at nearly age three, squeals with pleasure while swooping after them herself. Lady Cappelletta has been fed innumerable eggs and a countless weight of poultry-flesh. Was it dove, or partridge, or sparrow that at last did it? None can say. Her madness quiets as her breath grows shallow, her face swelling like the pig bladder blown full of air that my boys used to bat back and forth between them. No one speaks of it. She is too fearful. And Lord Cappelletto is too superstitious.

He hires a donkey to carry her in this year's Easter procession, while he walks before her beaming as he shows the whole city that he's finally filled her belly again. Ridden by an ass so long, she now rides one—a merry joke, though I've no one to tell it to. But some jokes tell themselves. During Mass, Lady Cappelletta lets slip such a passing of wind, it echoes against the arched ceiling of the cathedral. On the men's side of the nave, Tybalt's laugh breaks nearly as loud, setting Juliet giggling as well. I pinch a look at him and a thumb on her, until they hush.

Juliet's so big, I cannot hold her as I kneel, and so she must kneel herself, though her body leans heavy into mine when she grows tired. As for Tybalt—even on his knees he's now taller than his uncle. But he still mumbles during Mass, repeating by unsteady rote as I do, with none of Lord Cappelletto's prideful mastery of Latin.

Once we are back in Ca' Cappelletti, the Easter feast spread upon the sala table, Tybalt is the first to fill a trencher, and just as quickly fills his mouth. While Lady Cappelletta, elbows propped upon the dining table, falls into a doze, Tybalt's new-long arms stretch for seconds and then thirds, emptying the serving bowls of the wild boar braised in rosemary, wine, and walnuts, and then the roasted kid stuffed with parsley, veal, and fig.

The Lenten fast is hard on growing boys, but Lord Cappelletto is harder on him still. Last month, Tybalt finally bested his uncle at chess. After all the years of losing, he was so proud he'd won, he ran to tell me and Juliet and Lady Cappelletta, and did not understand why I tried to shush him. I'd not expected Lord Cappelletto to take well to being bested, and in the days since, he's seized every chance to needle Tybalt, insisting his nephew will do the Cappelletti more dishonor than five generations of Infangati or Uberti or Montecchi have.

"Your Latin is disgracing." He jabs his dinner knife into Tybalt's trencher to take back the last lamb-and-fennel sausage. "And your tutor tells me your figures and tallying are even worse."

Lord Cappelletto's words hit Tybalt like gut punches, hunching him forward, singeing his ears with crimson shame. Juliet, frightened for her cousin, climbs onto my lap and searches out a breast for what is her comfort, and mine. I ought to carry her off, to nurse her far from Lord Cappelletto, but I'll not abandon Tybalt.

"I try, Uncle." Tybalt's voice cracks under the effort of answering. "But words or sums upon a page dance before my eyes until I'm dizzy."

"Dizzy?" Lord Cappelletto snorts the word back. "Lazy. A lazy princox, and I'll not suffer it."

I share, if not Lord Cappelletto's severity, at least some worry over what will become of Tybalt. He does not fall in with the other boys his age, who roam the city looking for trouble. When he sneaks from his family compound, it is only to follow Pietro as he makes his circuit from one hive to another. And my husband says Tybalt's enthusiasm wanes when it comes time to haggle with the chandler or coax raw honey into carefully spiced comfits.

But anyone with sense can see that Tybalt is not lazy. He dances, and prances, and tumbles, burning with more energy every passing year. He still dotes on Juliet, so that whenever he comes into a room, she smiles at him like a coquette at a wealthy suitor. And, like that wealthy suitor's poorest and most desperate rival, Tybalt will do anything to please her. But these days, nothing he does seems to please his uncle.

I remember first Nunzio and then Nesto at thirteen, when a youth thinks he is too clever to be young, though truly he is too young to be clever. An age when he needs most what Tybalt's father is not here to give.

Broadswords hang upon the sala walls, each as long as Tybalt is tall and all decorated with the gilded Cappelletti crest. Tybalt loves to play at swords, just as his uncle loves to tally the profits of his investments—and to outdo the Cappelletti's rival families in currying favor with Verona's ruler. "They say Prince Cansignorio has sent to Brandenburg, to hire the city's finest master-at-arms to teach Count Paris and Count Mercutio." I speak to no one in particular, though I make sure Lord Cappelletto hears.

"Who says this?" he asks.

I shrug, as if to show it's on everyone's tongue, though truly it's only on my own. I've woven it out of thin air, and now I knot the loose strands into a tidy edge. "They may only be his nephews, but Prince Cansignorio rears them as though they're his own sons."

Lady Cappelletta jerks herself awake at the word *sons*. Lord Cappelletto makes careful survey of the low spread of her belly. "I will write my brother about securing a master-at-arms. It's time someone disciplined Tybalt."

Tybalt pulls himself up at the idea of training with a sword-master, Juliet hiccuping off my nipple to give him a milk-wet smile.

Lord Cappelletto's mouth puckers over how Tybalt's joy feeds Juliet's. And it is from those puckered lips that I hear the words, "And also time for Juliet to be weaned."

Weaned. If Lord Cappelletto took my breasts into his stubby-fingered hands, twisting like Sant'Agata's tormentors, it'd not pain me more than his uttering that word does. As though what flows between milk-mother and milk-daughter can be cut off with a single word. As though I'll let the dour cloister of Santa Caterina swallow all the light and joy of Juliet, just so he can bribe the saints into giving him a son.

I rouse Juliet early the next morning and tell her we must go see Friar Lorenzo. She knows the route as well as I. Grasping my hand, she leads me along the Via Cappello toward the Porta dei Leoni, turning south and east and south again through streets no wider than a donkey-cart. Although by night these tight passageways are so quiet you can hear the thrusting of a single vendetta-driven blade, at this hour they're crowded with women and children hauling and haggling and hanging laundry, the street more filled with noise than light. Juliet stops every tenth step to gape and wonder, wearing my patience filigree thin by the time we emerge into the bright sun before San Fermo, cross the churchyard, and duck into the entrance to the friary.

Juliet is always delighted to enter the Franciscan's cell. She raises her face, ready to hear him say how pretty she is, grown ever prettier since our last visit, though he'd not have thought it possible. Her little mouth loves to form the words *me fess* and share with him her childish misdeeds: how she's cried herself exhausted while refusing all my efforts to console her, or plucked a flower after I've forbidden it. I always nod solemnly as she speaks, repeating her odd-formed words so he can understand them. By my troth, I believe she only does such little wrongs for the joy she finds in adding her play-shrift to my weightier one, and having Friar Lorenzo in a single breath forgive us both.

But today the truest sin I have to tell is neither hers nor mine, so

I'll not say it. How can I confess that Lord Cappelletto is ready to make sacrifice of Juliet? I claim impiety instead, for laughing with Tybalt and Juliet at Lady Cappelletta's breaking wind.

I bow my head and Juliet, her lip trembling with regret, bows hers, as Friar Lorenzo absolves us. "Poor Lady Cappelletta, she suffers so," I say, when he has done. "She'd do anything to be cured of such windiness. And Lord Cappelletto would give anything to have her cured."

Friar Lorenzo's great ears brighten to hear *Lord Cappelletto* paired with *would give anything*. I may not know a word of Latin, but I've long understood the mendicant order's unspoken motto: do all you can for the poor—and take all you can from the rich. It's the latter he's at now, leaning his tonsured head over his stock of petals and powders, muttering about wild celery and cowbane, then mastic, cloves, and madder root, carefully mixing in drams of who knows what else. He grinds it all into a powder, pours the powder into a pouch, and affixes a tiny cross, so Lady Cappelletta and her lord husband will know it came from him. "Three scruples," he instructs me, "to be given her with sweetened wine, whenever the windiness takes her."

I accept the Franciscan's *benedicte* along with the little pouch. When we leave his cell Juliet wants to tarry as we often do, stopping first to visit the bright saints in the lower church, and then, in the upper church, to twirl beneath the dim ones peering down from the dark ceiling. But I've no time for church and saints, when for once it's Lady Cappelletta's help I seek.

Juliet, long too big for the cradle yet still too small for a needle, has learned to make toy bird or clay horse her companion during the slow hours Tybalt is with his tutor while Lady Cappelletta and I sit sewing. But though I've told her a thousand times that what is said in Friar Lorenzo's cell is a sacred confidence between penitent and priest, Juliet proves again this morning what I often say: two can keep counsel, putting one away.

"Ma'da," she says, for the formal *madonna madre* is still too much for her little tongue to master. "Ma'da, me fess, and Nurse fess, and Friar make it go way."

Proffering the pouch, I explain, "Friar Lorenzo sends a blessed remedy to soothe your suffering," and instruct her to call for wine. Not the pale trebbiano Lord Cappelletto has her drink, but a foreign-made malmsey as red as the flush it will bring to her wan cheeks.

Three scruples, and wine, and honey to go with. One goblet and then another, and the mixture so sweet and good, she drinks down a third. All that tinctured wine calms her ill-winded humors, and soon Lady Cappelletta is giggling like a child of eight and not the woman of eighteen she'll soon be. She says Juliet's play horse reminds her of the steed that was the pride of her father's stable, telling us how on holy-days the horse's mane was woven with ribbons and pearls to match her sisters' fair hair, and her own. She even sings a little song that they sang as all three girls rode upon its back. Juliet's eyes puzzle at hearing the bright melody from such a usually so sour source.

"Happy days of childhood," I say, though I know not whether she had even a dozen such days before she was married off. But I need her to help me give my Juliet such happy days—and happy nights—as she deserves, not a one of which will come to her if she is sent off to Santa Caterina. "You should tell Lord Cappelletto to get so grand a horse, so that you and Juliet and the new babe might ride like that, when the second gets as big as Juliet is now."

"I cannot tell my lord husband such a thing," she says.

Even the wine is not enough to nerve her. So I add what ought nerve any wife. "I should think there's much you'd like to tell him, for mousing after the pursemaker's daughters instead of doing his dowry-duty to you."

Though it's not my proper place to speak so, what more have I to lose than if Juliet is sent off to the nuns? But my words are like a swift-winged wasp circling before Lady Cappelletta's brow. Her eyes cross in confusion.

"A wife must catch the rat, when her husband's on a mouse hunt." I work the spindle quick, letting my words work her. "Even Prince Cansignorio keeps his natural spawn out of the castle, now that he's got a proper wife. A husband must show public pride for his lawfully begot, church-blessed children, and send the bastards away."

This is my pretty plan. If Lord Cappelletto is in want of a child to sacrifice, let the convent devour what children he's made outside his marriage bed. Though for all I know, he's had even less luck planting his seed among the pursemaker's daughters than with his wife.

I bid Lady Cappelletta take more wine, hoping it will warm her to what I'd have her do. "Tybalt says the queen upon the chessboard uses knight and rook to keep herself protected. Just so a wife, who keeps her children near to make her husband put his duty to her first." I drop my voice to a conspiratorial whisper, though in truth there's no one near enough to hear. "I knew of a woman once, whose husband became so overfond of his natural child he took it into their home, and sent his wife and lawful children off without returning her dowry-portion."

I do not add that the home was a mere shack, the wife a shrew, the dowry-portion a near-dead billy goat, and even so, the village priest declared the husband wrong and gave the wife back her rightful place—where she was made to raise her husband's bastard child along with their legitimate ones.

As we sew, I keep a steady pouring of wine into Lady Cappelletta's goblet and vinegar into her ear. When the dining hour draws near, I urge her to put on her wedding bracelets. She wears them like Tybalt does his father's castoff gorget-armor—believing it girds him for some imagined battle, though in truth it's too big to fit him.

Juliet, grown tired of her horse, begs for a length of ribbon. I give her three, and show her how to weave them into a braided diadem, which she carries into the sala, where Tybalt is already waiting. When Lord Cappelletto enters, Juliet runs to him with the bright crown in her outstretched hands, calling, "Me give pa-pa."

But he ignores the gift and does not bend for her soft kiss. "I must go to Mantua," he says.

Mantua is a spark that ignites Tybalt. "Will you see my father? When do you leave? May I come?"

"I will go." A mere three words, yet Lady Cappelletta heaves a sigh at all it took for her to say them.

Lord Cappelletto, surprised to hear his wife speaking at all, answers, "You'll not."

But he looks full at her as he speaks, rather than keeping his eyes on his trencher, or on Tybalt, or on anything else in all the room. When a husband looks away, he is done hearing what his wife might say. But if his eyes meet hers, she may pry upon that tiny crack, if she has nerve to answer back.

All that wine has surely nerved Lady Cappelletta, though I mouth *the pursemaker's daughters* at her, just to be sure. "My dowry-gold fills your purse," she tells Lord Cappelletto. "You've no need to seek another."

Tybalt looks with wonder from his aunt to his uncle. "You're going to Mantua to get a purse?"

"I'm going to Mantua because my brother is unwell." Lord Cappelletto's wrinkled features sag under the weight of his words. But they hit Tybalt even harder.

"Will you not let me see my father?" he asks.

Before Lord Cappelletto can reply, I say, "A child is much comfort to a parent at such times."

For once, Lady Cappelletta catches the meaning first. "Your brother will want to have his rightful son with him in Mantua." She takes her husband's hand and lays it upon her babe-stretched belly. "And you will want to have your own."

It's the first I've ever seen Lord Cappelletto find comfort in this wife. "We will all of us go to Mantua," he says, just to be sure he's the one who settles it.

I gather Juliet onto my own lap, whisper *Mantua* into her ear.

But before I can spin out tales of all the wonders I imagine we'll see there, Lord Cappelletto looks over, as if discovering Juliet for the first time. She beams at him like sunlight streaming through church glass, offering the ribboned crown again.

"Juliet Cappelletta di Cappelletto, we must go to Mantua," he says. He takes the crown and sets it on her dark hair. "You will stay here and be weaned, while we are gone."

I flash a look at flush-cheeked Lady Cappelletta. But she is leaning toward Tybalt, the two of them murmuring about their journey—both so caught up in their confidence, neither of them thinks of Juliet, or of me. They do not so much as mark Lord Cappelletto waving his long-pronged fork and telling me, "The child is to be done with crying for the dug, before we return."

For all Juliet's memory and more, our days have always started with Lord Cappelletto coming for his morning kiss. But these mornings, there is no Lord Cappelletto thumping his way into our chamber, nor any chance of Tybalt climbing through the window or sneaking in by way of the hidden tower door, and no Lady Cappelletta anywhere in Ca' Cappelletti. It was a furious flurry of preparations, afternoon stealing into night, before we saw all three of them off at the next dawn. Lady Cappelletta sobered back to her usual uncertainty as her husband guided her into the wooden box of the hired carriage. She begged Tybalt to sit with her among the household bolsters and brass-hinged traveling coffers that were lain inside. But he insisted on riding upon a post-horse just as Lord Cappelletto did, one hand clutching the leathered bridle while the other waved fare-thee-well to Juliet and me.

Juliet's eyes widen with unease a dozen times a day at having all of our household routines unsettled. Again and again, I remind her that they are gone. That the sun must rise and make his way across the sky, then sink down and disappear, over and over at least a hand-count's worth of times, and maybe two or three, before they will return. Then I ask what she wants to play, and let her whims set each hour of our days. Though these may be the last we'll have together, I'd not have her know. I'll not burden her with all the grief I feel, as I hold her and offer what Lord Cappelletto demands she learn to live without.

It's more than a week that they've been away. Juliet, playing the wood-nymph frolicking among the fruit-laden trees, bids me be her fairy-queen. So I'm plumped upon the bench beside the dove-cote as though it were my fairy-throne, when Pietro comes into the arbor. One of his hands curves around a sack that's tied off with a tiny cross. I realize in a chilling instant why Pietro has it, what Lord Cappelletto must have directed Friar Lorenzo to send.

As the cross catches the summer sun, my besotted lamb reaches for it. Pietro slips Friar Lorenzo's pouch to me, then flourishes his empty hand as though he's a court magician. Juliet, startled to find what she seeks gone, blinks out disappointed tears. But Pietro offers his other hand, which holds a second well-filled sack, this one smelling of cherries, clove, and cinnamon. Juliet snatches it, twirling with delight. She pulls out three honeyed cherries, stuffs them into her mouth, and resumes her frenzied circuit through the arbor.

I hate to see her cry. But I hate more to see her soothed so easily.

"What comfit will comfort her, once she's tasted this?" I wag Friar Lorenzo's pouch of wormwood at Pietro.

"The child finds other delights than the breast. So might the breast, and the rest of my beloved wife, find other delights than suckling the child."

He pulls me into the shade of the peach tree. A tender sapling when first I came to Ca' Cappelletti, these three years later it's grown big enough to bear plump fruit. Pietro plucks a peach, halving it with his bare hands. He grasps the pit in his strong teeth and spits it to the ground. Then he rubs the wet, ripe peach halves along my neck, across my collar-bone. Deep into my dress. Slicking my breasts with peach flesh, as juice pours down my belly.

His tongue follows, licking and probing. Reminding me a husband's mouth can be as needy as a nursling's. As needy, and as needed. July is hot even in this shadiest corner of the arbor, and I am hot, too. Pietro knows it, urging my hands to the most ravenous parts of him.

I'm dancing my hips against his when a sharp shriek ruptures the air. A shriek, and then an awful silence. And then harrowing sobs that pierce my heart.

I race through the arched passage into the courtyard, Pietro following. Juliet's sprawled beside the well. Tripped over her own impatient feet, her brow cracked open.

I kneel and kiss her bloodied head. But before I can ready a breast to soothe her wailing, Pietro takes her by her tiny shoulders, turning her away from me toward him.

"Did you fall upon your face?" he asks, as though any fool could not know that's what she's done.

He waits for Juliet to snivel back a sob and nod, then says, "A child falls upon its face, while a woman falls upon her back." He laughs, sweeping her up with his big arms so she lies gazing at summer's cloudless sky. "Will you not fall backward for a merry man, when you are grown and have wit enough to know more pleasures?"

Juliet stints mid-wail. She smiles up into Pietro's winking eyes and leaves off crying. "Aye," she says, though surely she cannot know what he means, never mind how many times she's been with me when I've fallen on my back for him.

He sets her down and runs a broad thumb across the ugly lump that's swelling from her brow. "A lesson every girl does well to learn, and you'll have a bump as big as a cockerel's stone to remind you of it." He laughs again, and she laughs too. Her tears forgotten, she runs off into the arbor to play.

I lean back, letting the well-stones take the weight of me. "She's too young for talk of rooster parts, and rutting people."

"She is growing. Soon she will be grown." He sits beside me, slipping an arm across my shoulders and pulling me to him. "Why not let the girl know what pleasures she'll relish when she's a woman?"

"She'll not ever get to relish them." I bury my head against him and tell him how Lord Cappelletto plans to send her to the convent as soon as she is weaned. "He'll take her first from me, and then from every worldly pleasure. She'll wither away in a cloister, so he can have his son."

My merry-tongued husband has no words at first. But then he sighs and says, "She's his child. He may dispose of her as he pleases. You've known that all along. But if we have one of our own—"

"She is my own." The words I've never said aloud come pouring out. A flood, an avalanche. "It's my milk that's made her. The bone and muscle and soft, smooth flesh of her, they're all grown from what I give. The hair upon her head, dark as my own, and those plump cheeks. There's more of me in her than of Lady Cappelletta, or even Lord Cappelletto. Anyone can see it."

"What they see is the Cappelletti crest. Upon her clothes, and this grand house. And on the signet ring with which Lord Cappelletto will seal the papers committing her to Santa Caterina." Pietro kisses me, not with his earlier passion, but with the same gentle comfort I offered Juliet for her broken brow. "You've always known this time would come."

I've known, of course. But by my troth, I've not known, too.

Have I not said that self-deceiving is the very way of human-kind? That in our hearts, we all wish to be fooled, and so we make fools of ourselves? There are coin-hungry husbands who every year contract for a different babe to be cradled at their wives' breasts, and hard-to-please fathers who will hire first one nurse, then fickly turn her out and seek another, and then another after that, so that their child ever suckles upon strangers. But what Juliet and I share is not, cannot, be like that.

I am a fool, perhaps, but even as Juliet shed her swaddling, learned to waddle then to walk and now to run, even as she's swallowed her first tastes of solid food—in all this time we've had together, I've not truly believed that Lord Cappelletto could ever be so heartless as to cleave me from her.

"I'll not lose her."

"No, you'll not. Novitiates, and even full-habited nuns, may have visitors. I'll take you to the convent whenever she's uncloistered."

How can Pietro's talk of some-day visits succor me, when I know I'd not survive the stretch of time between them? "How can I live even for one day apart from Juliet?"

"Three years, you've lived apart from me."

"And it was ten times three years that we had together first. Why can I not have even half so long with her?" My words fly sharp and heavy, like the rocks Tybalt hurls from atop the Cappelletti tower.

How can my husband argue with me over this? Does he not know what losing Juliet will cost me? Did he not grieve for our sons, and for the loss of little Susanna? Is my mother-love so different from what a father feels?

Pietro pulls himself away, rising to his feet. "Mantua is only a day's ride from here. Lord Cappelletto may return at any time. When he does, he'll expect to find her weaned. And if she's not, he'll likely put you out at once for disobeying him. You'll get no chance to bid *God-be-with-you-and-good-bye* to Juliet. No leave to see her, even on uncloistered days at Santa Caterina. Nor ever again to visit Tybalt."

What Pietro says is true. But every syllable of it forms a taste as bitter on my tongue as Friar Lorenzo's wormwood will be upon my breast.

"I must go to Villafranca. A day's walk each way, to haggle for what spices I can afford before I harvest this summer's honey. When I'm back, I'll not come here again. I'll not keep sneaking about, stealing time with you like I'm a thief taking what is rightfully Lord Cappelletto's." He leans down and kisses my hair, letting his words slip softly into my ear. "For thirty years we made a home together, through the worst that anyone could suffer. Since you came here, I've worn my patience like haircloth, waiting to have you back again. It's time for you to be my proper wife. Let me love you near, as I've loved you every day you've been away."

I close my eyes, feeling the sun pour its stern heat across my face as I nod to my beloved husband. But he cannot see how I rub my tongue against my mouth-roof, knowing his honey-coated words'll not take away this bitter taste.

For one last night, I nurse Juliet into milk-sweet sleep. Restless though I am, waiting for her to wake and take her final taste of me, she sleeps heavily, stirring only when the morning lark twitters outside the open window, and the sun begins to stretch its golden way into the room.

"Me pick?" she asks, studying me with drowsy determination. I nod, glad for this game she's loved to play since before she had the words for it.

She opens an expectant mouth and takes in the nipple of my left breast. As she suckles, she reaches her hand up to stroke my face, drinking me in until my left breast has no more milk to give. I wait in perfect anticipation for her to reach her mouth to the ripe right nipple. Then I pull her close, savoring her last latching onto me. Wondering if ever tender hearts could break more than mine will, and hers as well, when we are forced apart.

By day's full light, I cannot deny the truth in what Pietro said. Yesterday's bruise has deepened into a hideous purpled rise above Juliet's eyes. That sight alone might be enough for Lord Cappelletto to put me out. I'll not risk disobeying what he's ordered me to do. Not anger him so, he might never let me see Juliet again. So I pray to Santa Margherita and Sant'Agata and the Blessed Virgin Mother for such strength as only women show, as I loose Friar Lorenzo's cross-bound pouch.

I was not much older than Tybalt is now, when I had Nunzio, my firstborn, at my breast. I can still remember how he crawled up my belly and found the nipple for himself. They will do that, the clever ones, in their first hour. And from that first hour, for fifteen years my milk ran for my boys. And then, when I was long past thinking I would ever suckle babe again, it came once more. Seven I birthed, and seven I nursed. But after today, not any more.

While Juliet giggles and gambols about the arbor, I sit beside the dovecote to rub on the wormwood, the godly friar's way to trick a child to stop suckling. I flinch at the first dab, expecting it to burn like salt in a fresh wound. But crueler than that, I feel nothing.

As I coat myself with this bitterest of herbs, I sense a dark form suddenly rising. The bees—they're flying frenzied from the hive, the arbor filling with their thousand-headed hiss. They hover in a whirling mass in the hot, fruit-scented air before forming a furious, swirling cone between me and Juliet.

The slabbed bench slides beneath me, then drops away. The fast jerk flings me to the ground. Stones fly past. The dovecote cracks, birds caw. Bells across the city clang. Not rung with the pious care that calls the holy to pray, but as if some unseen demon's hand was smacking every clapper in Verona, intent on splitting all our bells to pieces.

I cling for a hellish eternity to the shuddering ground, wondering if this thundering from every side will ever end. Worried the world will no longer stand when it is done. And plotting how to drag myself to Juliet.

And then, in an instant, the earth stills. The eddying cloud of bees funnels back into their fallen hive. Birds soar from the crumbled ruins of the dovecote, screeching as they spread themselves through the arbor trees. Screams of agony seep into Ca' Cappelletti from Verona's streets. But not a sound comes from Juliet.

She's heaped on the ground. She does not sob, does not stir. Not even when I crawl near and lay a hand across her chest to feel for the quiet beating of her heart.

I pull her to me, pushing my breast into her gaping mouth. She vomits me out the instant she tastes wormwood.

"Goddamn the brown-frocked friar." The words are out before I know I've made them. Surely I'm the one who'll wind up damned, for that unholy utterance. Perhaps I already am.

The arch over the passageway to the courtyard has collapsed. I stumble over toppled hunks of marble, clutching glassy-eyed Juliet to me. The great Cappelletti crest that hung within the courtyard lies smashed upon the ground. But the well still stands. I thank the saints for it as I haul up a pail of water, the rope rough against my hands.

My legs quake so, I cannot tell whether the earth is trembling again. I scrub and scrub my bittered breasts, dipping my tongue to test the taste. Wormwood, wormwood, wormwood. I cannot rid myself of it. How can I make Juliet come back to me, to herself, without a milk-sweet breast to draw her here?

Leaving her beside the well, I scurry once more across the jagged pile of fallen stone into the arbor. I do not give myself time to think, or doubt, or fear, before bending to pry loose the lid of the cut-log hive. I plunge my hand inside, the waxy comb crumbling in my desperate fingers.

The first sting burns the wattle of flesh hanging beneath my elbow. Pain sizzles up and down my arm and across my hand, as a second bee stings, and then a third. Then too many to keep count.

I hold tight to the crushed bits of comb, zigzagging my way from the hive, shaking bees out of my sleeve. By the time I'm back in the courtyard, I'm so swollen with stings, it's hard to unfold my fingers. I slip the sticky comb between Juliet's gaped lips and beg her to take suck.

She begins to work her mouth, leaching golden honey from the wax. The sweetness soothes her, and soon she hums with pleasure. She reaches for me, squeezing my arm, which makes the stings pain even more.

We rock together in the day's heat. Cocooned in pain, and grief, and honeyed relief, while Verona's streets echo with terrified shouts reporting all the damage the shaken earth has wrought.

NINE

The servants have all gone pecking after their own pleasures since Lord and Lady Cappelletti went away, and the house-page is still not back at his post. Which means there's no warning before the horse is inside the Cappelletti gate. Lathered from being ridden too hard for too long, the beast brays as the rider jumps down. I recognize the heavy footfall on the stone path, the clanging of the broad silver belt. But I've no time to right myself and Juliet, and no means to make her swollen head and bruised face less frightful.

"Juliet?" Lord Cappelletto calls her name as a question announcing his return.

"Papa," she answers, opening her arms and raising her face in anticipation of his kiss.

What's sweet anticipation for her is sour worry for me. Lord Cappelletto left the most beautiful of daughters, and returns to find a seeming changeling for his child. All the easier for him to cast her off to a convent, and cast me from her forever.

But though he startles at first sight of her, he kneels and kisses her with keen father-love, then murmurs soft words only she can hear before kissing her again. His voice catching in prayer, he brushes his finger along her brow, gently tracing the bruise that's spread beneath her eye. "I rode straight from Mantua as soon as the ground ceased shaking, fearing you were hurt."

"Me was hurt. Me fall, and Nurse fall, and dovey-coo fall."

I seize upon what she says, nodding toward the fallen archway. "We were in the arbor when the earth quaked. The dovecote collapsed, and Juliet fell and cracked her brow. She cried for the dug, but having weaned her as you bade me, I comforted her with honey." Every word I say is true, even if things'd not occurred in the order that I tell them. But I put my whole heart into what I promise will happen next. "What's bruised on her will heal, and she'll be every bit the lovely Cappelletta di Cappelletto, pride of Ca' Cappelletti, before the dovecote is rebuilded."

Lord Cappelletto shakes his head. "It'll not be built again. Lady Cappelletta has borne a son—"

"Thanks be to God." I cross myself with my sting-riddled arm, though I'm unsure whether Juliet is saved. "A son, at last."

"Her last," he says. "Dead within the hour it came out of her, and dead she nearly was with delivering it." Grief bows his balding head. "The day we arrived in Mantua, her pains came on. The

Gonzaghe sent their own court midwife along with their physick, but neither one could save my son. Nor could the physick cure my brother." He clasps Juliet tighter, nearly smothering her against the dark folds of his new mourning cloak. "The physick is certain nothing more will quicken in Lady Cappelletta's womb."

Juliet wriggles her face free. Impatient with his talk of what she's too young to understand, she mews out, "Tybalt?"

She wants to know where her beloved playmate is. But Lord Cappelletto, bound by his own thoughts, says, "He'll be my heir. I promised my brother I'd take him as my own to keep our family's fortune complete."

Heir and *fortune* mean much to a man as rich as Lord Cappelletto. But what comfort can they be to a father-hungry boy like Tybalt?

Lord Cappelletto spends the rest of the day shut inside Ca' Cappelletti, so bereft he turns away even the prince's own messengers, though he sends out alms of loaves, oil, and wine to honor the memory of his brother, and of his last lost son. His days in Mantua have aged him by ten years, and he carries himself more burdened than the page and serving-man who, having skulked back to Ca' Cappelletti, are ordered to haul off the pieces of the crumbled archway and the fallen Cappelletti crest.

When, hours later, a carriage arrives, Lord Cappelletto himself reaches up to lift out Lady Cappelletta, grief seeding an unwonted tenderness for his nearly taken wife. She is more wan than ever, her amber eyes unfocused as he guides her gently to the ground. "Ma'da," Juliet calls, putting all a child's expectation into those two syllables. But Lady Cappelletta, flickering like a tallow-candle in a sudden wind, pays her no notice.

I kiss Juliet's dark hair, whispering that Tybalt is here, too. But what appears next is not Tybalt, though the delicate creature has his pretty eyes and poutish mouth, its well-shaped head crowned with the same long, soft curls. Juliet buries herself among my skirts, taking timid peeks at the beautiful being. A younger, softer, girlish version of Tybalt, with none of his awkward angularity. Nor his bold curiosity. Hesitating at the carriage opening, she crosses herself and recites some Latin prayer.

Lord Cappelletto nods at her piety. "Fear not, fair Rosaline," he says. "Tybalt, come help your sister down."

Tybalt is not eager to obey, I can tell from how long it takes him to make his way to the carriage opening, jump to the ground, and turn to lower this Rosaline out. His long face is made longer by grief, and he'll not meet my eye, nor Juliet's. As the last of the day's dusk seeps from the sky, he follows Lord Cappelletto up the stairs, Rosaline holding to his arm in imitation of how Lady Cappelletta clings to her husband, all of them cloaked in mourning.

I've promised Juliet what I've not got to give: Tybalt. Long after the compline bells ring, she lies awake in our chamber, waiting. Sobbing herself sick, she begs me to bring her beloved cousin. And so I go looking for him.

Lady Cappelletta is long settled in her bed, though whether Lord Cappelletto lies beside her or spends the night hours upon his knees down in the Cappelletti chapel, I cannot tell as I sidle past the antecamera to their chamber. All is still along the loggia overlooking the courtyard, the storerooms bolted shut, the entry to the parto room left bare. Inside the apartment on the far side of Ca' Cappelletti, I find only Rosaline. She's sleeping with a cherub's guiltless grace in the ornate bed that once held her parents, though in all my time in Ca' Cappelletti Tybalt's been the only one to lay his head here.

But tonight, no part of Tybalt is in the bedchamber. Nor in the study that sits beyond it, though he so dreads his tutor's lessons, I'd not expect to find him there. From the study window I look out over the kitchen roof and across the toppled passage to the arbor, to where the moon rises above Juliet's chamber. The dark silhouette of the family tower tells me where Tybalt must be. Where I must go to find him.

Despite the score of times Pietro's climbed the first storey of the tower stair to make his unseen way from the arbor into Juliet's chamber, I've not repeated the climb to the tower's top, not since that morning long ago when I first followed Tybalt up. By day the many steps were hard enough for me, but at night they're dark as pitch. Part of me is glad for it, for the darkness keeps me from seeing what I hear: the scurrying of rats or mice, I know not which, and the night-flapping of bats above my head.

I make my way slowly, for I've not got Tybalt's taste for adventuring—although I know what's urged him up the tower stair tonight is something else, something heavier on his heart. Turning up the final flight, I see him perched like a falcon upon the ledge at the tower top.

I whistle one low note as I approach. Afraid any more than that might startle him, send him tumbling to the street so far below.

"They took him." I can barely make out his words. His body is balled tight, his face buried against the sumptuous cloth of his mourning cloak.

"Death took him," I say, though I know too well what little comfort those words bring.

"They did it. I'm not sure how, and my uncle'll not tell me. But I know. I saw the swallow-wing."

I lay a hand on his head. It's feverish hot. "How could a bird—"

"Not a bird." Shaking off my mothering fingers, he points to one tower, then another, standing eerie guard over Verona. He does not pick every tower in every parish, only those whose bricked tops are notched with curving clefts, the same as ornament the city walls, and the prince's castle.

I know the pattern as well as anyone who lives within Verona, though I suppose I never noted how each cleft resembles the wings of a swallow raised in flight.

"The swallow-wing is the mark of those who hate us, because we're loyal to the Pope." Tybalt endarts his words like an archer shooting flaming arrows. "It was on the house where my father stayed. That's why they killed him."

Burning anger in a boy of thirteen only hides the more tender thing he feels. "He was not killed," I say. "He died."

"My mother died from giving birth. My new baby cousin died from being born. But why would my father die, unless some Uberto or Montecche killed him?"

What way is there to teach a child about the randomness of death? My own sons never heard a word of it from me, not in all their youthful years. Nor in that awful week when they lay ill, each too deep in his own agony to know when another of his beloved brothers slipped from us forever. No one could have imagined a thing as awful as the pestilence, until it came. But what good would it have done us to know such a thing could happen, in the years before it did?

"My daughter died, the day that Juliet was born."

Tybalt raises startled eyes to me, as surprised to hear those words as I am to utter them. But our own pain is all we have to offer when those we love are suffering.

"I miss my Susanna every day. But every day, I know I have Juliet, and you, to love. It's what saves me from wishing I'd gone, too, when Susanna went." I kiss his head. Not merely to comfort him, but to give myself a chance to take in his boy-scent, to warm myself with what burns in him. "You miss your father, as a son should. But Juliet is downstairs, crying for you. And Rosaline will want to see you when she wakes. And I need you, and so does Pietro, because we've no boy of our own. Neither does your uncle, or your aunt. We're none of us your father, but you are our dear Tybalt. In our love you'll find your solace, the same as I found mine in you and Juliet."

He does not answer, not aloud. But he lets me help him from

the ledge and lead him to the stairs. He slips a grateful hand into my sting-swollen one, and together we make our way back down.

Not knowing how many nights I've left with Juliet, I'd not waste this one in sleep. Whenever I begin to doze, I yank myself awake to watch her, nestled through the smallest hours of the night between me and Tybalt. They whispered long together before he fell into the deep sleep that grief brings, and she into the contented slumber of a child whose disordered world has been restored.

But Lord Cappelletto is more wakeful. The nightingale is still trilling when he pushes his way into our chamber. He's so rushed he's not stopped to break his night-fast, nor even to rinse the sleep-stink from his mouth. And so it's with the stalest of breath that he says, "We must go to Santa Caterina."

"Would you break your new heir's heart?" I keep my words a whisper, to let the children cling to their final hour of limb-entwined sleep. "I found him atop the tower ledge in the middle of the night, so bereft he might have fallen." I cross myself. "Or worse, if I'd not lured him down to take condolence from Juliet for the loss of his father."

Even in the pewtery pre-dawn, I see that Lord Cappelletto's features mirror Tybalt's grief. "He was my own and only brother. All I had, after the plague had done with everyone else I loved." Lord Cappelletto closes his watery eyes. "But what comfort was I to him, when years later it was his wife who lay dead? I lost him then, to his own anguish. Now I'll never have him back. He's left me with only a boy to fill his place."

"The boy will be a man soon enough." I hear in my own words the echo of what Pietro said of Juliet. Juliet, who neither Tybalt nor I can bear to lose. "We must take care that he'll not grow bitter before he's grown. He loves Juliet more dearly than he loves himself. He'll not be able to endure it if you send her to the nuns."

"To the nuns?" Lord Cappelletto does not bother to keep to a whisper, as he repeats what I've never let on I know. His words pull Tybalt full awake, and Tybalt's stirring rouses Juliet.

I kneel beside the bed, laying one hand on her head, and the other onto Tybalt's. "Just because God's not granted you a son, is no reason to banish your daughter." Let Lord Cappelletto take whatever pleasure he'll have in hearing me beg. "Please, do not shut Juliet away in Santa Caterina."

"You're sending her back with Rosaline?"

I cannot understand what Tybalt's asked, or why it makes his uncle crumple onto the edge of the big bed.

"No one is sending Juliet anywhere," Lord Cappelletto says. He pulls her onto his lap, as though to fend off any who might try. "I'd not even return Rosaline, if it were left to me. She is an obedient child, though not so winsome as my Juliet, and two marriages would serve the Cappelletti all the better, with what alliances a dowry as big as what I'd give would bring. But my brother would not have his daughter wed, not risk her to her mother's fate." He wraps an arm around Tybalt, holding the cousins together. "I suppose it's just as well. Rosaline'd not know how to pass back into a worldly house like this, having lived half her life already among the Holy Sisters."

Half Rosaline's life was scarce two years ago—not so long after that Easter Day when Tybalt told me what he'd heard the bishop say. The silver chalice Lord Cappelletti gifted to the Duomo must never have been meant to pay for Juliet's place in the convent. It was for Rosaline's.

Lord Cappelletto is like any man, ever wanting to produce an heir. But even in these wife-maddening years of trying to make a son, he's never stinted in adoring Juliet. My sleepy-eyed girl snugs herself against him now, and any fool can see she long ago won his heart.

With Juliet and Tybalt in the circle of his arms, Lord Cappelletto reminds me of the painting in his own bedchamber, the Sainted Maria holding the Holy Infant and his blessed cousin the Baptizing Giovanni.

And I might as well be the ass the Holy Family rode out from Bethlehem. I'm no more than a dumb beast that Lord Cappelletto can declare he's done with, now that Juliet is weaned. For what good is it to me to keep my girl from the convent, if I cannot stay with her?

"Rose-line go way?" Juliet asks, frowning when Lord Cappelletto nods. "But you and Tybalt and Ma'da stay with Nurse and me?"

She's my true heart and reads my very thoughts: whoever comes or goes, surely Juliet and I must be together.

"Yes, my beloved," Lord Cappelletto promises. "God and saints be willing, we will all of us stay healthy and well, within Ca' Cappelletti."

Juliet smiles across her father's arm at me, and I smile back.

Only when a lone morning lark begins to twitter, calling for a mate that does not answer back, do I wonder how I can tell Pietro that I'll not be coming home.

Lord Cappelletto insists Juliet join him and Tybalt as they accompany Rosaline to Santa Caterina. It's the first time she and I will ever be apart. But by my saints, it'll be the last.

Lord Cappelletto holds her tight against him on one post-horse, Tybalt and Rosaline matching their pose on another. "Honey nurse?" Juliet asks, looking down at me.

"You'll be back before the sun makes his way across the sky, and I'll be here," I say, not betraying my worry about where I must go, who I must see, in the scant hours before she, Lord Cappelletto, and Tybalt return.

My stiff and swollen hand works clumsily when, alone in Juliet's chamber, I wind my braid beneath a veil, as any decent woman does before going out. But as I step into the Via Cappello, a crooked-back crone creeps by, bare-headed. A wimple-less mother passes the other way, herding her unshod brood. All around me, women bow uncovered heads, taking careful steps across fallen stones. Surely they cannot all be prostitutes. No more than all the boys who hold out an imploring hand today were beggars just two days ago.

Walled off within Ca' Cappelletti, I'd not imagined all the devastation yesterday's quaking caused. Full buildings felled with families still in them. Shrieks of pain and plaintive prayers from under piles of rubble. I've seen Verona's buildings stand emptied by the creeping pestilence, but I never dreamt the city would face such reversed misery. Light streams through the gaping spaces where roofs and walls have fallen away, the sun beating hard on the bruised and bewildered who, having escaped a collapse, now wander with no place to go. Teams of men, grunting like beasts, struggle to unbury the not yet dead. Plastery dust swirls in the air, coating everything with an eerie pall.

Where in all of this is my Pietro?

Consumed with fear of losing Juliet, I'd not thought what threat the trembling earth might have been to him. Pietro's so strong he's ever been my strength—but passing among these ruined buildings, I realize that the men who lie lifeless beneath them were just as hale and every bit as hardy as my husband, until the quake came.

The wooden stalls of the Piazza delle Erbe now are broken heaps, and the few who've come out to sell are outnumbered by the hungry. One old man waves a cudgel, trying to hold off a pack of children who are snatching at his wares. Two of the bigger boys rush him, pinning him to the ground while the others rifle his stock like rats scurrying onto a new-moored boat. None of those who hasten past stop to help the man. Not even me. When I glance back after I've crossed the piazza, the children have already picked his goods clean.

Turning south, I see a trio of stubble-faced youth scrambling atop the remains of the metal-workers guild hall, stuffing what they loot into bulging sacks. Such shameless thieving makes me gape, until one pulls his dagger, flashing it at me. Hurrying away, I turn into a narrow street. Before I'm halfway down it, a shriek of timber splits the air, and a house-front topples into my path. A moment later, and I'd have been beneath it.

I double-back, twisting along one tight passage, then another, improvising routes around what the rubble blocks. I've never been so lost in broad daylight, and it's more by luck than memory that I find my way to the Via Zancani.

Although most of its roof tiles lie shattered in the street, our home still stands. Only when I see the barred door do I realize Pietro's not yet back from Villafranca. I cross myself and make a quick prayer asking San Pietro, his patron saint, to keep my husband safe. Then I hurry off again.

I'm not the first to seek Friar Lorenzo's aid today, and it's no short wait among those who line the windowless passageway outside his cell. In the press of people, there are some who share their suffering with any who'll listen, and those who keep their mouths shut tight, determined to hold what burdens them for the friar's ears alone. I fall among the latter and have no use for the former, too troubled about Pietro to take any interest in these strangers' misfortune.

When at last I step into his cell, Friar Lorenzo's customary "God give you peace" sounds wearied. He does not even wait for me to answer with *And peace to you* before he reaches for my swollen mitt of a hand and turns it over, examining my welts.

"Plantain leaf, a simple cure," he says. "If only there was so ready a remedy for what brings most Christian souls to me today."

Though the poison still singes up and down my arm, I tell him that it's not bee stings that brought me. "Pietro went earlier this week to Villafranca—"

"Well that he did, my child. The quaking there was not so great. Some cornices and lintels fallen to the ground, but not a single person needing to be buried."

The thick-cassocked friars gather news like magpies gather anything that shines, and I take comfort from his report. But so long as Pietro's unhurt, I'm not sorry that he's still far away. That I've time to plot and plan before he must hear what he'd not have me say.

"Bethanks to your wise dispensing of wormwood, Juliet is weaned, as Lord Cappelletto wished." I bow my head to show I know my place. "But his wife has lost another babe, and she'll not bear again. Poor Lady Cappelletta. So young married, and too soon marred."

I wait for Friar Lorenzo to cross himself and intone a prayer for her, before I continue. "The ones so delicate as she is often prove no better for rearing children than for bearing them. And so Lord Cappelletto wishes me to stay at Ca' Cappelletti and care for Juliet." Surely, Friar Lorenzo will wish it as well—if I make him see some especial advantage in it. "Lord Cappelletto dotes on Juliet more than most men do their daughters. Though who'd expect less from such a noble and pious man, and a most generous benefactor of the hallowed Church?"

Friar Lorenzo well knows how often Lord Cappelletto opens his purse to holy hands, and he makes quick calculation of all that it's worth to keep such a man pleased. "I'll need to draw up a new contract," he says. "Now that the child is weaned, you'll not earn the whole of Pietro's rent any longer, though as you say, I'm sure Lord Cappelletto will be most generous in what he pays to keep you."

The whole of Pietro's rent—this is the first anyone's bothered to tell me what price men put on what I am to Juliet. These three years past I've earned what in that time I lost: the cost of the home I left for Ca' Cappelletti. Each hour I stole at the Via Zancani, each time Pietro begged me to move back—all of it paid for with the very milk of me. More mine than in all the years I lived there, yet not mine at all.

"Such matters are beyond me," I say, fluttering a hand to smooth my veil. "But Pietro—he can be proud, like any man. Your godly counsel will do much to guide him to accept whatever Lord Cappelletto offers."

"I will speak to Pietro as soon as he returns from Villafranca and inform him of the new terms of your service," Friar Lorenzo says, eager to earn whatever payment he'll make for drawing up the contract.

I accept his absolution along with the pouch of plantain leaves. Taking my leave of his cell, I head to the lower church. It is the least grand part of San Fermo, yet it's always been my favorite. The paint is still being laid fresh on the frescos in the upper church, but the saints upon the columns down below are old familiars. They're always ready to hear my prayers and, if they offer nothing in response, at least they'll not ask anything of me, either.

On this of all days, I know what I need to beg of them. Of her. For it's the Holy Virgin whose favor I seek, and of all the many paintings and statues of her in Verona, it's the one in the lower church whose help I need. I know her face better than I do my own, for though I've caught an occasional glimpse of myself reflected in a puddle or a water pail, I've knelt gazing on her for countless hours. A century of fading has taken its toll on the golden crown around her head and the brightly patterned throne on which she sits. But time's not marred the pale breast where her Sacred Infant suckles. I'll beseech this Blessed Mother, who'll never wean her own Holy Son, to take mercy on me and ensure that what Pietro'll not hear from me, he'll listen better to from our holy confessor.

But when I climb down the steps, I see someone is already inside the lower church. A youth of Tybalt's years, he stands with his back to me. He's swaying and moaning, halfway between the image of my suckling Maria and a fresco of the naked full-grown Christ accepting his cousin's sprinkling baptism.

It's not the spirit that moves the youth. It's the flesh. I come up behind and pinch his ear. "Here, of all places, for the hand to be upon the prick—"

"The prick of noon," he laughs, "and sext will soon be ringing."

I raise a hand to slap such sacrilege from him, but when he turns to face me, my open palm goes to my mouth instead. It's Prince Cansignorio's impish nephew.

Though I recognize this Mercutio, he has no notion who I am. And well it is that he does not, for I'd not have anyone know I nearly struck a member of the royal household.

Mercutio wiggles his own royal member at me. "Half Verona has fallen—why not make rise what I can?"

Piety, debauchery—when the pestilence raged, there were those who chose the first, hoping to be saved, and those who indulged the second, fearing they would not. To desecrate a church with self-spilled seed—that's one extreme, to be sure. But it's said that in the sudden jolt of catastrophe, some who survive feel the dark premonition of their own eventual death. Mercutio may smirk with a youth's bravado, but I sense beneath it a desperate child's fear.

"Do not let the friars find you at that here." That's all the reprimand I can bring myself to give him, before I hurry off.

First Nunzio, then Nesto, grew to such an age, younger in some and older in others, when a mother must avert her eyes, and pretend she does not know what her son's hand does beneath his doublet hem by day and the bed cover at night. My sons indulged themselves with especial frequency, for they had Pietro's heat. Donato at all of nine was not long from discovering what already pleased the elder two. But before he did, they and their three younger brothers all were taken. Self-pleasuring, that simple sin, one among the many things they'd never know.

This Mercutio, and Tybalt, too—they're not much shy in years of those who brawl upon Verona's streets. And while Lord Cappelletto has grown keen to take his nephew as his heir, Mercutio's uncle may not be so kind. Prince Cansignorio killed his own brother to seize his place upon the throne. What chance is there that, once his sister's son comes of age, Cansignorio will deal differently with him?

The sun is at its highest by the time I turn into the Via Cappello, the sext bells tolling as I enter Ca' Cappelletti. Those sonorous tones resonate through my very bones as I wait for Juliet to come back to me.

If Juliet craves me like I crave her, she's done well hiding it, delighting in the game I've made of what I give her instead of my own milk. Bread soaked in wine. Porridged chicken fat. Barley in beef broth. I bade her close her eyes and guess what each was as I put it into her ready mouth. Such tastes, such textures for her pink tongue to learn as we sow the pleasure nursing taught us into something new.

I steal early out of bed to find some fresh delight to feed her. The air is hot and thick with fruit. I shudder, thinking of the wet peach flesh Pietro rubbed me with, just four days past. Why not share such succulent fruit with Juliet?

I hurry down into the arbor. But I stop fast before I reach the peach-laden tree. The beehive's been righted, its seal replaced. I smile and turn this way and that, dancing my skirts as I search for where Pietro waits for me. Behind a tree? Crouched by the ruins of the dovecote? Within the entry to the tower stair?

No, and no, and no again. He's not anywhere. The twittering I hear is only the morning lark, not the whistling tease of my hiding husband.

Something thumps upon the kitchen roof. I look up expectantly, as though my great bear of a Pietro might be there. But of course it's only Tybalt, sprung from his own rooms and calculating whether he can leap across the fallen archway onto the ledge that leads to Juliet's window.

Catching sight of me, he bounds to the roof edge and jumps

down. He lands nimbly on those cat feet, dives into an elegant somersault, and brings himself up facing me.

"Have you seen Pietro?" I ask.

"Is he here?" Hope widens Tybalt's eyes. Which tells me he's not
seen my husband since before going to Mantua.

Is this Pietro's way of punishing me? To come before I've risen,
or after I've gone to bed, and leave this sign that he's been without
bothering to see me. *I'll not keep sneaking about, stealing time with
you like I'm a thief taking what is rightfully Lord Cappelletto's.* But
what greater sneaking is there, than for a husband to come so near
yet not take his willing, wanting wife?

"The hive's upright, and the lid is back in place." I feel a fool for
saying aloud what Tybalt can see with his own eyes.

Feel yet more foolish when he thumps a proud fist against his
chest and says, "I righted it myself, and I put my ear to the trunk to
check the hive-noise. I even swept the dead bees away and watched
to be sure the rest were gathering pollen again. I did it all, without
even being bid to."

Tender Tybalt, ever hungry for my praise. Or better still, for
Pietro's.

"Pietro will be pleased with you." I let the compliment settle
like a richly woven mantle over his broadening shoulders. "He's
probably tending some of his other hives. Perhaps you can find him
and let him know what you've done. Surely he'll want to come and
admire it himself."

Tybalt's never been a boy who's easily put off, not by one so
soft-hearted as Pietro. Let him convince my husband to come here,

and I'll work my own greater persuasion once he arrives. For though I schemed to have Friar Lorenzo be the one to tell Pietro I'd not be returning home, there's that which I saved to say myself.

No lord would risk his child's wet-nurse tainting her milk by receiving her husband's seed. But now that Juliet is weaned, what objections could Lord Cappelletto have to me fulfilling my conjugal duty to Pietro, so long as it does not interfere with my caring for Juliet? Pietro and I might even enlist Friar Lorenzo to write it into the new contract, such terms as say that Pietro may come to me here, or I go to him, openly. And with a frequency we've not had these three years past.

I pluck a blushing peach from one of the fruit-laden boughs and offer it to Tybalt, then pick another to bring upstairs to Juliet. I'll ready the slices while she sleeps, so she can wake to the delicious promise of what I tasted when Pietro was last here.

Summer's sun melts the hours. They pour one into another, and still Tybalt stays gone. As the day grows hot, then hotter, sweat streaks my face and neck, bathes my back and belly. Juliet's unceasing chirruping makes my head ache. It's no ease to me when, after I at last settle my little one into her nap, the house-page comes scraping and scratching to tell me Lady Cappelletta summons me to keep her company. I cut tooth against tongue to keep from telling him a wet-nurse is no lady's waiting maid. Wet-nurse I no longer am, and to stay with Juliet, I must be whatever the Cappelletti will want of me.

Lady Cappelletta lies a-bed, still worn with the jaunce from Mantua. Or so I'd supposed, until I enter her chamber and see the vinegared way she waves me near, her wedding bracelets clattering. "Sing to me," she commands. "And not the dull religious droning Lord Cappelletto favors. I want a pleasure-song."

Surely she wants more pleasure than I can trill forth. "If you are sorrowful—"

She cuts me off with a quick snort. "What sorrows have I?"

What am I to answer? *You are wed to an old goat who's not given you a living son, and for all your beauty, even in your youth you already look more misused than I at my age do.* "None, unless you say so," is what I say aloud.

"None indeed, now that the learned physick tells my lord husband he must be done rutting with me." A newfound contempt curls her mouth when she speaks the phrase *my lord husband.* Before I can puzzle over it, her ring-laden fingers drum a quick cadence against the wooden bedstead, demanding I match a bright-paced tune to it.

I sing, fast then faster still, my breath short and shallow as I struggle to keep pace with her hurried rhythm. When the song is done, she says, "The journey to Mantua was so rough, the infant fell from me, pulling my womb out with it. The midwife and physick made me soak all night in a bath of mugwort and fleabane, before that cursed womb could be shoved back inside. They stuffed a linen full of pennyroyal and spikenard into me, to keep it in place. I was more dead than not, and begged them to let what lingered of me go."

"But by God's grace, you survived." As though she should need me to remind her of it.

"I survived because the esteemed physick did not wish to upset his Gonzaghe patrons by losing a patient whose husband is so close an ally to Prince Cansignorio." All hint of the timid girl she's been is gone, leaving instead a young woman who puts me in mind of a foal struggling to take to its legs for the first time: unsteady yet certain she's mastering something she'll make good use of. "I made the physick promise that if I lived, I'd need not suffer Lord Cappelletto to take his pleasures on me again."

"A wife's duty," I begin, as though I might yet explain the pleasures Pietro and I take in each other, to one whose husband is so ill-matched as hers.

"My duty's done. I delivered him his son. What fault of mine if it did not live beyond the hour I bore it?" It's more than an ill-fated laboring that makes her face less soft than it once was. The calculating glint that's come into her eyes gives her a newly hardened beauty. "He's got Tybalt for his legal heir. That was my idea, though I took care my lord husband heard it from his dying brother's mouth. The boy has no mother—he'll not turn me out when I am widowed."

Her conniving is no match for my own, for though she may feel her way upon a foal's ready legs, she lacks the cunning of a mare that's run as many courses as I have. "If Lord Cappelletto makes a son outside your marriage, he might yet change his will." Might turn even against Juliet, if a canny mistress pushes him to it.

"Lord Cappelletto is firm only in his faith," she says, "his eel too slithery to seed even one of the pursemaker's daughters. He beseeched every saint in heaven to send him an heir, not believing such piety could go unanswered, until his brother's final confessor convinced him that his legitimate son's death was punishment for breaking his church-made vows to me. He'll do penance by giving dowries so the pursemaker can marry off every last daughter, and hew to his marriage vows henceforth." She gives a smile that lets the sharpest of her teeth show. "Tybalt well earned his place, conveying to me all that was whispered at his father's bedside."

I'd not have thought that Lady Cappelletta and I could be so much alike. She young, and rich, and wanting only to keep her husband from her, and I at my age plotting to find a way to draw my husband back to me. But in our choice of go-between, we are the same. Faithful Tybalt. On who else can we rely?

Lady Cappelletta bids me sing another song. While I warble it out, she tells me, "I've not forgot it was by your urging that I went to Mantua." Those calculating eyes shimmer with the same hard contempt they showed when she spoke of Lord Cappelletto. But this time, she lets me see it's meant for me. "You convinced me to try what nearly killed me. If I'd stayed safely here, I'd not have suffered any of it."

I'd not intended any harm to her. Not thought what toll my goading might take, so consumed was I with keeping Juliet from the convent. But what way have I to tell this to Lady Cappelletta?

Quick feet cross the antecamera, and in one great rush Tybalt enters the chamber. "Half the hives are harvested. But the—"

Lady Cappelletta cuts him off. "Is that a proper greeting for an heir to give his aunt?"

Tybalt drops his eyes from mine, bowing his head to kiss her hand. "God give you good-den, dear Aunt."

"When did you last make your prayers?"

"Yesterday. When my uncle and my cousin and I took Rosaline to Santa Caterina, we joined the Holy Sisters at their Mass."

"You must pray every day, as Rosaline does, for the souls of your departed parents."

Why must she pester Tybalt about his prayers, making him dwell on what he's lost, just when he has news to give to me?

"You're to go once a week to Santa Caterina, to make memorial devotions with your sister," she tells him. "And on the other days, pray here with Juliet. Rouse her now, and have her make *amens* with you."

"Juliet is tired," I say. "It's best she rest through the hottest of the day."

"My lord husband insists it's not too soon for his adored daughter to learn how one day she will pray for him, and for me, when we are gone."

Death sat so near to Lord Cappelletto the week past, he supposes its bony hand will soon reach for his wrinkled one. And so he wants to be assured of what is every parent's due: a dutiful child whose prayers will ease his way to heaven when his time comes.

"I'll make sure they do as Lord Cappelletto wishes." I rise and nod for Tybalt to lead the way from the chamber. He is the heir now. It'd not do for him to follow behind me.

But as soon as we are in the sala, I lay a halting hand on his shoulder. "Half the hives are harvested," I repeat, "but?"

"The rest are left heavy with wax and honey." He tells me how he traced and retraced Pietro's usual routes, surprised not to find him collecting from one hive or another, or making his way between them.

"Perhaps he's bargaining with the chandler," I say.

"A beekeeper cannot bargain until he knows how much wax his bees have made this season, Pietro's told me that a dozen times. It will be weeks of separating honey from comb, before he sees the chandler."

With all his heeling after Pietro, Tybalt knows my husband's business better than I do. But I know my husband's heart. I need Tybalt to bring him to me, or to discover where I might find him, so I can ease him to accept my staying at Ca' Cappelletti. "There are many ways to move about Verona, and more than one bridge crossing the Adige. You must go out again—"

Scarlet tinges his ears, his shoulders hunching into the same curve as when Lord Cappelletto carps at him.

I'll not treat Tybalt so, not add to what already grieves him. "Juliet will be glad to have you wake her," I say instead. "She misses you when you are gone."

The thought of her lifts his chest. Juliet never wants a thing from Tybalt but his companionship. Not Lord Cappelletto, nor Lady Cappelletta, nor even I can say the same.

Our chamber glows in the afternoon light as he shakes her softly from her sleep, lifts her from the bed. She kneels drowsily beside him while he stumbles through his Latin and she mumbles her made-up imitation of his prayers. Another day, I might take joy in seeing them bow their heads together. But I can barely bide myself until they utter their *amens*. If Tybalt cannot find Pietro for me, I must plot some way to seek him out myself.

I don my veil and tell Juliet, "You say your prayers so well, perhaps we should go to Friar Lorenzo, so he can hear them for himself."

"Me pray," she says, greedy for the praise she knows he'll give. "And me fess to Friar."

But the name that brightens her face shadows worry onto Tybalt's. "Friar Lorenzo bade me tell you to come see him. He told me I must not forget."

Something catches deep inside me. "When? When did he tell you this?"

"This morning." Tybalt pulls at where his doublet collar rubs tight against the fresh bump of his Adam's apple. "He called to me as I passed the friary on my way to check the first of the hives."

Friar Lorenzo must have spoken to Pietro. But if my husband leaves it to the Franciscan to give me his response, surely it cannot be a happy one.

"Fess to Friar," Juliet repeats, sliding her sweat-damp hand into mine.

"Tomorrow," I say. "Or the day after." I'm in no hurry to hear Friar Lorenzo repeat whatever angry words Pietro has for me.

Juliet tugs my hand. "Fess now."

"You said that you would go." Tybalt's voice cracks as he takes my other hand. "He'll think that I forgot."

Is this not why I hold myself from returning home to Pietro? To soothe and care for Juliet, and for Tybalt, when not another soul in all the world marks what each of them needs? With their doubly insistent grip upon me, I force myself into the Via Cappello.

Heat thrums from buildings, streets, every surface of the city, even with the sun slanting to the west. Though the cries and confusion caused by the quake have ebbed, something sinister hangs over Verona, the souls of those crushed beneath fallen buildings lingering in the heavy air. Tybalt and I hold Juliet between us, and for once I do not smile at how he keeps a ready hand upon his dagger hilt, as we seek out an unblocked route to San Fermo and the friary.

A dozen needy beings crowd the corridor outside Friar Lorenzo's cell, and I worry how I'll keep Juliet from growing tetchy until it is our turn. But I worry more when the Franciscan comes out to call the next expectant in and, seeing us, waves me ahead of those who've been here longer.

In the cool quiet of his cell, he dips his tonsured head to Juliet, keeping his eyes from meeting mine. He blesses her and takes the kiss she offers for his narrow cheek, then blesses Tybalt and tells him to take Juliet into the lower church to make their prayers.

"Me pray already. Me fess now." Even pouting, Juliet is a pure and pretty thing.

"The lower church—" I begin, but find I've no words for what I've seen Mercutio at there, not ones that I would say before Tybalt and Juliet. And whatever Friar Lorenzo has to tell me weighs thick enough in this close space, I know it's not meant for them to hear.

I join Juliet's hand to Tybalt's, and give his shoulder an easy urging from the cell, promising a comfit for every pillared saint they pray to before I come to find them. Though how I'll convince Pietro to spare me comfits to gift them when he'll not even speak to me directly, I cannot fathom.

Once they're gone, Friar Lorenzo tells me, "Hunger can turn even good men cruel. And terror brings out the very worst, or the very best, within us."

If I were in need of homilies, I'd come to Sunday Mass. "What does Pietro say?"

The Franciscan rubs at where his eyelids droop from want of sleep. "Yesterday at dusk, a mother and daughter were making their way back from the public fountain, when a brace of rowdies laid hold of them. They had no riches, nothing to steal but the few worn garments they'd just scrubbed clean. This was no satisfaction to the ruffians, who tried instead to take from the daughter what no Christian girl wishes to give. The mother screamed for them to stop. Pushing herself before the child, she begged them to take their pleasure upon her instead, and leave her daughter be. A passing stranger, hearing her, swung at the two villains, and the mother snatched the child and ran off. They found shelter in Sant'Eufemia, where the priest gathered half a dozen clerics to take them home. By the light of the clerics' torches, they came upon the man who'd been their savior. He'd been stabbed and left dead in the street."

He touches fingers to brow, to heart, to both sides of his chest. "Angelica, it is with a heavy heart but all Christ's redeeming love that I tell you the man who died so nobly was your Pietro."

"Tell him I will leave Juliet." The words twist out of me, some unseen blade tearing them from my gut. "Tell Pietro I will come home before this very day is through."

"It is too late for that, my child. Your husband is gone. I saw him for myself, afterwards."

Pietro cannot be dead. That is the truth, the certainty, that cracks open my chest, jolts me into motion. Out of the cell, away from this lying Friar Lorenzo.

I must get Juliet and Tybalt. I'll take them back to Ca' Cappelletti, then go myself to find Pietro. The Via Zancani will be seeped in evening shade by the time I reach it, the door to our house swung wide to let fresh air flow in. I'll coax the kitchen ashes into full fire, and Pietro will pour our wine, singing with me as I cook, as he always used to do. As he's always meant to do again.

TEN

"Nurse wake?"

Juliet buries a tear-streaked cheek against my neck. Beyond the curve of her head, I see Tybalt, crouching with a worried stare. Above him dark lines mark out a low-curved ceiling, the paint an eerily familiar hue. Too somber for Ca' Cappelletti, and the hard stone digging flat against my back tells me I'm not in bed. Before I can ask where we are, why we are here, a hand reaches over from my other side.

"It is well you are awake, my child." Friar Lorenzo's touch is icy as he marks a cross upon me.

It all rushes back, every wretched thing the blessed faint let me forget. "Nothing can be well. Not without my husband."

The Franciscan unfolds himself. Standing on the step above the landing to the lower church, he speaks down to me. "If Pietro is in a better place, we must be glad for that."

"Po go way?" Juliet asks. "Like Rose-line?"

The friar tugs at one of his great ears. Waiting, wanting me to say it. But I'll not.

"Pietro's dead?" Tybalt's two words explode against the arched ceiling. They shiver down the walls, rumble across the floor, and crawl up my spine, to pound between my eyes.

"Yes, my child," Friar Lorenzo says. And then, because what holy man does not love to hear himself speak, he adds, "This life is but our bitter passage to the next."

Juliet burrows tighter against me, though surely my little one cannot know what he means.

"Shall we pray for Pietro now, as I do my father? Or must we wait until the funeral?" Tybalt's voice breaks, then settles into the careful rote that years of his tutor's beatings have taught him. "My father's funeral procession had eight horses, and wound through the city for an hour, and his Requiem Mass was said in the biggest church in Mantua." He sits straighter in his mourning cloak. "How many horses will Pietro have, and how long will we walk?"

"Such processions are only for rich men," I tell him. "The bishop does not open the Duomo doors to bury one as poor as my Pietro."

Friar Lorenzo hisses at my sacrilege. "Rich or poor, every loss we suffer is God's will. He gives us mortal life that we may pray, and do good, and earn our eternal place among the righteous."

What place have I earned, refusing my husband what he begged of me: that I live with him as a loving wife should? Did he hold out hope that I was coming home? Or did he die knowing I'd determined to stay away?

Did Pietro rush at some swift-bladed ruffians because I'd left him, even left it to Friar Lorenzo to tell him I'd chosen Juliet over him?

I twist onto my side, my arms cocooning her against me. This is my comfort, and my curse: to choose this child, the single salve for all I'd lost. Not realizing I'd lose yet more.

Friar Lorenzo lays that icy hand upon the back I've turned to him. "What's tomb is—"

"Doom." I cut off his holy platitude with my hard-learned truth. I'll not let the celibate speak to me of wombs. Not when I've left Pietro without a single living child to pray for him, as Tybalt does his father, and as Juliet one day will for Lord Cappelletto. "Bury him as you will," I say. "I'll have none of it."

The cloister bell tolls, calling the Franciscans to vespers. Friar Lorenzo cannot bear to leave us without uttering a final, "May God have mercy on his soul, and on all of us."

Once he's gone, I let Tybalt lead me back to Ca' Cappelletti, where I bury myself in my own tomb, built of my guilt and my grief, and of Juliet's commiserating tears.

Hot as it is, even with the sun disappeared and the stars flung against the sweltering sky, lying restless through the night all I can think of is the rime-frosted day when Pietro and I first said farewell, and what followed from it. He'd returned to his village to give his family the news that we were to bind ourselves as married. While he was gone he sent me a love-gift. A handkerchief, of no fancy material. Just a little trifle to carry the scent of him. Or so I thought.

To a girl of twelve who has no more than chores for company, the fortnight a lover is away seems an eternity. I tucked the handkerchief into my dress so that I might always have it, have him, with me. On the day Pietro returned, he asked for it, and I slipped a hand to where I'd kept the kerchief close against me.

I did not find it. Did not even have sense enough to hide my surprise.

"What's the matter, Angelica?" he asked.

"Nothing, now that you're back." I nuzzled his chest, knowing I could well take in the smell of him, and his taste and touch, without that bit of cloth.

But he pulled away. "There is something special in the kerchief's weft I want to show you."

"You sound like a fabric merchant, trying to prove his prices are fair."

For once, he had no heart for teasing. "That kerchief is above any price. My mother wove it." This was the first he spoke to me of her. "It was the last thing she made before she died."

I saw then all it meant to him.

I bowed my head. "I've not got it."

"Go fetch it, then."

"I cannot."

"You've thrown it away?"

"Of course not. I . . . ."

192

As my words trickled off, Pietro's voice rose. "You gave it to another?"

"Never."

"Well then, where is it?"

In the month we'd known each other, I'd never seen Pietro angry. But I'd seen my father beat my mother many a time, knocking the very teeth from her head, for far less than losing such a precious thing.

Surely it was fright that made me answer as I did. By punching my fist hard at Pietro's face.

In an instant, his much larger hand flew up. But not, as I feared, to hit me. Only to wrap my wrist in his broad palm, to keep me from hitting him again.

Whatever pain flashed along his jaw was nothing compared to the deeper hurt that showed in his eyes. My arm went slack in his tight grip.

He dropped his hold on me, turned, and left my parents' house without another word.

My mother offered me no comfort, saying only she'd raised a fool, for even at twelve I should have known better than to raise a hand to a man, whether before we were wed or after. When my father came in from the fields, she bade me tell him what had happened. He beat us both, screaming that he'd not find another one so gullible as Pietro, to marry me to without a single denaro of dowry. For what had he got to give, even to be rid of such a stupid daughter? He threw me out of the house. Not for the night, for good.

The moon was three days shy of full, and I did what any herder does, when something is lost from the flock. I began circling slowly outward, seeking after it. Searching not with my eyes on the horizon for the low, wooly form of a sheep, but with my gaze to the cold ground, willing the handkerchief to appear.

It was no easy task. The moon was well on its descent when, crossing Agostino diMaso's land, I glimpsed something in his pigsty. There, trudged deep into the half-froze mud, was Pietro's treasured handkerchief. How the pigs had gotten it, and why once they had it they did not chew it up entirely, I could not know. I worked the cloth free and carried it like a martyr's relic to the icy creek edging Agostino's fields. Though I scrubbed it against a rock until my fingers bled, the kerchief'd not come quite clean.

I brought it to Sant'Agnese, our village church, meaning to ask the priest to write a letter to send with it to Pietro's parish. But there was no need for a letter. Pietro had gone straight to the church from my parents' house, hoping to take holy council. Finding the priest gone, he'd slept all night before the barred church doors.

Though he'd always seemed man enough to me, at twenty he was still in truth a youth, and the softness in his sleeping face taunted me with all I'd lost in striking him. As I laid the folded kerchief on his chest, he grabbed my wrist. Full awake at once, he held me for a silent instant, as he had before stalking from my father's house. But now he pulled my wrist, drawing me down onto him. Pressing my fingers against the intricate weave of the soiled kerchief, he told me of his gentle-hearted mother and how indulgently she loved him. He said he wanted to make such a mother of me, once I was his wife. Which, when the priest returned an hour later, I soon was.

Not a hand was raised between us after that. Nor was one ever raised to the son I bore that year, or any I bore after. Even in his hottest youth, Pietro never needed to prove himself by beating wife or child. There are few enough like that, and I never forgot it was my own foolishness that almost cost me my Pietro. I always swore I'd not take such risk again.

Why did I ever leave him? How could I have let myself lose him?

I could go now. Climb the tower steps once more. Dark as it is, I could find my way up, perch like Tybalt at the tower's top, and look upon Verona. This city where Pietro and I came so young and full of hope, holding nothing but each other's hands, to build a life. A life so filled with death—our sons, our daughter. But always, we held to each other. Now, with him gone, I'll not hold on. I'll look upon the world and let myself slip free. It would be so easy to let the heavy thing inside me have its way. Let loss be the weight that carries me down, down, down, until I'll never have to bear this grief again.

I close my eyes, imagine swaying in the hot air, feeling myself fall. But something stabs sharp at my back. My eyes fly open, and I turn. The statue of San Zeno towers over me. The fishing saint of fair Verona, his unseen hook plunging deep into me. Pulling me back. Because it is forbidden to die this easy, longed-for way.

Pietro well earned his place among the righteous. And surely all our little ones are there as well. All my lost beloveds together, waiting. What would I be, to damn myself from them for all eternity? Hooked here, I'll not let myself make that last climb up the tower steps and leave this mortal life. Though by my troth, it's all I long to do.

"Eight comfits," Tybalt says, climbing in through Juliet's open chamber window sometime in the ripening morning hours before the terce bells toll, "as you promised." He sets down a sack as big as a pillow-casing, casts off his mourning cloak, and slides one hand into the other tight-pulled sleeve of his dark doublet to draw out the candies. Softened from the heat, each is fragrant with some surprise of quince, or fig, or apio, and laced with cinnamon, ginger, or clove. And all of them emanating the unbearable sweetness of honey.

Juliet snatches one of the comfits. She runs to the far side of the bed, slipping it into her mouth before I can stop her.

"Where did you get these?" I ask Tybalt.

"I woke at dawn and went to the Via Zancani. I knew there would be comfits there."

"You broke into a dead man's house to steal candy?"

"Pietro always brought us sweets. He'd want us to have these." He holds the candies out to me.

I cannot bear to taste what my husband made. I do not deserve to hum with delight in his handiwork, as Juliet does, working the sticky comfit with her tiny teeth. I nod at the sack. "What else have you thieved?"

Tybalt draws up the bag, reaching in and pulling out the Virgin's portrait that hung upon our wall. The one Pietro gave me when we wed, trothing ourselves together until death forced us apart.

I tell Tybalt my cockly-eyed familiar has no place in this grand house, where fine images fresco the walls.

"My uncle says you may hang the Holy Mother here, and wishes she may bring you comfort," he says. "And he gives his leave for you to take Juliet and me with you today, when you go to the Requiem Mass."

Lord Cappelletto gives me leave to do what I'd not asked of him. I've never once spoken Pietro's name to him, and I long ago forbade Tybalt to ever mention my husband before his uncle, to keep safe my place with Juliet. But what does that matter now?

Of all the house, Lord Cappelletto's the one who might truly know my grief, because he knows his own, kneeling nightly before the Madonna in his chamber and praying for the cherished wife he lost. Yet I'd not share my most private hurt with him.

Tybalt entreated Lord Cappelletto from some belief my mourning must take the same shape as his does. It's Tybalt who wants this. Tybalt who's put on his finest garments, the seams strained from how fast he's grown, to go to the Requiem Mass.

"Afterwards, I'll finish harvesting the hives," he says. "I'll collect the wax and honey, and separate them out. I helped Pietro enough times, I'm sure I can do it on my own. But I've no way to make comfits. When the honey's ready, I'll sell it to an apothecary who'll work with it himself, as the chandler does the beeswax."

"Is this all you can think of, honey and candles and candy—even with Pietro gone?"

"Bees die each day, but the hive goes on," Tybalt says. "That's what Pietro taught me. He said the ones who gather pollen may never taste the honey it will make. He told me it's why he loved the bees. The way they build, creating combs not for themselves but for the future brood. Like the men who lay a church's marble cornerstone knowing they'll not live long enough to pray within the finished nave." He draws a deep, wavering breath, laying a hand on his mourning cape as if to touch his own great grief. "Pietro said this is why we must take care in tending them. The hive must live, and in its life we'll find our hope."

I'd not known such things about a hive—or about my husband. Never understood why the bees that afrighted me could so comfort him. What other things had I been too afraid to hear from him? What else about Pietro will I now never know?

Tybalt urges me to braid my hair and ready Juliet, so we'll not be late. When I set my jaw and make no answer, he says, "I did not want to go to my father's funeral, until my uncle said I must. He said that we must show everyone the strength of our piety, even when we are bereaved. But the friar says we go for God, to implore him to take my father's soul, and now Pietro's, into heaven."

"Those are a nobleman's reasons, or a clergyman's," I tell him. "Not a woman's." Not a widow's.

My whole life I've seen them. You can tell which ones truly loved their husbands, some wailing and pulling hair and clawing at their own faces, and some still and stony silent as they kneel through the Requiem Mass. All listening from under their dark veils as though something in the priest's impenetrable Latin might meliorate their grief.

But what could lessen my loss, what can console me, now that it's too late to beg Pietro's forgiveness and give myself wholly back to him?

I busy myself with calling Juliet to me, dabbing her face and untangling the knots sleep worked into her hair. "We'll not go any-where," I tell Tybalt. "The streets have grown too dangerous."

"I'm not afraid." He pulls himself tall, widening his shoulders as broad as they'll go. Which is not nearly broad enough to carry all he thinks he can.

"What good did a fool's bravery do Pietro?" I lace my words with enough venom to sting us both. "A full-grown man, and the brace of murderers left him in the street to die."

Juliet whimpers. I've pulled her hair too hard, and made her hear such ugly things. Shrinking from me, she reaches for Tybalt. He bends to her, offering her kisses and a second comfit. Distracts her with her toy bird before he straightens up again and kisses me as well, the same tender way my sons did.

"I'll go alone. I'm Tybalt, king of cats, and I'm not scared. I loved Pietro. And you said that he loved me. I'll kneel and pray the Mass for him, even if you'll not."

This is how he leaves us, Juliet playing with that beady-eyed bird while I stand at the window staring out at the hive thrumming in the arbor. Wondering over what parts of Tybalt are yet boy, and what are already man, that make him able to face what I cannot.

Tybalt is the nimble king of cats, and the legal heir to Lord Cap-pelletto. But who am I? Not who I've been for more than thirty years. No longer Pietro's adored wife. Nor Juliet's wet-nurse. I gave up my husband for her—but what am I to her now? What will I be a year, a decade, hence, should God make me live so long without Pietro? What is a milk-mother to a child who's been weaned?

I'll not forget how she turned away from me, seeking solace from

Tybalt instead. And worse than her turning away was the moment before, when she looked at me just as Pietro had when last I saw him—the last I'll ever see him. The same accusing look almonding her eyes, the same surprised hurt stippling her still-bruised brow.

Like a clapper smacking hard against a bell, it hits me. Rings hard at my temples, reverberates across my head, down to my heart. It makes my arms shake, and my legs. I turn from the window, sun-blind as I look back to Juliet. In two strides I'm beside her, swooping her up so quick her toy bird tumbles to the floor.

"Nurse?" She is too startled to utter any more than that, as I carry her back to the open window, hold her in the brightness of the light. And realize what surely has been there to see all along.

Her coarse, dark hair. Her deep brown eyes. Friar Lorenzo himself marked how much they are like mine. Colored by my milk, he claimed. But the shape of those eyes, how they sit in her face. The way emotions dance across her features. It is a face I know better than I know my own, and yet I've not recognized it until now.

It is Pietro's.

I know what Lord Cappelletto, with his treatise-reading, feared. It's why men draw the nursing contracts as they do: to keep a husband's humors from tainting his wife's milk, and transforming the nursling's features. But what I recognize is not just in her features. It's the child's very nature—for is not my sweet, loving Juliet more like Pietro than like Lord Cappelletto or Lady Cappelletta?

Surely this is something more than milk or taint. All these years, Lord Cappelletto's seed could no more quicken into healthy babe in Lady Cappelletta than Pietro's could help but make strong babies in me. Except for their first, and our last. How could we make something as weak as Susanna, to not live a single day, and they make such a precious, lasting jewel as my Juliet?

How've I not seen it before, not known how truly she is mine? For surely she was mine even before she sucked the first milk of me, mine before I even knew she stirred within me. Mine, as she could never be the Cappelletti's.

Why else would Friar Lorenzo arrange for me to come here, yet howl at me, over and over, about being only a wet-nurse? Who else but he could know what happened the day two daughters were born, both brought to him for baptism, but only one survived? The priests are ever saying we must trust God's plan for us, and with all their Latin learning making us believe they always know such plans better than we ever can.

I breathe in the honeyed spice of the remaining comfits, more redolent than all the incense of a Requiem Mass. I swear by the Sacred Maria and the Holy Infant and every heavenly saint that sits among them, I still cannot believe I've truly lost my husband. That Pietro could have slipped from this life without bidding me farewell.

This is the loneliest, the most unbearable, part. To have not said one last *I love you*. To have the last we said not be a true good-bye.

But lonely as it is, I am not alone. Tybalt's father left two children, Tybalt and pious Rosaline, to pray for him. Pietro suffered six sons lost. But still she is here. Our final, secret, stolen one. Kneeling beside me in this light-filled chamber before the Holy Mother that Pietro gave me, the two of us praying as we take one final taste of his honey on our tongues.

PART TWO

1374–1375

ELEVEN

I keep my place beside the sala window as Lady Cappelletta, Juliet, and I sew. Purblind as I've grown, none begrudge my standing where the light is better. Nor do I mind being where the view is better as well, for my aging eyes are keener for what passes below than for the stitch my needle makes. Verona's spring bustles with donkey-carts sloping off the bridge from the far side of the Adige, heading for the Piazza delle Erbe. Wine barrels are heaved into houses full, or hauled out empty. Veiled women and thick-bellied men hurry toward some urgent task, or stop to gossip in the street. The Via Cappello is like a river thick with barques and barges while I'm tethered in port, watching every thing and everyone that sails by.

But the top-gallant is here inside, Lord Cappelletto flapping as noisily within the sala as a high-masted sail in a blustery wind.

"We'll serve ravioli of wild boar simmered in spring herbs, to start. Next, veal stuffed with saffroned pigeon, leek, and fava beans. Then chicken, sausage, and Lake Garda carp, layered with dates and almonds and laid inside a pie. It will be the finest wedding banquet Verona's seen since our own."

"My lord husband has forgotten," Lady Cappelletta says, without bothering to raise her eyes to his, "the feasts we ate when Cansignorio was wed a decade past."

"More sumptuous than ours, as is a prince's due. But no better than a plowman's meal before furrowing a barren field, as it turned out to be." Lord Cappelletto takes a certain pleasure in pitying Cansignorio, who has neither sons nor daughters by his lawful wife. "This may not be a royal marriage, but we'll reap plenty of delights when it comes to fig and pear compoted in rosemary and anise. And almond-porridged quince, and cherry-and-rose tarts. And peaches braised with gingered honey." He smiles at Juliet. "I've not forgot who keeps a ready tooth for sweets. Do you not, my love?"

Nearly fourteen, and still Juliet blushes with full innocence. But Lady Cappelletta's own innocence is long gone. She's become well-practiced in disdain, and serves up her scorn in overly abundant portions. "We've much to do to get the trousseau finished," she tells Lord Cappelletto. "Juliet is slow with a needle, and such distractions do not make her any quicker."

Though Lord Cappelletto has all a man's ignorance of needlework, he waves away her chiding. "A rushed stitch is like a rushed courtship," he says. "What comes together overhastily is too easily undone."

Courtship and *come together* jolt Juliet. Her needle pierces a finger, and she gives a startled cry as red drops fall upon the sheet she sews.

"That's the only pricking there'll be upon that bedsheet," I say, to bring a laugh from Lord Cappelletto before worse comes from his wife. "Enough it must be for all the Holy Sisters of Santa Caterina." I add that last to remind them that the convent trousseau we're making for Rosaline'll not be truly hers, every stitch of it to be held in common among the cloistered nuns.

These months we've spent sewing, and the long night of feasting to come—all of it to consecrate what none of us would wish for ourselves. Prince Cansignorio's childless marriage is no more barren than Rosaline's Christly one will be. But Tybalt tells me his devout sister wants nothing more than chastity. At her age I surely wanted chastity—though only in the sense I was in want of it, delighting as I did in my marriage bed. But those days are forever past, and what I am in want of now are delights Rosaline'll never know. She long ago donned habit, and as soon as she was deemed of age she happily professed her vows. This season she is fain to consecrate them, and Santa Caterina is glad for it. The convent, like all the Holy Church, dearly loves its ceremonies, for every one of which Lord Cappelletto gives generous dotal alms.

I take the bloodied bedsheet from my blushing Juliet, rubbing comfort onto her injured finger with the soft of my thumb, and hand her a pillow-casing to finish instead. "Salted water will bring such a stain out," I say, "as many a tearful bride learns the morning after her marriage is consummated."

That brings a knowing smirk from Lady Cappelletta. It goes unnoticed by her husband, who busies himself with cataloguing the esteemed guests he'll invite to feast in honor of the newly mendicanted Rosaline.

Juliet's usually so heavy in her own sleep that I may drowse late as I could wish and still rise first from our long-shared bed. But she's full awake before the prime-hour bells ring on the Sunday Rosaline is to be consecrated, kneeling before the statue of San Zeno while peering expectantly at me. As soon as I unlid my eyes, she asks, "Is my cousin a better girl than I am?"

To wake with such worries is to not know what true worry is. But my dearest lamb ever struggles to bear Lady Cappelletta's carping. And it is no easy thing for even such a light as Juliet to dwell in the shade of the ever-pious Rosaline.

I pat the sheet beside me, waiting for Juliet to settle back in bed and proffer a good-morning kiss before I answer. "Rosaline is good at being good, but it is much better to be better at much."

"Such riddles, honey nurse." She snuggles against me. "Can you not tell me if I am the precious jewel that you and my lord father Cappelletto and my holy father Friar Lorenzo all say I am?"

Why does the age that in boys brings boastful confidence in girls bring only doubt? There'd been naught like this in all my years of raising sons, or in rearing Tybalt. But Juliet of late puts me in mind of a bud you need protect, lest a sudden storm tear loose its newformed petals before it flowers to full bloom.

"Rosaline is a tambour, taut and well put to the task of giving off a steady beat. You are more a well-stringed lute. Full of bright notes and pleasing melodies"—I lift a lock of her hair and dance its end along her neck—"so long as the right hand plays upon you. Now, out of bed we must both be, and readying ourselves to go to Santa Caterina."

This is enough to satisfy her, though it's no full part of all that I might say of what and who she is.

When my heart first seared with the pain of losing my Pietro, I ached to claim her for my own. But what would my word have been against Lord Cappelletto, who believes with all his own heart that she's the sole fruit of his loveless marriage, the same girl the city's finest midwife delivered of Lady Cappelletta? What more proof would he need than what lying Friar Lorenzo would gladly give to keep so rich and influential a patron satisfied? For that is what I puzzled out, in my grief-filled sleepless nights: who else but Friar Lorenzo could have managed it, and why else would he have done it? To preserve a wealthy, powerful family's joy, for which they ever bestow gilded thanks upon the Church—even if it meant yet more grief for me and Pietro. With a single deceit he fooled us all, rich and poor alike. None would believe a brown-cloaked Franciscan of being so duplicitous, so what good would it have done me to accuse him? I'd not risk being sent away from her. Not hazard the tie I yet have to my daughter.

So I've forced myself to keep kneeling before my confessor, never letting the slightest sign of what I know flicker in my eye. With Pietro gone, I've need to be shriven only once or twice a year, and in those infrequent visits Friar Lorenzo's not sensed anything amiss. Harder is holding my secret from my own darling girl. Too young she was at first, to understand. Too young to keep such a confidence. And even now—how could I take her from so grand a house, and force on her a life without name and fortune? Each day her belly fills with the Cappelletti food, and their fabrics clothe her finely. Each night we sleep entwined on the Cappelletti linen. I've let that be enough, for now.

I could not love her more even if all the world knew how truly she is mine. And soon my bud will blossom to full bloom, and I'll know the time is right to tell her.

It's no easy thing to find a conveyance grand enough to suit Lord Cappelletto yet narrow enough to pass through Verona's crowded streets. Once the convent dowry is packed inside the carriage, there's barely room for four to sit within in any comfort, so it's just as well that Tybalt insists on riding post. Though the weather's warmed, he still wears his cloak trimmed in marten fur, for I've not had time to take the winter lining out and sew in this season's taffeta instead. He carries himself with the confidence earned in years of daily practice with a master-at-arms, and Lady Cappelletta smiles and admires the handsome figure he cuts upon the horse. So handsome, so admirable, is Tybalt, she must turn immediately to Lord Cappelletto and make great show of forbidding him from trotting off beside his heir. This is the closest to kindness she comes, to keep her aged husband from mounting a steed and thrusting himself into the saddle, for which surely he's grown as ill-suited as all the other mounting and thrusting she long ago forbade him. And so Tybalt gallops ahead alone, as the rest of us wend more slowly out of the city and across the river, to where Santa Caterina nestles on a gentle hill above Verona.

Slow as we've come, still Lord Cappelletto insists there's time to descend into the catacomb and clear the cobwebs from his family crypt before the convent ceremony. Juliet cannot bear the sight of bones and begs to walk the Stations of the cloister instead. Lady Cappelletta gives her leave to do so, though she relishes the visit to the tomb herself—I suppose to be sure Lord Cappelletto's first, beloved wife remains quite dead.

I stay with my Juliet. In the near two years since she turned twelve, my girl's not been allowed to leave Ca' Cappelletti, save to make her shrift to Friar Lorenzo, or to walk behind Lord Cappelletto in a holy-day procession. A rich man's marriageable daughter is like his wife's dowry-jewels—a precious treasure to be kept under lock and key, shown only when he deems it to his family's advantage. Soft as Juliet is, it's not been hard on her to be penned in, her days filled with whatever sewing and singing I devise to divert her. But I'm glad to escape the confines of Ca' Cappelletti, to be brought beyond the city walls, and walk among the cloister garden smelling its mint and thyme and fecund dirt. To breathe in their pungent promise, and know that spring is the season of possibility.

Even Juliet senses it, laughing and pointing at plant and peacock and every pretty view. All talk of tombs forgotten as she wanders along the venerative path, infused with as much awe for what grows in the garden as for the Christly acts commemorated at each Station. I'm glad of it. Glad that even here, she is as full of love for this life as the encloistered Rosaline is for the holy hereafter. Surely God and saints'll not favor less her liveliness.

After we make our prayer at the final Station, Juliet's mouth curves into a sly smile. "I've a surprise to show you," she says, bidding me close my eyes as she steers me along another of the convent's paths. It is a contenting thing to be led by my near-grown Juliet, her gentle touch guiding me as she chitters to herself about which way she means for us to go. She stops us with a giggle, and opening my eyes I find myself facing a statue of Santa Caterina.

Towering over us, Caterina's colors dazzle in the sun. Her cheeks flush pink, the red of her lips nearly as deep a ruby as her gown. The bright green robe held by two angels above her saintly gilded crown contrasts with the deeper green of the martyr's palm she holds, which is dotted with golden dates. Her other hand clutches a dark brown torturer's wheel. Mysterious gold letters are worked into the holy book that opens at her breast.

"I came here once, when I was a girl," Juliet tells me, as though I could forget that day. "When I saw this statue, I thought that it was you."

"Me? A virgin saint?"

"Do not tease me, Nurse, for what did I know of such things?" She points to Santa Caterina's wheel. "This seemed so like your spindle, and her hair is fixed in braids like yours."

"Most of the women in Verona wear their hair in braids." Reaching beneath where Juliet's unplaited locks fall from her Cappelletti cap, I give the lobe of her ear a loving tweak. "And what I cradled at my breast was more precious than any book could be."

Soft cooing sounds from behind the statue. "A songbird," says Juliet, "and we've not a crust of bread to feed it."

"A cat," I correct her, "and he'd not be satisfied with any less than two full loaves."

The cooing turns to cawing laugh, and Tybalt steps out from where he's hid. "Is a convent walk a place to play, and are you yet of such a pranking age?" I ask, though my smile shows how glad I am to see him.

"Does the cruel virago scold," he hunches out his head and wags a finger, before straightening himself tall again, "even when a goodly man places candles before a godly saint?"

"A goodly man," I repeat, mocking him in turn, to Juliet's delight—for she and I still see the boy, the youth, that Tybalt's been, though at twenty-three he's eager to believe none can detect it. "Does that not depend on whether what you offer is a narrow taper or a well-thickened votive?"

I reach into the wooden chest he carries, feeling for the familiar shape of candles. But what I touch instead is an unexpected form. Drawing it out, I see the offerings Tybalt's brought are carved in the shape of the Holy Mother. I lift this one to my lips to offer prayerful kiss. I breathe in the sweet scent, pressing my thumb until it makes a slight burrow in the beeswax.

"Did it come from our hive?" Juliet asks.

"Harvested from the one within our arbor, and the others that I—"

The convent bell cuts Tybalt off. He nods for me to place the votive upon the altar at the statue's base and makes a quick prayer as I touch its wick to the one that already burns low there. Carrying the near-full chest in his hands, he offers one elbow to Juliet and the other to me. We slip our arms through his, walking three abreast across the cloister grounds. Honey-scent, spring, Juliet, and Tybalt—all of this warms me.

Though convent-dowries and what the Sisters sell of their vineyards' yield keep their church well, it's not so large as some within the city. Christ, like some Mohammedan sultan, takes many brides at once, and the churchyard teems with the families of all those who are being consecrated.

"I pray you, sir, let us pass," Tybalt says to a man so broad there is no easy way around him.

The man turns and, instead of stepping aside, takes quick survey of Tybalt. "Whose son are you?"

Such a question, meant to insult any full-grown man, cuts all the worse with one who's spent so much of his life fatherless.

"I am Tybalt Cappelletto, brother to Rosaline who will be consecrated a Sister of Santa Caterina within the hour. And I should like to kneel and pray for her long service to the Holy Church, rather than standing here squabbling with you."

But the man'll not move. "You bring so small a chest of candles, Cappelletto?"

Tybalt takes a half-step forward, crooking his elbow to maneuver Juliet behind him. "I bring such a goodly store each week. Our candles burn day and night in every chapel and before every holy statue at Santa Caterina, as the Sisters say Mass for our noble family."

The man smiles as though Tybalt is a hind with one foot caught in a well-strung trap. "Fifty boxes of candles a year, is that all the Cappelletti offer?"

"Candles to keep filled the score of gifted silver candlesticks that bear the Cappelletti crest, and a wedding cassone overflowing with trousseau linens." Having risen from the catacomb and pressed his way through the crowd to find us, Lord Cappelletto takes even more than his usual pleasure in cataloguing his own calculated benevolence. "Along with silver plate for the church altar, and another two chests filled with enough of Prato's finest wool to make full-skirted habits for every Sister here. And a plot of tilling land near to Villafranca, rich soil that the Cappelletti've held for five generations, ever since it was given to us by the Pope's decree for besting some rebellious mountain peasants with unfounded pretentions to nobility."

Lord Cappelletto spits the last part, but this thick mule of a man only shrugs. "Rich dirt, perhaps, but poor compense for all the Cappelletti slaughtered by their fiercer, braver foes, in that generation and the next." He swells his belly all the larger, to be sure we cannot pass, and nods at Tybalt's wooden chest. "I suppose you may be so indulgent for a niece. Would that I could do as much for my goddaughter Augusta Infangati, who consecrates her vows today. But as a man with seven sons, I must take more care in stewarding my family's fortunes."

Son and sons, is that all this man talks about? I'd curse him and every son he has, and be done with him so we can settle ourselves to prayer. But it's not a woman's place to speak in public, and Lord Cappelletto'll not leave off so easily.

"A burden it must be, to know your family's wealth will be so divided and diminished, when the whole of it has never been even half what we Cappelletti have." He tips one ear, as though pondering some great question. "But perhaps that's not all there is to the matter. Even one as poor as Il Benedicto makes tithe out of his meager means, yet it's said the Montecchi never tally the church's portion as fully as you ought."

Marking how the name *Montecchi* shoots an angry twitch along Tybalt's jaw, I lean close and whisper to him what I dare not say to Lord Cappelletto. "A nice quarrel to have before a church, while Juliet waits to kneel and pray, as do your aunt and pious Rosaline."

The Montecche is already thundering back at Lord Cappelletto. Tybalt cuts him off, shoving the box of candles into the man's fat gut. "I make a gift of these to you, that you may give them to the church to celebrate your goddaughter, and none of your sons suffer a pennyworth of loss for it. Come Uncle, Coz, and Nurse, let's show the Sisters of Caterina the reverence that's their due."

He ducks around the man to walk beside his uncle, taking care that Juliet and I follow unharmed.

"You were right to put your duty to Rosaline before such bickering," I tell Tybalt, when we reach the church door.

"I'd not put anything before my family," he answers. "I care not how large a man's fortune is, nor how many sons he's spawned. But I'll not forget how the Montecche insulted me, and Rosaline, and our uncle, and the Holy Church as well."

There's only so much insult given as what we choose to take. But high-born Tybalt, braised like the tenderest veal cutlet in all

Lord Cappelletto's talk of family honor, will not see that. So I turn instead to Juliet. She's laid a hand upon Lord Cappelletto's arm and whispers some pleasant word to coax a smile from him. Such affection is more than his wife ever offers, and any who look upon Lord Cappelletto can see how he treasures it. Treasures her. He smiles and says, "Darling daughter," kissing her farewell then hurrying to take his place among the kneeling men, while Juliet and I join Lady Cappelletta on the women's side of the nave.

Darling she is, and daughter, too. Milk-daughter, and more, to me. Let Lord Cappelletto call her what he will. He's as blind with would-be father love as Tybalt is with hot rage over whatever slight he's sure the Montecche made. Mannish pride on either side, and Juliet and I have naught to do but bow our heads and pray among the women.

Rosaline'll not see us once the Mass is done. The stone-faced prioress nods approvingly at all that Lord Cappelletto gifts the convent, then announces that Rosaline is so moved by her newly consecrated state that she's vowed not to speak for an entire week. And she'll keep a holy fast for just as long, consuming nothing but the Host.

By my saints, this Christ is a demanding husband. To ask a wife to forego the pleasures of a conjugal bed, and have neither words nor food to fill her mouth instead.

Lord Cappelletto scowls at this proroguing of his planned feast. He's thinking of the powerful guests he's longing to impress, and of ravioli and savory pie and all the other already-prepared dishes that'll not keep another week. Lady Cappelletta, who's learned to love an evening's revelry since her husband, grown too old to dance, leaves her to terpsichore among his guests, shares his displeasure. But Tybalt's jaw softens at the prioress's pronouncement. Though I wonder what in his sister's self-denying devotions so pleases him, I give Juliet's chin a loving chuck and say, "It's just as well to wait the feast. For all we've sewn of Rosaline's trousseau, there's been little time to array Juliet, and Lady Cappelletta, as finely as we ought for such a fête."

The thought of getting up greater finery satisfies girl and woman both, and Lord Cappelletto's hairy fingers busily tally how much can be made of another week of preparations. Tybalt catches my eye with his own, endarting his gladness to me before taking his leave to untether the post-horse.

Plodding as the carriage ride is, still we arrive at Ca' Cappelletti before Tybalt. Lady Cappelletta hastens to the upper storage room and unlocks the cassone that holds the finest of the household fabric stores. "The zetani, at last," she says, pulling out a length of cloth as azure as Santa Maria's own celestial robes.

Juliet's slim fingers ripple along the velvet-embossed silk. "Does my lord father bid it, Madam?"

That she calls Lady Cappelletta by the same *Madam* as I do is comfort to me, though to hear her mouth form *father* for Lord Cappelletto always sets a sharp shard in my craw.

But *bid* is the word that catches for Lady Cappelletta. "This zetani was pawned to him in payment for some debt so long past, the color fades along the folds." She raises an eyebrow in careful calculation. "Surely even my lord husband'll not begrudge us fabric enough to make new sleeves for his dear daughter, and his wife."

Juliet raises pleading eyes to Lady Cappelletta. "Can I not have a whole gown of it?"

It's not greed but a child's innocent delight that makes my girl ask. But such innocence only draws a frown from Lady Cappelletta. Indulgent as Lord Cappelletto is with Juliet, my girl's not noticed he's harder with his wife.

"No simple stitch will pull such well-wefted cloth to proper shape," I say. "Which means we'll have enough to do to get sleeves cut, set, and sewn in one week's time."

The soft zetani scents our fingers with the rosemary that's kept it free of worm and moth, and I know my Juliet will shine in so rich a color worn against the pale yellow stripes of her gown. But it seems whatever rest I'd hoped to have once Rosaline's trousseau was done will never come, for we work long past the evening torches being lit. Although I keep a ready ear for Tybalt's return, I never hear him. Such is the man that he's become, still prancing on cat paws though he's long grown—yet oftener and oftener keeping counsel only with himself.

It's a short night's nap I get, because not long after the lauds bells are rung trumpeters pierce Verona's sleep, summoning Prince Cansignorio's most trusted advisors. Lord Cappelletto responds to the blasts like a hound to the huntsman's whistle, rushing down into the still-dark street to join the hastily called council.

I swing open the window in our bedchamber. "Why let in such chill?" Juliet murmurs, snuggling deeper beneath the bedclothes.

I do not worry her with an answer as I lean out to smell the air. No fire, no powder. The city's quiet, except for the peals of the trumpeters, the hoofbeats of their horses, and the clatter of the lords answering the call. But after I pull the window tight within its case and turn back to the room, a shiver catches me. Not of cold, but of something else. Some foreboding makes me cross myself and ask safekeeping from my Virgin before I climb once more into the bed where Juliet, fast asleep again, breathes a steady rhythm into the still room.

By the time Lord Cappelletto returns, the sun is high and the whole house is long awake. He barks down in the kitchen before storming his way into the sala.

Lady Cappelletta, practiced at ignoring her husband's moods, does not even turn her head when he enters. Juliet wraps the length of zetani she is working around her shoulders, wanting Lord Cappelletto to take some pretty notice of it, and her. "Will I not make a fine sight at the feast?"

But for once his brooding brow does not raise in joy at Juliet. "There'll be no feast," he says.

This at least works a response from his wife. "Does my lord husband not wish to celebrate our brother's daughter Rosaline's most holy state?"

Brother, Rosaline, and *holy state*—she offers all three when any one of them ought to be enough to catch his heart. But none do.

"There's been fighting," he tells her, "upon Verona's streets."

"Surely there has." I answer fast, in case his words have frighted Juliet. "As happens on so many nights, while we are safe inside."

"This was not some night-brawl in a remote corner of the city. There's blood spilt among the Scaligeri monuments in the Santa Maria Antica churchyard. Prince Cansignorio, fearing some treason, has forbidden any gathering of lords outside his council chamber until the culprits are caught."

Such is a man's reasoning, which makes everything that happens have to do with him. Cansignorio, who with cold heart and quick hand killed one brother and keeps the other chained within a prison cell, knows well how easily traitorous thoughts can turn to deeds. But with a woman's wit, I sense something else at play.

I let out one cough and then another, hacking louder and louder until Lord Cappelletto orders me from the room to take wine and water.

Needing neither wine nor water, I swallow my false coughs and head instead for Tybalt's rooms. But he's not there. Not in the courtyard. I spy him at last in the arbor, staring at the beehive.

I cannot move on so fleet a foot as he does, and, keen as his long-ago lessons from the master-at-arms have made him, he calls, "Good day, dear Nurse," without even turning.

"A good enough day for those who did naught last night. But for any who scaled the compound walls and went—"

"Will you not come close," he cuts me off, "and look at this?"

I've no use for bee watching, and he well knows it. But to talk to Tybalt, one must talk as Tybalt will, and so I edge closer to the hive. At a limb-hole of the log, a mob of bees savages some winged foe like fierce-jawed dogs tearing at a fox.

"Why do they attack one of their kind?"

"Not one of their kind," he corrects me. "An intruder, who snuck into their hive to steal their honey. Do you not see the difference?"

I'll not get near enough for my old eyes to mark it. But he leans yet closer, admiring the raging insects. "It's said the bees are more like us than the English or French or Germans. Always seeking for what is sweet—but when something goes amiss, fast to fight to defend their hive."

"A foolish sacrifice, to waste one's life just to sink a single sting."

He turns, ready to tell me I am wrong. But my gasp overruns his words. A finger-long cut crusted with blood slices his cheek. "You're hurt," I say, as if to dare him to deny it.

"It's but a scratch, and well worth the greater damage I did the Montecche."

"That pompous old man? He must be your uncle's age."

"It's not him I fought, but one of his precious sons. Less precious now, for the hurt I've done him." He smiles, and the cut snakes into an angry curve. "Insult they gave us, and injury I gave back."

Insult, ever insult. The Cappelletti honor is like that finely worked zetani. A pretty, precious thing, though in truth too delicate. The poor who cloak ourselves in coarse woollen bigello, which bears a host of blows, can only wonder that the zetani of a rich man's honor is so easily marred. And so often in need of avenging.

"Prince Cansignorio believes both insult and injury were meant for him," I tell Tybalt. "When he discovers you're the culprit—"

"He'll not know. I took care to meet the Montecche when only stars were watching, as he returned alone from a night of drinking."

Is there no way to make Tybalt see the danger in what he's done? "The Montecchi will cry for justice."

Tybalt laughs as though I've truly turned into the foolish old virago he teases that I am. "Will the man whose blood I drew denounce me publicly, and admit to all Verona how clumsily he fought, and how easily I bested him?"

He unseals one end of the log hive and daggers off an edge of comb. The bees arc around him, intoxicated by the sweet scent of their own handiwork. But none offers an angry sting. It's as if they believe him one of their own, and know he means no enmity to them.

He holds the dripping comb out to me. "Honey will keep the cut from festering. Will you not offer a careful rub and a kind word, to have me healed?"

For all the sauce and swagger with which Tybalt wields a weapon, deep within he's still the lonely child who's ever needed me. Needs me as much as I need him.

I take the comb and dab honey along the angry stripe that mars his cheek, as I tell him about Prince Cansignorio's decree. "Your uncle'll not be pleased to learn you're the cause that cancels Rosaline's holy-wedding feast."

This cools a little of his hot pride. "My sister deserves more banquets than all Verona has the means to give. But she's too saintly to care whether we feast her. And my uncle, who values naught more than the good name of the Cappelletti, must be glad to have his heir defend it."

Tybalt speaks the words *his heir* as one might speak of *his silver belt* or *his ermine-lined gown* or *the fee-simple of his landed holdings*. Lord Cappelletto's taken Tybalt as his heir, but never given in return what Tybalt so longed for from his father, and found only too briefly in Pietro.

I slip the comb into his pouting mouth so he can suck the remaining honey from it, as he learned to do when Pietro first set the hive here. I wait until I'm sure the sweetness is on Tybalt's tongue before I say, "Lord Cappelletto loves you, and Rosaline, as surely as he loves Juliet."

He chews the comb until he's worked all the golden honey from it, then spits the palish wax upon the ground. "My uncle loves Rosaline for being pious, which he hopes will bring the favor of God and Church upon our house. He loves me for matching honor to that favor, so long as my first honoring act is unwavering obedience to him. But Juliet has his purest love."

Quick as my words come, he lays a long finger against my lips before I can utter any of them. "Hush, Nurse. We both know it's true, and you know I'll not resent it." He smiles again, and the glistening honey on his cheek makes this curl of the cut appear less sinister. "Juliet is as charming as Rosaline is good. Any man might love her. Why would her father not?"

I'll not answer as I could. Not dare betray to Tybalt what I've not let anyone know that I know: who her true father was. "You'll have to stay within Ca' Cappelletti until the cut has healed, to keep clear of Prince Cansignorio's suspicion. But there'll be no hiding it from your family."

I lead him out of the arbor and through the courtyard, stopping to collect some wine before we climb up to the sala. Though for my part I might prefer some aqua vitae, wine is all Lord Cappelletto drinks. And so I pray the vin santo will be enough to calm his ire, and to let flow Lady Cappelletta's full sympathy for Tybalt, which runs as deep as my own.

It's Juliet who first catches sight of us as we enter the sala. Paling at her dear-loved Tybalt's bloodied cheek, she cries out, the zetani sliding from her lap and pooling on the floor.

Lady Cappelletta's amber eyes flicker with surprise, then horror. "Who's done this to you?"

Lord Cappelletto, who stands at the window, turns to see what's amiss. Spying Tybalt's wound, he demands, "What villain is this within my house, jeoparding our family by raising a weapon against the prince?"

I step between them. "He's not jeoparded—"

Lord Cappelletto cuts me off, pushing his way to Tybalt. "Are you yet a child, hiding behind the nurse's skirts?"

"I'm neither villain nor child." Tybalt draws himself to his full height, dwarfing Lord Cappelletto. "I raised a weapon only to defend our family. Glad I was to do it, and to pay this simple price"— he runs his smallest finger along his sliced cheek—"for the pleasure of spilling a greater quantity of Montecchi blood. Such was their due, for insulting our gifts to the Holy Church."

Lord Cappelletto's mouth sharpens to a pucker, as he takes in Tybalt's words. But then it broadens as he laughs, pulling Tybalt into his arms.

"Dry your womanish tears," he tells Lady Cappelletta and Juliet. "Tybalt's done right. Done as I did many a time when I was of his age, to pluck the crow of the Montecchi and their allies." He claps a hairy hand upon his nephew's back, like a knight patting his stallion after a victorious joust. "Prince Cansignorio's quick to take a slight where none is given. But he's got no part in this private quarrel between families. So long as none know the part you played last night, it'll be but a short delay before the edict's lifted, and we feast for pious Rosaline. And for brave Tybalt."

It's not love of the sort Pietro showed Tybalt, that tender echo of what he felt for our own sons. But it's all Lord Cappelletto offers, and Tybalt drinks it in like a bee sucking nectar from a blossom.

One note, then the next, then yet another—they fly so swift from Tybalt's lute, I can barely draw air in fast enough to match singing to them. Together we turn such a bright tune that Lady Cappelletta hums along, one foot tapping as she sews.

Such is not enough for Juliet. Her sleeves done two days past, the needle now holds no interest for her. Bearing herself with perfect grace, she hops and turns about the sala. A pleasing sight to match each pretty song. But she longs for a chain of other dancers.

"Might not my lord father—"

Lady Cappelletta's smile sours. "Your lord father has much to do, tallying rents and tributes."

She's always glad for the long hours her husband spends in his study bent over his correspondence, and gladder still when he leaves Ca' Cappelletti entirely, which he's done much this week and a half past. Lord Cappelletto's impatient for any chance to be in Prince Cansignorio's presence, showing the Cappelletti loyal.

His going out makes harder Tybalt's staying in. After so many days with little to do but pluck tempestuously upon the lute strings, Tybalt's chin hangs, and his shoulders slope.

"Dance with me, Coz," Juliet says, "while Nurse sings for us."

But even she cannot draw off his sulk. "I prefer to dance with steel rather than with silk."

Such poetry, just to show he's still eager to spill blood. "It's dancing with steel that's gashed your face, and left you closed inside among the ladies," I remind him.

He makes no answer, which upsets me more than the bitterest rebuke. This quiet, brooding Tybalt—he steals in like evening's shadow creeping across a room, pushing out the bright, loving boy we adored. Would my sons have sullened so, if they'd lived to such an age? Would they have turned away from me, as Tybalt of late so often does?

Juliet reaches out her hands to me. "Nurse, you must make yourself my partner. Come, I'll hear no plaints about your corn-riddled feet or achy hips." She widens those familiar eyes in such a way as she knows makes it near impossible for me tell her no.

But I'm suddenly in such a sweat as if it were the height of summer, or some devilish spell raged over me.

"I must have water," I say, laying my needlework down and standing myself up. This is my well-worked compromise for the hours I spend in Lady Cappelletta's presence: I'll not ask a by-your-leave-may-I-m'lady of her, as the common servants must. Instead, I annouce what I intend to do and set myself to doing it, unless I am bade otherwise.

"I'll go withal." Tybalt's quick onto his feet, as if accompanying me to the courtyard well offers some great respite for his restlessness.

His coming along does not please me, for ruddied as I feel, I might plunge face and neck, arms and chest, into the water trough, were he not near. Instead, I must settle for long sips from the well-cup.

Tybalt's mouth twists in thought as he watches all I swallow. "Bees need to drink, just as we do." He points through the passage-way to the arbor, toward a low clay bowl near the hive that's filled with a pebbly mound over which he's poured water. "It's not rained in weeks. The other hives must be without water by now." Tipping his head, he surveys the top of the compound wall. "Perhaps to-night, I can replenish them."

"You cannot," I say. "You must not." Flushed though I am, that portending shiver shakes over me. "Your cut's nearly healed. Surely the bees can wait another week, until you can go safely through Verona's streets."

"In a week, we may have lost whole hives. Pietro's hives."

"I'll go." Why do I promise such a thing, though the bees frighten me? It's hearing how he speaks of Pietro. Esteeming my husband's memory is the one honor I understand. "If you'll invent some excuse to satisfy Lady Cappelletta, I'll go early tomorrow, when it's yet cool."

He is a sly fox and I'm the fat hen, I see that from the smile that spreads along his face as he tells me where each hive is set and how to reach them, saving for last the ones nooked within the walls of Santa Caterina. He knew I'd not let him journey so far with the prince's edict still in place.

Small sacrifice it is for me. Shut away all this time, I long to roam the city and wander through the countryside beyond its walls.

"It'll take all morning, and much of the afternoon," I say. Longer, if I dally in places of my choosing.

"You'll need to save the hours after noon to go to the Mercato Vecchio while the fabric merchants have out their finest wares."

"Do you mean for me to dress the bees, once I've watered them?" In truth, the thought of walking among those crowded stalls, bright colors dazzling my eye as my hands work their way across silk, samite, and Damascus cloth—that delights me, whatever reason Tybalt has for wanting me to go.

He takes my plump hand, raising his long arm and twirling me beneath it as Juliet would've had me do in her capers around the sala. "The bees need no more dress than a dusting of bright pollen. But our dear Nurse deserves something prettier than that old morello to wear to Rosaline's feast."

His words stop me mid-turn. For near eleven years, I've worn naught but mulberry-dyed cloth. I've not minded my widow's weeds, bought with what was made selling off Pietro's few garments, and the scant furnishings and kitchen things we'd owned.

I wear my loss for all the world to see, for it's all I've left of my happily wedded state. Or nearly all, aside from our Madonna, and Pietro's three linen shirts. Well darned they are by now, but still I ever wear one beneath my dress, the last hidden rub of him on me. Only my precious bedmate Juliet knows how I yet keep something of his against me. But even she does not suspect how I hope the dull morello worn atop those shirts washes any brightness from my face, keeps anyone from noticing the way my coloring matches her own.

I drop my hand from Tybalt's. "Sumptuous colors come at great cost. They're meant for such as Juliet, and Lady Cappelletta."

"Pick something golden, then. The color of new-minted coins, and the flowing honey that brings them." He reaches for the cup, dips it once more into the well bucket, and holds it tippling full to me. "Half all the harvests' profits are your due. Will you not spend them?"

This is a well-worn argument between us. The boy who, through all his tutor's beatings, never cared to reckon sums has turned into a man who faithfully tallies how much each season's wax and honey yield, and figures to the last eighth-denaro the half-share he insists is mine. I've not touched any of it, letting Tybalt store those coins along with the wages Lord Cappelletto pays each quarter for my minding Juliet. As though the things I do for Juliet, I do for money—no more than Tybalt tends Pietro's hives solely to take a partner's portion of the little sum to be earned at it.

Another flash of heat rises over me. I accept the cup, swallowing down the water while Tybalt reminds me for the hundredth time that the coins sit in a box hidden beneath the arbor-hive. The bees guard our lucre, which is made from robbing them. "Take all of it, if you wish. And take my hooded cloak as well, so that at each place where there's a hive, they'll know I've sent you."

"And what of Juliet?" I ask. We both know this is no journey on which Lord Cappelletto would allow her.

"I'll play the knight-gallant for her, and give her dances as well as songs, and jousting games, and every piece of play her pretty heart desires." Grown as he is, he's got less patience to dote on Juliet, though she longs for his attention as much as ever. I nod to let him see how pleased I am that he'll please her.

Taking quick measure of my gladness, he asks, "And while I amuse my cousin, will you carry a message from me to Rosaline?"

The slightest crease rises between his eyes, and I begin to wonder if all the talk of watering bees or buying cloth was but a ruse, so that he could ask this of me.

"Of course." The fat hen is not so fast outfoxed, for I'm glad to be privy to whatever confidence he sends his cloistered sister. "What shall I tell her?"

"No need for telling." He draws a folded page from his doublet sleeve, already sealed with a fat dollop of blood-red wax. "I've got it written here."

"Written—for Rosaline?" Perchance the girl can read, the Sisters of Santa Caterina needing to be learned enough to spend their days bent over holy books. But to write is to keep confidence from me, and Tybalt well knows it. "There was no need for you to struggle with a pen," I say, mouthing Lord Cappelletto's ready reminder of

Tybalt's flaws, "when I'd have no trouble remembering your message, and repeating it to her."

Unkind it is of me, but if the words hurt Tybalt, he gives no show of it. "Rosaline prefers me write, so she may keep the missive and read it over in any lonely hour."

I'd not believe pious Rosaline passed any lonely hours, living among a convent's worth of company and devoting herself to her holy wedded Christ. I pack my tongue close among my well-cracked teeth to keep from saying so to Tybalt, as I tuck the letter into my own sleeve.

TWELVE

It's good I've got the girth I do. It draws up the length of Tybalt's cloak, the excess fabric folded over the twice-girdled silver belt he's lent me. A rich man's finery works like a faery-tale spell. Wrapped in it, I slip into houses as grand as Ca' Cappelletti in every parish of Verona, each with a hive within its hidden garden. There are yet more hives nooked into the very walls that encircle the city, and tucked in trees that edge the fields beyond the walls. None question me busying myself about the hives, cloaked in fine camlet embroidered with the Cappelletti crest in gilded thread.

I imagine Pietro as I go about, how carefully he must have chosen each place, how wily he was to site his hives so well. Log or cork, woven fennel stalk or wooden chest—I'd not known there were so many ways to house a hive, each selected to suit where it's placed. And nearby, always some simple dish piled with pebbles where water's meant to be.

Tybalt's talked so much of how Pietro loved his bees, I try to feel for the tiny creatures some small part of what my big bear of a husband felt. As I tip the jug I carry, the bees dance with expectant delight, the most adventurous ones touching down on one of the tiny rocks, drinking from the shimmery surface even before I'm done. It's not unlike tending a flock. Though it was my family's poverty that put me to shepherding, I came to relish roaming beyond the sinister confines of my father's house, the dull familiar of our little village. I passed happy days among my sheep, soothing any nighttime pangs of solitude by burrowing myself against a warm, woolly companion. It's comfort to think Pietro felt the same, venturing out from the Via Zancani to set one hive and then another, slowly casting a buzzing skein around Verona and the countryside beyond.

As I make the steep climb to Santa Caterina, the ruts formed on the narrow path by hoof and cart and carriage all work hard upon my feet, the borrowed belt clanging an uneven rhythm to match my unsure pace. I empty the jug in careful swigs, husbanding a few drops onto my sleeve and pressing the dampened cloth against the hot nape of my neck. The sun stays close on me, drawing his course along the sky as I rise above the city, until at last I stand before the convent gate.

Setting down the water jug, I use both hands to tug upon the bell-pull, feeling for the resistance that weighs the weathered rope, a metal answer to my effort. This is how our lives are marked and meted out. The tolling of the hours of a day, the Sunday of a week, the holy-days of a year. And then the rings like this, tolled to tell that somebody's arrived. And the other kind, rung from parish church when someone's departed. Only when I led my flock to pasture could I forget such a great and brassy sound, forget that in all the universe there was something louder than bleating sheep, or a wolfish howl, or the most fiercely raging storm. Louder than any noise I heard upon the hills.

An-gel, an-gel. In the awful time when we lost all, the death knells rang day and night, knocking my heart from its rhythmed beats and stunning the breath from me. Pietro would gather me in his great arms, so that his broad chest was all I could know of the world. Pressing his lips to my ear, he whispered *an-gel, an-gel,* over and over, matched to the pealing of the bells. Angel, each one of our boys was become, as though their souls rode to heaven on the tolls. Angel, Pietro said I was, his Angelica here on earth.

I want to hear my husband's comforting *an-gel* once again. But the high-pitched clanging of the bell upon the gate to Santa Caterina offers only a keening questioning.

Metal slides against metal, the hasp swings, and the wooden door gives way. I'm faced with a woman near my own age, or so I guess from what the wimple shows of her gaunt face. Her hands are rubbed raw, the odor of lye clinging to her.

"I'm here to tend the bees," I say, lifting the jug. She nods and turns without a word. I follow her inside, wait while she slides the hasp shut. She points me to the well and, before I've drawn the water to refill the jug, silently disappears back into the laundering shed.

Tybalt's told me where to find the half a dozen hives nestled among the convent grounds. As I bend to pour water at the first of them, set within the vineyard wall, a lone bee flies inside the gape of cloak below my chin. I stop stone still, anticipating the hot anger of its sting. But I feel instead a gentle tickle as it crawls along the curve of my collar-bone. The creature makes curious survey of my tender flesh, such as none has done since death stilled Pietro's insisting kisses. Tybalt's spoke enough of the workings of a hive that I know this bee was hatched no more than a few months past. But still I cannot help thinking of it as my husband's. I close my eyes, shutting out the world that's easily seen, and wonder if in its oddly pleasant prickling there's some message from him.

"Pietro, our girl's near grown. Lovely and loving as only we could make her. Fresh as the milk and sweet as the honey that's fed her. And Tybalt—at last to raise a boy who's lived to be a man. You'd be proud of him. But husband, how I miss you. Just as much today as I ever have." I wait, wanting for some answer. But all I hear is the steady hum of the insects entering and exiting the hive. The shivery sensation along my neck is gone, whatever bee was there flown off to join the others, unrecognizable to me once I blink my eyes open to the bright sun.

I make my way from one hive to the next, the convent grounds familiar from my recent visit, though to move about them, even to breathe the same scent of earth and plants, feels different without Juliet and Tybalt. The land slopes gently here, and at the farthest hive, I turn back to look across the low wall that encloses the convent. Spread in the valley below, encircled by the Adige, is Verona. I search for the familiar shape of San Fermo, then the soaring campanile of Sant'Anastasia, and try to pick out which of the household towers rising between them is Ca' Cappelletti.

Does a bee feel such a pull for its hive, as I do for the teeming city? Is each nectar-gatherer as devoted to its queen as I am to Juliet, that even on so short a flight, there is always the longing to be back with her?

The bee is more practiced at parting from its queen, for it takes flight each day. I've not been away from Juliet since the morning more than a decade past when, newly weaned, she rode here with Lord Cappelletto and Tybalt, to bring Rosaline back to the nuns. I still miss those first years. Sometimes I believe I'm living them again during our nights of enlaced sleep, when all the world retreats and Juliet's bed becomes a tiny ship in which the two of us drift, dreaming together.

I can feel the wonder of her at each age she's been. Tiny baby, plump toddler, fast-growing girl. The near-woman she is now. I'd keep her this age forever if I could, though part of me is impatient to see the lady she'll soon be—and to have her know all she is to me.

That impatience quickens my pace to the final hive, set near the statue of Santa Caterina. But when I round the curve in the path, the water jug slips from my hands, smashing to the ground. The bees. They're everywhere. Crawling on the outside of the hive, irrupting onto the ground below it, infesting every nearby leaf and stem. Fear shivers over me as I watch the dark, creeping army. And then, in a frenzied instant, every bee alights at once. Like Biblical locusts blotting out the sky, they swoop together toward the saint.

They land upon the book she carries, which disappears beneath the writhing swarm. The great mound of bees teeming Santa Caterina's breast seems a perversing of every statue, every fresco, every image I've ever seen of Santa Maria suckling the Holy Christ.

I thought that it was you. A tremor shudders my own breast, as I remember Juliet's words. What have I to do with such an awful-omened thing?

I sidle away, too frighted to turn my back lest the bees come after me. As soon as I round a curve in the path and can no longer see them, vinegary fear pumps through my legs, and I race across the sloping grounds to the convent gate, thrust back the metal bar, and heave the hasp free. Shoving open the gate, I stumble down the winding path.

It's a clumsy-footed scramble to the city, tripping over Tybalt's too-long cloak. And over my own dripping dread. Just as I reach the Ponte delle Navi, something slams hard against me from behind, knocking me face-first to the stone span. Bone cracks as blood fills my throat.

"Dirty Cappelletto." Each syllable comes with a boot kick, the last of them pitching me onto my side.

"What's this?" Another voice, uncertain. "A maid in a man's cloak?"

"Made to pay, she'll be," the first, angrier man says. "Though what I'll thrust in her is not what I'd thrust into that knavish Tybalt."

A thud—and then a weight on me. That same man, cursing. And another, pummeling him with a wrathy, "The devil take you, for attacking a woman in broad daylight."

I try to push myself up, but the slightest lift of my head sets the world swimming. I cover my face while they brawl over me.

The shouting spreads, and the sounds of fighting, too. Like tinder igniting into an ever-growing ring of flame.

Someone grips my wrist, peels my arms from my face. A careful finger pries my eyelid up. In the blur, I make out brown cassock, and Friar Lorenzo's great gaping ears.

He pulls me to my feet and guides me from the fray, which spills from the bridge into the piazza. Edging past the swinging fists and flashing daggers, we slip around the massive hind-end of San Fermo and take shelter in the arcaded churchyard.

The noise of the clash is muted within these holy walls. But that only makes the pounding in my head sound louder. "No farther," I say. Or try to, the words swallowed in a bloody gurgle.

It is enough for the friar to make out my meaning. He sets me upon a bench and unrolls the sleeve of Tybalt's cloak. Bunching the gilt-embroidered edge against my nose, he bids me hold it tight to staunch the blood.

I nod, but even that slight movement shoots pain through my skull. Friar Lorenzo hies to his cell, returning to offer both poultices and prayers. Neither brings me relief. With a rip of pain along my side, my stomach twists, and I heave out a putrid stream onto his holy robe.

When I croak out an apology, Friar Lorenzo waves the words away. He has all a Franciscan's devotion to the wretched—coupled, perchance, with some scheme to appeal to Lord Cappelletto for the gift of a new cassock. He moves to make the sign of the cross upon me, but his *benedicte* is drowned out by a thundering of horses' hooves and the angry trumpets of Prince Cansignorio's royal guard.

"Thank Christ, they'll put an end to the fighting," Friar Lorenzo says.

It's true, the lance-wielding guard will scatter the brawlers. But

Tybalt, who drew his sword to answer so small a slight as he imagined the old Montecche gave him at the convent, has his hot-headed match in a thousand other young men of Verona. As I mark the blood that's soaked into the gold-threaded Cappelletti crest embroidered on his cloak, I wonder whether it will take more power than the prince has, and a greater miracle than Friar Lorenzo can pray forth, to calm them all and bring a lasting peace to the city's streets.

Though Friar Lorenzo offers his arm to lead me back to Ca' Cappelletti, once we make our slow way out of the churchyard and enter the piazza, he stops to survey the handful of youth who, too wounded to run off, are being held by the prince's guard.

Each breath sears new pain into me. I long to be a-bed and have Juliet lay her pretty head beside my throbbing one. But I'm caught quick while Friar Lorenzo weighs the worth of delivering me to Lord Cappelletto against what he might amass here. The Franciscan'll not easily forego a chance to offer succor to any who are hurt. He must want to tend the injured brawlers, and to plead with the guard to have mercy on them, which will surely earn him the favor of the young men's powerful families.

Another horseman cantors up the Via Filippini. He wears Cansignorio's own colors, the carmine of his high-hemmed doublet and well-turned leg setting off his night-black mount. It's as if an over-earnest hand has copied over the prince, creating a younger, handsomer, and less haughty version of Verona's ruler.

"Is this some new treason against my uncle?" he asks.

Nephew to a prince—surely the greatest gain is to be made by catering to him. "Young cocks, Count Paris, you know how they crow. But it's only some ancient grudge, rupturing anew. No treason is intended." Friar Lorenzo presses his palms together and bows his head as though he's begging for the count's guidance to solve a great dilemma. "I might treat both their anger and their injuries, and thus do my rightful duty to Verona's ruler by calming such disturbances to our streets, if I were not pledged to escort this goodly widow to Ca' Cappelletti."

The count, though no older than the brawlers, bears his princely connection with great pride. "I'll guide the widow," he tells Friar Lorenzo, "while you remedy the rest." He unhorses himself, leaving the reins to one of the guard, and offers me his arm. "If it pleases you?"

It pleases me to look upon such a pleasant face. And yet it pleases me not, to be bloodied and stained in his handsome presence.

"May the saints bless you for your benevolence." I lean unsteadily on him, forcing my features not to betray how badly I ache as we walk along the Via Leoni. "Surely Lord Cappelletto—"

"Sure Lord Cappelletto surely is, as I've seen often enough in my uncle's council chamber." He smiles, and despite the pain I do, too. Few there are for me to smirk with, about Lord Cappelletto's pretensions. "You are by blood or by marriage, a Cappelletta?"

That wilts my smile. "Neither," I say. What binds me to Juliet is something I cannot explain. Not to this noble stranger. Even with Juliet herself—we've no words for what we share. "I care for Lord Cappelletto's daughter."

"Is she of an age that requires much care?" He gives a curious glance to my mannish cloak.

"She's a girl for whom none can help but care. Including her devoted kinsman Tybalt, who dotes on her while I am off upon a pressing errand, gifting me his own cloak to do it in."

"A greater kindness it might have been, had he not been so generous."

Savvy this Paris is, discerning what I've not wanted to admit to myself. Tybalt put me into danger by bidding me wear his family crest while the Montecchi seethed to avenge themselves on him.

"You seem to be a man who knows much of kindness." And being a man, like all men happy to be praised. So happy that haply in lapping up my flattering he'll forget whatever he's surmised about me and Tybalt. "We've no feast fit for a count prepared," I say as we turn into the entry to Ca' Cappelletti, "but perchance we can decant some of Lord Cappelletto's finest Carmignano for you."

Before he can answer, Juliet's merry laugh rings from the loggia. "There you are, at last." She hurries down the stairs into the courtyard. "Tybalt and I spent the morning collecting blossoms from our arbor, so I could make you this."

A bright garland, worked with more love than skill, drops to the hard ground when she sees my bloodied face.

"What's happened to you?" She covers me with kisses like a mother cat licking a hurt kit, then issues a curt, "Raise a bucket from the well," ordering the count as if he's one of her family's man-servants. He wordlessly obeys. She does not notice the bemusement dancing on his lips as she undoes the fazzoletto scarved around her neck and dips it into the water he's drawn.

I mark that, and more, as Juliet gently washes me. All the love with which I've fed her, she gladly feeds back to me. She may not have the learned friar's knowledge of medicinals, but her tenderest mercies do me more good than any holyman could.

Paris drops to his knee, gathering up the garland and offering it to Juliet. "She ought to be a-bed. Perhaps I—"

Juliet gives no notice to the kneeling count, keeping her worried eyes on me. "Are you tired, Nurse?"

"I should like to lie down, though to climb the stairs may be much for me," I say, imagining myself carried in the arms of the handsome count and laid beside Juliet in her great bed.

But Juliet, my innocent, asks, "Shall I call for Tybalt?"

The name throbs pain through me. I shake my head, which worsens the hurt, and tell her I can manage without him if I might lean upon her. She wraps her dainty arm around my thick waist and draws my hand across her narrow hip. Wrapped together, we walk like a single lopsided creature up the stone steps, Paris watching until we disappear inside.

Once we're in our chamber, Juliet unclasps my borrowed belt and removes the soiled cloak, then unravels my braids and works her own ivory comb through my hair. Undressing, undoing, freeing what's confined—her tending echoes how I've put her to bed, how many thousand times.

She settles me beneath the bedclothes and pulls wide the window, letting in the fruit-ripe arbor air, before setting beside me. "Am I a good nurse, Nurse?"

"So good that I'm a lucky sufferer."

But the lock upon the tower door turns, and my luck turns with it. Tybalt swings his way into the room. The sight of my swollen features stops him short.

"Stung?" he asks.

"Struck. By some unruly youth who mistook me in your cloak."

"Dishonorable dog." The score along his cheek pulls taut. "I'll pay him what he's due for treating you so."

This is the difference between the warmth of Juliet and the heat of Tybalt, the measure of what each will do believing they do it for me. "And what will he pay you, in return? Or pay me, or Juliet, or anyone of us?"

"It is our honor—" he begins.

"It was her blood." Juliet lays a protective hand against my cheek. "Better saved than spilled, if that's the cost of honor."

"Do not let Lord Cappelletto hear you speak so, Coz."

She draws her hand to her mouth so fast you'd think it burnt. Juliet does not bear harsh words well. Especially when they menace with the threat of harsher still from Lord Cappelletto.

"Cansignorio's nephew knows that I am struck," I say. "If he tells the prince, they'll soon discover it was you who drew the first blade."

"Who'll trust what that pleasure-loving Mercutio says? He's overfond of the Montecchi, and even the prince knows it."

"Overfond of much, Mercutio is." I flash a look toward Juliet, to warn Tybalt not to utter any more in front of her about pleasure-loving Mercutio's debauchery, rumors of which are enough to shock all of Sodom and half Gomorrah. "But it's Paris who happened upon the brawl and brought me home. Let him advise the prince on how to settle it. He seems a fair man."

"Fair to look at," Tybalt says. "Your sight's not harmed, nor is your lus—"

"Truly, my head aches. Juliet, would you call for some aqua vitae to soothe me, and a plate of walnut-candied figs?" I take care to name a delicacy she'll crave along with the drink I want. With a devoted nod, she's off to have both brought.

Once she's gone, I tell Tybalt, "You must watch what you say when Juliet is present."

"What harm can unchaste words do chaste ears?"

I know well how easily unchastity undoes the chaste, especially at such an age. But before I can answer, something in his own words draws Tybalt's attention. "What reply have you from Rosaline?"

Rosaline—when the bees teemed Santa Caterina's breast, I forgot about his message for her. But when I tell Tybalt what I witnessed, he waves off my terror.

"A harmless swarm, flown from a hive that's grown overcrowded because I've not been to collect their comb and honey." He lectures as though I am a thick-witted child. So when he says, "I must gather them into a new hive, and bring the missive to my sister," I do not try to stop him. I'd not realized what risk there was to me in going out wrapped in his cloak, and mayhap he'd not known it either. But if it's danger for him to lurk about Verona, that's his own doing. I'll stay safe inside with Juliet, as I'm meant to be.

As I pass back the letter, he says, "The bees are nothing for you to fear. As for the Montecchi, I'll give them more than even for the hurt they've done to you."

I make no answer as I wait for him to go. And for Juliet to

return with the sweetness of the figs, and the numbing flow of aqua vitae.

Lady Cappelletta'll not bear the sight of me, banishing me from the sala like a thief from the city. What offends her is my swollen nose, though it's the smash to the back of my skull and the boot-blows to my side that more trouble me. How am I to see my own hard-used face? But I cannot help but feel the thudding ache across my head and the groaning pain in my gut—and half a dozen times a day the flashing of that feverish heat, which I might've hoped the beating had knocked out of me.

Still, I have my truest comfort, for Juliet begs leave to tend me. And so we've the days, like our nights, to ourselves.

"How do you feel?" she asks me for the hundredth time.

Like I've had my head bashed in, my body bruised, and my nose broke. But instead I say, "Funny, how sharp my smelling sense has got. I can detect each fruit and flower in the arbor, the way a keen ear perceives the separate notes within a harmony."

"Can smells make a harmony?" she asks. "Is that not a lovely riddle?"

Juliet is lovely, yet no riddle. No convolution or dual meaning in her, still taking delight in such simple games as she and I conceive for ourselves. "Rosemary and roasted veal make a harmony."

"That is taste, not smell."

"Close your eyes," I tell her. "Can you not conjure both? How the sweet-sharp rosemary scents the roasting flesh, perfuming the air around the kitchen in the hours before you sit in the sala and taste how tender and succulent the meat."

The tip of her nose twitches as I talk, her pink tongue peeking from between her lips. I press my tiniest finger to it. Her lids fly open, and she laughs. "Tell me another."

"No." I give her only a single heartbeat of disappointment before adding, "it's your turn to tell me."

"Minted lamb stew?" So tentative, until I nod. Assured of my approval, she catalogues a rush of toothsome dishes as would do the Pope's chef proud. "Pork and ginger pie. Piacentine cheese in fennel sauce. Partridge and pine-seed ravioli. Plum and cardamom tart." Wonder wrinkles her pretty brow. "Must it always be food?"

I bow my brow to hers and slowly tilt my head from one side to the other, as though I'm rolling out a delicate crust. How that simple touch soothes us both. "It may be whatever you wish."

Her eyes rove, landing upon the statue of San Zeno. "Incense and a woolen habit," she says.

"That's Rosaline's harmony, as sure as beeswax and the steel of a Toledo blade is Tybalt's."

"And what is mine?"

"When you were a newly born babe, you smelled like softest down, brazier-warmed swaddling bands, and my milk." No need to speak of what soiled the swaddling, which I was quick enough to clean. "Now you're a rose that's freshly bloomed, a dancer's flush when the tempo's fast, and a spice-and-honey comfit."

She purrs at the first part but frowns at the last. "No more food, Nurse. We agreed to it."

To believe I agree to whatever she demands—she's not so far off in that. "And would you not eat such a comfit, if I offered it?"

She grabs at my sleeves. "Have you been hiding comfits?"

As we make mock battle over imagined candies, heavy footfalls thud their way to the chamber door. Lord Cappelletto calls, "Is my Juliet within?"

"Why not enter," she answers with a laugh, "and find out?"

She's not noticed how the man who once barged in at any hour now stops, always, when he's without to ask if she's within. Or rather, if she's noticed, she's not reckoned why. Lord Cappelletto has no worry that he might open the door to an empty room. His concern is that opening it unannounced, he might see more of his daughter than a decent father deems right, now that the bodices of her gowns grow tight across her chest. Juliet is too pure-hearted to fathom the worry her tenderly budding body could work into Lord Cappelletto—or what else it might work into another man.

If he'll not gather her into his lap as he did in years past, still he's pleased to have her give each of his cheeks a kiss. "Nurse is nearly better," she tells him, "for I've given her good care."

He nods without so much as glancing my way. "Well that you're done with it. Prince Cansignorio gives permission for us to feast Rosaline this Sunday, thanks to a member of his household who made the plea for me." I'd expect resentment to tinge such words, for Lord Cappelletto likes to believe he speaks directly into the prince's ear and needs no one to intercede for him. But I hear something else instead. A glimmering of some hope Lord Cappelletto has for even greater alliance with the Scaligeri.

"You shall wear this for the dinner, and the dancing afterward."
He slips an emerald ringed in gold upon her finger. The stone is as
big as a cherry and as green as the first leaves in spring. "A jewel as
lovely as my Jule."

"How heavy it is," she says.

"You do not think it too archaic, I hope."

She smiles reassurance at him. "An old style, but a pretty one.
Was it my mother's?"

"No. It was—" He draws a short breath. "It was Juliet's."

"Another lovely riddle, that a ring can always have been mine
though I've never before seen it."

I'd not let out the answer to that riddle. Not let on what I think
of how he means to spoil her by gifting her his dead wife's rings.

"The color will shine against my zetani sleeves." Juliet twists the
ring one way, then the other, as though screwing some unvoiced
doubt into its place. "Although the pale hue of my gown'll not show
it nearly as well."

"Why not have a whole dress of the zetani, then?" Lord Cappelletto's no wiser than a fly, carried by carefree wings into the silken
tangle of her carefully stretched web.

But I'm the one who'll be mope-eyed from working silken strands
to finish a new dress by Sunday. "We've no time to sew a gown," I say.

"I can buy time," Lord Cappelletto says. "A dozen sempstresses'
time, if Juliet requires it."

Juliet takes her eyes from the ring to beam at me. But she
raises a hand to her own nose at the reminder of my bruised face.
"May we make it a masked ball? I might be the summer sky, in an

azure gown—and my lord father bedecked in gold could be the shining sun."

She means to find a way for me to hide my face so I might join the feast. And she knows to make best case with Lord Cappelletto by letting him believe she thinks only of what ought delight him.

"Have you forgot we fête to honor Rosaline's consecration of her vows?" he asks.

"Rosaline might mask herself as virtue," I say.

"Or a saint," suggests Juliet. "Would it not honor her order for her to dress as Santa Caterina?"

"No." I answer too fast, my chest prickling with the memory of the teeming bees. "Lord Cappelletto is right." I bow my head as though begging his pardon. "Rosaline must come only as her pious self, whatever mask and costume anyone else might wear."

To be told he is right is enough for Lord Cappelletto. He does not mark how Juliet and I've bested him into consenting to a masquerade, as he nods assent.

I suppose there is some convolution to Juliet after all, though I'm the only one who discerns it. And with that same discernment, I espy the swirl of carmine in the courtyard in the days that follow, as Paris visits Lord Cappelletto's study.

I say naught of it to Juliet. Not yet. Handsome as he is, a meet match for my girl, I savor our last however long it will be, when she and I alone share such a love, a heart, a bed as we've enjoyed these near to fourteen years.

The household boils over with servants, the loutish staff familiars lording themselves over the score who're hired on just for the days of frenzied preparations. Wine barrels are thumped up the stairs to edge the sala, plate burnished till it shines, unlighted torches positioned ready to be blazed. I've never gained a liking for the cook, who begrudges every bite I've eaten in all my years within Ca' Cappelletti, and it pleases me to hear how he bellows at all hours for some inept hireling or other to fetch obscure ingredients, his kitchen fires smoking long into the night.

Even Juliet grows burdened before the week is done. Eager though she is to feel the swish of the zetani as it drips in long folds to the floor, she struggles through the hours spent holding herself statue-still as the city's finest sempstresses huddle close around her, their hurried needles flashing.

I sit nearby, my back to them to keep my bruised face hidden as I work my own needle, securing jeweled birds and enameled stars and every sky-born wonder onto the headdress that will crown Juliet come Sunday night. Lady Cappelletta twins my task, adorning the ocean-green samite that will be her headdress with mermaids and dolphins and mysterious creatures of the sea. Her gown is of the same fabric, the thick gold ribboned into the cloth shimmering like sunlight beaming upon watery waves. It's the dress she wore to Prince Cansignorio's wedding banquet more than a decade past, seamed narrower now than it was then, when her belly swelled with one of her many ill-fated pregnancies.

The dress cost so dear, I'd have thought it'd have to be the Pope's wedding banquet before Lord Cappelletto let her don it again. But for this feast he spares nothing, showing off every connection he can to the Scaligeri. Flower-entwined ladders to match their crest are set against the courtyard walls, the banqueting table festooned with marzipanned dogs like those on the Scaligeri livery, each wearing a Cappelletti cap of jellied quince. The morning before the fête, he rouses Lady Cappelletta from their broad bed before the terce bells ring, insisting she accompany him to Mass at Santa Maria Antica so they can see the Holy Sacrament raised up by the Scaligeri's priest's own hand.

He'd have Juliet along as well, but if Paris is what I suppose, there'll be time enough in years to come for her to kneel and open her mouth for regal communion. I bid her feign the heavy breath of sleep while I plead for Lord Cappelletto to let her lie in bed a while longer. "She's overworn from standing so many hours," I say. "She must rest, to look her best tonight."

This brings an indulgent nod from Lord Cappelletto, and an envious glare from Lady Cappelletta, who must wish she'd been as clever in making the case to stay a-bed herself.

But once they're gone, Juliet'll not fall again to slumber, nor let me. "How can you sleep on such a day as this promises to be?"

"Like this," I say, closing my eyes and gaping my mouth. I throw a clumsy arm atop her and make great mocking snores.

She laughs but wriggles free, waving aside my urging for another hour's doze. "Do you not recall what it is to be young, and eager for a ball to start?"

"We had no balls when I was young."

She gives one of my grayed locks a gentle tug. "Were you born in days so ancient, they'd not yet invented feasting, and dancing, and masquerades?"

"There were feasts and dances and masquerades, but not for those so poor as I was."

"Honey nurse." Her voice is thick with pity. As though to not don a fine gown was the worst suffering there was to my girlhood. "What did you have instead?"

I've always been careful not to speak to her of men like my father. What does such a pretty, petted child need know of cruelty? Instead I spin a tale of my first spring with Pietro. He still carried his hunter's bow, and we wandered together by day, and by night slept beneath the open sky. What more music did we need than his voice joining mine in song, what dancing beyond the hot rhythm of his hips against my own?

"But did you not want for company?" she asks.

"If I did, I'd fashion tiny cups of acorn caps and hazelnuts, and we'd have marmot, squirrel, and black-grouse to dine."

"Did you, truly?" The hints of woman in her melt away into a girl's delight. As though she's still of such an age to believe in enchanted beasts.

I lay a solemn hand to my heart. "Pietro and I had marmot, and squirrel, and black-grouse, and we dined." When I drop my hand and smile, she sees the joke, and we laugh at how easily I've pranked her. But before the girlish part of her fades away again, I ask, "What do you remember, of Pietro?"

"I remember a room, where I would play upon the floor. There was a man there, taller than my father, who always kept a sack of sweets. He'd come here, too. You were happy when he was here, but he was happier when you were there. How do I know that, who was happy where, when it all seems more like a dream than some true thing? If I try to conjure the man's face, it's only Friar Lorenzo's features that I see."

"Your memory plays tricks on you. Often we'd visit them both in a single day, but there's not much of Pietro in Friar Lorenzo." Yet much of him in you.

I dare not tell her that. Not yet. Such privity it would be, and thus better kept until her future is secured, and neither she nor I must rely upon the Cappelletti.

"Sometimes what I think I remember of Pietro seems only what I've heard told by you, or Tybalt." The name douses me like a hard rain, and she marks it. "Are you still cross with my cousin?"

Tybalt's held himself from us all week, haunting the world beyond the Cappelletti walls. By my troth, though it's been hard on her, I've not minded. He makes the injury done me solely what serves him—as though my bruised body is measured only by the insult to his honor. I know it's what he's learned during all the years he's listened to Lord Cappelletto cataloguing ancient slights. But there's deeper hurt in Tybalt treating me so than came from all the blows and kicks the brawlers gave me.

Perhaps I've been too soft with him these long years, believing the mother-love for my lost sons might find and fill in him the longing for his own lost mother. But all that soft has made him hard, and harsh, and ever more hot-headed. What love he's got from me and Juliet, and even Lady Cappelletta, has kept him from seeking what young men ought: the kind of love that might quell raging youth into courting, and settling to marriage.

"He's like a horse too long unbroke," I say, "that now'll not be bridled, and would throw off any who try to ride him." My pun's too bawdy for Juliet to ken it, so I offer a more sober answer. "I'm cross with how Tybalt crosses—"

Bloodthirsty shouts cut me off. The sound of metal clashing metal echoes along the Via Cappello.

"Bend your knee, and clasp your hands." I nod toward the Madonna as the alarm is rung. "Pray to the Holy Mother to keep the parish safe."

My own knees bend, though only enough to carry me from the bedchamber into the sala. The common servants have already shucked their labors and got their heads stuck out the windows to get the better view. As I jostle my way among them, calls for clubs, hook-bladed bills, and spears rise from the street. A crowd is gathering below, accursing first against the Cappelletti, then at the Montecchi, for sparking the violence. On either side of me, servants cheer and jeer by turns, as though donning Cappelletti livery has made them take their master's fight as their very own.

Blasts sound from unseen trumpets. Where the Via Cappello broadens into the Piazza delle Erbe, there's a flash of carmine. The crash of fighting ceases, and Prince Cansignorio's voice reverberates against the buildings, though by the time his words reach Ca' Cappelletti, they're too obscured for us to understand.

"Nurse? Are we safe?" Juliet has crept unseen into the sala. When I turn from the window to answer her, the servants surrounding me turn too, elbowing each other and whispering at the sight of Juliet still in her nightdress, no cap on her head and her hair yet held in plaits.

"We are as we were," I say. "Safe within the walls of Ca' Cappelletti."

"And my lord father, and my—"

"Safer still, within church walls." I hie to answer, to hide the truth: the fighting may well have caught Lord and Lady Cappelletti as they passed through the Piazza delle Erbe. Would Lord Cappelletto call for a long-sword to join the fray? Or tremble and cower behind his wife? Either way, surely he and she remain unharmed. Whatever sparked was fast extinguished, and the alarm that tolled was not followed by any death knells. I take Juliet's hand. "Come, we've much to do before tonight."

I guide her back into our chamber, where we braid my hair and unbraid hers, arranging mine as I always have, and hers to hold new fullness around her face. "Is it not dull, to ever wear your hair the same way?" she asks, tying a length of morello velvet to the tails of the two long braids that hang upon my back.

"Saints, widows, and happily wedded matrons all plait their hair," I say, though at nearly thirty Lady Cappelletta still wears her hair as a well-born maiden does, most locks loose, strung through with pearls and precious beads. That's her vanity, and her husband's, too. Although she's not as just-plucked fresh as when I first came, still there are few faces so fair in all Verona, an artly work kept framed by flowing tresses and the jeweled Cappelletti cap. As though beauty might be mistook for happiness. "When you're wived to a worthy man, you'll want no more fashion than to keep him faithful."

"Wived?" She pulls at my shoulder, turning me to face that face so like the one to which I was once wived.

"To a worthy man," I repeat. "Like Pietro." My heart quickens. For all the times I've spoke of my lost husband to her, I've never till now breathed to her the thought of the husband who'll be hers.

Her heart must ever match my own, for it raises a flush into her cheeks. "And where would I find such a worthy man? Shall I climb mountains and ford rivers and seek out unknown kingdoms, as would-be lovers do?"

"I've sung you too many fanciful troubadour songs, if you believe that's what real lovers do." What can I say, to ready her for what I suppose Paris will propose? For ready she must be to answer right, and too undesigning is she to imagine it herself. And yet, dare I speak of him, if I do not know his heart? But then, what heart would not want Juliet?

I'll not speak the name, and raise her hopes, before he plights his troth. I draw her hand in mine, tracing my pinkie along her palm like some sooth-telling Egyptian. "There is one nobly born, pleasing of features and true of heart, who'll see in you, and be to you, such spouse as any would be glad to get."

She giggles, flushing deeper. "You tickle me."

"And yet you've not drawn your hand away." I kiss her palm, fold her fingers to hold the kiss in place, and lay that hand between my breasts. "You've had my heart for your whole life, and soon, I promise, you'll have another. Do not forget mine, when you find his."

"I'll not. I cannot." She flutters open her fist, her fingers trembling as she presses the kissed palm against me. "Will you not come with me, when I am married?" She bows her head, unsure. "If such a thing really is to be."

"It is to be, though whether in this season or in one to come, I cannot say. You're too sweet a fruit to go unpicked." I give her cheek a gentle pinch. "And near enough to being ripe, you must be ready for it. But worry not, I'll go with you. Always and wherever." My talk of fruit sets my stomach grumbling. "We ought eat now."

"Eat now? When there's such a feast to be served in a few hours?"

This is how artless my girl is, that she would think she might eat her fill while she sits before the honored company, rather than pushing her portion around her plate without lifting a bite, to show herself dainty. I am a woman of many appetites and never connived like that myself, denying one fleshly pleasure in the hopes of garnering another. But I've watched Lady Cappelletta and the Cappelletti's noblish guests long enough to know what's expected at a so-called feast. "There's still much I must teach you," I tell Juliet, and bid her call the serving-maid to fetch from the cook a sampling so we can taste now what she'll not swallow later.

THIRTEEN

urse. Nurse."

The urgent cry wakes me confused. In my dream, nurse I did. I was a six-teated creature, and each fed a mouth of ferocious hunger. An agony of pleasure, to feel those tugs upon my willing dugs. Until a seventh mouth opened onto me. Finding no nipple, it sucked against my very flesh. Sucked more than milk, for milk gives life, and this took life from me until I'd nothing left to give the other six, nothing left even to save myself. The pleasure turned to searing pain. A burn upon my skin that blazed to roast the very heart of me.

"*Nurse.*" Lady Cappelletta is as insistent as whatever tormented my sleep. As I rise to go to her, the twinned faces of comedy and tragedy fall from my lap to the floor. It's the mask Juliet and I made to hide my marred face at the masquerade. I'd bade her find a stick we might attach to it, so I could fan it back and forth when the sudden heat flushes over me. She went, and I waited, and in the afternoon's great warmth I dozed just long enough to dream. And to wake to this shrieking.

I hurry from our chamber through the sala and the antecamera to Lady Cappelletta, who greets me with, "Where's my daughter? Call her forth to me."

She might well have called Juliet herself, as summoned me to summon her. But Lady Cappelletta likes having someone to do what she wills.

I trudge out, calling, "Juliet, my lamb, I bid you come." But my dear lamb is like a ladybird, flitting about. My talk of courtship has given wing to her heart, and sent her fluttering to some corner of Ca' Cappelletti. "Juliet? Juliet?"

By my lost maidenhead, I grow red repeating her name until, simple as you please, she steps out from behind the heavy curtain that hangs across the entry to Tybalt's rooms. "How now? Who calls?"

"Your mother," I say. As if in this moment when she stands celestial in that zeitani, Juliet might hear me claim her as my own. But remembering the impatience in Lady Cappelletta's voice, I shake the thought from my head and follow wordless as Juliet presents herself in the antecamera to the Cappelletti's bedchamber. "Madam, I am here. What is your will?"

Lady Cappelletta smiles. Not approvingly, as loving mothers do, but disapprovingly. One of Juliet's sleeves has come loose. Her coral necklace is askew. There is a golden blush of pollen midway down her skirt. Lady Cappelletta takes silent stock of all these flaws.

I step between them. With a single swift motion, I hitch sleeve, straighten necklace, and sweep skirt clean.

Lady Cappelletta frowns at my now-yellowed hand, frowns deeper when the emerald upon Juliet's finger catches her eye. "Nurse, give leave awhile. We must talk in secret."

Secret shoots a jolt through me. What secret can she have to share if not the one I've guessed already, which Lord Cappelletto must have bade her convey to Juliet?

I ought to turn and go. Let Lady Cappelletta tell what I anticipated. I'll hear it soon enough. Juliet holds no secrets from her beloved bedmate. But it will be a long night, a lot of wine. Many guests, and jests. Hours of dancing, though I've too many corns upon my feet to join in. The house will be so thick with merriment, there'll be no time between now and dawn for me to draw Juliet aside, draw out from her what Lady Cappelletta means to share in confidence. If I'm to be of use to my girl on this auspicious night, I must know now.

I wait in the doorway like a flipped card hanging in the air before it chooses which way to flutter and fall, while Juliet pouts at Lady Cappelletta.

Lady Cappelletta'll not suffer anyone's pouting but her own. She looks as if she might order me to close Juliet up in our chamber for trying her. But she'll not. Not with the evening's esteemed guests nearly to the door, where they'll expect to find Lord Cappelletto's family turned out to welcome them.

She waves her thin wrist as though she's just remembered something. Which perhaps she has: remembered that if I'm gone and she says something that fills Juliet with grief or fear or over-joyed exuberance, she'd have to be the one to soothe her. And Lady Cappelletta is too well-primped, too eager to make her own way to the sala, to risk that. "Nurse, come back and hear our counsel."

All ears I am to hear it, but still she pretends there's some rea-son of her own she's kept me here. "You know my daughter's of a pretty age," she says. A pretty way for her to put it, when I know Juliet's age to the hour. By my few remaining teeth, I know it better than I know my own. "She's not fourteen."

"She's not fourteen," I say, as though Lady Cappelletta has not just said it. But I say it looking at Juliet, while Lady Cappelletta spoke looking at her own reflection in the well-polished silver tray that hangs upon the wall. As if to be assured she's not long past such years herself. "How long is it now to Lammastide?" I ask, though Juliet and I both know. We count the days each night, be-fore we fall to sleep.

"A fortnight and odd days." Lady Cappelletta does not keep the same exacting tally as we do.

"Even or odd, of all days in the year, come Lammas Eve at night, she'll be fourteen." To the day, to the hour, I know it. Those days and hours that I'll not forget. They make me tell what once was my dearest truth, which I hold even dearer now that I know it for a lie. "Susanna and she—God rest all Christian souls—were of an age. Susanna is with God. She was too good for me." As though Juliet is not too good for Lady Cappelletta.

"Eleven years it is," I say, "since the ground quaked, the day that she was weaned." As if the earth rended itself out of grief at seeing

Juliet put off my breast. "She could run and waddle all about, and fell, and broke her brow."

Juliet has ever loved to hear my stories of when she was her littlest, so I tell the tale of that day. I do bear a brain for memories, and a tongue as well that loves to speak, and on I prate until Lady Cappelletta stamps a foot and says, "Enough of this. I pray you, hold your peace."

What I hold is not my peace but a pretty piece of Juliet's past, and I'm so keen to share it, I tell yet more of when she was a toddling thing, a falling girl, and Pietro saged how she one day would be a woman and fall as women do, for a man.

This brings a flush to Juliet, turning her face bright against the azure of her gown, like the reddened sun dawning into fresh sky. When I talked to her this morning of falling for a man, she hung eager on each word. But that was done between the two of us. Now, before Lady Cappelletta, she waves my words away. Dark eyes pleading above those blushing cheeks, she says, "Stint, I pray you, Nurse."

Pray I do, with all my soul. "God mark you to His grace, you were the prettiest babe that ever I nursed," I say, adding with great care to catch Lady Cappelletta's ear, "If I might live to see you married once, I have my wish."

My wish, and my felicity. We'll make a handsome household with Count Paris. And soon enough there'll be babes of my dear babe that, if I cannot suckle, I can at least succor, and raise. A lasting part of my Pietro, and a joy of my old age.

"Marry," says Lady Cappelletta, taking to my hint like a shad swimming for some worm wriggled on a hook, "is the very theme I care to talk of. Tell me, daughter Juliet, how stands your disposition to be married?"

She only calls Juliet *daughter* when there is some especial reason playing mother suits her, some praise or prize to seize herself. But Juliet slides her eyes to me and watches for my careful nod before she answers. "It is an honor that I dream not of."

True enough. Too giddy a girl to sleep this day, and why should she save only for a dream what I've told her will be waking true? "An honor," I repeat, with a wink to her. "Were I not your only nurse, I'd say you'd sucked wisdom from the teat."

Lady Cappelletta smooths the seagreen samite over her own never-tasted breasts, reminds us how often ladies of esteem younger than Juliet are already made mothers. Recalls that she herself was delivered of a babe when she was not much older. And for once says the very words I hope to hear. "The valiant Paris seeks you for his love."

"A man, young lady." This is what I say? At such a moment, to sound such a thick-witted fool. But why not be a joyous fool, to know my Juliet'll have so fine a match? Count Paris may not carry the spice-and-honey scent of my Pietro, but surely he can be something near to what my bee-sotted husband harvested. "Lady, such a man as all the world. Why, he's a man of wax."

My wax Lady Cappelletta must immediately outdo. "Verona's summer has not such a flower," she says.

A flower handsomer by far than the old shrub to which she's wed. Mayhap that is her part in this, for I'd not expect her to delight in being made a grandame, and have all Verona reminded she's no longer any summer flower herself. But to gather such a flower to her by marrying Juliet to him—

"Nay, he's a flower," I say, to pluck what's budding from Lady Cappelletta. "In faith, a very flower." I rub one pollened hand against the other, and think of all that the bees take from such lovely flowers, to make the delicious drip of honey that Juliet so loves.

But Lady Cappelletta is done with flowery talk, and makes a bookish speech to Juliet, about pens and lines and what is writ along the margins of some dull tome or other. Books? Who cares what lays between the covers of a book? What matters is what lays between the covers of a bed. To remind them both of this, I place a loving hand upon Juliet's taut belly, as if to warm her womb to what it will receive, and say, "Women grow by men."

I might add that first men grow by women, for it's time Juliet was taught how to play a pricksong so more than music swells. But better to save such talk for when we are far from Lady Cappelletta, who has no ear, no taste, for bedroom harmonies. My Juliet shall learn from me the lessons that I learned laying with Pietro, and know what pleasures a warm-humored wife can take, and give, within a marriage bed.

Footsteps sound from the compound's entryway—not just the scuttering of servants but the first of the guests already arrived. "Speak briefly," Lady Cappelletta says, "can you like of Paris's love?"

Now her eyes, like mine, are on Juliet. I cannot say what Lady Cappelletta sees, but I see in this one moment all Juliet's life. And all of mine. I see summation of all my joy, comfort for all my sorrows. I remember what it was to be such a creature, and have that

ram of a Pietro come tupping upon me. I want such years of pleasure for her. But I see too that she is still a tender lambkin, not sure
even how to answer without first taking private counsel with me.

"I'll look to like, if looking liking move." She pauses, choosing
her words with care. "But no more deep will I endart my eye, than
your consent gives strength to make it fly."

A clever rhyme, and I reward it with another wink, to show
she's a good girl for saying it so. Let Lady Cappelletta believe it's
her consent, and her lord husband's, Juliet speaks of. My girl and I
both know what we together can make fly.

But what flies now is one of the newly hired serving-men. He's
not been here a week, but already he's as indolent and insolent
as any who've ever served within Ca' Cappelletti. Rushing in, he
treads hard upon my foot before making a bootlicker's bow to Lady
Cappelletta. "Madam, the guests are come, supper served up, you
called, my young lady asked for." He slides his slithery eyes over Juliet. I'd have him out for that, but, catching my glare, he adds, "The
nurse cursed in the pantry, and every thing in extremity."

Cursed—hearing that, I might name an extremity into which I'd
put, if not everything, at least the serving-man and pantry-maid and
any others who dare try tell me what's my place. I've seen dozens
like this one come and go in the nearly fourteen years I've been
here. I'll outlast him and his impertinence. Or if I'll not, it'll only
be because I'll go with Juliet when she's wed to Count Paris and
become mistress of her own house.

"I must hence to wait," the servant says, as though he means to
wait table, when by my holidame, I suspect what the wastrel waits

is only a chance to pinch some cups, and some choice meats, and the pantry-maid as well. "I beseech you follow straight."

"We'll follow." Lady Cappelletta barely gives curt nod to dismiss him, before shooting one last judging squint at my dear girl. "Juliet, the count awaits."

As soon as Lady Cappelletta passes out of the room, I grab Juliet about the waist and swing her round. Nose to nose, like a mama cat admiring her kitten's whiskers, I say, "Go, girl, seek happy nights to happy days."

The cook's plucked a half dozen peacocks, stuffed them with fried oysters and spiced oranges, roasted all in belly lard, laid each upon a silver platter, and arranged the feathers back upon them. When they're served, the forty guests who've come to dine stamp their feet in delight. Iridescent feathers shimmer as knives thrust and carve the birds.

All through the sala, young men make great show of sucking meat from quills and offering them as adornment to the loveliest ladies. Tybalt did as much for me, years past. A pretty bit of flattery to an old woman. But tonight he sits somber beside the sister whose features are so like his own, except that while his are edged with truculence, hers sit prim enough they might still every wavering feather. Rosaline wears a dun-colored habit, the crucifix about her neck as big as an assassin's dagger. Though Lord Cappelletto and the other revelers raise goblet after goblet to drink her health, not a sip passes her pure lips.

I might pity the poor girl, who'll never know the delights Juliet is to find in Paris's bed. But what Rosaline cannot know, she'll not miss. She bows her head and crosses herself, over and over through the dinner, shocked at the company's indulgences. The goodly nun eats only lettuce dressed with lemon, followed by a handful of fresh grapes. Nibbling like a rabbit among hounds until she can bear no more, when she leans and whispers to Tybalt, who rises and leads her from the room.

The rest of the company makes up for her restraint. Having had our fill of peacock, we're served the flakiest of focaccia, the pastry filled with egg-basted turtledove. Next comes fig-peckers braised with four kinds of olives, then pheasants covered with fried squid, followed by veal mortadella simmered in fava beans and mint. Lord Cappelletto flouts the sumptuary law, keeping keen eye to make sure the trencher nearest Prince Cansignorio's nephew is always the first filled.

Though Juliet sits across from Count Paris, she does not raise her gaze to his, the shyness natural to her age ripening to coyness by my morning's tutelage. She tilts her head to mine, feeding me from her trencher with her own hand, like I'm her pet. Hiding my bruises behind my broad palm, I eat all that she demurs, waving off only the boar's head covered in pomegranate. Too toothless at my age to burst the rosy seeds and taste the succulence inside, I've Juliet to savor what I no longer can. I bid her nibble upon those pretty seeds as we gossip like old women and giggle like young girls, ahum with our wooing news.

When the rose water is brought in finger bowls, I fuss over Juliet, carefully turning my own ill-used face from the company while I dab at her mouth and work the silver-and-ivory pick I wear about my neck to clean her teeth. She's too grown to need such tending, but it occupies me while the lesser servants clear away the plate and push aside the tables. The diners don their masks, and I raise mine. More guests arrive already in their costumes. Lord Cappelletto drones a pompous speech about the days when he wore a merrymaker's visor, though his bulbous nose is so frightfully large it's impossible to imagine the mask that could've covered such a thing. "Thirty years, since I last danced," he says, raising an uncertain eyebrow to some other shrivelled codger, "or only some five-and-twenty?"

Who cares which it was, I wish to say, impatient for him to give lute and pipe leave to play so Juliet may prance to her finer future.

Wax or flower, whichever Paris is, he shades easily among the masked revelers. Not so his cousin Mercutio, for not by his face alone has that debaucher made himself known around Verona. Mercutio wears his doublet so short, it shows every whorl and flourish upon his gilded codpiece. He's a nearer relation to the prince than Paris is, which may prove perilous. Rumors swirl through the city of how Cansignorio plots to have his bastard sons rule after him, and all Verona knows how Cansignorio disposes of relations he deems rivals. Although it's hard to imagine lascivious Mercutio taking any interest in the throne—unless perhaps there were a shapely maiden or two seated stark-naked upon it.

The summer night grows dark, and the house is thick with torchsmoke. I try to keep sight of Juliet among the dancers, but the rings and chains move quick, and my old eyes weary with peering through my mask-holes. Searching for a place to sit, I spy Tybalt at the edge of the hall, sliding his sword in and out of its scabbard.

"Freshly stained?" I ask, nodding at his blade.

"I drew during this morning's fray, but had no time to drive my hate home before the prince's guard came calling peace." Disappointment smolders along his face, as it did when he was but a boy, longing for his far-off father's company.

"Did I not tell you I'd no desire for your vengeance?"

"I heed you, Nurse, as I try to heed my uncle. But neither you nor he can dissuade me, when it's my sister I defend."

"Rosaline?" What sort of brute would attack a nun? "Was she—" I search for the word, imagining the folds of her habit hiding such bruises as I bear. "Is Rosaline unwell?"

"She is well." The words bring no softening to what pinches hard in him. "Too well, too fair, too wise, wisely too fair. She's caught the eye of a certain cursèd rakehell who woos and woos, and will not hear her *no*."

This must have been what he wrote so secretly of in his letter, why he was so impatient for her reply. The wall around the vineyard of Santa Caterina is low enough for a lusty man to climb. And many a girl or woman who's shut up in a convent for want of a proper dowry would be glad for a clandestine suitor. But not pious Rosaline. She'd not be hit by Cupid's own enchanted arrow.

"What harm can unchaste words do chaste ears?" I repeat what fell from Tybalt's own mouth, in hope it'll cool his too easy temper.

But Tybalt's like an iron held so long in the fire it glows of its own accord. "The scoundrel haunts the convent. Offers gold enough to seduce a saint, in hopes Rosaline'll ope her lap to him. To know some fiend plots to use my sister so—"

"Is only to know what moves a man." Pietro, I miss you now anew, for surely you might better speak to Tybalt of what I know he needs. Might bend his ear with more merry tales than Lord Cappelletto's droning on of family honor. Might convince him to seek a more pleasurable thrusting than what men do with swords. "It's time you thought of such pursuits yourself. Not to cast your eyes upon one pledged to chastity, but to set your heart on some hartless hind." I conjure all the love I've ever felt for Tybalt. "You've an affectionate nature. Why not make an honorable suit, and take a bride?"

"It's not for me to take, but to be given. My uncle will arrange a wife for his heir such as suits him, when he deems the time is right. I'll have naught to say about it, except to mutter the church vows when I'm told I must. What joy is there in that?"

I search across the sala, hoping to catch sight of Paris empalmed with Juliet. Though the dancers are a blur, my own palm quakes with the thrill of imagining their hands joined. "Lord Cappelletto can arrange a winsome match," I say. "If you but speak to him—"

"I've tried to speak my part, endeavoring to tell him that this villain who would seduce my sister has dared come here enmasked to find her. And am told, *be patient,* and *take no note of him,* and *he shall be endured.* Am told I must keep the peace within Ca' Cappelletti, even with one not worthy to be granted it." He draws sword and strikes, his well-handled blade slicing a single blood-red thread from a nearby tapestry. "I'm the one who's always told to guard our honor, yet when I try am called by my own uncle a *goodman boy,* a *saucy boy,* and a *princox.*"

"Your uncle says many things that would better go unuttered, and are best unheeded." I stoop and pluck up the silken strand, looping it to form a bright bud I nestle between my breasts. But I cannot raise even the smallest smile from Tybalt. "You are a good man, and no boy. Saucy at times, but who does not prefer a sauced meat to a dry one? As proud a cock as any prince, but no princox."

Nothing I say soothes what rages in his eyes, or loosens the tight grasp on his hilt. Hoping wine will do what words will not, I go to find him a full goblet, and myself one as well. But before I can make my way back to him, I hear, "*Nurse, Nurse,*" shrilled in that voice I'm suffered to obey. I empty both goblets in swift gulps, stash them on a window's sill, and turn to present myself to Lady Cappelletta.

I'm flushed with the wine, but she's flushed with something else, the samite pulling low upon her bosom as she leans close to Paris. "Nurse, I crave—" Paris arches an eyebrow at the word, which makes her flush more—"a word, I crave a word with Juliet. Fetch her here."

Fetch, like I'm a hound and Juliet some slobbered-upon bone. But I nod and curtsy. Let Paris see Lady Cappelletta for what she is, and see me as a worthy part of Juliet's dowry. Juliet, who I find not among the dancers but, after seeking everywhere, discover in an alcove speaking to one of the masked guests, a thin and tallish fellow. "Pilgrim," I hear, and "prayer," and "book." Can my Juliet be so simple-hearted, wasting an evening's revels in such dull talk? Duller even than what Lady Cappelletta might have to say.

"Madam." I speak boldly, for surely Juliet'll be glad to be called away from such as this. "Your mother craves a word with you."

Hearing me, and realizing she's been overheard, Juliet flitters like a pale moth and is gone.

"What is her mother?" the fellow asks, his callow voice an odd match to his well-jeweled mask.

What is her mother? I might count all heaven's stars before I could count the ways I can answer that. "Marry, bachelor," I say. If he's a clever man, he'll know what I say next is as untrue as a married bachelor would be. "Her mother is the lady of the house, and a good lady, and a wise and virtuous one."

Though he's not so handsome above as Paris, nor so well-formed below as Mercutio, still he has a boyish pretty mouth below his mask, and a pair of shapely arms. I press myself close upon those arms and say, "I nursed her that you talked withal." And nursed enough wine tonight to take this stranger into my confidence. "I tell you, he that can lay hold of her shall have the chinks." Chinks of the precious dowry coins Lord Cappelletto will gift Paris, whole cassoni of which could be worth no more than her treasured maidenhead. With that bit of bawd, off I go after Juliet.

But the wine pounds in my head more steadily than my feet pound upon the floor. I'm whirled this way and that among the press of people, until Lord Cappelletto orders the musicians done and the stairway torches lit. I find my lambkin standing to the side, watching the departing guests. She pulls me near to ask who this one is, and that, just as she's done since she was a girl of six, wide-eyed at all the finery worn to a fête.

When she points to the pretty-mouthed one, I tell her I know not his name. My knowing not is not enough, and off she sends me to find out. But this guest I ask does not know, and neither does that. And so I go on inquiring, until I feel a grope upon my rump, and turning quick collide into Mercutio, who laughs and tells me the pretty-mouthed youth is called Romeo.

The name means naught to me. "What Romeo?"

"Romeo Montecche."

Such a rascal is this Mercutio, to prank me with false words. I parry back, "What man is mad enough to bring a Montecche here?"

Mercutio roars open-mouthed, and says he is the man, and if a saucy maid will call him mad, she'll get what she deserves. With that he swats my bottom, sending me stumbling. When I right myself I keep on my way until I'm back beside Juliet.

"His name is Romeo, and a Montecche." All Lord Cappelletto's bitter railing about the ill-blood between their families ought to make the name Montecche familiar to her. But her startled eyes fill with such confusion, I add, "son of your great enemy." I take care to whisper, for if Tybalt hears a Montecche's here, and him already in such angry spirits—

But when I look about for Tybalt, he's nowhere in the room. How long is it since I had sight of him? He might be lying in wait outside for the would-be seducer. If he sees instead a Montecche passing from his uncle's house, Tybalt'll follow him into some dark corner of the city to lay sword to him. Or not to him, but them, for Romeo leaves with Mercutio and half a dozen of the other maskers. Tybalt is hot enough to try them all. Which worries me so much I only half hear Juliet reciting some verse twining hate and late, and love and enmity.

I cup a hand to my ear. "What's this? What's this?"

Even in this near-extinguished light, I feel the warmth of her blush as she answers. "A rhyme I learned of one I danced withal."

A pretty bit of poesy from Paris, it must be. I'm impatient to have her tell it to me, that I might know what count to take of the count who courts her. But before I can bid her repeat it, Lord Cappelletto calls, "Juliet."

"Anon, anon," I answer, for I'll not make her face him alone.

We find him misty-eyed and musty-breathed, speaking of fathers and daughters and the honor it will be to unite his house with the Scaligeri. Hearing him, Juliet goes green as a spinached egg. Only my quick catch keeps her from fainting to the floor. "It's late," I say, "and the torches make for close air on such a hot night." With no more by-your-leave than that, I steer my girl away to our bedchamber.

"What've you had to drink?" I ask, when we're shut up alone.

"Naught but water. Like Rosaline."

Naught to drink, nor to eat. Weak she must be. I take my leave and hie to the kitchen, snatch from the voracious serving-man the most delicate remaining morsels, and tuck a vessel near-full of wine beneath my arm. Laden, I return to find the chamber door pulled fast to me. I call once, twice, and a third time, worrying that she's fainted. But, ear to the door, I'd swear I hear her speak, answered by a second voice sounding farther off. Tybalt, perhaps, climbed up to her window as he did so many times in childhood. Could he have found a heart for such frolicking tonight? If any could call him to it, it would be Juliet. Her bounty is as boundless as the sea, her love as deep—

Paris's wooing must be catching, for my thoughts to weave into such lovers' verse. "Juliet," I call once more, arms aching from all I carry.

The door flies open. Juliet's no longer the pale moth, nor the Florentine's greened egg. She's pinked, and pleased, and pulls me inside, and shuts the door behind me, and waves away all I've brought. Steals a look toward the moon-lighted window and asks, "Nurse, what hour is it?"

The answer throbs from my sore head to my swelled feet, paining every part in between. "So late of night, it's better called early on the morrow."

She fills a silver goblet with rubied wine, and passes it to me. "Will it be long till the hour of nine?"

I mark the pearly tooth she works into her lip, and know there's more tolling than the city's bells. Perhaps it was another man's voice I heard without, a more smitten heart than Tybalt's calling as she stood in the window as shining fair as the East's own sun. "The lauds are already rung. Next will be the prime, and after those the terce, that ring the hour of nine. Are you so well wooed, and your heart so fully won, that you forget such simple things?"

The question makes her laugh, and cry, and throw her arms around me. So furiously am I hugged, the goblet drops, splashing wine across us both. My morello hides it well enough, but the beautiful zetani's ruined.

I tut at her. "Lovestruck though he is, if he saw you now—"

I only mean to tease, but Juliet digs sharp nails into me. "What do you mean? Will he not be true, when he sees me for what I am?"

"What you are is good and goodness." I rock her in my arms, like I did when she was but a babe. "Have no worries, you've won his whole heart. If it's already early on the morrow, then by my saints, this will be the day that you are trothed to Paris."

"Paris?" The name falls like a curse from her mouth.

"Juliet, did he not please you? You dance, and trade rhymes, and hurry night into morning so you may see him anon." I meant to teach her art enough to earn a noble match. But not so much as to tease and toy, and risk losing what any girl ought be glad to get. "His love's declared, so you may trust it. If you care for him, be plain about it. Elsewise, you are unfair to Paris."

"Would that I were unfair to Paris. What do I care if he finds me fair?"

I catch her chin in my hand, look close into her eyes. It's not a flirt's pretty pout that pulls at her features. Rubbing my broad thumb along her soft cheek, I stop a tear. "So you do not love?"

"Love? Of course I love. Has my heart not rushed along with yours, each time you repeated how you felt when first you saw Pietro? All these years I believed I swelled with the very flush you did, just to hear it told. Until tonight, when at last I felt such love myself, and knew it a thousand times more wonderful than even your words could tell it." She lays her head upon my neck. All the slim of her nuzzles against the girth of me, and her heart sounds as quick within my chest as it does her own. "I do love, dear Nurse. But this love I have is not for Paris."

"Then for who?"

She lifts her head and turns half away. "What is *who*? Who am I,

277

or you, or any of us, when love makes changelings of us?" She closes her eyes and I swear by the Madonna, she is more beautiful than I've ever seen her, standing bathed in moonlight. "What if I were not a Cappelletta? Would I still be who I am?"

"Yes." The word forms like a holy prayer upon my lips. Or more, for it is my dearest prayer answered. I search that moonlit face. Does Juliet sense at last what all these years I've held from her? "You'll always be a precious jewel, even if you're no Juliet Cappelletta."

"And what if I were the very opposite of the Cappelletti?"

"The very opposite of what they are, is the very thing Pietro and I ever were." The words that always seemed impossible to speak now melt easily from me. "Poor we were, without a name or fortune. But we loved, and were happy, and made in our happy love—"

"What if I were a Montecche?"

Her words are like a needle drawn too hard. They bunch my brow. They make no sense to me. "But you were not born to the house of Montecchi."

Some strange sentiment tremors across her. "Not born," she says, "but what if I were wed to it?"

Is there a heart that knows a heart better than a mother knows her child? For I see now what was right before my nose some hour past. "Romeo, the one you spoke withal—is he this love?"

"Romeo." She sighs to say his name. "No rose could be more sweet. No man more meet." Tears shine in her eyes, and something more shines upon her lips. "I do love, and Romeo is the one I love, and Romeo loves me."

The hard stone floor seems to shift, the very earth sliding from beneath me. Paris—such a match would he be for my girl. I could not conjure more kind, more handsome, more well-placed than he. And this Romeo, some near relation to the very Montecche who punched and kicked at me, believing I was Tybalt. Which could I possibly want for Juliet?

But when she buries herself against me and asks, "Why must I always hate where I'm told the Cappelletti hate, and love only where they bid me love?" I will my legs strong, that I may bear the sliding and the shifting. Glad as I am the Cappelletti's ancient quarrels mean naught to her, I'm gladder still when she almonds her eyes at me and says, "Surely you'd not have me wed a man who moves me any less than Pietro moved you."

To have her love as Pietro and I loved—this is the one legacy I've to give. How could I wish for her the match Lord Cappelletto makes, if it'd be no more loving a marriage than his own? Would I have her so miserable with wealth and rank as Lady Cappelletta, when I know how even on our hungriest days love fed me, and Pietro, and all of our boys?

This is the lesson the rich never learn. A full heart lasts longer than a full belly. And a well-carved bed hung with finely painted canopy and curtains is no great fortune to the wife who finds no pleasure there.

But little as I care what Lord Cappelletto wants, there's another among the Cappelletti who yet concerns me. Juliet and I've heard Tybalt curse the Montecchi long enough we both know such a wooing will not sit well with him. When I remind her of this, she smiles the very way she did when she toddled after Tybalt as a tiny thing.

"My cousin'd do better to love than hate, you're always saying so yourself. By my lesson, he can unlearn this generations-old enmity, and learn to love where love's well won. For how can he despise all Montecchi, once his dearest cousin is become one?"

It took so small a slight to drive Tybalt to take up a sword in this ancient feud, I'd not have thought there'd be any way to convince him to lay it down again. But I want to believe that what was best in the boy can yet govern the man. If her love can temper Tybalt's hate, he'll be the better for it.

And if my body still aches with keen reminder of what vengeful wrath can wreak, what fault is it of Romeo's? My own vile father's violence did not taint my marriage. Why would Romeo's Montecchi blood stain Juliet's new joy?

"If he loves you as Pietro loved me, he'll win my consent. But first I must know if his heart is as true as yours."

"At nine, you shall know. I told him I would send to him at that hour." She's so lovestruck, she kisses my lids, and lobes, and the great wine-soaked, morello-covered bosom of me, as she says, "Your eyes must be mine, and your ears, and your heart as well, so you can judge by light of day the truth of what I feel tonight."

Judge I will. For Juliet is all to me. If I might see her married—not merely once, as I said before Lady Cappelletta hours past, but well, as she begs of me now—then truly my mother's heart will beam fuller than moon, and sun, and all the fairest stars I set upon her headdress.

FOURTEEN

Though Juliet and I barely doze a dozen winks between us, the rest of Ca' Cappelletti clings to heavy slumber. Slipping from our chamber before the terce bells ring, I move through a hushed house. The remains of feast and fête litter sala, stairs, and court-yard, the snores of lord and servants the only sounds within the compound. Despite my haste, I stop within the arbor. The bees are already in flight, scenting the morning yeasty-sweet with brood and honey, their bodies goldened by their loads of pollen. I whisper to them of what fills Juliet's heart, and mine, as though they might bear my words to my departed husband as they soar into the sky. It's all I want, to share love's happy tidings with him. But my eye catches on one of the Scaligeri-style ladders that'd been put up within the courtyard. Nestled instead beneath Juliet's window, the flowers twined to it crushed last night by Romeo's eager boot. My sore side aches as I wrestle the decoration back to its former place, so none will wonder who climbed so close to speak to her.

Stepping into the Via Cappello, I nearly collide into Tybalt, who's pulling at his glove with the satisfied expression of a cat licking cream off its paw.

"Where are you rushing to?" His eyebrow arches. Not with the boyish curiosity with which he'd pose endless questions to me or to Pietro, but with a cocksure man's quick censuring.

"Juliet suffers from last night's excitement, I must fetch remedy for her." Not one false word in that, though together they conceal the truth. "You've risen early," I add, to heave his mind from her and me, "though perhaps part of you rose late, moved by some beauty found among the fêting dancers. And having moved something in her, the part that rose first now rests, as the rest of you must rise at this hour to hasten home." With a wink, I ask, "Who is she, Tybalt?"

"Not she, but he." His chin thrusts forward, drawing his long face even longer. "I've done as my uncle bade, letting him play generous host to the rogue who'd rob my sister of her greatest treasure. But the villain's gone out from our house, and I've left a challenge at his own for him."

I wish I could run a hand through Tybalt's curls and ease away this sour humor as I soothed so many dark moods that shadowed his boyhood. But he's too old to let me lay comforting hand on him. Too old to know how young he yet is—though Juliet, younger still, may be the one who'll calm for good what rages in him. All I can do is cut short his talk of bloody-bladed revenge by pulling my veil full upon my face. Carefully covering the last of the bruises that remain from when I was mistook in Tybalt's cloak, I leave his smoldering hate to seek Juliet's new-kindled love.

The Piazza delle Erbe is already thick with vendors hawking and customers haggling. I fan away the swelting air, wondering how I'll recognize Romeo unmasked in the day's light. The only familiar face I pick out in all the thronging crowd is Mercutio's. He's perched upon the piazza fountain as if he's peering up the Madonna's statued skirts. There's barely a stitch of cloth upon him as he splashes in the spouting water, defying any who pass to chastise him for defiling the public font.

Mercutio may know no morals, but he knows well Romeo. And so I make my veiled way to him and say, "God ye good morrow." For which I get back naught but filthy bandying.

I survey his smirking companions, marking which seems to wear the mouth I met yester-eve. Easy enough to choose, as the sleepless youth wears the same doublet and hose, as well. When I artfully ask where I may find young Romeo, this very one says, "Young Romeo will be older when you have found him than he was when you sought him," before admitting he's the fellow who bears that name.

Well said that is, and I tell Romeo so. Cleverness is a rare enough trait among young men, as Mercutio himself proves, interrupting me to recite some randy rhyme that's all hare and hoar without much wit. He carries on until at last Romeo waves him and the others off.

I wait till they're well gone before I speak. "My young lady bid me inquire you out," I say, though I keep what she bade me convey to myself. I'll not open her heart to him, until I discern what he might be.

Even unmasked, this Romeo is not so handsome as Paris. Though I suppose some might find him comely, with light locks falling to his shoulders. There's a brooding in his eyes and at that pretty mouth, tinged not with Tybalt's gall but with a wistful melancholy that might easily move a heart as soft as Juliet's.

"The gentlewoman," I begin, though it startles my own ears to hear my girl called such. Did I not mark the girlish way she giggled and flushed yestermorn, when first I spoke of her marrying? Those words must've softened her eye to Romeo, and charmed her ear to whatever he whispered to woo her. "The gentlewoman is young. If you lead her in a fool's paradise, if you deal double with her—"

Suddenly I wish, if not for Tybalt's sword, at least for some steely way to show this Romeo I'll not let any hurt to Juliet go unanswered. Even a mother bird has beak and claws to defend her nest. But what have I to raise against a man?

I lean wordless toward Romeo's narrow chest, as if to show I'd peck him clean if he does her harm.

Romeo raises a knobby-jointed hand in protest. Lays that hand upon his heart and swears it swells with love for her. With quavering voice he says, "Commend me to your lady."

He's wise enough to ken I'm what will bring him and her together. Or, if I doubt, keep them apart. Surely only a pure heart can discern all I am to Juliet, when such as Lord and Lady Cappelletti still deny it.

I promise to tell Juliet well of him. "When I say how you protest, she'll be a joyful woman." That word sits easier with me now, for surely this teary Romeo will gently make a woman of her.

My answer draws his pretty mouth into a proper smile. "Bid her devise some means to come to shrift this afternoon," he says, "and there she shall at Friar Lorenzo's cell be shrived and married."

By my Sainted Maria, what am I to make of this? To honor her straightaway in holy marriage, that is as it should be. But to have them joined in the very cell where as a babe I brought her, the place where when she toddled I first modeled to her how to make good shrift—I might've been glad for it, had I not guessed years past what trickery the Franciscan performed when my girl was baptized there.

"Friar Lorenzo agrees to marry you?"

Romeo swells with youthful pride at having secured the Franciscan's approval. "He says a happy alliance it will prove, that turns our households' rancor to pure love."

I nod. Calculating as Friar Lorenzo is, I'll not be outdone by him. None knows better than I how well he holds secrets, and if he weds Juliet to Romeo, surely neither she nor I will bear any sin or blame from it. Who else would marry them, without the consent of the Cappelletti?

Romeo presses a florin into my hand with the same certainty with which a priest lays consecrated Host upon the tongue. But with my tongue I tell Romeo I'll not take even a denaro. What I do, I do not for gold or silver but for love of Juliet. And then, because I know I must win his love as well, I tease Romeo as I've long teased Juliet and, in happier times, Tybalt. "There is a nobleman in town that would fain lay knife aboard, and husband a meal of my mistress."

At this Romeo goes pale as a clout. Has no one taught him the jesting my darling ones and I've enjoyed? No matter. It's a pleasure he can learn from me, while Juliet learns other pleasures of him. "She'd as lieve see a toad," I assure Romeo, "a very toad, as see him."

I prate on about when Juliet was a prating thing, making careful study of how Romeo hangs ravenous on each word, hungering to know more of her. Before I take my leave, I remind him to keep no counsel, that we must hold this marriage secret.

He swears his serving-man is just as true to him as I am to Juliet. But how can a common servant be all I am to her? True in what I do, if not in what I've let her believe I am. Surely the time is near to tell her all, though how am I to deliver such unexpected news?

In wondering at it, I nearly miss what Romeo says next. Love-sick, he prattles as a poet might of tackled stairs and top-gallants of joy, until I discern that he means for me to meet his man a little while hence, and receive some ropes by which Romeo'll come to Juliet to consummate tonight what the friar will officiate today.

Tybalt's never needed ropes to reach our window, cat-nimble climber that he is. Nor did Pietro, directed by me to mount the tower stair and pass into the bedchamber to mount me. But this Romeo wants to believe himself a clever sneak, and so I indulge him, promising to collect the ropes and set them where he may scale his way to her.

Taking my leave, I do not turn directly back to the Via Cappello. I need to ready myself for the quick of it—my Juliet, wedding this day. Crowded as the Piazza delle Erbe is this morning, I conjure the quiet of it on that Lammas Day fourteen years past when Pietro brought me to Ca' Cappelletti. Even in this heat, my body still shivers with that ache, that longing for babe newly born, and freshly lost. Or so I thought.

Wandering through Verona's streets, I make seven circuits around the city. First for Nunzio, my eldest. Then one after the other for Nesto, Donato, Enzo, Berto, and their littlest brother, Angelo. This is the gift and curse of memory. Though we bury our dead, we cannot ever bid a final good-bye. I circle past the places that hold especial rememberances of each of my boys, some that I've not let myself indulge since I was swallowed up within Ca' Cappelletti all those years ago. I save Pietro for last. His is the longest loop. There's not a place in this city that does not echo of him. Of us. Again and again I whisper what makes me miss him as keenly as I ever have: that from our love a new love grows, and soon Verona will bear new memories, of our Juliet and her Romeo.

The sun's climbed high by the time I return to Ca' Cappelletti. Juliet secrets herself in the arbor. Sitting in the shade of a poperin tree, she worries the ring Lord Cappelletto set upon her finger a week past. But the dazzle of his emerald'll not hold her attention once she sees me. She's on her feet asking, "Honey nurse, what news?"

Honey nurse, that sweet that gave her life. Sentimental old fool that I've become, emotions grow so thick in my throat, not a word is able to escape me.

Her color fades. "Good sweet nurse—why do you look so sad?"

"I'm aweary." I take the place she left upon the bench. "My bones ache from what a jaunce I've had."

"I would you had my bones, and I your news." She tugs at me with the same impatience as when she was three or four and thought I held some candied comfit from her. "Come, I pray you, speak."

Jesu, what haste. "Do you not see that I am out of breath?"

But Juliet was never one to be stayed. Nor have I been one to stay her. "You have breath to tell me you are out of breath," she says. "And take longer in making excuse why you delay, than the whole of the telling would take. Tell me simple, is your news good or bad?"

If it were yesterday, I'd jest with her as I often have, and tell her she knows not how to choose a man, and blazon Romeo with faults he does not have, and bid her go serve God as nunnish Rosaline does. But it's as if she's unlearned her girlish love of waggery in this little time she's known wistful Romeo.

"What a head have I," I say instead. "It beats as if it would fall in twenty pieces. And my back, and side. Beshrew your heart, for sending me about, to catch my death."

These words are better meant for Tybalt, chiding earned by what I got when last I ventured from Ca' Cappelletti. But Juliet at least hears them with a loving and not a wrathful ear. "By all my faith, I'm sorry you're not well. Sweet, sweet, sweet nurse." She kisses my head and lays a gentle hand upon my side, which ache less under her caring touch. "Tell me, what says my love?"

How can I not answer those pleading eyes? "Your love says, like an honest gentleman, and a courteous, and a kind, and a handsome, and I warrant a virtuous—" But why do I court for Romeo? Does my love count for naught? "Where is your mother?"

"Where is my mother?" She repeats the question with such wonder—is this at last the time to tell her? Can she have already guessed the truth? But her eyes flick to the arched passage to the courtyard. "Where would she be? Why, she's within."

Is this any poultice for my sore and sorry bones? That she'll not even know me for her mother, that all I am to her is messenger?

"Lady Cappelletta is within, but my heart is without, as only you know, Nurse." She smiles, and sighs, and takes my hands in each of hers. "And without you, what comfort has my heart?" Her soft hands are still small against mine, gripping with a child's fretful need. "Come, what says Romeo?"

Those eyes flash familiar at me, and by all my years of loving her, and loving my Pietro, I know there's time enough for her to learn what I really am. That it'll better wait till she is wed, and perchance on the way to being herself made a mother. For now, there's naught she'll listen to but what she wants to hear.

"Hie you hence to Friar Lorenzo's cell, to make your shrift." I loose my hands from hers to tuck her wayward hair, straighten her sleeve, and smooth her skirts as I've ever done, although in truth such beauty needs no bettering. "There stays a husband to make you a wife."

The blood comes up in her cheeks, scarleting my pure lamb. I flush as well, the sudden fevering that's struck me half a dozen times a day during these weeks past flashing over me once more. But for all the heat, we wrap arms around each other, joy echoing with joy as we breathe air fruited by peach and poperin pear. Breathing together that sweetest of anticipation just before lips part and teeth sink in, and juice and taste explode upon the tongue.

Though I'd lieve not ever let her go, I pull away first, so I'll not feel what it is to try to hold her longer than she would be held. "Get you to San Fermo, and take care none see you till the friar's done his part. I must fetch the roping ladder by which Romeo'll climb to you once the day turns dark." I've been her age. Knowing what stirs a heart, and other parts as well, I add, "Though I'm the drudge, and toil in your delight, you shall bear the burden that'll come at night."

She laughs and blushes deeper. So new-woke with love, she twitters like a wanton's bird. Reciting some pretty poesy, she calls parting such sweet sorrow, gives me a giddy kiss, and turns away to meet her match at Friar Lorenzo's cell.

It's no easy thing to watch her leave alone. But I must think for both of us, and be ready for what comes after the marriage vows are trothed. And so I kneel next to the arbor hive, careful not to block the bees as they stream forth. Sliding a hand beneath the cut log, I draw out the box Tybalt long ago hid there.

It's no fine cassone. Not carved by a skilled hand, nor painted with some impressive scene, nor tooled in precious leather. The box he chose is simple, to attract no notice. Even the bees fly blithely by as I lift the lid and remove the sack that lies within, my fingers clumsy as I undo the knot. When the pouch opens, I rock back and pour what the hives and I have earned into my lap. Though it's not a hundredth of what Lord Cappelletto'd give to dowry Juliet, it'll buy what I'd have her have. A new drawn-thread bedsheet imported from some far-off port, to lay upon with the husband only she and I and Friar Lorenzo will know she has.

I count out enough to purchase a sheet as wide as her broad bed, slipping the coins inside my gown. Handful by handful, I work the rest into the sack. Twist and tie it, and lay it in the box, then slide the box back into place. Tybalt must not notice it's been moved. Must not question me, on this of all days. But Tybalt seems to have forgotten the bees. The clay bowl beside the hive is dry. I draw water from the courtyard well to give the honey gatherers, before making my own bizz-buzzing way from Ca' Cappelletti.

Romeo's man is little more than a boy, and for all Romeo swore he was good at keeping confidence, he's no good at keeping time, and so he keeps me waiting in the day's hottest sun. When at last he arrives with the roped ladder, my thirst's so great I'm grateful he slips out a bulging skin filled with aqua vitae, so we can drink to the marriage of his master to my mistress. A happy omen, for my first sampling of such was on the day I wed Pietro. My new husband taught me to taste the fiery liquor with his own tongue, and sang a merry rhyme to ease me to it. *The first sip is bracing, the second's a blessing, the third's your last care in the world.*

I sing the foolish verse to Romeo's Balthasar, as he tells me he is called, and he sings it back to me in a wavering contralto. Though I miss the deep resonance of Pietro's basso, I'm glad to have another voice mingle with my own, celebrating the vows Juliet and Romeo have by now already made beneath Friar Lorenzo's cross. Once we empty the skin, Balthasar bows to me and I make curtsy, and we go our ways. Mine is toward the Mercato Vecchio, where I must find among the fabric merchants a bedsheet fine enough for Juliet's parting with her maidenhead.

Just before I reach the marketplace, a flash of regal carmine catches my eye. I draw back, for the last man I want to see today is Paris.

But it's Mercutio who stumbles from the nearby passageway, his carmine robe stained with a darker crimson. A sword drops from his hand, metal clattering against street-stones as he curses Cappelletti and Montecchi.

I espy within the passageway a second sword. Wet with blood and being slid by a quaking hand back into its too-familiar scabbard. My eyes catch Tybalt's, and in that instant I read his terror at what he's done.

Mercutio lets out an animal's anguished howl. He cries, "A plague on both your houses," and crumples to the ground.

FIFTEEN

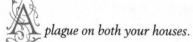 *plague on both your houses.*

If Mercutio's many fornications are not enough to send him straight to hell, for this spiteful oath alone he deserves damnation. How could anyone wish such suffering as the plague brings, not just upon the Cappelletti and Montecchi but on all Verona? For the pestilence'll not stop at the boundary of one house without stealing its awful way into another. None knows that better than I do. So though I should cross myself and pray for Mercutio's departing soul, instead I spit and say, "May the devil have you."

Then I look back toward Tybalt. But he's gone.

Tybalt, my last boy. As near a son to me as I'll ever have again. And as much in danger now as mine were on that awful day they stole into our plague-dead neighbor's house.

I know what I am, and what I'm not. Much as I ache to protect Tybalt, I turn the other way. Back to Ca' Cappelletti.

Though Cansignorio might eventually have killed his nephew himself, the Scaligeri honor'll not bear anyone else having slain him. When the prince pronounces the punishment for taking Mercutio's life, all I feel for Tybalt'll be not a pennyworth of help to him. But Lord Cappelletto—surely he'll cast every bit of favor he's ever curried with Cansignorio to save his heir.

Only when I reach Ca' Cappelletti do I realize I still carry Romeo's cords. I secret them outside the compound wall, then hurry into Lord Cappelletto's study.

When I burst in, the old man jerks up, astonished. He's been dozing among his accounting books. A happy fool, whose joy I rob by saying, "Prince Cansignorio's nephew is slain."

I need Lord Cappelletto strong, need him at his most conniving. But he shrinks, so small and weak and old. "Paris? Slain?"

"Not Paris. Mercutio. Stabbed in the street by Tybalt."

This brings him to his feet. He reaches out an unsure hand, and I offer my arm to steady him. "Where is he?"

"He vanished when Mercutio fell." The tolling of bells and blasting of trumpets drown out any more I might say.

Lord Cappelletto bolts from behind his desk, shouting for me to show him where last I saw his heir. And so we rush together through the courtyard and out of the compound, Lady Cappelletta, alarmed by how her husband cries out Tybalt's name, hastening along with us.

The street where Mercutio fell is already thick with people. Prince Cansignorio stands in the middle of the keening, kneeling crowd, far changed from the bravadoed young man who first seized Verona's throne. Looking upon his sister's slain son ages him well past his not-quite-forty years.

"Which way ran he that killed Mercutio?" he asks. "Who began this bloody fray?"

A youth steps forward. One of the ones I met at the fountain this very morning, though it seems a century ago. He bites his thumb, and points with it past the prince.

My knees buckle beneath me. They'll not support the weight of what I see. Tybalt, sprawled motionless upon the ground.

The same ground rears up at me, and something roars inside my head. My stomach twists and fills my mouth. The thundering resolves into words, shouted by that pointing youth.

"There lies quarrelsome Tybalt, who killed brave Mercutio. And who for that crime, was slain by young Romeo."

Each sharp word stabs into my heart. Tybalt, killed. Romeo, his killer.

Lady Cappelletta rushes to where the young man points, wailing for her nephew. Dumbstruck, Lord Cappelletto follows, falling to the ground and cradling his heir in disbelief. What enfeebles him inflames her. She clamors back to the prince. Throws herself upon her knees, kissing his knuckles and kneading his fingers, pulling his hand to her heart. "Romeo slew Tybalt," she says. "Romeo must not live."

"Not Romeo." Lord Montecche erupts through the crowd, pushing his way between Lady Cappelletta and Cansignorio. "He was Mercutio's dear friend, and concluded only what the law otherwise would end—the life of Tybalt, who laid your nephew dead."

The prince swings from one to the other like a weathervane caught in an angry wind. None seem to breathe, no heart to beat, until he speaks. "Tybalt disturbed our peace, and for that paid the proper price. But Romeo took what it was my lawful right alone to take. Let him hence in haste. Banished, he may live. But if he's found again upon Verona's streets, that hour is his last."

Cansignorio calls for his guard to gather up Mercutio and carry him to the castle to be prepared for burial among the other Scaligeri in Santa Maria Antica. The crowd follows, eager to insinuate themselves into his princely grief. Only Lord Cappelletto, Lady Cappelletta, and I remain. And Tybalt, our dear Tybalt.

Creeping close, I cannot keep my eyes from the wound upon his chest. His face, his hands are already deathly pale. But that dark, wet mark—it seems the only thing alive of him.

I tear tooth into my tongue till I taste my own blood, hating myself for every harsh word I've had for Tybalt of late. I wish with all my soul that I could take them back. Why did I not keep him from this fatal fight?

Lord Cappelletto shakes his head like a dog trying to loose a porcupine's quill from its nose. "Why would Tybalt raise a sword against the count?"

"Honor." Lady Cappelletta spits the word at him. "All your talk of honor, of your precious family name. All the ancient prideful grudges of the Cappelletti. That's what laid him dead."

Lord Cappelletto touches the gold crest worked upon the hilt of Tybalt's sword. "The Cappelletti had no enemy in Mercutio. He was a relation to the Scaligeri, I'd not have wanted Tybalt to—"

"It was not for you," I say. For in this instant I realize what must have caused the quarrel: Tybalt was more like my Pietro than I've realized, dying not for some foolish male honor, but to protect precious female virtue. "Tybalt knew there was a rakehell who was trying to seduce Rosaline. He beseeched and besieged her, and would not let her be. Even came into your house to find her. Tybalt tried to tell you, but you'd not listen to him."

Lord Cappelletto loses what little color the shock of Tybalt's death had left him. I know my words have hit the mark. Know, too, it does not matter. So what if he's as sorry as I am, to not have stanched what stormed in Tybalt?

Blade, street, blood. They're Tybalt's death, just as they were Pietro's.

Lord Cappelletto pulls at Tybalt's cloak until it covers that awful wound. "I'll take him to Santa Caterina, to our family crypt." He crosses himself, plodding out each deliberate word. As though he must convince himself that Tybalt's truly gone. "Best not to make too grand a public funeral, with Cansignorio's own mourning turning him against us. I'll have Rosaline and her convent Sisters pray a month of private Masses for our Tybalt, God have mercy on his soul."

Lady Cappelletta grips one of Tybalt's lifeless hands, refusing to let go. Though it's no woman's place to travel with a body to its burial, she insists on going with him. Insists with the same wildness in her eye that haunted the years in which her womb squeezed forth one ill-formed creature after another. Her madness blazes like a fire, warming Lord Cappelletto, and me as well. Weak as this blow has made us, its her fierce strength we need.

Lord Cappelletto nods, agreeing to let her come. Turning to me, he says, "You must tell Juliet."

If all of heaven's angels sang in one great harmony, it'd not sound sweeter than what I hear as I approach Juliet's chamber: her lilting voice weaving love lines into an adoring tune. From the doorway, I watch my newly wedded girl take each of San Zeno's statued hands in one of hers, swaying as though she'd dance the saint about the room. Giddy, she twirls herself from him and catches sight of me. Taking a half-step back, she studies my grief-struck face. "Why do you wring your hands?"

I look down at my hands, as though they'd speak. Wishing they might, and save my tongue the torture of answering her. "We are undone."

She stares at me, and I know those words are not enough. My eyes swim past her, searching out the window and across the arbor to what were Tybalt's rooms. "He's gone. He's killed. He's dead."

Juliet stumbles backward, catching herself against the holy icon. "Can heaven be so envious?"

"Romeo can, even if heaven cannot."

Her eyes, her mouth gape in confusion. "Romeo?"

"I saw the wound, here." I lay my hand in the tender flesh valleyed beneath my ribs, and something sharps inside me. As though the same blade that felled Tybalt gouges me as well. "Tybalt, the best friend I had. I never dreamt I'd live to see him dead."

"Romeo slaughtered, and Tybalt slain? Who lives, if those two are gone?"

I live, and she lives. Always my same awful fate. Despite this grief great enough to kill us both, through the pitiless mercy of some unseen saint we yet survive. "Tybalt's dead. Romeo killed him, and is banished."

"O God." She reaches for me, the same desperate babe who howled for me all those years ago. "Did Romeo shed Tybalt's blood?"

Such cruel relief, to still have her to comfort after all I've lost. I hold her fast against me, letting her grief curse out. "Serpent heart, hid with a flowering face. Beautiful tyrant, angelic fiend. Just opposite to what you justly seemed. Spirit bowered from hell, paradised in such sweet flesh. O, that deceit should dwell in such a palace."

"There's no trust, no faith, no honesty in men," I answer, stroking her hair and laying kisses on those precious locks. That her fond heart must learn such hate so young. "Shame come to Romeo."

Juliet yanks herself from me, so fast her emerald ring gouges my soft flesh. "Blistered be your tongue. Romeo was not born to shame."

Were her curses not for Romeo, but for Tybalt? "Will you speak well of him that killed your cousin?"

Quick as her anger came, it just as quick is gone. She knuckles her hands into her eyes, as if to blind herself to our terrible fate. "Shall I speak ill of him that is my husband? Is he a villain who killed my cousin, if that villain cousin would have killed my husband?"

I grab each of her thin wrists, pulling those angry fists from her reddening eyes. She blinks once at me with surprise, and then a second time with the same steely resolve I watched harden Tybalt. "My husband lives—this is all comfort. But some other word you said, worse than *Tybalt's dead*."

I shake her wrists, as if to jerk such thoughts away. What's worse than *Tybalt's dead*, so long as we both live?

Before I even force aloud the question, she answers. "Tybalt's death was woe enough. But *Romeo is banished* cuts like ten thousand *Tybalt's dead*."

Tybalt, who loved and was loved by her for fourteen years. Who held her dear from the first day I bore her to this chamber. Whose face, and voice, and doting touch were the second she learned after mine. How does she shed tears over this living Romeo she's known but a day, and forget it's a lifetime of our dearest Tybalt that's lost to us?

"Lord and Lady Cappelletti are already at Santa Caterina," I say. Surely if she sees Tybalt lying in the Cappelletti crypt, his heart stilled by Romeo's sword, she'll share the weight of what shatters me. "Will you go to them? I'll bring you there."

She shakes her head and pulls away from me, stumbling backward into our bed. For all the day's heat, her teeth begin to chatter. She pulls the bed curtain around her like a shroud. "Romeo, my three-hours husband, was meant to make a highway to my bed. But it's death, not Romeo, that'll take my maidenhead."

She does not speak these words to me, but to some specter only she can see. It frights me. Not because such madness is so strange, but because it's so familiar.

Have I not gazed longingly upon that same specter? Not ached to have my own life end, rather than bear the grief of living through the loss of those I loved?

Pietro's tight hold bore me through the burying of our sons. Rocking Juliet in my arms anchored me through mourning my

Pietro. Loving what's in this life is the only remedy for death. If Juliet'll not let me hold her through this fresh loss, what harbor will either of us find for our grief?

I bow my head to my cockly-eyed Madonna, silently begging for her aid. All the answer I get is what Juliet whispers through her clattering teeth. "I, a maid, die maiden-widowed."

I'd not leave her for all the world. Nor look on the Montecche ever again. But hearing *I* and *die* dance together on her tongue, I know I must do something. "I'll find Romeo," I say.

I make her swear she'll stay inside our chamber while I'm gone. Whatever her despair, there's naught here with which she might undo her life. She promises, saying she'll not leave her wedding bed. She pulls the ring from her finger, pressing it into my hand to take to Romeo.

I cup the weight of it in my palm. This precious thing Lord Cappelletto gave her, which now she'll have me gift to Romeo—the one who is to her dearest loved, and by the Cappelletti and my own heart hated most.

I wit well enough where to look for Romeo: where any lovesick sinner goes to be absolved. But for once, the corridor outside the friar's cell is empty. His door, ever open to any who are in need, is instead shut fast. I knock, cracking my knuckles so hard I expect the wood to splinter beneath them. But the door'll not budge.

Leaning close, I hear voices within. I rap again with even greater might. From the other side, Friar Lorenzo asks who knocks and whence I come. Asks as though he must take care who is let in. Does this not confirm what I suspect? Surely Romeo hides here.

I might turn away, fetch some men from Cansignorio's guard, and lead them here. Why not let the prince deal Romeo a blow as fatal as the one Romeo dealt Tybalt? But uncertainty worms within me. "I come from Juliet," I say.

The door swings open. Friar Lorenzo waves me inside and latches the door after me.

The Franciscan stands alone. "Where's my lady's lord? Where's Romeo?"

He crooks a finger to a prayer niche cut within the cell. "There on the ground, with his own tears made drunk."

Romeo is huddled against the wall. Blubbering and weeping, weeping and blubbering. As though it's him, and not Juliet, who suffers for what he's done.

"Stand up." I jab my foot at him. "Stand, and be a man." Did Juliet dare compare this sniveler to my Pietro? "For Juliet's sake, rise and stand."

"Do you speak of Juliet?" He raises his head, his voice wavering like a child's. "How is it with her? Does she not think me a murderer, for having stained our joy with blood removed but little from her own?"

For all Tybalt's love, it's my blood, not his, that's little removed from Juliet's. And with all that blood's heat I answer. "She says nothing, sir, but weeps and weeps." What harm is my lie, against his greater sin? I'll not use any words of hers to comfort him. "She falls on her bed, and starts, and calls *Tybalt*. Cries *Romeo*, then falls down again."

"*Cries Romeo, then falls*—as if my name slaughters her, as my cursed hand killed Tybalt." He draws his dagger. "In what vile part of this body does *Romeo* lodge? Tell me, Friar, that I may cut it from me."

With quick hand, I snatch the knife. I want to point it to his chest and drive it home. Want to feel it pierce flesh and organ and draw warm blood. To know it is my sharp thrust that drains all from Tybalt's killer.

And yet—if you've ever plunged a knife to butcher a newly slaughtered sheep, you know how hard it is to drive blade into flesh. But that is naught compared to what it takes to pull out the knife that's been so keenly driven in.

I watched Mercutio fall. I saw my Tybalt felled. Both haunt enough. Slaying Romeo would no more earn back Tybalt's life than good Tybalt's death did Mercutio's. It'd only leave my own hand guilt-stained as well.

I fling the dagger across the cell. It hits the floor and spins. Stops, pointing not at us, but at the bloodied Christ crucifixed above the Franciscan's narrow bed.

"Would you slay yourself, when happiness is yours?" Friar Lorenzo is so consumed with reprimanding Romeo, he pays no mind to me. "Juliet, to whom you vowed your love, yet lives. Tybalt, who would've killed you, you slew. The law that might punish you with death asks only exile. For each of these, you might be happy. And yet you whimper and would die miserable."

Romeo totters in shame, which pleases his confessor. "Go to Juliet, and give her comfort," Friar Lorenzo tells him. "But be mindful. Do not stay too long. Be gone before the night-watch makes its rounds so you may pass safely to Mantua, where you must stay until I've time to blaze your marriage, reconcile your families, beg pardon of the prince, and call you back to Verona. Saints be willing, we'll have more joy then than the Montecchi or the Cappelletti have known in the generations since this ancient feud began."

The marriage blazed, the families reconciled, Juliet and Romeo dwelling happily together for ever after. This is what she wants. What I, loving her, should want as well.

May Tybalt's saints forgive me—but what death took is taken. Whatever serpent has slithered into our Eden, poisoning our joy, I'd not let the devilish creature steal Juliet as well. So when Friar Lorenzo tells me, "Go commend this to your lady," I nod my assent and force out thanks for all his counsel, before I turn to Romeo.

"My lord, I'll tell my lady you will come." My lord, I call him. For if Juliet's fate is now entwined with his, mine is as well. I slip the emerald from my finger, and hold it out to him. "Here, sir, a ring she bid me give you."

He kisses the ring, and kisses my own hand for delivering it. "How well my comfort is revived by this," he says. He cradles it as gently as Juliet did a wounded bird when she was but a girl of eight, while I tell him where to find the ropes by which he'll breach the arbor wall and reach my darling one.

I spend my night in the Cappelletti tower. Where else can I go, while Romeo takes my place beside Juliet? Tybalt's bed is empty. But I'd not lie within his darkened chamber, thinking of him already laid inside the Cappelletti tomb. Instead I climb, as he so often did. I make my way to the tower top, where I've the stars for company. Trying to forget the sight of Tybalt's lifeless body, I pray for his everlasting soul, gone from this world with all the rest I've loved.

All, save Juliet.

Juliet, who in these same hours learns what I could never teach: the pleasure of a husband's touch. Even at my age and in my widowhood, my body still quakes remembering the shivery explosions I felt when I first lay with Pietro. Love. Lust. Loss. Inseparable companions.

Lightning's bright shock and thunder's heavy grumble burst the small hours of the night, loosing heavy rain upon Verona. It's as though heaven itself weeps with me. When the first streaks of dawn lace the easterly sky, I steal my way back down to Juliet. But just as I draw near to her door, I hear above the tempest Lord Cappelletto calling Lady Cappelletta to go to Juliet.

Juliet—although she's ever a slug-a-bed, surely this once it's not the lying down but what rises up that occupies her. Romeo cannot yet be twenty, and at that age, they rise and come and rise again with such quick ease, my lamb must have passed a night well full of cock-struts. But now, it is another cock that crows, the morning lark that sings, and Lady Cappelletta that caws. And so I'll not tarry with a knock.

I cover my eyes, open the door, and call, "Madam." Madam, for my lamb is wooed, won, married, and maiden no more.

"Nurse?" she answers, and I enter. From behind my hand I peek at Romeo, half-lit by the candle that burned all night before my

Blessed Virgin. He's a scrawny thing without his doublet, not broad and strong like my Pietro, nor even so well muscled as Tybalt. Still more a boy than I'd guessed him to be.

"Lady Cappelletta is coming to your chamber." I might as well be speaking in the tongue of a Far Eastern trader, dull-eared as Juliet is for me, being so full-eyed for Romeo. She gazes soft at him, and hears me not.

I turn my own uncovered gaze on him, as hard as hers is soft. "The day is broke. Be wary, look about." My warning works fast on him, and I leave young love to its fare-thee-wells.

The sala, so teeming full during the masked ball the evening before last, seems cavernous now. As I step inside, an eerie moaning echoes through the shadowed room.

A trick of the storm, perchance, the wind catching some loose shutter. But the moan sounds again, so close I let out a startled gasp. It's coming from Lord Cappelletto, who sits alone within the dark. With weak voice he calls, "Angelica?"

I've not heard my name spoke aloud in this house in all the years since Pietro's been gone. Would not have thought Lord Cappelletto even knew it, though I suppose it was writ upon the contracts Friar Lorenzo brought him so long ago. I've always been only *Nurse* to him. Though when he says, "Is that you, Angelica?" my name sounds like some delicate thing he treats with care.

I've never known Lord Cappelletto young, but now he seems more than old. Shaky, and sapped. "It's late," I say, as though sleep were any remedy to him, or me.

"Late? What hour could be so late, so dark?" He nods toward

the window, which despite the summer heat is shut fast against the storm. "When sky's sun is set, the earth drizzles dew. But for the setting of my brother's son, it rains downright." Dark as the shuttered sala is, I sense more than see how deeply our newest grief etches his face. "Tybalt took so strongly after Giaccomo, it's like losing him again. Like losing both at once."

I lay my hand on his. I expect it to feel cold, an eel hooked from the fishmonger's basket. But it rests warm in mine. More comfort than I'd thought I'd get from him. "He was a good boy," I say, "and would have made a better man, had not hot temper taken him."

"We were born to die, and I'll not fault him for being quick to defend Rosaline." His eyes search out the place along the wall where Tybalt's sword once hung. "Poor broken girl. Even as she sobbed and wailed for her murdered brother, I bade her repeat to me before the Holy Abbess of Santa Caterina what she'd confided to Tybalt. How the rakehell, eyeing her at prayers within the church, pressed a secret suit. With words, and deeds, and every sort of flattery, tried to seduce her. Offered his Judas coins to buy the purity she's vowed to keep. Even masked himself and came into my house, plotting to take his lust on her."

Tybalt was always so quick to find some insult to the Cappelletti honor, I'd half-believed he'd imagined the plot to corrupt Rosaline. But I might have known Cansignorio's lascivious nephew would seek some debauched pleasure with such a pious girl. "May the saints forgive Tybalt. And may the devil take Mercutio."

Lord Cappelletto gives a fierce shake of his head, crossing himself to fend off the taint of such damnation. "Not Mercutio. He only stepped between them. It was Romeo Montecche who ill-used my niece."

Romeo who tried to seduce Rosaline?

Romeo, who finding her already gone when he arrived here, sought another just as innocent.

Romeo who pressed his silver coin on me for offering Juliet to him, like a lamb led to a sharp-toothed wolf.

Romeo, who lies right now in our bed. Taking what he could not pry from Rosaline, from Juliet instead. Horror grips my throat, tears into my chest. How can I have been so big a fool, and let my precious Juliet be ruined?

Juliet, ruined.

Lord Cappelletto asks, "What's that you speak?"

Have I said those two most awful words aloud? But he's not heard them clear, for with watery eyes he asks, "How is my girl, my all?"

"She has much to weep for." More than she yet knows.

"Poor child, she'd wash Tybalt's corpse with tears, though by Prince Cansignorio's decree we cannot grieve publicly for him. But I've remedy for that. We'll honor Tybalt after we've won the favor of the Scaligeri once again." Resolve settles across Lord Cappelletto's shoulders. Whatever shared sorrow shrouded us together is quick forgot as he nods a command at me. "Come, let us see how Juliet takes the gladder tidings Lady Cappelletta brought her."

What happy word can Lady Cappelletta have given Juliet? What relief could it be against this terrible truth I bear?

I follow Lord Cappelletto into the chamber. My darling lies on the bed, shaking with silent sobs while Lady Cappelletta stands turned away from her.

"How now, wife?" As Lord Cappelletto speaks, I slip past Lady Cappelletta to stroke what silent comfort I can onto Juliet's down-turned head. "Have you delivered to her our decree?"

"Ay, sir." Lady Cappelletta ducks her chin, so she'll not have to meet his eye. "She gives you thanks, but will have none."

"Will have none?" In two swift strides, Lord Cappelletto's beside the bed. He hovers so close, his angry spittle hits us both. "Are you so proud? So ungrateful, when I've found a worthy gentleman to make you a bride?"

"Not proud." Juliet's voice is so small we all must strain to hear her. "And not ungrateful. But I cannot marry where I do not love."

"Cannot marry? Do not love?" He swoops his claw of a hand into her hair, yanking her from the bed. "As you are mine, I give you to my friend. I'll fettle you like a horse, and ride you out on Thursday. Then shall you be made Paris's wife."

Juliet wraps shaking arms around his boots, weeping and beseeching. But Lord Cappelletto berates my darling as he too often did poor Tybalt. "Disobedient wretch. I tell you this: you'll stand and make your vows in church on Thursday, or never after look me in the face."

He kicks her away, and reaches his hand to Lady Cappelletta. "Wife, did we ever think ourselves blessed, that God lent us but this only child? Now I see this one is one too much, and we've a curse in having her."

God lent? Not God but the friar, who borrowed and lent. Who

with secret deceit took what I will ever love and gave my babe to this man who could so quick turn hate on her.

"God in heaven bless her." I curve my great body over her trembling one. "You are to blame."

Lord Cappelletto gapes as though he's forgot I'm here. "What's that, my lady wisdom? What blame is there, when day, night, work, play, alone, in company, for fourteen years all has been one care to me: to have her well matched. The more so since Tybalt's lost, and Paris is all that's left to be a son to me. A gentleman, noble, fair, and honorable."

He shoves me aside, wrenches Juliet up by her shoulder. "Whine and pule if you will, but if you'll not wed, you'll not house with me. You may beg, starve, die in the streets. I'll have naught to do with you." He crosses to the door, but turns back once more to speak to me. "Thursday is near. Look to your heart, advise her well."

Juliet raises her tear-stained face to Lady Cappelletta. But just like the hind caught by the hound, she could not even protect herself, and she cannot pity my poor girl. "Do as you will, for I am done with you," she says and follows her husband from the room.

Juliet sinks back to the floor. I cannot coax her to her feet, have no strength to carry my full-grown girl back to our bed. So I settle next to her, weighing how the very thing I wished for her just two days past now works such misery on her: for good and handsome Paris to want her for a wife.

Romeo, Romeo—over and over she whimpers his name. My darling does not know that fiend for what he is. And I'll not tell her. Not shatter more her already breaking heart by revealing how falsely he's dealt with her. Not let her know how stupidly I let it happen.

How long we sit like this, her sobbing and me scheming, I do not know. There is no bell to mark it, no clock tower to tick it off. Only the once-ferocious storm, which flashes quiet as suddenly as it started, melting Juliet's wails into urgent words. "Oh God, Nurse. By my husband on earth and my faith in heaven, what am I to do? Comfort me, counsel me. Have you no word of joy?"

Of joy, no. But of good counsel, yes. For all I want to tell her—that she is no Cappelletta, that there is naught Lord Cappelletto can take from her that values more than all I have to give—I know the fool I've been. To let myself be fooled, and let so much be nearly lost.

If Lord Cappelletto turns her out, what life is left her? Could I go begging for some household to take in the Cappelletti shame and let us live as scrub maids in their scullery? So soft a girl as Juliet would not last a week at that.

And if her secret marriage to Romeo is exposed—what then? I'd not trust her for another hour with that deceiver. I wish no less than bitter death for him. For what he did to Rosaline, to Tybalt, and worst of all to my Juliet. I'll not let the world know the only thing a lady has to trade on he's already pried from her.

Mother though I am, there's nothing I could do to save her, if it were not for Paris. Paris, who offers name, fortune, family. And even love. What more can she—can we—ask?

"Faith, here it is. Romeo is banished, has naught in all the world, and can make no challenge to you." I rush through this barest mention of him, then slow my speech to ease her to what more I have to say. "I think it best you marry with Count Paris. He is a lovely gentleman. None is so fine, so fair, and you'll grow happy in the match."

This stints her sobs. She raises eyes I'd swear can read the very depths of me, and asks, "Do you speak truly from your heart?"

"From my heart, and my soul." I make a cross over the first, to show I swear upon the second. "Or else beshrew them both."

"Amen," she answers. Adds, in yet more piety, "Go in and tell them I am going, having displeased my Lord Cappelletto, to make shrift and be absolved by Friar Lorenzo."

It does not lessen a mother's love to admit some of her babes are born obedient, while others ever struggle to assert their will. My Juliet has always been a good girl. A girl whose pleasure lies in pleasing. Whatever spell vile Romeo cast on her, it must weigh little compared to what wills her to obey me, and Friar Lorenzo, and even Lord Cappelletto.

Lord Cappelletto. Brutal as he was to her this morning—as I'm my father's daughter, I know how much a woman, a girl, will do to appease the brute who beats her. Though I'd deal more vengefully with him, I'll bide my hours and bear his presence till Thursday comes and she's wived to Paris. What is Lord Cappelletto's anger, when with my loving counsel she'll open her heart to the prince's noble nephew, and earn herself a safe and a happy future?

SIXTEEN

Juliet bade me tell Lord and Lady Cappelletti where she's gone, what she's agreed to do. And so I make my way to the kitchen. The ever-drudging cook is mashing a great mound of dates into a mass of capon livers, working knife and pestle quick as Lord Cappelletto prattles on about boar and basil salsiccetti, leek and chickpea migliacci, roasted eel minced with mint and parsley to be cooked with walnuts and almond milk into a crusted pie. Dish after dish he says the cook must make in only two days' time.

Lady Cappelletta's slim fingers finick against her mourning cloak. "Is it not too soon to throw a marriage feast?"

Lord Cappelletto swats away her question as he might a fly that's settled on the freshly slaughtered lamb. Outside the Cappelletti walls, every parish, every guild, every holy order in Verona unfurls its banners to parade in Count Mercutio's funeral procession. But he's as deaf to all of that as Tybalt, lying entombed, is. Deperate to be sure he'll marry his house to Paris, he signals a serving-man, listing out a mere dozen guests he deems it seemly to invite to the ill-timed feast.

As the serving-man departs, Lord Cappelletto catches sight of me hovering outside the doorway. His anger flashes fast again, but I step inside with a contrite curtsy. "Juliet is chastened. She's gone to make penance to Friar Lorenzo."

Lady Cappelletta glances to her husband to gauge what he will make of this before setting any emotion of her own upon her face. Lord Cappelletto only mutters, "May he chance to do some good with the peevish, self-willed child." But he piles heavy hope that Friar Lorenzo will succeed, ordering everyone within the house to the exacting preparation he deems necessary to celebrate Paris being wed to Juliet.

I'm set to picking herbs from along the edges of the arbor. Leaden-headed and swollen-eyed, I reach beneath thyme and parsley leaves to dig my hands into the warm, moist earth. I need the reassuring feel, the fecund smell of what can grow new life. Bees weave in and out of the herb beds, eager to be back at their gathering now that the rain is done. We work together, I making my green-burdened trips to the kitchen as they make their golden ones to the hive. In one of my passes through the courtyard, I catch Juliet's light step in the entryway. "See how she comes from shrift," I say to Lord and Lady Cappelletti, surprised myself by how merry she looks.

"How now, my headstrong, where have you been gadding?"

Stern as Lord Cappelletto's raised eyebrow seems, lurking in his *my headstrong* I hear a fond affection, laced with the barest regret for how cruelly he's used her.

"Where I have learned to repent the sin of disobedience." She kneels and then, as though kneeling is not enough, folds prostrate on the hard stones. "Pardon, I beseech you. Henceforward I am ever ruled by you."

I might roll my eyes and urge her up, pinch her for so overladening her performance. So ill-practiced is she at deceit, she play-acts overmuch to hide her dalliance with Romeo. But Lord Cappelletto is well-fooled. Grinning like the chimpanzee paraded in the prince's menagerie, he summons the house-page, instructing him to bear this news to Paris.

Juliet pulls herself up and says she's already met the count at the friar's cell. "I gave him what love I might, within the bounds of modesty."

She plays the part so well, I clap my hands together, then must pretend I only clasp them tight in prayer, and thank aloud the saints who bless Ca' Cappelletti with this propitious match.

Lord Cappelletto nods, offering amen. "May God bless the reverend holy friar. We and all Verona are much bound to him."

Bound to him Juliet and I most certainly will be, for concealing everafter her first marriage. Bound with us, Friar Lorenzo would be, if any hint of it escaped.

"Nurse." Juliet must also feel the weight of our shared secret. "Will you help me sort such ornaments as you think fit to furnish me tomorrow?"

"No." Lady Cappelletta pecks out the word like a hen going after a worm. "Not till Thursday will you be wed. That's hardly time enough—"

"Go, Nurse," Lord Cappelletto interrupts her. "Go with her now, and ready her, and we'll all be off to church tomorrow."

He hums "Heart's Ease," a lover's ballad, while Lady Cappelletta clings as close to him as a sundial's shadow does its pointer, reminding him of how little time there is for so much preparation to be done.

Juliet sorts spiritless through her collars and hair garlands, keeping her gaze from mine. Her silence tells me how she yet yearns for Romeo, and how little she looks forward to the next day's wedding.

No mother wishes a hasty marriage upon her daughter. Nor a loveless one. But I know there are worse fates than what faces Juliet.

We were born to die. Though Lord Cappelletto spoke the truth, he said only half of it. We are born to die, but born also to live before we're dead. When I lost Pietro's kerchief and was sure I'd lost him as well, I spent desperate hours wishing my life already done. And once he was truly gone—but by then I knew what at Juliet's age none can fathom: the grief we think will drown us we'll learn somehow to bear. And the joy we'd swear is ever lost to us will seep back again.

I rub a sprig of rosemary I've snatched from the kitchen garden against the pillow-casing, to mask any lingering musk of Romeo.

"Be sure to wait until Paris is well in his cups before you lead him here tomorrow night. Do not suffer a servant to bear a torch, and let the candle before the Sainted Madonna burn low before he hitches up your gown."

"Do you think me so hideous, he must be drunk and blinded to have me?"

"It matters not what I think, but what he thinks." What man does not wish to believe he lies with a virgin—and how many girls and women have lied as well to let a man believe he does? If Paris harbors any doubts within the dark, by morning light there'll be this stained sheet to dispel them. "He'd not seek you for a wife, if he did not find you pleasant to look upon. Did he not say as much, when he met you at San Fermo?"

"He said my face was his, and I'd no right to slander it." She turns that face from me, as though I've no right to it either, since telling her to let him claim it.

I step close anyway, twining the rosemary twig into her hair like it was a lover's nosegay. "And his face, did you find it fair?"

"I tried not to think of what was fair, and unfair."

Is it her age? Or the Cappelletti wealth that she was raised in? Which leads her to believe the world is fair, when all my life and loss have taught me that it's not?

I kneel beside the grand cassone at the bottom of her bed, lifting out the lifetime of clothes stored there. Saved once for her, preserved since she's outgrown them for the children she'll soon bear. Such delicious hours we'll have when those babies come, hoarding their soft, their warmth, that milk-sweet scent between us like a miser's gold. Paris'll not begrudge such a mother as I know she'll make, with me to guide her.

I unroll the precious garments piece by piece, starting with the tiniest ones. I need only the slightest glimpse of each to recall her at the age she wore it. The striped pelisse she wriggled in just out of swaddling. The rose-robed cherub who'd shriek as I chased after her. Dark gray stripes to suit the child who pushed me off with angry fists but who, when tears welled in my eyes, spilled out her own as she clambered into my lap to kiss and be kissed comfort. Out of a quilted purple gown that carried her from her sixth year to her seventh tumbles the toy bird Tybalt gave her when she was but a babe. She long loved the little plaything, crying miserably when it was lost, until doting Tybalt said he'd got her a real bird to replace it. He led us down into the arbor, pointed to a nest within the medlar tree, and told her the warbler there was hers, which she might come watch any time. Only, she must not cry, for that would scare the timid bird away. Our dear Tybalt was clever as he was kind, and many a tear dried that year from no more than a mention of her bird.

When I hold the toy to Juliet and remind her of Tybalt's deed, a scowl pulls across her face. "Such trickery, so young. Little wonder he came to such an awful end."

Trickery. To come from her, who being deceived by Romeo has learned so fast to put on her own deceptions. Pretending the grateful daughter before Lord Cappelletto while forgetting all affection for Tybalt.

"Do you deny the love you bore Tybalt, out of some allegiance to Romeo?" I brush her cheek, as if to sweep away the speck of her resentment. "You must put such things from your heart, now that you'll marry Paris."

"There is much I must put from my heart now that you've counseled me to wed the count." She twists away from me. "What affection should I bear Tybalt, who struck down the cousin of the man I am to marry? Does not a husband's grief outweigh his wife's? Would you not have me mourn Paris's kinsman Mercutio, and curse the hand that killed him?"

Though I study her hard, I cannot tell whether she is true in this wifely submission, or still playacting at contrition. "Does Paris ask this of you?"

"Paris asks to kiss what he has yet to wed." She shudders. "That is the man he is. One who'd take advantage of maiden innocence."

Pure of heart and thick of head—is that what I've raised her to be? Kissing true-natured Paris the day before their wedding vows is far better than laying with false-tongued Romeo in an illicit marriage. But before I find a way to tell her that, she crosses herself and adds, "God save me from becoming such a harlot as could want a man who'd have her without first making her a Christian wife." She raises a hand to her mouth, going so wide-eyed that now I see for certain she is playacting. "Oh, Nurse, I have forgotten—you did as much at twelve with that Pietro."

This is too much for me. That she'd slander me a harlot, and mock the very love tales she's begged me to repeat so many times to her.

I'll not hold my tongue. I'll tell her how vile a villain her Romeo is. For what good is a willful colt, until it's broke? But not left broken: I'll bridle her to bridal be by offering a model of a proper marriage, telling how she sprung from that most wonderful love between me and Pietro. Once she knows, and there's no secret left between us, then we'll—

"Are you yet busy?"

Juliet and I both startle at Lady Cappelletta entering the bedchamber.

She shows no more joy than usual for Juliet. "My lord husband would have me offer help to you."

"I've culled what's needed for tomorrow." Juliet waves a quick hand to the trifles she's set out, before bending her knee in imploring curtsy. "If it please you, I would be left alone to pray the heavens to smile upon my state, which as you know is cross and full of sin."

This pleases Lady Cappelletta, to think Juliet so awful. I'm sure she'll leave us to ourselves.

But then Juliet straightens her leg and looks entreating into Lady Cappelletta's eyes. "Let the nurse sit up and be a help to you, for I am sure you've your hands full all, in this so sudden business."

Juliet'll not meet my gaze. Need not meet it, having grown so bold as to put me out. To put me to waiting on Lady Cappelletta, who sizes me up like I'm some dumb ox upon the trader's block, for which she'll drive a pinchfist's bargain. "Take these keys," she says, slipping a ring from her belt, "and fetch out the banqueting cloth. Scrub it to lay upon the table."

I might out-argue Lady Cappelletta, or best her into believing she does not want my labor after all. But I'll not beg Juliet to let me stay while she's caught in such a mood.

The hour's late. The too-little sleep she got last night raws her nerves. I'll leave her rest alone this once. When I steal back hours hence to tousle her awake, I'll tell all that's in my heart, for her to carry when she stands beside noble Paris and makes true marriage vows.

Just past her door, I think I hear her call me back. Does she yet long to be with me the way she did when she was a littler girl? But what can I do with her tonight but play out once more the dismal scene we've already had? I'll not chance more sore words between us. I must let her be alone long enough to be glad of me again. Just till morning. There'll be time then to tell her, first of Romeo's deception, then of my own. After which we'll never let another secret forge its way between us.

"Fetch more spices."

"Look to the baked meats."

"Find dates and quinces from the pantry."

Cocks crow, curfew bells ring. Three o'clock comes and goes, but Lord Cappelletto'll not leave off ordering me about. Ordering me, and cook, and every servant in the house. Lady Cappelletta watches over him, muttering how nothing's kept him up so late since the last of the pursemaker's daughters was married off. He says she wears a jealous hood that unbecomes her. Such an unhappy house from which to send forth any bride. But this is the last day Juliet and I must abide beside such misery. I can hide one final time behind the hedgerow of their bickering. Slinking to the woodpile that's stacked where the dovecote stood, I lie down for a doze.

I've not slept long when the serving-man seeking logs awakens me. A perfect logger-head he is. But before I've run my tongue through half the ways of telling him what wooden fate I wish him, pipe and lute sound from the courtyard, and the house-page announces Paris is arrived.

I hurry to the courtyard, where Lord and Lady Cappelletti buzz about the count, who's dressed in the same deep mourning for his cousin that they wear for Tybalt.

Paris looks past them, lays pinky finger beneath his eye, and nods smiling to me. He means to say my bruises are well-faded. I'd thought as much, peering at the polished plate set out in the sala, but his kind notice reassures me. Will not my Juliet do well, matched to such a man?

"Hie, Nurse, make haste," Lord Cappelletto says. "Go wake Juliet. Trim her up, tell her the bridegroom's come."

One come, one gone, and she's got the better of the bargain, the second so excels the first. It gives my tired legs strength to mount the stairs. As I cross the loggia I keep my sights on handsome Paris beaming eagerly below, as though he alone can draw joy into the Cappelletti courtyard.

"Why, lamb," I call as I enter Juliet's chamber. She's got the bed curtains pulled as tight as on the coldest winter night. "Why, lady, why, love, sweetheart. Why, bride."

My slug-a-bed's sound in her sleep. Stealing every pennyworth of rest, and well she does, for Paris'll give her none tonight. Will give her all, I mean—so oft she'll have no rest. Marry and amen to that, and may God forgive me, and her, for deceiving him.

This will be our last hour alone together, and I must make the most of it. Must find the words, the way, to tell her what she really is. What, and who, and how she came to be here, and why I've hid it all so long. This is the dowry I've got to give. Not coins or gowns or plate, but love. Love such as she's only known from me, yet love she's never known for what it truly is.

Such love surely is enough. I'll rub her in it, like a scented oil. Wrap her with it, like the finest cloth. Adorn her with it, like jewels strung in that dark, thick hair that's so like mine, and looped around her smooth young neck and dainty wrists. I'll kiss it onto those almond eyes and tell about the day I first saw it in them. The bittersweet of losing Pietro, only to find him again in her.

I'll tell it all in this precious hour. Our last hour alone. Yet not alone, for I feel Pietro with me. Feel there is in gallant Paris some echo of my own great-hearted husband. I'll make her feel it as well, so she'll know why I'm sure he's meet match for her.

"Lady." I draw back the bed curtain. "Lady, my lady."

Juliet's dressed. She must've been unnerved to wake alone. To rise so early and get herself into her clothes, only to falter and lie lonesome down again.

"What a bride you'll be, already in your bed. Should I send the count to you directly?" That ought to rouse her. But still she sleeps.

I lay loving hand against her shoulder to shake her awake. Lay loving hand and feel her cold.

But no, it's me who's cold. An icy stone sunk to my stomach. A freezing through my heart. For in that touch, I know. A bitter shivering jitters my joints, rattles the teeth in my head, makes me curse the day that I was born.

Born to live to find her dead.

Dead. Dead, dead, dead. My numbed lips form the word, over and over. A whisper, a roar, I cannot tell which. Until Lady Cappelletta comes in calling, "What noise is here? What's the matter?"

What am I to say? My last child, my only life, is gone.

How can she die and leave me living?

Lady Cappelletta comes near the bed. She looks on Juliet and screams. So loud I grab my darling's hand. And find clasped there an empty pouch, its loose drawstring tied off with a cross.

The numb, the cold, heats to searing pain. I hide the pouch within my own fat fist. Use that fist, and the other, to beat my head for being such a fool. A fool, and fooled.

Lord Cappelletto rushes in, then crumbles to his knees. "Death," he says, his own face waxy as a funeral mask. "Death is my heir and steals everything from me. Tybalt stabbed, and Juliet taken with him, broken-hearted from grieving for her cousin."

The musicians are still playing in the courtyard. Thrumming out their happy tune, not knowing bliss has turned to loss. My Juliet dead, never to know the last good act Tybalt tried to do, and how untrue her beloved Romeo. Me, not knowing as I should have, the instant death took her. Not knowing when I could, I should, have saved her.

My fist's clenched fast, keeping clasped the awful truth. Between the Cappelletti's wails, I steal out of the bedchamber, through Ca' Cappelletti and off to San Fermo, to find the man who killed her.

A scaffold rises inside the upper church, and some exalted painter barks down to his assistants. Another saint is being martyred on the wall. Barbara perhaps, or maybe Dorotea. Brushes dip into garish colors to depict the virgin's torturous demise. As if those who come to pray do not have enough of death in our own lives, and need frescoed instruction in fresh grief.

I hurry past, down into the dank of the Franciscans' cloister. There is the usual dismal press of sniveling children, shame-faced husbands, wretched wives, and crag-faced crones outside Friar Lorenzo's cell. A lifetime of misery, seeking such relief as we're told only the Holy Church can give.

Pushing my way through, I heave against the door. It gives way, revealing Friar Lorenzo bending his fervid ear to a blushing maiden like a worm wriggling into ripe fruit flesh.

"Benedicte, and God give you peace." He smiles at me like I'm a child. "But you must have patience as well as penitence, Angelica, and wait your turn."

"Damn your *benedicte*, and your God. And you." I fling the empty poison-pouch at him.

Shock grays his face. But only for an instant, before he wills his features back to composed. "My dear Ginevra, you are absolved. Go forthwith to the church of San Zeno for the morning Mass." In one swift motion, he ushers the maiden out, latches the door against any other entries, and turns to hover over me. "Angelica, I did not—"

"Did not want what punishment you'd get, if it was learned you ministered an illicit marriage. So you hid the deed with poison."

"No." He snatches up the pouch and secrets it among his cache of medicinals. "Juliet came to me in ungodly anguish. She raised a blade to her own breast. I only gave her what would still her hand, as you stilled Romeo's."

"If only I'd stilled his heart along with his hand. But he lives, while my Juliet is dead."

"Not dead, Angelica, though it's comfort that you think so."

What comfort, in seeing, touching, keening over her lifeless body? What good to him in denying she is killed?

Friar Lorenzo touches the tips of his fingers together, steepling his hands to lecture me. "What appears as death is not always death. No more than what appears as virtue always is true goodness. The remedy I dispensed has put her into a sleep so deep that she seems a corpse."

It's nearly more than my worn heart can believe. "She lives, truly?"

I make him swear to it, before Christ upon the cross. I want to trust his words, to let them melt away this tight hold of loss.

"But why?" I ask. "What could set her to such deception?"

"With her marriage to Romeo consummated, Juliet could not be married to the count, though all within Ca' Cappelletti would force her to it. To save her from such sin, I deemed it best to let them think her lost. Once they've laid her within her family crypt,

I'll send word to Romeo to bear her to Mantua, where they may live in secret joy."

How could he, could she, have plotted to keep such a thing secret from me? "You'd've let me believe Juliet was dead, and bid her live far-off in Mantua without me knowing?"

"Did you not tell her to wed Paris, knowing she was already bound in the eyes of God to Romeo?"

This is why he turned my girl against me? I spit out what Romeo is, what he's done. But Friar Lorenzo offers not even a flicker of surprise.

"You knew?" I'm still the fool, to need to ask. For what does he not know, sitting all day in this cold cell listening to what's most intimately told?

"Romeo is not the only man in Verona who, courting what he could not get, would come to me for counsel. Such groans, such sighs, do I hear. But no more than that, concerning Rosaline—no sin done, none confessed. Her virtue was enough to save them both. When he turned his heart instead to Juliet, and found in hers a welcoming return, I only offered holy blessing to what they'd begun. Thus was Romeo saved from sin."

"And Tybalt?"

"Romeo proclaimed a cousin's love for Tybalt, but still Tybalt raised a sword at him. As Romeo tried to beat down the bandying, Tybalt struck Mercutio. Only then did Romeo, mad with grief, lift his own blade." Friar Lorenzo pinches at his Pater Noster beads like a merchant plying abacus to calculate a profit. "God knows, I'd bring them both back if I could, and bind the families to peace as I intended. But what death takes from us we can only have again in heaven."

I've no need for him to tell me so, when everyone I've ever loved is lost to me.

Except Juliet.

If what he says is true. If my girl still lives. If for once I'm given hope instead of grief.

The deepest place within my chest aches. Just as it did when I swelled with milk, and all I sought was the sweet pain of her suck. Hope instead of grief.

But even such hope carries a sharp edge: this potion Friar Lorenzo's given her must be some semblence of what he used to convince Pietro that our infant daughter was dead. Twice, he's stolen her from me.

"Death did not take Susanna. You did." The secret I've long kept spills from me—for what have I to lose in letting him know now all that I know? Why hide how much I loath him for all he's put me through? "Because we were poor and could make no grand gifts to the Holy Church, you stole our living baby and gave her to the wealthy Cappelletti, letting them believe that theirs survived. Deceiving us into accepting that ours was dead."

A hideous line throbs across his forehead, pulsing angry blue. "Who told you this, Angelica?"

Told. As though I must be ever told, the way a stupid beast must be shepherded. As though I'm no more than some dumb animal, and cannot figure for myself how I've been used.

"Sainted Maria." I see her before me, bare-breasted and beatific as she suckles the sacred babe. But in Friar Lorenzo's narrow cell there's no image of the Holy Mother. Only Christ, tortured upon the cross. "By the Sainted Maria, there are things only a mother knows."

He gathers himself within the thick folds of his cassock, searching out words to convince me I am wrong. But I unlatch the door and take my leave of him.

Though the morning's bright by the time I return from the friary, Lady Cappelletta's gone to bed, having taken wine enough to slumber heavily. Lord Cappelletto sits alone with Juliet. Staring dull eyed, his voice so wearied I must bend close to make out what he says. "The earth has swallowed all my hopes but her. Left only this one poor thing to rejoice and solace in. But cruel death snatches even Juliet from us."

By his *us* he means the Cappelletti. I once believed his losses measured as heavy as my own, and together we took comfort as we prayed for all those death stole away. But I'll not find such fellowship with him today. He's settled the Cappelletti cap once more upon Juliet's head, and condoles himself by cataloguing how grand the funeral cortege will be. What he could not do for Tybalt, condemned as Count Mercutio's killer, he'll conjure instead for Juliet, heralded across Verona as Count Paris's betrothed. A procession led by her godfathers Cansignorio and Il Benedicto. Entire religious orders burning candles for her soul. The prince's council carrying the Cappelletti banner and shields. Finely decorated horses clad in the family colors. And Paris walking shoulder to shoulder beside Lord Cappelletto, the carved bier before them, and atop it Juliet.

"Juliet," I repeat, impatient as I am to be rid of him. "I must ready her." Immodest it'd be for a father to watch a full-grown daughter's final washing and anointing.

He leans nearer to the bed. As he brushes a fare-thee-well hand against her cheek, my heart catches, sure he'll sense whatever life pulses within her.

But grief's too constant a companion for him to disbelieve it. "Dress her in the green samite," he says. The finest gown in all the household. Lady Cappelletta'll not be pleased to learn she'll never again wear it. "It was my first Juliet's. She was married in it."

Have I ever envied wealthy Lady Cappelletta? Pietro could not have afforded even a patch of so fine a fabric. But my husband never would have dressed me in a dead woman's clothes, never made me feel there was anyone or anything he cherished more than me.

Lord Cappelletto's eyes go to Juliet's finger. Mine cannot help but follow, though I know he'll not see what he seeks there. "Where is the emerald ring?"

I tap a fingernail against one of my yellowed teeth, as if I might chisel out the right half-truth to tell him. "She was not wearing any ring when she fell prostrate before you yesterday. Perchance it was given over in Friar Lorenzo's cell, where she made her shrift."

Every stitch I speak is true, though I sew them together in such a way that they cover over all I know. Let the scheming Franciscan, ever covetous for gems and plate and finery, explain to Lord Cappelletto what's become of the Cappelletti jewel.

I bow my head and cross myself, muttering how lucky it is to be claimed just when one has a freshly shriven soul. Lord Cappelletto murmurs amen, and sighs, and stands, and says he must go down to the family chapel to pray for Juliet, and for Tybalt.

At last my girl and I get our hour alone together. Though by my holidame, I'd not have this be our last.

I climb into our bed and turn my head over hers, hoping to feel her breath upon my cheek, as I did when she was just a babe. But I sense nothing. I lay my ear onto her chest. Something throbs between us. Heart, blood, love. I cannot separate what's hers from mine.

I let the full weight of my head sink onto her, wrapping my warm body against her immobile one. "Dearest lamb, how you frighted me. Did you feel so despairing you thought you'd need deceive me, when all I live for is your happiness?"

Raising her too-still arm, I kiss her palm and cradle it against me. And then I tell her.

Tell how twice I did not let myself fathom what with my mother-love some deepest part of me surely must have known. The first, when I woke uncomprehending one last child had quickened in me, and in my astonishment labored two long days to bring that tenderest infant out. How Pietro's weeping told me it was lost, and how by the Virgin's grace I came here to her. How this was the second time I was so unperceiving: sure as I was that my milk, my love, my tender care was what fed her, it took years before I realized it was more than milk that bound us. How blood and bone and every bodily humor tie her to me, and to my lost Pietro. "I am your mother." The words glimmer in the golden air. "You are my daughter."

How many times have I imagined saying this, imagined what surprise and joy and deepest love she'd offer in reply? How I've wanted to have her know why what I give her will always be so much more than what Lady Cappelletta offers, why what lives in her of my Pietro weighs more than every jewel and cloth and coin Lord Cappelletto ever could bestow her. I've longed to tell, and have her wrap soft arms around me, and weep with joy-filled relief to know our dearest truth, and mayhap confess to me she'd long before sensed it for herself.

But there's no joy-filled relief. Not for her, lying senseless to all I say. Or for me, who might as well've whispered into an empty cask, sealed it up, and cast it in the Adige to bob away unheard.

The brazier's been tucked away unused since winter warmed to spring, but in this full heat of summer I light a fire in it. Cool as the water is when it's drawn from the courtyard well, I wait for the fire to take the chill from it before I dip a fazzoletto cloth in, wring it out, and touch it to Juliet.

The last I looked upon my boys was when I washed each one before Pietro bore them off to be buried. Six beautiful bodies, speckled with black spots. *God's tokens.* So enchanting a name for such a horrific sight. Like insects swarming across their thighs, their arms. Those specks were worse than the plague's raised boils, which at least appeared angry, insolent. God's tokens were a more awful marring. Delicate pricks death took over and over, gently eating its way across the flesh of all my darling sons.

But not my daughter. Juliet's body is perfect. Perfectly quiet, perfectly still. Perfectly lovely.

Downstairs, Lord Cappelletto reads out some version of the liturgy Friar Lorenzo long led me in. Friar and lord can have their learned Latin prayers. I've something more holy, my hands cleansing every precious part of her.

Did I think just two nights past she was her most beautiful by moonlight? Lying here, bathed in the day's full sun, she is more pure, more beautiful, than anyone or anything I've ever seen.

From the first day I held her, I bathed and swaddled her so many awestruck times. I remember every inch of her. But I mark the difference, too. How heavy she's become. The infant I craved and cradled as though she were still a part of me is now this full-grown body I must roll carefully, dipping the soft cloth over and over into the warmed water as I slowly trace my way across her. I wash the length of her fingers and stretch of her arms, the curl of her toes and the curve of her legs. With her back to me, I part her hair, tucking it to either side to reveal the blades of her shoulders jutting like an angel's wings. The smooth rounding of that bottom I wiped when she was at her littlest. I swear, though I know all of her, my most familiar is yet a mystery to me. Could so lovely a child, a near-woman, have grown from me? Could she be so nearly lost so young?

Would she really have left me, letting me believe that she was dead while she went off to Mantua to live secretly with Romeo? I'd not have thought she could hold so much from me. But I've held all I know of who she is, and what he is, from her.

What he is. This is the one thing I've still not confided, even to these now unhearing ears. I'd not made her know it yesterday, hoping ignorance might ease her to forget him and make a loving wife to Paris. But if she'd sooner take her own life than live wedded to any but Romeo—or, living, beshrew me heart and soul just to be with him—then I must hold my motherly tongue. I'll not tell what still wears upon my heart, to keep her from shoving me away again.

With caked rose petals and rosemaried oil, I anoint my daughter. The bright floral fragrance dances with the sharp woody one. Can scents make a harmony? Yes, as surely as Juliet and I have, and always will.

In those first awful days and months without Pietro, how I craved him. My body ached to have those great paws of his upon me, the cinnamon-sweet scent of him and the tickle of his whisper in my ear. I was half-mad even just to hear the timbre of his voice again, and to use my own to say all the things I'd not realized till too late I'd never have a chance to tell him.

To not have bid good-bye to Pietro. Or to Tybalt. All I would've said and done to keep that boy from harm. Or even just to show my deepest love before I lost him.

It was no different even with my sons. When they lay infected with pestilence, we knew we'd not have them long. But Pietro and I'd not utter anything we thought might fright them, and so left unsaid what otherwise would've filled their final hours.

Always, death has robbed me of this chance to speak my fullest heart to those I love. Until Juliet.

It'll not be long before Lord Cappelletto comes to claim her.

I must make for her some sign so that waking in the Cappelletti tomb, she'll know I know that she yet lives, and be comforted by my love as she shivers alone among ancient bones, beside death-struck Tybalt.

Never have I wished I could write, or she read, until now. To have the power to close my hand around a pen and mark words upon a page that her hungry eyes could claim a whole day hence— what remedy that'd be, when I am far from her.

But I must clever out a way to make myself known without words. Did not the touch and taste of me soothe her, when she knew naught but a baby's babbling? Just as the rub of Pietro's linen shirts still succor me.

This is what I have to give our daughter. I slip one of the precious three shirts I've saved over her head, smoothing the well-worn cloth across her tender breasts. A far coarser weave than Juliet has ever donned, although she's snuggled many a night against the faded fabric, all that came between us in this bed. I work the samite gown in place, careful to hide any trace of the secret shirt beneath it. Though it's richer to the touch than the frayed-thin linen, the samite's green sallows my girl's cheeks.

I bend to give her one last kiss, and taste the friar's potion lingering on her lips. Loathe as I am to leave her when we've so little time together, I'll not have her wake to such bitterness.

I hie down the tower stair into the arbor. The air is filled with pollen-coated bees, hurrying their precious treasure into the hive. When my toddling Juliet could not abide the wormwood taste of me, I plunged a desperate hand into the waxy comb, and earned a dozen searing stings. But as I unseal the hive today, bees alight along my arm but do me no more harm than they did Tybalt, as they arced with grace around him. I dip my fingers carefully inside and lift them away honey-coated. With the other hand I replace the seal before hastening back to Juliet.

I work my broad thumb between her lips, spreading its honey on her tongue. My three middle fingers coat her pink gums and pearly teeth, the littlest one saved to trace a honey kiss upon her lips. These lips through which my suckling girl first knew me.

These lips which, with this honey, will once more drink in all my love for her.

SEVENTEEN

All Verona believes a rich man's daughter is being laid dead within his family tomb today. Why would they not? The parish bells toll it. The holymen and noblemen who don mourning bands and accompany the gold- and fur-trimmed bier pay solemn tribute to it. The poor huddled on the benches placed to line the cortege route earn their coin by witnessing it. And Lady Cappelletta and I peer down from the sala windows, watching all of it.

Roused by Lord Cappelletto and dressed in a silk mourning gown covered by a vair and ermine mantle, a ruby necklace newly clasped to set off her garnet cross, with sapphire rings on every finger and a gold-and-sapphire garland in her hair, Lady Cappelletta dutifully rent and wept and caterwauled during the long hours of the vigil. Cursing the Montecchi and mourning the twin loss of Tybalt and the samite gown, mayhap, if not Juliet.

I let my grief for Tybalt swell to tears as well, so none would wonder why I'd not cry over my nursling's seeming corpse. But as the death knell tolls, the procession candles burn, and the cortege snakes away from Ca' Cappelletti leaving us behind, our eyes are dry, and our words are few. Insistent as she was on clinging to Tybalt, Lady Cappelletta showed no such interest in accompanying Juliet's body to the Cappelletti vault. Lord Cappelletto, ever calculating what makes best public spectacle, must be glad she's not forgotten a woman's proper mourning role now that so many Veronese are watching.

We wait side by side, each wound in her own thoughts, until it's time to leave for the Duomo. No ordinary church will do for Lord Cappelletto, nor for Count Paris, who sends the prince's own liveried carriage for Lady Cappelletta. In the thick July heat, she heaps the fur hood beside her on the bolster. I sit opposite, watching Verona's streets slip past.

When Juliet awakes, I'll not hold from her what she is to me, what I am to her. But I'll serve her better if she keeps me ever close. And so I'll feign for Romeo the very love she'd have me feel. But I'll not forget the evil that he's done. Plotting to debauch a nun. Deceiving and defiling innocent Juliet instead. Trying with his Judas coins to make me a common pander. Running his murderous blade through our beloved Tybalt. For all that, I'll show to him the same false heart by which he beguiled Juliet. If she's to travel to Mantua to make a household with him, then I must go withal, biding my time while I tend her.

Juliet need never know how cruelly Romeo's served her, so

long as I secretly serve him the ruthless same. Perchance I'll find an apothecary in Mantua who'll minister an unaccustomed dram, a poison that'll do to Romeo what Friar Lorenzo's potion only pretends on Juliet.

And what then? What will become of her once he is dead?

Many a wife who's too soon widowed finds youth and beauty can win for her another, better match.

Lady Cappelletta draws back her veil, amber eyes wide as she repeats, "Another, better match?"

Her astonishment brings on my own. I'd not realized I spoke that part aloud, so fiercely did I want to convince myself it could prove true. Before I can work my tongue into some half-truth to shade my meaning, she asks, "What man would have me, when all Verona knows I cannot bear again?"

It's Lord Cappelletto's eventual demise, the only possible end she can hope for her own loveless marriage, that troubles her. Not yet thirty, but haggard-eyed as she stares out at the banners bearing the Cappelletti crest hung all along the route. "Tybalt gone, Paris lost to us." Worry curdles her words. As though the fear I first saw eddying over her when she lay in the parto bed has never ebbed. "What's left for a widow, when a husband leaves no heir?"

Rosaline and her Holy Sisters line the Duomo steps, the answer to her question. Few among them shine as Rosaline does with pious light. They stand identical in their wimples and habits, except for the youngest orphans, the ones who've no means of donning sacred cloth until some wealthy sinner buys absolution with a bit of dotal-alms charity.

Whatever dowry portion returns to Lady Cappelletta when Lord Cappelletto dies, however much beyond that he might choose to bequeath her, without nephew or son-in-law to serve as her protector, she'll end up in a convent. Just as I would've these years past, without Juliet. What else is there for a woman with neither heir nor husband?

But Juliet, still in the bloom of youth and blessed with my fertile humors—surely she'll fare better. She's barely older than I was when Pietro found me, and she'll have me to search out such a man as—

The carriage stops. Paris waits in the piazza to hand us down, his face pocked with grief. Handsome, young, and powerful. Yet so easily unmade by the despair death dances down on even the most fortunate.

Lady Cappelletta leans heavily on his arm, grateful for one final chance to hold to him. I bow my head, following in mock obedience to take my place among the mourners.

"Angelica." Friar Lorenzo winnows himself from the mass of brown-frocked Franciscans gathering to make their procession into the church. He grasps my elbow, whispering fusty breath into my ear. "The thing you spoke of in my cell, about Susanna. I cannot know what has given you such thoughts, but I must tell you—"

"You've told me already." For once, it's my eyes that bear down on his, searching out a hidden sin. "What appears as death is not always death."

He draws back as if I've slapped him. The piazza is filling with whole companies of friars, nuns, and well-ranked priests, all handsomely paid by Lord Cappelletto to be here. Behind the holy orders crowd finely dressed members of Verona's most powerful families—although only the ones who bear no enmity to the Cappelletti. Or who hide such feelings today, when the family is high in Prince Cansignorio's and Count Paris's favor. Friar Lorenzo runs a lizard's tongue along his wine-stained teeth. But he'll not dare speak another word as the assemblage swells around us.

I turn from him to file into the cathedral with the rest of the women. Banners and pennants with the Cappelletti and Scaligeri coats of arms hang from every wall within the Duomo. The air is sweet with beeswax, so many candles burning along the altar and before the rood screen that the whole apse of the church seems ablaze.

What appears as death is not always death. Is this not what Christ, looking down at us from upon his cross, is meant to tell? Is this not why we pray for the everlasting life of those who've passed, and search for every trace of them in the features of their children? Why I carry such careful memories of my boys, believing that so long as love for them lives in me, they're not truly lost. Why I still wear my husband's shirt, and wrapped Juliet in one as well, so his touch, his smell, might keep him close to us. How I know my own dearest lamb will rise again, as surely as Christ himself did from his tomb.

Chanting fills the cathedral, the deep voices of priests and friars surging from the chancel, joining with the harmonious swell of nuns secreted within some hidden choir. Their voices arc along the vaulted ceiling and reign back down over all who kneel to honor Juliet. The holy music hums within my very bones, as priests and deacons bless and incense and kiss sacred text, every familiar ritual meant to earn eternal life. *What appears as death is not always death.*

No more than what appears as virtue always is true goodness.

The thought pulls tight across my chest, squeezing the breath from me. *What appears as virtue.* Hundreds of Veronese kneel before me, yet my eyes cannot help but search the gilted openings within the rood screen, seeking out the back of Friar Lorenzo's tonsured head.

My holy confessor's practiced such deceptions, always cloaking them in seeming virtue. Stealing a poor woman's newborn babe, and thinking it recompense enough to contract her as servant to the rich family who unwittingly receives it. Groping so many years after a lord's wealth, only to snatch his greatest treasure, a daughter entered into marriage without her father's lawfully required consent. Counseling a mere child to play at the sin of taking her own life. Making mockery of my grief, along with Lord Cappelletto's and Paris's, by letting us believe one dead who lives.

And now, this greatest sacrilege. How can the Franciscan hide behind his own piously clasped hands praying a false Requiem Mass, and suffer me to do the same, when we both know Juliet yet lives? Unless—

Unless she does not live.

What if he's lied to me once more, and Juliet is truly dead? What if he tricked her into swallowing his poison with promise of some secret rendezvous with banished Romeo—and tricked me as well with the promise my precious girl survives?

He took the cross-tied pouch from me, the only proof of his

part in this. If I speak a word against him without that, I'm nothing but a heretic and madwoman.

A heretic and madwoman. I pray to the Holy Mother and all my saints that's all I am. A heretic for bending knee and bowing head through false Requiem. A madwoman, frantic with fear until I can see my girl, my heart's delight, awakened from feigned death. Smiling and speaking and laughing once more.

All around me, people rise, turning to make their way out of the cathedral. I'm carried along by the close press of bodies, like a broken shard tossed into the Adige. Taken one last time to Ca' Cappelletti.

Fur-lined mourning robes, a quarter-mile long funeral procession, silk flags and gilt banners and a hundred blazing candles—and still there must be more to mark the mourning of ones so rich as the Cappelletti. They host a feast as well, the sala thrown open to welcome Verona's most godly and most powerful, who gorge themselves on our grief.

The Requiem Mass was enough for me. I'll not bear the banquet. So I steal my way downstairs, through the courtyard and the arched passageway into the arbor. I kneel one last time beside the beehive, drawing out the box Tybalt husbanded beneath it, grateful for the coin-heavy sack inside. Enough to keep Juliet and me in simple household. I secure the sack within my dress and replace the box, praying my thanks to Tybalt and telling myself I must do what he meant to. For his sake, and Rosaline's, and most of all for Juliet's.

But can I do it? Can I, after all, bring myself to kill even such a villain as Romeo?

Something crackles in the air behind me. Paris.

He slips into the arbor, bouquet in hand, to stare up at the window of Juliet's bedchamber. As if by the very power of his royal gaze he might conjure her there. I give a loud *amen*, so he'll think I kneel in prayer.

He whirls my way as though half-expecting her, then makes a quick half-bow to hide his disappointment at discovering only me. "You do not dine with the others?" he asks.

"Grief thieves me of my appetite."

"Grief thieves us both of more than that." He draws a pink rose from the bouquet, its petals barely opened into bloom. "So tender a heart she had, to die of mourning her beloved cousin."

So tender a heart he has, to believe that. Though I might have thought the same of Juliet, before Romeo preyed upon her.

"A too-loving nature. She had it since she was a babe." My words are true enough to satisfy us both.

I'd not've thought I'd care for company, but Paris draws me gently to the arbor bench, asking me one thing and then another about Juliet, as a babe and then a girl and lastly a young woman, and I'm as glad as ever to tell.

"You make me love her more with every word," he says. "And hate myself for hastening her death." He slides his thumb along the rose's stem, searching out a thorn. Pierces himself just for the awful pleasure of the pain. "Lord Cappelletto urged patience when first I asked for her hand. But once Tybalt was killed, he wanted no delay in trothing her to me. He told me to stop her tears with joy. But times of woe are not the time to woo."

"I urged her to it, too." For all I must hold secret, it's good at least to share as much as that. For it was my championing Paris that drove her to the Franciscan's cell. If I'd been more careful in my counsel, perhaps she'd not have turned to the conniving friar.

And yet, I see from how deep Paris's sorrow cuts that I was right in this: he is the one man worthy of her. Not just a handsome face, a full purse, a powerful uncle. He's a heart that's truly noble. If Romeo had not snuck in seeking Rosaline, what happy future might my Juliet've had with Paris?

I am a fool to indulge such thoughts. Yet what is a fool but one who hopes?

From all my life's grief, I'd forged these weeks past a single hope: that if Juliet and Paris wed, she might make a well-loved and loving wife. It's a hope I cannot help holding, even now.

Paris knows naught of how Juliet was beguiled by Romeo. But he knows Romeo is Tybalt's killer, the sworn enemy of the Cappelletti, and by his own princely uncle's royal decree banished from Verona. Who better to rid us of Romeo? If Paris discovers Romeo's intended trespass, surely he'll take it for villainy and drive him off while Juliet yet slumbers, saving me the sin of poisoning him.

When my girl awakens among the cobwebbed bones of a hundred rotted Cappelletti, beside poor Tybalt's slowly mouldering corpse, what if, trembling with terror, she finds Romeo's abandoned her, and discovers handsome Paris guarding her instead? Seeing his grief and then his gladness, surely she'll realize for herself his worth.

Desperate I must be, to try it. But if in such desperation I can bring her a true and goodly love, then I must.

"Such pretty flowers." I nod at them as if there'd not been any bloodied pricking. "I'd take them to where she lies now, if curfew were not so near to being rung."

Paris's mourning cloak is embroidered with the Scaligeri shield, and he pulls himself tall in it. "The guards must let me pass. I'll bear her the bouquet."

And water it with tears, no doubt. So much the better, for wet lashes will show well the love that shines in his fair eyes. "Be sure to have a steady torch, so you can stay to pray the matins and the lauds for her." To linger long enough to dispense with Romeo so I'll not have to, and then find your wildest prayers come true when my lady awakes.

He bows again and takes his leave. Alone, I make one final climb up to Juliet's chamber. While the last of the feast guests stumble full-gutted from the house, I pray we'll not to Mantua after all.

EIGHTEEN

'm up before sun or morning lark, walking toward where dawn's first light pinks the eastern sky. I've not ever been a patient woman. I'll not keep myself from Juliet.

Last night it seemed wily to send Paris to her. To believe that when she sees the noble affection in him, it will win such corresponding love from her as it does from me. But in the restless hours since, I've worried her eyes remain too blinded by Romeo's deceit. That I alone can wipe them clear. As I did whenever some childhood malady—

"What noise?" A man steps from a darkened doorway, his blade drawn. "Who's there?"

"A mourning woman." I quaver my voice to match my morello

cloak. "Making my way to Santa Caterina, to pray for one who's lost."

"Move past, or you'll be the one that'll need praying for." With his free hand, he raises a flannel to his face. "This house is sealed up with the plague."

Plague.

The word hits like a slap. What worse omen could this eerie hour hold than the news that the pestilence's come again to ravage Verona?

The old imagined swelling throbs beneath my arms, the awful tidings driving me faster up the road to the nunnery. As though I might outrace Mercutio's last curse.

I've not got Paris's regal right to order a gate open, nor the strength to scale a convent wall. But the entry to Santa Caterina is already swinging wide, which sends me even quicker across the grounds.

I stumble in the dark beneath a yew tree. Trip across some unseen thing, heart thundering as I fall sprawled beside a lifeless body.

The seeming corpse shivers out a snore. It's pimply-necked Balthasar, moaning with some troubled dream. A new knife-slice of terror shudders up my spine. If Romeo's got to her before Paris—

I pull myself to my knees, find my uneasy way onto my feet. Head bent, I search out the winding path and hurry on.

Just as I near the entry to the catacomb, something wraps icy around my wrist. A too-familiar voice says, "Angelica, we must make haste from here."

The only haste I mean to make is to Juliet. But Friar Lorenzo has such a hold on me that though I twist and shove, I cannot push past.

"Has Romeo already come?"

"Yes, come unbidden," Friar Lorenzo says. "The messenger who should have born my missive to Mantua was quarantined within a pestilence-ridden house."

"The plague is truly here again?" Why do I ask, as though I do not within my bones already know? Know once it's come, all that it might take.

He nods, murmuring some self-preserving Latin. "Romeo, ignorant of my scheme, believed Juliet was truly dead. And now he's gone."

Romeo, gone off again. This gives me hope enough to ask, "And Count Paris?"

"Both he and Romeo departed in a single unkind hour."

Unkind, and worse, of Paris to leave Juliet. I'd not've believed it of him. Mayhap he was afrighted by the sight of her newly woke from what he thought was death. Or worse—perchance Juliet, without me here to advise her, refused Paris with the tiding that Romeo's already wedded and bedded her.

"Where is she?" I ask. "Where is my Juliet?"

He nods toward the crypt.

"You left her alone within the tomb?"

"God forgive me, I left one who would not leave." He gropes with his free hand for his Pater Noster beads, the way Tybalt from the time he was a boy would touch unwitting fingers to where his dagger hung. "Juliet swore she'd not come away, although I begged her to."

"Well that she disobeys you, when your intent was to give my girl to live in secret exile with the false-hearted Romeo. But you're well practiced in stealing such a daughter from her parents."

He tightens his grasp on me. "I never stole, or switched, I swear it." But then his grip loosens, and he shakes his head. "And she'll not live with Romeo."

This last makes me so glad, I break free of him. I must get to my girl, must comfort and counsel her. I quicken past, worried Friar Lorenzo will follow. But some alarm sounds beyond the convent wall, and he scurries off, unmanned.

The stone steps down to the catacomb lead me into as deep a dark as swallowed me during my night climbs in the Cappelletti tower. Upon the final step, I'm hit by a stench that turns my stomach. The putrefied stink of what's become of Tybalt.

Groping my way along the dismal passage, I thump my leg into a mattock. It lies beside a crowbar at the entrance to the Cappelletti crypt, along with a hundred fallen petals shaken from what was Paris's bouquet.

No. Not petals. The crimson spots are blood, slicking the marble floor.

"Juliet? My lady, my lamb?" My words sink unanswered into the dank, cold vault.

A dropped rush-and-tallow torch glows just inside the entry. I raise it up, and by its smoke and stink discover the crimson spots puddle into a carmine pool beneath Paris.

He lies motionless, his chest bearing a wound I know too well, a match to what felled my beloved Tybalt. Paris'd not had time to strike before he was struck, his sword half-drawn as the last of life slips silently from him.

God forgive me for bidding him come here. And God damn Romeo, who surely was the one who killed him.

A chill shivers over me. If Friar Lorenzo was mistaken, and Romeo is yet here after all, hidden as he waits to smite again—

Tipping the torch away from me, I call again to Juliet. I step deeper into the tomb, and the light catches a face grimaced in bitter death. It's Romeo, his pale hand clutching an emptied apothecary's vial.

Self-poisoned, I suppose. But what comfort is dead Romeo without my living Juliet?

By the friar's mark, Paris and Romeo were both departed in the same unkind hour. But not Juliet.

"Dearest lamb. My darling girl." Why does she not answer me? How could she have voice to refuse Friar Lorenzo but not to call to her beloved nurse? "Juliet. Susanna. Juliet."

Something rasps back at me. Low and wretched, all the world's agony shuddering in it. As I turn, my torchlight glisters along the bands of gold ribboned through Juliet's green gown. And the shining silver hilt of a dagger, jutting from her chest.

The sight pierces my own heart. I drop the torch, grasp the hilt in both hands, and tug. A gurgling suck shudders up the knife as it rips free from her.

Letting the dagger fall, I cradle her to me. "My loveliest one, I bid you. I beg you. Do not leave me." Blood oozes through the thick samite, and the thin linen shirt beneath it.

I am too late.

If only I could carry her from here. Could will life back into these chilling limbs. Could breathe my breath into her, though it cost me my last gasp. I'd die willingly that she might live. But all my love cannot stanch what's already lost.

I bend my head to her breast and, baptized in the final warmth that seeps from her, beg forgiveness for not saving her.

What mother would not cling to her own child, would not hold, and hold, and hold one final time? But horse hooves thunder in the distance, along with the shouts of the night-watch coming toward the catacomb. I'll not stay here while strange men blaze torches to gape and gossip over my innocent girl, nor listen to them weave around my blameless babe some sordid tale.

I kiss Juliet. I mean to hold all my life's love within this single kiss, to bid with it one last good-bye not just to my girl, but to Pietro, and our boys, and even Tybalt. But already death has sucked the honey of her breath, leaving only the bitter truth of mortality.

With that terrible taste upon me, I turn back through the dank air of the catacomb and climb the worn stone stair. At the top, I waver. I might steal unseen into the church and offer up Ave Marias for Juliet's departing soul. But what good could my prayers do her? What good have they ever done her, or me, or any that I loved?

A brace of watchmen hastens from beneath the yew tree, bearing Friar Lorenzo and Balthasar between them. I duck around the far side of the church, shivering even as midsummer's light begins to blaze the darkness into day. It's not yet Lammastide, yet an eternity since I walked these spreading grounds between Juliet and Tybalt, all the possibility of spring binding the three of us in promised joy. What God could take them both so quick, so young?

The God who's taken all I ever loved from me. The God whose saints have always failed me.

Beshrew my soul, but this is what I think as I round the convent path and come upon the statue of Santa Caterina. I ought to bend knee, beg forgiveness, and seek comfort from her. But for all the holy icon's brilliant golds and greens, the robust pinks and red catching the rising sun, can I not see it's just dull stone that lies beneath the paint? Only hard rock, quarried and carved into the image of a woman who did naught but suffer and die, because she thought Christ wished it of her. What Christ is that? What saint for me to bow and beg to? What model for a living, loving woman, who's never wished to be a martyr—and who never dreamt death could steal so much, and leave her alone alive to bear it?

The last time I stood before this statue, bees writhed thick upon Caterina's breast. Now every bee is gone, the relentless buzzing silenced.

I wish they were still here, clustering on me instead of her, sinking their thousand-fold stings into my breast. I crave the burn and swell and itch of those stings, a torment to match my shattered heart. But even the sweet agony of such pain is denied me.

A swarm is harmless. Pietro said as much, and so did Tybalt. What I witnessed was just bees gathering themselves to build a new hive. But what is left for me to gather, what can I build, without Juliet?

Water pools at the foot of the statue. The lingering last of the summer storm, half a dozen bees floating dead along the surface. Another awful omen. Or so I think, until I notice a single still-living bee crawling beside the water, seeking some purchase so it can drink without succumbing as the others did. Lowering my hand into the puddle, I spread my fingers, knuckles crooked to rise above the water. The bee climbs onto the thick joint of my littlest finger, holding safe on me while she bows her head and drinks her fill.

She lifts effortlessly into the air once she's done. I try to track her flight, but in the glint of sun she disappears.

Other bees must share her thirst. This is all I let my troubled mind think of, as I rise and snake my way to the convent well. Drawing up the bucket, I dip my cupped hands in. Carefully cradling the water, I cross back and forth to the pebble-filled dishes set by each hive. But I do bear a brain, and as I work it seeps into thoughts of when Tybalt, yet a boy, took over the tending of the bees. How I'd scolded him, not understanding what comfort he found in doing as Pietro'd done. Not realizing that this was how he grieved: by breathing in the raw sweetness of honey and humming along with the unwavering buzz of bees.

Not just honey—the air around the hives smells yeasty with brood, each egg tucked within the comb bearing the promise of a future bee. It sharps through me: that promise, that hope, rubbing against the cutting pain of all I've lost.

On the far side of the grounds, the convent bell is already tolling death knells for Paris. For Romeo. And for Juliet. The solemn peals mark another day in which prince and lords will make their way into a church, kneeling as high priests intone the Reqiuem Mass while unseen nuns chant within their hidden choir. But I'll not go to hear the half-familiar Latin sung. Not smell the incense spicing the sweet beeswax of the candles Tybalt brought here. Not gaze upon my beloved Virgin clinging to her sacred babe. I'll not fool myself into finding comfort in such things. Not fool myself, as I've ever done.

Was I not fool enough to let Juliet deceive me? A fool to believe she'd not been capable of such a thing, even as I helped her deceive the Cappelletti. A fool to think I knew her heart, that it was ever one with mine. A fool to trust that I would always have her.

But worst—to have been fool enough to lose her. To lose her to such a violent death.

This is what, fool that I am, I've tried hardest not to know: what awful hand drove the dagger into her?

A fatal vision dances before my too-imagining eyes: Paris, discovering Juliet in Romeo's embrace and stabbing a jealous blade into her, before Romeo slashes avenging sword at him.

But surely it cannot have been so. Even horn-mad, Paris'd thrust only at Romeo. He'd never have harmed Juliet.

That villainous Romeo might have snuck back to take some final perverse vengence on the Cappelletti, slaughtering noble Paris and stabbing my trusting Juliet—this I can believe. But why would he not skulk off again? If all Romeo wanted was to kill, and kill, and kill again, why would he stay and take some deathly draught?

Who else could have, would have, slaughtered my dear lamb?

Friar Lorenzo—once he learned his morbid plan was thwarted,

he must have rushed to the catacomb. Rushed yet arrived too late, and discovered Paris already killed by inconstant Romeo, who then, with some twisted desire, drank poison in a final violation of the Cappelletti tomb. When Juliet awoke, Friar Lorenzo, afraid the night-watch would discover them, must have pleaded for her to leave with him for some other secret place. Frightened, my girl would have refused to go.

The friar must have wanted mightily to hide his part in all these dreadful dealings. Was he so desperate he plunged a dagger to silence Juliet?

The man who absolved me of my every sin. Who the Holy Church has given the power to bless and shrive and shepherd human souls. Who's hidden his own crimes from the world: the illicit marriage, the feigned suicide, the web of lies he wove that's left fresh corpses littering the Cappelletti crypt. I know them all, as he well knows. And this is how at last I know who slew Juliet.

Friar Lorenzo, having killed Juliet, could not have suffered me to live. He'd've had to lay me dead as well, to bury all I know.

Scheming and fawning and deceiving he might be. But he's no killer.

A fool I've been. A fool I am. But not fool enough not to realize that her own hands must have driven the knife that pierced her heart, stealing the life I gave her.

My precious lamb, how could you?

The answer shivers over me. Do I not know what it is to love so fiercely, to feel loss so keenly, that death seems a welcome respite? Could I not choose this very moment the metal-sharp edge of a well-honed blade, the bitterest of poison draughts, a headlong plunge into the deep, wet well? Does each not promise a final relief from love's greatest grief?

The sin of suicide. How strongly it seduces. Wherever Juliet's soul has gone, mine could follow after. What hell could there be in an eternity with her? Whatever we'd suffer, we would be together.

But I cannot forget the others. Pietro. Nunzio. Nesto. Donato. Enzo. Berto. Angelo. My first love, and our six cherished sons. They are waiting, too—in a place Juliet now will never reach.

I'd have given my life to save her. But I'll not take my life and lose them as well.

NINETEEN

I pull the edge of my widow's veil down over my neck and tuck the corners inside my dress. Then I pass my hands close to the torch so they'll bear the scent of smoke. Unsheathing my newly purchased knife, I cut the first warm slice. It's the day before Lammas Eve. Time to begin my harvest.

I'd not paid much heed when Pietro taught Tybalt about the working of a hive. Or, in the years afterward, when Tybalt repeated what he'd learned, eager to offer me something of my lost Pietro. But now I gather every memory, skimming all I can.

It's the warmth that most surprises me. The heat from countless thousand bees clings to the sticky weight of what I take from them, as though something lives and breathes and beats within the golden liquid covering the comb. My thick hands have never been more grateful, more careful, than cradling their warm honey-coated wax into the rounded pot.

I'd not anticipated how fast the pot would fill, or how heavy the full pot would be. How I'd struggle to lift it, and how careful I must be to bear it off upright. Each step chinks the sack of hidden coins against me. Though I'll bruise purple from it before the harvesting is done, there's solace in feeling the weight of my long-saved soldi and denari, an assurance there'll be more to come. Pestilence snakes once more across Verona. No one can say for how long it will ravage, who'll be lost before it's done. In such times, the righteous will call for candles, and the wicked for bodily delights. Wax for one, honey for the other, and either way a well-earned sliver to keep me.

The harvesting takes longer than I expected. A half-day, and I'm still at the first hive, deciding how much comb to take, how much to leave. I must calculate what each family of bees will need to survive the winter, and what they can spare for me. To survive, to spare, to be spared. I'd not have thought such choices would be mine. But I labor with the same droning purpose as the bees. Relying on them as they rely on me.

While I work I imagine the weeks that'll follow. I'll skim and strain my many pots as what I've gathered slowly separates. I do not yet know who or where the chandler is that I might bargain with, how my long-past years of marketplace haggling will serve me now that I'm to sell instead of buy. Tybalt spent whole seasons clinging close to Pietro, without either of them suspecting how soon he'd be left to carry on alone. None of us ever dreamt such tasks would one day fall to me.

I suppose the hives will need me less as the days cool to autumn, frost to winter. I'll have time then to take my coins to the Piazza delle Erbe, or maybe all the way to Villafranca. I'll trade for spices and teach myself to make comfits such as Pietro sold. For this, more than linen shirts or even our cockly-eyed Madonna, is what he's left me.

I'll never again be what I've been. Not wife, or nurse, or mother. But I'll not be servant to such as the Cappelletti, nor shuttered away in a convent, either. I've my little buzzing livelihood, enough to keep me in my two rented rooms not far from the Via Zancani— and yet much further than I ever thought I'd come.

Thinking of comfits growls hunger into my stomach. I slip a slice of comb into my mouth and suck the honey off. Savoring the taste, I reach greedily for more comb. I sense too late that a bee is crawling there. In a startled flash, she sinks her only weapon in. The burn, the sting, the too-familiar pain shoots through my clumsy finger. For weeks it will ache me. But it's worse for her, for in that angry instant she is dead.

Did I ever fear bees? Was I afraid of how a sting might hurt me?

I cradle the poor bee in my palm and weep for costing with my carelessness her life. A foolish sentiment, but I'll not forgo it. What would Pietro think of me shedding tears over a bee? I imagine he might whistle, just to nettle me. But then he'd pinch the stinger out. Kiss the pain away. Rub honey where I hurt. Tell me how he adores me, how glad he is to see how I've grown to love his bees. He'd remind me of what I already know: loving what's in this life is our only remedy for death.

But I also know the more you love, the more you have to lose.

I weep for him. For her. For me. But then I press close my veil to dry my tears. I wave my swelling finger near to the smoky flame and heave myself back to my task. Whole hives still need my tending.

The days are short, the winter long. And on many of these darkened days, I hate her.

How could I not? She took everything. Everything I gave. Everything I had. Or thought I had.

Not just took. Killed. The bloodied violence of it, that is what maddens me. How she drove the dagger in. How she'd not cared who she hurt with that single stab.

Not cared for anything but Romeo. Not cared for me.

Who could love her more than I did? Who could lose more than in all my life I have?

The hate comes on quick, like the heat that's flashed over me the year past. My face goes red, my body sweats with it. But then just as quick it's gone, leaving me grief and guilt instead.

I raised six sons and then reared Tybalt. Watch boys turn to men, and you'll learn how they're drawn to danger. But I'd not known how fragile a girl can grow in the season she starts to ripen into a woman.

This is what shatters my heart, over and over again. That I'd not known, not seen, not ever sensed how fragile she was. How she could be so unlike me.

My father's beatings. The first great plague. Pietro's sudden slaying. Bit by terrible bit, every awful thing that ever happened to me taught me to survive. Not like my girl, who never suffered aught. Never suffered because I was ever near to tend and cosset her. Never suffered and so could not bear the slightest sorrow, the hint of unfilled longing, the least glimmering of loss. And so was lost herself.

Should I have let her suffer? Would it have taught her to survive?

Or was it better to keep her short life always sweet? Sweet as a taste of honey on the tongue.

You cannot live long on only honey. You cannot survive without tasting much that's bitter. Wormwood coats life's dug, and that's where we must suckle.

Slowly the days stretch and warm. Winter melts toward spring, and I wake half-thinking it's already Pentecost, though we're still in Lent. As the sun glows outside my waxed-cloth window, I rise from bed and ready myself to visit the hives.

The bees have roused themselves as well. They're already soaring out, seeking the first of the year's blooms. Pietro once said a hive was like a parish church, but to me each hive seems more like its own teeming city. The bees who guard the entryway, the others who fly far off to gather. Those that stay inside, turning collected pollen into precious nectar, and the ones deepest within who tend their brood. By some miracle each knows what it must do to keep the whole thrumming hive alive. This is the beauty Pietro found in tending bees. This is what finally comforts me.

I feel my husband's presence most here, near one of his hives. Tybalt's presence, too. My boys I feel more whenever I carry my tithe of beeswax candles through the streets where they once played, to San Fermo where they prayed. But my last—my Susanna, my lamb, my Juliet. I feel her against me, always. Carried like fragrance on a rose, like mother's milk on a baby's breath, like pollen goldened on a soaring bee.

AUTHOR'S NOTE

Juliet's Nurse isn't a book I expected to write—it feels more like the book chose me. My focus has always been on intersections of American history and literature. But after I finished *The Secrets of Mary Bowser*, a novel based on the true story of a slave who became a Union spy in the Confederate White House, the title *Juliet's Nurse* suddenly came to me. I pulled my copy of Shakespeare's play (which I'd last read in high school) off the shelf, and reread it in a single sitting.

I was amazed and intrigued. Although the events in the play take place across just five days, it hints at loyalties, rivalries, jealousies, and losses that extend far back in time. Shakespeare places the young lovers squarely at the heart of his play: Romeo has by far the greatest number of lines, followed by Juliet. But the character who speaks the next largest number of lines is not the head of either the Capulet or Montague households, nor the prince who rules Verona, nor the friar who first marries the lovers and later orchestrates Juliet's feigned death. The person to whom Shakespeare gives more lines than all of these characters is Juliet's wet-nurse—a woman whose very presence within the Capulet household seems curious, given that when the play begins Juliet has already been weaned for eleven years. What did Shakespeare see in her? What can we see only through her eyes?

Bawdy and clearly of a lower class, the nurse as Shakespeare presents her seems out of place among the cultured, wealthy Capulets. Her name, Angelica, is mentioned only once in the entire play. But in the very first scene in which she appears, the nurse reveals that she lost her virginity at age twelve, that she is the widow of "a merry man," and that her own daughter was born on the exact same day as Juliet but did not live. Writing *Juliet's Nurse* gave me a chance to explore this tantalizing, troubling backstory—while also offering a new, historically rich view onto the action at the heart of Shakespeare's tragedy.

Romeo and Juliet is the best-known play in English literature and the world's most cherished love story. Taking on such a popular literary work—a perennial high school reading assignment, a staple of theater companies around the world, and the source for powerful reimaginings from *West Side Story* to Franco Zeffirelli's classic film to the electrifying *Romeo+Juliet* starring Leonardo DiCaprio and Claire Danes—is no small task. When I traveled to Verona to conduct my research, I was astonished to learn that more than half a million people come to the city each year to visit sites associated with *Romeo and Juliet*. This deep attachment to Shakespeare's play convinced me there was an audience hungry for the story revealed in *Juliet's Nurse*.

Focusing on the nurse forces us to ask one of the most terrifying questions any person can face: What would it be like to lose a child? Delving into the history of wet-nurses, I learned that the arrangement described in the play was quite common: wealthy families in this era preferred to employ a wet-nurse whose own infant had recently died, and who thus had "fresh" milk to devote to their child. Imagine the intensity of losing your newborn, and then, that same day, being given the chance to nurture another baby—yet always knowing your relationship with her is tenuous, subject to the whims of her parents.

Now imagine experiencing those things in a world so different from our own. Violence was a regular feature of city life in fourteenth-century Italy. Divided allegiances to the ruling prince, to the Pope, and to increasing their own power and property drew wealthy families into bitter, bloody rivalries. Though most households in Verona had fewer means than the Cappelletti or the Montecchi, in the steady rhythms of daily urban life, everyone—from the poorest of the poor to the merchants and artisans we would think of as the middle class to the richest nobles—was driven by forces of honor, piety, and myriad local alliances and rivalries as they struggled to survive.

Understanding this time and place was crucial to exploring Angelica's story. Although Shakespeare tells us the season in which the play's tragic events take place—late July, just before the August 1 harvest holiday of Lammastide—the year is never mentioned. But important hints abound. The inclusion in the play of Prince Escalus (Shakespeare's version of the Scaligeri family name) places the events before 1405, when the Scaligeri lost power and Verona became subject to Venetian rule. And in the pivotal scene in Shakespeare's play in which Mercutio is killed, he exclaims not once, not twice, but three times to Romeo and Tybalt, "A plague o' both your houses!"—perhaps the most dreadful curse for anyone alive at the time.

Plague first came to Italy in 1348, bringing unfathomable horror: in less than two years, between one third and one half of the entire population was dead. In some places, the death toll rose as high as 60 percent. Think of what your town would be like, what the nation would be like, with so much of the population suddenly gone.

Imagine the terror Mercutio's dying words would have struck in the Veronese, who knew firsthand what plague meant, for those whose bodies rotted away, and for their bereft survivors. In Shakespeare's play, Juliet has no sisters or brothers, and Lord Capulet tells Paris, "The earth hath swallow'd all my hopes but she." Even the most wealthy and powerful families were vulnerable to the loss of their children, a tragic and haunting experience that in *Juliet's Nurse* affects both the hired wet-nurse and the affluent family she serves.

What was it like to live in the wake of such devastation? How, without our modern understanding of the effects of emotional trauma, did individuals make sense of their experience and move forward with their lives, despite all they'd lost? These are some of the questions *Juliet's Nurse* answers.

Ultimately, Angelica's experience parallels one of history's great paradoxes: the horrors of the plague contributed to Europe advancing from the medieval era into the Renaissance. The death of large segments of the population created new opportunities for survivors. Peasants moved from the countryside to cities. Young men enjoyed professional prospects beyond their family's original standing. The loss of so many spouses and betrotheds caused shifts in how marriages were contracted. New markets for luxury and everyday goods emerged, as international trade flourished—bringing with it advances in transportation and the intermingling of European, African, Asian, and eventually New World cultures. As Friar Laurence reminds us in his first speech in Shakespeare's play, what's tomb is womb. The Renaissance was the rebirth following the plague's enormous death toll.

But the story also resonates in our own era. *Romeo and Juliet* ends with the suicides of the teenage lovers, following the violent deaths of other young men. Weaving Angelica's story around these incidents from the play pushed me to think deeply about violence, despondence, and suicide. What would enable Angelica to withstand the anger and grief that destroy so many of the other characters? What larger lessons can we learn from her?

This became the overarching theme of the book. *Juliet's Nurse* probes the relationship between loss and endurance, because in life, as in the novel, suffering exists not in opposition to, but as an inevitable experience of, survival.

LEARN MORE

isit www.loisleveen.com to learn more about the medieval and Renaissance history of Verona, Italy, and to find reading group questions and resources for teaching *Juliet's Nurse* along with *Romeo and Juliet*.

ACKNOWLEDGMENTS

Novel writing can sometimes be as sweet as honey, and other times as bitter as wormwood, and I offer great thanks to many sweet people who've kept me from turning bitter.

Rosemary Weatherston is such a keen reader and dear friend, she keeps making both my life and my books better. David Garrett proved ever collegial in helping me access myriad scholarly sources. Carol Frischmann, Naseem Rakha, Kathlene Postma, and Shelley Washburn read the draftiest of first chapters and convinced me that I really had a book. The Newberry Library supported my research with an Arthur and Lila Weinberg Fellowship, and Judy Wittner opened her home to me during my time in Chicago. Dr. Michael Slater and Dr. Shoshana Waskow provided medical counsel on a variety of fictive injuries and diseases. Obscure materials on medieval beekeeping and church practices were located by Janie Rangel and translated by Armanda Balduzzi and Hanna Hofer. The far-flung participants in the Medieval-Religion, Mediev-L, and MedFem LISTSERVs gave me insight into the period that shaped my characters. I've consulted more scholarly books and articles than I can list here, but suffice it to say that without the work of many academics, I couldn't have created this novel.

Here in Oregon, the wonderful members of Portland Urban Beekeepers not only provided a hands-on understanding of beekeeping, they taught me the power of a welcoming hive. Multnomah County Library is truly a treasure, and I am always grateful for its resources and its dedicated staff, and indebted to the voters and government officials here (and everywhere) who understand that library funding is critical to the well-being of the entire community. I continue to be sustained by readers and by the bookstore and library staffs around the country and abroad who eagerly embraced my first novel, *The Secrets of Mary Bowser*, and whose enthusiastic nagging about when I'd have another kept me from procrastinating as I wrote *Juliet's Nurse*.

William Shakespeare endowed Angelica with just enough intriguing backstory, while also providing an inspiring model of literary appropriation. Laney Katz Becker proved once again that a sage agent benefits an author at every step of the process, and words can't say how much I appreciate all she and her colleagues at Lippincott Massie McQuilkin do to help me write the best novels I can and to connect readers around the world with them. In our very first conversation, Emily Bestler won my heart when she told me that because her name is on every book, she cares about each one as much as the author does, and she's proven it true time and again. She and Megan Reid are not only savvy readers (and re-readers), they are also so warm, supportive, and funny that it is always a pleasure to work with them, even when they make me toil much harder than I ever thought I could. Any author might feel lucky to have one such editorial team, but I am extraordinarily blessed to benefit as well from the astute input of Anne Collins. Readers often do not realize how much goes into the making of a novel, but I owe a great debt to Jeanne Lee, Hillary Tisman, Mellony Torres, Alysha Bullock, Adria Iwustiak, Amanda Betts, and many, many other people at Emily Bestler Books/Atria Books and Random House Canada for this beautiful book you (or your e-reader) now hold.

As ever, my deepest gratitude goes to Chuck Barnes, who has read countless drafts, engaged in spontaneous plotting sessions, put up with a too-often very moody writer, and courageously suffered through a research trip to beautiful Verona, Italy. Here's to a love story that is always a comedy, and never a tragedy.

Award-winning author LOIS LEVEEN dwells in the spaces where literature and history meet. She is the author of the critically acclaimed novel *The Secrets of Mary Bowser*. Her work has appeared in literary and scholarly journals, as well as the *New York Times*, the *Los Angeles Review of Books*, the *Chicago Tribune*, *Huffington Post*, *Bitch* magazine, the *Wall Street Journal*, the *Atlantic*, and on NPR. Leveen gives talks about writing and history at universities, museums, and libraries around the world. She lives in Portland, Oregon, with two cats, one Canadian, and 60,000 honeybees.